In
Arra

MIRA LYN KELLY
ANNA CLEARY
JULIA JAMES

MILLS &
BOON

Published in Great Britain 2014
by Mills & Boon, an imprint of Harlequin (UK) Limited,
Eton House, 18-24 Paradise Road, Richmond, Surrey, TW9 1SR

INDECENT ARRANGEMENTS © 2014 Harlequin Books S.A.

Tabloid Affair, Secretly Pregnant!, *Do Not Disturb* and *Forbidden or For Bedding?* were first published in Great Britain by Harlequin (UK) Limited.

Tabloid Affair, Secretly Pregnant! © 2010 Mira Lyn Sperl
Do Not Disturb © 2011 Anna Cleary
Forbidden or For Bedding? © 2010 Julia James

ISBN: 978 0 263 91183 1
eBook ISBN: 978 1 472 04478 5

05-0514

Harlequin (UK) Limited's policy is to use papers that are natural, renewable and recyclable products and made from wood grown in sustainable forests. The logging and manufacturing processes conform to the legal environmental regulations of the country of origin.

Printed and bound in Spain
by Blackprint CPI, Barcelona

TABLOID AFFAIR, SECRETLY PREGNANT!

BY
MIRA LYN KELLY

Mira Lyn Kelly grew up in the Chicago area and earned her degree in Fine Arts from Loyola University. She met the love of her life while studying abroad in Rome, Italy, only to discover he'd been living right around the corner from her for the previous two years. Having spent her twenties working and playing in the Windy City, she's now settled with her husband in rural Minnesota, where their four beautiful children provide an excess of action, adventure and entertainment.

With writing as her passion, and inspiration striking at the most unpredictable times, Mira can always be found with a notebook at the ready. More than once she's been caught by the neighbours, covered in grass clippings, scribbling away atop the compost container!

When she isn't reading, writing, or running to keep up with the kids, she loves watching movies, blabbing with the girls, and cooking with her husband and friends. Check out her website www.miralynkelly.com for the latest dish!

To Mom and John,
with countless thanks for showing me *true love*
and *happily ever after* aren't just for stories.

CHAPTER ONE

FLASHBULBS exploded. Shutters snapped like automatic fire around him as reporters from rags of all caliber called for attention, each voice clamoring to rise above the rest.

"Mr. Evans!"

"One more over here!"

Beneath the awning of the exclusive Chicago hotel, Nate Evans offered up a stock smile, responded to a few light questions with a handful of ambiguous words and waited for the question he knew would come.

It didn't take long.

"Mr. Evans! Care to explain your sudden absence from the social circuit these past months?"

The question shot through the early autumn evening, silencing all others with its gathering strength while narrowing the focus on him like an interrogator's spotlight.

They knew when they were onto something.

But he was ready for the assault. Invited it.

Feigning surprise at the inquiry, Nate paused in mock consideration before answering. "Guess I've been so caught up in business, I hadn't realized I'd gone off the map."

His answer wouldn't satisfy even the most limited curiosity. And more than that, it was a lie. He'd spent the last six months laying low. Flying under the radar to avoid notice while the nightmare of his life slowly, painfully, worked itself toward an unsatisfactory resolution. Six months out of the limelight, away from the cameras, only to find his absence conspicuous enough in itself to fuel new rumors and speculation as to the cause.

Who's the beauty behind this bachelor's broken heart?

The squelched headline had hit him like a sucker punch to the gut and he'd spent a fortune making it go away. Buying time. But if he didn't get a stranglehold on the situation, the trash hounds would dig and dig until they found the truth. And then they'd keep digging, making such a muck and mess that the dirt slung in their quest for ratings would reach anyone and everyone even remotely tied to his life.

His dad didn't need that.

Neither did Bella, the tiny baby who'd dragged a commitment from his jaded heart with a fist too small to wrap around his thumb. She was pure and precious and new. And though she didn't belong to him, he'd sworn to protect her from whatever hardships he could. And preventing a media circus from assailing her home and her mother—who wasn't in any shape to defend against it—was top on the list.

Which brought him to tonight. The first who's-who gala event available to spin the press off his scent.

He smiled his best cat-about-to-give-the-canary-a-go smile for the cameras. "Better find out if any of the ladies still remember me." And with that parting sound bite, he jogged the few steps through the grand entrance, looking for all the world as though he didn't want to miss a minute. As though he wouldn't rather be in his physician's office turning his head to the left to cough, than heading into the "society wedding of the season".

He needed a diversion—and the sooner the better. So this was it.

He'd dive headfirst into tonight's sea of swank and silk, in search of the biggest scandal. He'd reel in a beauty he could splash across the tabloid pages. Someone with enough hook she'd drag the press's interest out of the past and secure it in the now.

Someone who knew the score.

That was the touchy part, because, when it came to his dates, Nate didn't do soft. He didn't do love. And he didn't do forever. He made certain his women knew what they were getting into with him—and then he did them with enough attention and skill they didn't care there wasn't anything deep or lasting between them.

Scanning the throngs of social elite gathered within the gold-domed ballroom, he searched for a like-minded wave-maker. Except after barely five minutes, Nate realized he'd miscalculated—and in no small way. Finding a woman to flaunt was easy. There were at least a hundred willing candidates batting thick-fringed lashes at him. But with each toss of perfectly coiffed hair and every lingering glance, the apathy that had kept him so easily unattached these past six months turned to something darker.

More suffocating. Everywhere he looked, false claims and secret agendas lurked beneath the guise of enticement, and he found himself backing away rather than closing in.

And then he saw her.

Payton Liss, slinking through the crowd, using every evasive technique at her disposal to dodge the conciliatory hand pats, air kisses and general gossipy blood sport that occurred post nuptials—regardless of the social strata involved.

The good girl from his past. Brandt's little sister. Miss Off-Limits herself.

Payton didn't need his money. She wouldn't want his name. And she'd help him regardless of what went down with Brandt all those years ago because she habitually did the right thing.

Or make that, she *mostly* did the right thing.

The corner of his mouth quirked as, while he watched, she pilfered a dinner roll from the table closest to the kitchen access hall and slipped stealthily out the door.

Nate's feet were moving before his brain had even finished processing the plan.

Neck deep in a cloud of ill-fitting taffeta and tulle, Payton Liss pressed her shoulders into the wall behind her. Stretching across the floor of her hideout—a miraculously unlocked utility room, discovered purely by accident three weddings before—she braced a foot against the door and straight-legged with the determination of a second-string bridesmaid on the run.

"Not a chance, Nate. The women will sniff you out. Go find your own storage closet."

Between the gap of the door and frame, ice-blue eyes slid over her, bringing to both mind and body the heart-pounding effect that gaze once elicited. "You open this door, Payton, or I'm heading straight back into that reception—and I'm telling every schmuck I can find you're alone in here…crying." The last word he delivered with the smug satisfaction of a man who knew he'd already won.

Her breath caught as she stared in outraged indignation. "I am not crying!" Hiding, yes. Sulking, some. Crying, not a chance.

"It'll be like open season. Every guy intent on snaring himself a top-floor job in Liss Industries moving in for his white-knight moment. And the talk…"

Her stomach seized. It was the talk that had driven her into hiding in the first place.

The "Poor Payton" talk.

"…Such a good girl…so desperate for a wedding of her own…so disappointed when he left her…what her father had wanted, but what did he expect…"

She couldn't stand the sound of it anymore.

They were all wrong. But even if she bellowed out the truth, no one would believe her. She'd done too good a job for too long of forcing herself into the mold of a quiet-souled, docile-minded lady who didn't exist. And for nothing. In the end, no amount of perfect behavior could save her father from the weak heart that had plagued him the last fifteen years of his life.

Pushing back the well of emotion that still rose at the thought of losing him the year before, she shook her head. Nothing could upset him now. No defiant choice or willful stand for independence. He was at peace and, though his death broke her heart, it also set her free.

But no matter the changes she made, no one could see past the illusion she'd perfected to the real woman trying to break free. Which was why this had to be the last society event. She needed a life. One she could live on her own terms.

To try and set the record straight before she escaped would leave her sounding *petty*—the perfect complement to pre-existing *pathetic*.

No, thank you—

The bored sigh directed her way snapped Payton back to the present. To Nate, quite literally sticking his head back into her life after walking out of it all those years ago. "Last chance, babe, or I talk. Lot of hopefuls out there tonight waiting for a shot."

He'd do it, too, the bastard, she thought, giving into the inexplicable smile that seemed to rise from the ashes of every memory she had of the man. Nearly every memory anyway.

Nate knew no limits when it came to getting what he wanted. And now—after a decade with little more than the most limited greetings passing between them, and only when absolutely necessary—he wanted to get into her hideout.

"Now, Payton."

With a reluctant sigh, and then a second, louder, more pointed version of the first, she gave up her hold on the door and scooted into a seated position against the wall where she'd arranged a pile of linens to pad the floor.

"Fine, come in. Just hurry up before someone sees you."

"Smart girl." He shouldered through the door, closing it with the sweep of one foot behind him. The swift, fluid move, executed with Nate's signature masculine economy of motion, took her back to the days of watching him tear across the soccer field. Fast and strong and skilled. Damp strands of sun-kissed gold whipping about his face as he drove toward a goal.

She hadn't been able to take her eyes off him.

Even now, attempting to pry her gaze from the man-sized version of the boy she'd wanted so badly, she only managed to skirt from one hard-planed, deep-chiseled element of his physique to the next.

It was no good.

He was more devastating in the looks he'd grown into than any man had a right to be. The waves atop his head were a few shades darker and a bit shorter, but remained utterly tempting in their unruly disarray. He was broader in the shoulders and chest, still athletically lean and exuded a power and confidence that dwarfed the world around him. Particularly in his tailor-made tux with a bottle of champagne hanging loosely from his fingers. The personification of careless elegance.

Intimidating in ways to which she was normally immune.

But then, this was Nate. It had been different with him from the start. He was everything she never let herself be.

Finally she asked, "What are you doing back here?"

His cool blue gaze locked with hers, and the corner of his mouth twisted upward to the slightest degree. "Looking for you."

Not in the imminent seduction way it sounded, she was certain. Nate didn't think of her like that and never would. She peered up from her spot on the floor, waiting for him to elaborate, but he glanced around the small room instead, taking in the shelves stocked with miscellaneous serving equipment, a rolling cart, table dressings. "Nice place you've got here. Built-in sound system and everything," he said with a gesture to indicate the strains of "Get Down Tonight" filtering through the walls.

"Thanks, it's coming together quite nicely, I think. A few more weeks and I'll be ready to entertain."

He cocked a brow at the makeshift seating she'd assembled. His gaze darkened. "Not expecting company now, are you?"

Heat splashed up her neck and cheeks as she realized what her little sanctuary might suggest to a world-class player like Nate. "No, no." She shook her head, her hands flapping as her explanation tumbled out. "Just settling in for the long haul. I shouldn't be seen leaving for at least another hour, but with all the talk I just couldn't stand to stay."

"I get it. They're like a pack of vultures out there." He gave her hip an indelicate nudge with the toe of his shoe. "Move it, I want in on the nest."

Inching over, she made room as he knelt down—the heavy muscles of his thighs flexing beneath the hug of his trousers—and settled against the wall beside her. Her heart-rate went up with the temperature in a room she'd been sure was cool only moments ago.

Arms balanced atop his bent knees, he held the champagne in one wide palm, brushing his thumb through the condensation accumulating on the heavy glass. "What I can't understand is why the hell you would come alone. And I'm praying it isn't because you were hoping to hook back up with that chump ex of yours, Clint."

Payton rolled her eyes. Too much to hope that Nate wouldn't have heard the gossip surrounding her breakup. Yet another reason necessitating her imminent escape from the social scene. "No. God, no. This is my worst nightmare. I'd planned to come down with something contagious and unexpected and not be able to attend at all. But a bridesmaid beat me to it and I got promoted up from guest. Lucky me."

Nate's mouth twisted down as he looked her over. "If you say so."

She laughed out a breath and then turned, falling back into the conversation that had always come so easily between them. "Well, what about you? It's a wedding…and you've scored a slot on the world's most eligible bachelors list three years in a row. You'd need a date on each arm to escape unscathed. But stag? I'm amazed you made it out of the ballroom without the single girls setting up a numbered queue to get served."

"Get served?" This time it was Nate who laughed, letting his head loll back against the wall behind him. "Payton, Payton." He caught her with a questioning glance. "What kind of talk is that from a good girl like you?"

She stared at him, her heart skipping a beat as his focus shifted to her mouth.

"And why am I the only one who gets to hear that lip of yours?"

She couldn't have him looking at her like that, particularly when he had no intention of following through. She could handle her attraction to him, she'd done it for over half her life. Managed it. Tamped it down and stuffed it away. First because it was futile, and then because it was misplaced. But now… The last thing she needed was Nate reminding her of what she couldn't have. Flirting when he'd never see her as more than Brandt's little sister. The *good girl*.

Enough. She needed to know what the man who walked out of her life with barely a word all those years ago wanted

with her now, and then she needed to get him out of her space
before she did something stupid. Such as catch a bit of that
unruly hair between her fingers and test its softness against
her lips. "What do you want?"

The question hung between them. Nate raised the bottle to
his mouth, tipping it back for a long swallow, before turning
and pinning her to her spot with the full intensity of his gaze.
"You. I want you, Payton."

CHAPTER TWO

"I NEED you to pretend we're involved. That we've been involved for the last month, actually."

Nate watched as Payton blanched and then went to beet, sputtering at length before she finally nailed that single-word demand for clarification. *"What?"*

Well, he hadn't expected her to simply agree and climb into his lap.

And, man, as much as he liked the hot flush across her skin, he definitely didn't need to think of Payton's lush curves and petite frame curling into the seat of his thighs. Not a good idea at all. Never had been.

"Take it easy, princess. Have a sip." He offered the champagne, only to have it pushed back at him. With a shake of her head, a silky blonde spiral sprang free at her temple. The first ruffled feather.

She was staring at him now, those big brown eyes wide with disbelief. "You want me to pretend we're together?"

A nod. "But you hadn't wanted us to get caught."

Her face screwed up. "Excuse me?"

How was it he managed multibillion-dollar deals without batting an eye when he couldn't spit out a simple illicit proposal with any clarity or finesse at all?

Letting loose a frustrated growl, he pushed his fingers into his hair, giving it a good tug at the root. "Here's the deal. The press is on me. Digging into something I don't want dug up. I need a distraction. Something juicy they can sink their teeth into. And I need a friend—someone I can trust—to help me pull it off. You're perfect. You're well known, respected, and everyone will believe you wouldn't want a relationship with me publicized."

"Why not?" she asked, and the way her brow furrowed in genuine confusion had Nate wanting to laugh.

"You're Payton Liss. You want a respectable husband. A tidy family." He tipped the bottle again and downed another swallow before turning back to her. "A blue-blood name."

And everyone knew Nate wasn't about marriage. There'd been a time, back when he first hit the financial papers, that women lined up with "love" in their eyes and a prenup in their purse. Talk about a turnabout for the kid who couldn't get a commitment for the prom because he didn't have a trust fund. But he wasn't a man built for love and lasting. And he didn't get played. Soon enough, the women in line weren't looking for anything more than he was. A little company and a lot of sweaty sex. Sure, the occasional fortune hunter still got her silk panties in a twist over his refusal to tie the knot…but on the whole, there weren't a lot of misconceptions about what he had to offer the women he dated.

A good time. On his terms.

The soft brown of her eyes seemed to go hard beneath his stare, her body still, her voice cool. "If those are my priorities then why would I have an affair with you?"

"Because I'm the best kind of forbidden fun," he answered with a cocky smile promising it was true. "A bit of slumming after things didn't work out with Clint. A palate cleanser before the next blue blood gets in line."

"Slumming?" she asked, incredulous. "You could buy and sell my family three times over."

Sure he could…now.

"The name thing," he offered with a shrug. "Old money versus new."

Payton's lips parted, then firmed into a tight line. A pretty pink stained her cheeks as she moved to stand. "No one would believe something so ridiculous and insulting."

Nate caught her wrist, pulling her back down. "Everyone believes it." He gently chucked under her chin. "But even if it's not true...there's still Brandt."

Brandt. The only reason she might say no.

She huffed, irritated. "Yes, and I don't particularly want my brother's wrath coming down on me over you—not without a good reason."

"How about this. Go along with my plan because it'll give the talk about you a whole new flavor. No more pity over that idiot not marrying you. They'll be shocked...and *jealous*."

Payton's expression lightened as she focused on some distant spot beyond the snug walls of their utility closet before returning to him. "Confidence is a real problem for you, isn't it?"

"Hey, you're the one who suggested the numbered queue." But his humor faded as he searched her eyes. "I need this. I need the press to stop looking for what I've been up to the last six months. I need them to think they've already found the big secret. That it's you. People will read a million reasons into why we didn't want it public.... Hope that Clint would come around. The animosity between your brother and me. The fact that women who date me aren't doing it in search of a happily ever after. Let them guess."

Payton's gaze shifted restlessly around their small space.

This was supposed to be it. The last society affair. She was getting out of the papers and getting on with the life she'd been working toward. The life where she was judged on her merit rather than how successfully she wore a gown or what the press reported her priorities to be.

But Nate would never have come to her if his secret wasn't important.

And she had to admit some brazen bit of her psyche, too long neglected, reveled in the stir the name Payton Liss paired with Nate Evans would cause. Definitely talk of a different flavor.

Brandt would be livid. Though her inward snicker quickly turned to pause. Whatever had transpired between Brandt and Nate hadn't been washed away by the passage of time. After ten years, the mere mention of Nate Evans put her brother into a lather…and she still didn't fully understand why. As she didn't understand why Nate had closed himself off from her so abruptly. So absolutely.

Casting a sidelong glance at the tuxedo-clad villain himself, she realized this could very well be her chance to find out.

"What happened with Brandt? Why did you hurt him that way?"

Nate's jaw set, the muscle jumping once before he answered. "Maybe Brandt deserved to be hurt a little."

Her brother had done a lot of things over the years she couldn't condone. Couldn't understand. In the back of her mind, she'd always suspected—

"Maybe he deserved worse." The ice blue of Nate's gaze raked over her in one slow, telling sweep before it locked back at her eyes. "I could have done worse."

Her mouth opened, to gasp or deny, only nothing came of it but a slow leaking breath that might have been regret. She would have given Nate anything. Done anything he asked.

If he'd decided to use her as a means of payback or revenge or whatever motivated him back then, he would have found no resistance. Only the eager willingness of a girl desperate for him to see her as a woman. And the repercussions… "Brandt would have gone nuts."

Nate let out a bark of laugher. "Yeah, well, it wasn't concern for your brother that stopped me."

A tide of warmth washed through her and she stole a glimpse his way. Her hero, always and in the most unconventional ways. Only he'd walked away from her as if their friendship meant nothing. "Where've you been all this time?"

Her quietly posed question brought a pause, and the faint lines around his eyes lost their laughter. "The last six months I've spent mostly in Germany." He shifted in the nest, stretching out one long leg before them. "Babysitting a new venture that didn't take off the way I'd anticipated."

It wasn't what she'd meant. She'd been thinking more of where he'd been for the past ten years. They'd been close. They'd been friends. And then one day, he just wasn't. Except now he was back. Asking her to be the friend he needed to help him.

"Do you want to tell me what this is all about?"

Nate ran a wide palm over the heavy line of his jaw. "Honestly, I'd like to get out of your little home-away-from-home here."

Pushing to his feet, he dug into his pocket for a handful of bills he then tucked under the champagne bottle left atop the rolling cart. "What do you say?" Catching her hand, he pulled her up with him. "Strength in numbers, right? We head back into the reception and give 'em something to talk about?"

It was tempting. Made even more so by the warmth radiating up her arm from Nate's casual touch. She didn't want it to end, but as he led her out into the kitchen access hall Payton's steps dragged.

Nate turned, seemingly amused by her hesitance. "What?"

"I need to think about this."

The idea of the talk surrounding her laced with something other than pity was thrilling, and the opportunity to spend some time with Nate again—well, she didn't quite know how she felt about that. If it was even possible for her to pretend to have a relationship with him at the same time she was pretending her attraction wasn't sincere. What she did know was that Nate wasn't a man to ask for favors lightly.

He *needed* her.

Still, a decision of this magnitude deserved at least one night's consideration. "Give me the evening and I'll call you tomorrow."

Ahead the door to the ballroom opened a crack as a waiter or someone prepared to back through it. Payton took a step in retreat, only to have Nate draw her to a stop.

"Here's the thing, Payton." His blue eyes had her now, cool and deep and dangerous. Captivating. "I've already thought about it. This is a prime opportunity and the results will benefit us both."

He'd already— "What?"

His loose grasp on her hand shifted, tightened as though he thought she might bolt. "Trust me," he urged in a tone of pure seductive persuasion.

Her chin shot up. She'd known Nate back when he was cultivating that tone and, while she couldn't say she was exactly immune, she wasn't wholly susceptible either. "No."

He could forget about luring her in the way he did every other man, woman and child on the planet. She knew how he operated and the last thing she needed was another overbearing man trying to control her.

She wasn't one of his devotees—some Wall Street junkie determined to live as Nate lived and follow in the footsteps of the financially infallible. And she wasn't one of his bimbos either, hanging on his arm and every whim. She was Payton Liss, determined to secure her independence, and she wasn't giving into this man just because his voice stroked like rough velvet over her every independent thought!

The corner of his mouth quirked up a degree and something

about his smile, one she'd seen countless times before and
knew promised pure mayhem, put all her senses on alert. Her
stomach jumped and she tried to escape.

"Oh, no, you don't," she gasped, backing down the hall
with Nate matching her step for step, still holding her hands
captive within his. She glanced over her shoulder, and nervous
laughter erupted with the realization she'd somehow ended
up moving toward the ballroom rather than away. *Stupid.*

"Come on…trust me."

That grin!

"I *don't* trust you," she shot back, her pulse rocketing in
response to the predatory intent blazing in his eyes. She'd be
a fool to trust a man leering at her like that—as if she'd made
his week with this little game of cat and mouse.

"You should," he cajoled, this time taking a step into her
space. "I've got a knack for making things work."

Payton peered up at him as he drew her closer—to the
point where their feet tangled, legs touched. He was so bad.
So incredibly, *unrepentantly bad.*

"You're arrogant," she accused, laughing as she nearly
stumbled into his chest.

"You *like it*," he challenged, with a pointed jut of his chin,
just daring her denial. But, God help her, she couldn't. She'd
always loved his crazy confidence. Nate's unwavering ability
to fly in the face of convention and come out on top. He was
free and, contrary to popular opinion, didn't take himself too
seriously…so neither did she. Only, if Nate pulled her any
closer, "serious" would become inevitable.

Her hands moved ineffectually to his chest. "What are
you—?"

But then the door to the ballroom pushed fully open and,
with an expertly maneuvered tug, Nate caught her up against
the hard-cut planes of his body in a hold so provocatively
intense she couldn't think of anything beyond the miracle of

its fit. Ice-blue eyes slid over her in a chilling caress that left her skin pebbled with goose bumps.

Flashing a quick wink, he caught the back of her neck. "Trust me. I've done this before."

Lips parted in protest, Payton didn't manage a word before he moved in and, with deadly accuracy, captured her mouth beneath his.

CHAPTER THREE

THE kiss was blatant and intense, a showy play of passion that bowed her in a delicate arch, caged by the unyielding iron and steel of Nate's powerful frame. Firm, smooth lips moved over hers in a back and forth rub so skillfully seductive she could only sigh under their assault. Give into the idea that, if she wasn't going to escape the spotlight as she'd planned, there were plenty worse things than being exposed while discovering what it was to be kissed by Nate Evans.

It was *all consuming.*

There was something undeniable in his touch, something chemical, instinctual and wholly unexpected. She didn't understand it—couldn't defend against it as, locked in his hold, her body and mind pushed into overdrive.

Eyes closed, fingers flared at his shoulders, she tried to brace against the curl of anticipation licking through her belly. Remind herself that Nate's mouth sliding against her own was just for show. For whomever had opened the ballroom door—the door that remained open if the volume of the music spilling into the hallway around them was any indicator. It was a kiss for the gossips. For their individual self-serving interests. But not for their hearts or souls or even their libidos. Only the deafening rush of blood speeding past her ears—the heat of it surging through her veins, awakening her body in ways she couldn't deny—suggested otherwise.

Any second he would stop. Pull away and take this fantasy, a lifetime in the making, with him. But until then...

Payton clutched at the hand-stitched lapels of his jacket, her body curving into his. She'd call it a good show, call it anything Nate needed to hear, but the honest truth was no fantasy had ever measured up to this moment and, audience or not, she couldn't control her physical reaction to a kiss she'd dreamed of since she was thirteen.

Her fingers skimmed over the contours of his broad shoulders, following the column of his neck until they threaded into the thick silk of the curls at the base of his skull. The forbidden luxury of her hands in his hair, coupled with the seductive pull of his mouth against her own, was too much— too good, everything and not enough all at once—and drove a soft, pleading moan past her lips.

Nate stilled, his mouth fused with hers.

Oh, no, he'd heard her. Heard the sound of desire in a kiss scripted for deceit. She couldn't move, couldn't breathe— couldn't quell the frantic beating of her heart or her desperation to take this insanity further.

And then a breath, warm and wet, slipped between her suspended lips, carrying the gruff response to her needy plea. "Payton."

Tension charged the air around them, a current jumping from each point of contact to the next.

What was this?

The arms that held her circled tighter, slipping into something wholly different than the embrace of a moment ago. Into a slow, sensual exploration of his hands across her body.

Heat radiated from his touch like a hot claim, waking her every nerve. Every sense. Every desire.

She needed to stop.

Nate obviously read her renegade moan as a call to spur him further. To up the charade. Only Payton was already in over her head. Her body couldn't decipher the real from the imitation. And—as his tongue licked at the corner of her lips, eliciting a shudder that racked her from top to toe, had her opening wider to the exquisite sensation of Nate Evans seducing her with his mouth, his tongue, his teeth, and the soft rumble of his groan sounding between them—she slipped beneath reason, drowning in need. She wanted him. More than his kiss. She wanted everything he could give her, show her.

Only, already it was ending. His lips eased from hers by degrees until only the barest brush of skin and breath kept contact. That lingering touch, suggesting he, too, was hesitant to break away.

A kiss so carnal, so hot, couldn't have been—

Don't be stupid. Of course, it could.

She was dealing with notorious Nate, playboy extraordinaire and on a worldwide scale as she heard it. She was out of her league. Out of her mind. And potentially spoiled for life because of one insane, staged make out she hadn't had the sense of self-preservation to defend against.

But Nate had caught her off guard. And within the decadent span of that kiss, every fine strand of lingering attraction toward the boy he'd been wove and wound itself into an indestructible tether to the man he was now.

Oh, she was in such trouble.

Breath ragged, she tried to focus on the shadowed planes of the face only inches above her. Taking in the harsh drawn features she knew so well—the strong cut of his jaw, chiseled lips, that once-broken nose—she couldn't bring herself to meet his eyes. To see his thoughts or risk he'd see hers.

Gaze fixed on the breadth of the shoulders shielding her from the reception, she waited for him to step back and reveal his latest conquest. Then it would be over.

Only she didn't want the seduction to end.

Her hands slipped down to his chest, palms pressed flat against the definition of pure masculine form. If he could sneak up on her like that, she could grope him a bit while she got her breath back. It was only fair. Except the feel of his hard-packed physique beneath her hands wasn't doing much to calm her. The flex and pull of his layered muscles. The beads of his nipples. Hard and enticing. Forbidden little playthings that, once found, she couldn't leave alone.

Nate's hands clamped around her wrists, stilling her shameless exploration as his breath punched out in a cough.

What a fool to think this could be hers.

Pulling herself together, she managed to make light of a situation that was anything but. "You could have warned me," she laughed, praying the sound was more convincing than it felt.

A second passed. And then another. Her eyes closed against the rising ache in her chest. The crazy sense of despair she didn't have any right to. She wanted more. Wanted to be the kind of woman a man like Nate took home. But he'd already said it once. She was the good girl.

He took her chin between his finger and thumb. Her gaze lifted to his and her breath caught. Strain deepened the lines etched around his mouth and blatant hunger darkened his eyes. His jaw jumped with a tension she couldn't believe.

"Warned you? No." His gruff voice was low and serious, not the jovial Nate she knew so well. He held her gaze, considering, and then slowly the corner of his mouth turned up. And closing the distance between them, he answered, "I don't think I could have."

Hell, this was Payton Liss twining her arms around his neck, melting into his kiss with a breathy sigh—a sound that was all sex and need, and doing very bad things to his imagination. Brandt's little sister whose grown-up curves burned against his body, heating his blood like liquid fire. Miss Off-

Limits herself, with her fingers wound tight in his hair, opening that lush mouth of hers in a sweetly seductive invitation, begging him to take. And he wanted to take. To hell with however many sets of eyes were trained on them through the open door at the end of the hall.

Except, as of that moment, Nate didn't want to share.

He didn't want to play pretend. He didn't want anything but the private continuation of the kiss that just blew his mind. There had to be a hundred reasons why giving into the need surging through his veins was a bad idea. Only, he couldn't think of one. All he could see, and with a sudden, vivid clarity, was that Payton Liss belonged in his bed.

The music faded, quieting to a muffled hum that resonated through the hallway around them.

Straightening, Nate shot a glance over his shoulder. The door to the ballroom had closed—whoever opened it having come, seen their fill and left. Whether they'd recognized Payton he had no idea, but they'd seen someone in a rather conspicuous dress. Which was enough for today.

His focus turned back to the unexpected lure in his arms, his gaze touching on each delicate feature of her upturned face. Lingering on her mouth as the brush of his thumb across her kiss-swollen bottom lip set off an all too satisfying shudder.

He wanted her. As he couldn't remember wanting before. And she was willing, in his arms, looking up at him with eyes asking for one thing. *More.*

Only with a woman like Payton, *more* could mean *way more* than what he had to offer. She didn't know the score and didn't play for fun. He couldn't risk her reading promises he had no intention of delivering on into the kiss they'd just shared.

"You know I'm not the right kind of guy for you, Payton."

It was a warning. Plain and simple. To both of them.

One he fully expected her to heed.

"Maybe I don't want the 'right kind of guy'." She swallowed, the color rushing to her cheeks as she held his stare. "Maybe, this once, I want the kind of guy who can give me a night no one else would dare."

CHAPTER FOUR

HER words shot like an electric current straight to his groin. Nate was a man accustomed to taking what he wanted, how he wanted it. Because of who Payton was, he'd been willing to exercise more restraint than he ever did. But with that soft-spoken gauntlet thrown, there was no going back. "Then we need to get out of this hall. Now."

Her eyes lit, the seductive curve of her lips stretching as she reached for his lapel, urging him back toward her storage closet. "The nest."

He let out a bark of disbelieving laughter and stopped her with a firm hold at her wrist. Spun her back with a tug. "Not a chance, princess. For what no one else would dare...we're going to want a bed to land on."

With that promise hanging between them, he grabbed her hand and pulled her toward the kitchen doors just as a busboy stepped out pushing an empty clearing cart. Nate caught him and slapped a fifty with his business card into the kid's palm. "Get your manager and tell him I want the best room you've got...in the next five minutes."

Four and a half minutes later they were alone in the Executive Suite, Payton's toes breezing inches above the carpet as Nate crossed to the bedroom, his mouth covering hers in an urgent, possessive claim staked with tongue and teeth and lips. Suspended in his hold, she caught the dizzying spin of the room from the corner of her eye an instant before her shoulders met the damask.

Oh, God, yes. They were feet from a bed and Nate had backed her against a wall instead.

Heart slamming, her fingers balled in the fabric of his shirt as she opened to the slow thrust of his tongue. Followed the measured retreat. And moaned as he thrust again, her body flaming to life with the knowledge this was real. More than some fantasy. More than a charade. Her every sense heightened and homed in on him, drowning her in the taste, touch and smell of *Nate*. The sound of his ragged breath. The look of hunger in his eyes before he went to her throat—his mouth devouring the sensitive spot where neck sloped into shoulder with an assault of gentle suction and grazing teeth, swirling tongue and hot, wet breath that infused every cell of her being with sensual achiness.

His hands covered her breasts in a kneading caress and then, fingers curling into the neckline of her dress, he pulled the fabric down, releasing them to perch atop the bunched taffeta. Groaning with pure male satisfaction, he pressed his mouth to the top of one mound and then the other, making her feel as though she were the gift to him, rather than the other way around.

"You're so soft."

And he was hard, every bit of him firm and taut, solid-packed man making her feel like a fragile doll in his grasp. This was the man of her every forbidden fantasy, exceeding them all with his kiss alone. This was Nate. And there was no way that kiss was as good as it got.

"Please," she gasped, asking for more of something she couldn't imagine but knew he could give.

"Please?" he growled, lips caressing the swell of her breast, the wet trail of his tongue miraculously teasing cool and searing hot in equal measure.

"Please, I want you." For so long and for so many reasons.

His head lifted and she saw the challenge rising, the glint of seductive mischief blazing in the blue of his eyes. "Just me?" he taunted, his hands sliding down her hips, over the curve of her bottom to the backs of her thighs. "Or me…doing things no one else would dare?"

Her breath caught, her lips parting for a response she couldn't fathom. And somehow, amid the overwhelming desire and surging lust, a whisper of delighted laughter slipped free.

How could she be laughing when her body was about to burst into flames? She'd never known a seduction like this. Never thought it could be playful and exciting and hot and insane all at once. But then she'd never been with Nate. And thinking about the man whose mouth should be classified as a weapon of mass destruction, she realized he was all of those things and more.

She didn't know what to expect from a night with him, particularly one he seemed to have taken as a challenge. Or exactly how far out of her league she was. All she knew was no man had ever looked at her the way he was looking at that moment. As if there was no part of her he wouldn't possess.

And God help her, she wanted him to have her. "Yes."

Hands slipping down the contours of his chest, over the ridged terrain of his abs, she curled her fingers beneath his cummerbund.

"Yes, she says," he chuckled gruffly, the hands at the backs of her thighs fisting in the excess fabric of her skirt. Lifting. Handful above gathered handful, until the heat of his palms covered her bare skin. "I used to think those curls of yours were the only untamed things about you. But it's not true." He licked and sucked at the tender swells, making them plump with his attentions. "You're wild."

A surge of pleasure having nothing to do with sex shot through her at his statement. Simple confirmation of what she'd hoped, needed to believe all along. He could see her—who she really was—when no one else had even thought to look. He was the only one.

She needed him, just one person who didn't get swept up in the tide of lies and rumors, the sea of untruths that even she perpetuated. One person who saw the faulted, fallible girl hiding behind all the muted perfection and stifling 'right' choices. He hadn't judged. Hadn't told. Hadn't done anything but laugh or chuck her under the chin when the real girl behind the princess snuck out to visit him.

"You could always see me," she whispered as those big hands moved over her legs from back to front. Torturously close and painfully far from where she wanted him to be.

Nate took a knee, and, with the layers of tulle and taffeta bunched over his arms, slowly pushed the mess of it above her waist. "Good God, this is a lot of skirt." Skimming a hand up her leg, he found the scrap of her lingerie. Made an appreciative sound that had her body instantly responding.

"Without a lot beneath it." He caught her knee and hooked it over one broad shoulder, taking her weight in his hands as her balance shifted to her standing leg.

"Nate!" she protested, unfamiliar with such intimate vulnerability—but the only response from beneath her skirts was a shocking, open-mouthed kiss that burned through the fragile silk between them and stunned her silent. She hadn't been expecting it—she'd thought he'd slip her panties down and take her against the wall. That was as daring as her imagination had gotten, but this—she'd been totally unprepared for the mind-blowing effect of a man at his knees before her.

Her breath held through the first languid sweeps of his

tongue, then escaped on a cry at the teasing bite and soft nuzzle of a man whose powers of seduction knew no limits. Never had she dreamed of anything like the hot, wet sensation of Nate's forbidden kiss skillfully coaxing her along the path of pleasure. His hands covered her bottom, giving it a hot, firm grasp that started the slow slide of molten desire through her core. His tongue stroked with a gradual increase of pressure until something too long restrained pulled hard at the reins of her control. Her fingers clutched his shoulders, knotted into his hair then shot back again—seeking purchase, a hold, an anchor amid the rising tide of her lust.

"Oh, God!" she cried, sucking air in desperate gulps as her body coiled tight beneath his ministrations. "I don't…I can't…" Her hands flew to her face as her knee buckled. But Nate had her, took her weight in his arms as he moved with the rhythm of her hips. Sodden silk gave way beneath the press of his tongue at her entrance, a cruel tease that left her panting, pleading for a release just beyond her grasp. And then, with a low growl, he held her to him as his rough kiss took her over the edge and through the free fall of pleasured abandon.

Releasing her leg from his shoulder, he set her back to her feet.

Half dazed, she barely registered his long arms snaking around her back. Suddenly the catch of her gown was open and all that dress was slipping free into a pool of shimmering lavender at her feet—leaving her standing wide legged, in a pair of sodden, pearl silk panties and four-and-a-half-inch heels. It was crazy after everything that had happened, all she'd let him do already, but under the sudden exposure her arms moved instinctively to shield herself.

Nate leaned back on his knees, his brow creased with intensity born of desire, his gaze trailing hot across her skin.

"No." Brushing her hands aside, he stood before her, his chest rising and falling with the efforts of his restraint. Need

raged in his eyes. Lines of strain bracketed his mouth. The
corded muscles of his neck stood out in stark relief.

For her.

Her hands relaxed at her sides as she leaned back into the
wall allowing this devastating man to look his fill.

And then she was in his arms, beneath the renewed assault
of his kiss. His guttural response scoring her lips as he pulled
her into the unmistakable hardness of his ready body. Wide,
strong hands skimmed across her back, her hips, her thighs in
a reckless exploration that left the surface of her skin tingling
with a deep radiating awareness, pulsing into the very center
of her. It was electric and erotically invasive. It was insanity,
and with every passing second she gave in more.

"I want you…" Sensation shot through her, making control
a thing of the past. "I've wanted you…for so long."

Nate let out a low groan, his hands tightening over the
curves he'd once sworn never to touch.

For so long…

This was Payton. Brandt's little sister. With her wide-eyed
innocent stare all but guaranteeing she'd fallen under the misconception he was someone she could trust. Not tonight, she
couldn't. He couldn't look out for her best interests, not with
those breathy moans and little teeth working at his ear while
her bare breasts pressed against his shirt. Not with the taste
of her sweet on his tongue.

But if she'd been carrying some kind of torch—

He couldn't ignore what everyone knew. She wanted the
happily-ever-after. The down-on-one-knee, white-picket-
fence, pram-around-the-park fantasy. And while most women
wouldn't make the mistake of imagining him in that role,
Payton had a bad habit of seeing him in ways no one else
could. God only knew what she was thinking now. "We've
got to stop," he gritted out. But the fingers at his waist only

clenched tighter as her lust-clouded gaze drifted hungrily from his mouth to his eyes and back again.

"No," she gasped, reaching for him and sending his body into some kind of lust-induced free fall from rational ground.

No? He'd heard the word before. Could quite easily imagine it slipping past Payton's lips. Only the context was all wrong.

But then those soft lips were pulling at him, her breasts pushing against his chest and suddenly his hands were moving down the sleek line of her, settling over the bones at her hips and—

Damn it, he didn't want to stop. Didn't want to have to bring reason and rationale into something that was so good as pure instinct and response, but he wasn't a kid and he knew all too well about the consequences of diving headlong into a skirt he didn't belong in.

"Payton, wait," he managed, ignoring the wounded look in her eyes as he held her still. She needed to understand. "I'm not looking for marriage."

"Okay." She nodded, her gaze already targeting his mouth as she leaned into him again, making him wonder if she'd actually registered what he said at all. That was a risk he couldn't take. He set her back a pace, having to check that the woman driving him past sense was who he thought. Payton. Hot, demanding Payton, with her slight fingers brushing against his navel as she tried to get into his pants. Heaven help him.

"I'm serious. Look at me." Warm brown eyes, smoked with need, blinked wide as she peered up at him.

He wanted her so much it hurt. And yet, he still couldn't give in. Not yet.

"It's not just marriage. What's been going on with me—Payton, I can't do a relationship. I don't want one."

The pounding of his heart filled the seconds before she

answered. Something he didn't want to consider flickered in
her eyes. Remorse. He knew better—but before he could drag
his own ass outside to kick it, something new surfaced in her
gaze. Resignation. Acceptance. And then the spark of what
could only be described as clarity and determination.

"Do you want tonight?"

How could she even ask?

Yes, he wanted tonight. But tonight was all he wanted.
Well, that and Payton not getting hurt. Just two consenting
adults having a good time with no expectations. Only sometimes good girls like Payton got the wrong idea when they
were making out with guys at weddings. Something about the
tux triggered those saccharine fairy-tale fantasies and then
suddenly they started attributing all kinds of meaning to an
event that began as a little sordid groping in a back hallway.
Sometimes they thought if they played along, things would
change—the guy would change.

But he wouldn't. He *couldn't*. And he wasn't about to let
Payton believe otherwise.

Only before he could open his mouth, she was pulling his
face to meet hers. "Stop looking at me like I'm some little girl
you have to protect." Her hands drifted lower, running down
his chest to settle low at his abdomen again. "See me as the
woman who wants a single night with you."

It couldn't be that easy. That straightforward. Except the
stare meeting his own shone with an intent of purpose he
couldn't mistake.

She wanted him and she understood this wasn't the beginning of forever.

It was tonight. He had one night—a mere handful of
hours—to give her what no other man would dare to.

Oh, yeah.

No more second-guessing. No more wasted time.

Sweeping Payton into his arms, he strode to the bed and

tossed her—wide eyed and squeaking—back into the pillows.
Followed her down, getting off on the fact he had her naked
but for a scrap of silk and those incredible heels that were
driving him nuts…and he was still decked out in the full tux
minus the jacket. That worked for about two seconds before
he was backing off the bed, taking those tiny panties with
him. He wanted inside her more than he wanted to revel in
some fantasy.

Working the studs free, he had his shirt half off before the
sound of her voice halted his actions. "Nate?"

His head snapped up to where Payton lay reclined, one
knee sliding slowly against the other. Fighting past the rise
of pure lust at the vision of her there for his taking, he sent
up a silent prayer she hadn't come to her senses. "What?"

The pink tip of her tongue slipped in a moist trail across
the swell of her bottom lip. "Hurry."

He swallowed hard. The shirt came off in a spray of onyx
studs clattering against whatever surfaces they reached, followed immediately by the cummerbund, pants and the rest.
Body taut with need, he rolled on a condom retrieved from
his pants, unwilling to be careless with either of their futures,
and then he was on her again, losing himself in the feel of
her mouth, the press of her breasts and the glide of her knee
against his hip as she melted in his arms.

It was torture, but he held himself in check as he pressed
his length at her entrance. His gaze holding hers, silently offering one last chance to change her mind.

Maybe it was all the memories he had tied up with her. Or
that he couldn't quite stop thinking of her as the girl he wanted
to protect from the guys like him. But whatever nonsense
he'd let take seed in his mind, Payton swept it away with one
head-back, body-arched gasp of pure need…

"Please." And then as though that weren't enough,
"Ye-e-e-s-s-s," when he began to move.

Oh, yeah, he liked the sound of that at his ear as he pushed into the tight clasp of her body. Too tight to thrust hard, he gritted his teeth through the measured penetration, pulled back, only to sink again, slowly taking her deep and then deeper still, repeating again and again until he was buried to the hilt.

Her lips were parted, a suspended breath hanging between them. Looking into her eyes, he held, lost in something too good. Too perfect a fit. Too intensely right.

Her body gripped him with the rhythmic pulse that signaled she was close, and his jaw clenched hard in his fight for control. He followed her every gasp and sigh, learning exactly what she liked, what made her crazy. And when those delicate hands moved down his body, from his shoulders to his arms to his back, clutching at him as if she needed to hold on…it satisfied him in a way he didn't even want to contemplate.

She was incredible. Coming apart in his arms even as she begged him for more.

Hell, yes, there was more. A whole night's worth of more. Payton didn't want to be the good girl tonight, and after six months he needed to be bad.

CHAPTER FIVE

PAYTON roused herself from a sated state of lethargy, peeling back her eyelids only to encounter a tangle of curls blocking her view. Shifting slowly, she reached up to shove the mess from her eyes—halting at the slow rise and fall of a chest beneath her cheek.

Nate.

She swallowed down the burst of joyous excitement as images, sensations and whispers of the night before bombarded her waking consciousness.

He'd been so gentle with her the first time. So careful. And then after that—

Her toes curled deep beneath the sheets at the thought of all they'd done.

Everything.

They'd made love, over and over again. Nate waking her with his hands, his mouth. A seductive growl accompanied by his rising need. Nothing planned. Nothing proper or polite about it.

Incredible.

"What's got you smiling so early?" Nate's morning-rough voice stroked over her like a soothing caress, bringing her attention to the hard line of his stubbled jaw and the soft amusement in his blue, blue eyes. They were intimately wound together. Arms and legs and bare skin everywhere. It felt good and, though today they wouldn't be lovers, Payton wasn't about to rush from the bed or give up the warmth of his body, the steady *thump, thump* of his heart sounding beneath her ear, or the shelter of his arms around her. She couldn't. Not yet.

For now, they were comfortably entwined. Or at least they were until Nate reached down her back with one hand and pinched her bottom.

"Hey!" she squeaked, ineffectually trying to pinch back at skin too muscle packed to give.

"The grin. Tell."

Inching her bum out of pinching distance, she raised a brow. "So desperate to feed your ego?"

"Mmm, so it's an ego-feeding grin. Tell me more."

She took a deep breath, weighing the temptation to share her indecent revelation. He'd never judged her before...but this was different. Telling in a way she wanted him to know but was afraid to reveal. After what they'd done last night, she might have finally killed the *good girl* misconception, and owning up to what had her smiling—the part beyond finally being in his arms—might negate all the progress she'd made. Casting a sidelong glance his way, to that devilish smile and waiting stare, the temptation proved too much to resist. Her eyes squeezed shut and she fessed up in a rush of breath. "I'm thinking you're the first notch in my bedpost."

There! That wasn't so bad. It was freeing, in fact. And—

Her eyes blinked open as Nate froze beside her, every muscle in his body gone taut and his breathing at an abrupt halt.

Her chin pulled back. Not quite the "partner-in-crime" kind of response she'd hoped for.

He couldn't be *insulted*. But now that she thought about it, she wouldn't feel great about being described as a notch either.

"You weren't a virgin." The words rasped out more plea than question or statement.

Momentarily stunned, Payton could practically feel his cold dread at the thought she'd saved something so special for him. That the night he'd given her on condition it be casual be so spectacularly significant. That she'd deceived him.

"No!" Her hands flew to the sides of her face as she shook her head in vehement denial. "I wasn't a virgin, I promise! I meant 'notch' like uncommitted. Sex for sex's sake." The beginning of her reckless adventure. He didn't need to know how special being with him truly was to her. After today it would never be an issue again. She wouldn't let it be. "Don't panic, please."

Nate's relief was a palpable thing, like a rush of air back into the room, the return of pressure with a whoosh.

"I wasn't panicking," he scoffed, pushing to one elbow on his side. "Pretty little princesses don't make me panic. Especially not when they are…" he lifted the sheet for dramatic effect, offering a quick leer at her prone body before meeting her eyes again "…naked."

Relief washed through her at the ease with which he recovered, but a lingering tension remained and his expression turned serious. Concerned.

"Are you okay about this, Payton?" Catching a wild curl with his finger, he pushed it over her ear. Let his mouth pull into a crooked twist when it sprang free and bounced back in front of her eyes. "With last night being the only night?"

She took a steadying breath. "I am if we go forward as friends."

In those first minutes after the kiss became real in the hallway, she might have indulged in a fantasy where there could be more. A little longing or hope. But she'd quickly understood it wasn't a romance in the making. And though a part of her cared for Nate on a level she couldn't acknowledge to him, there was another part of her excited by the raw rush of her very own too-good-to-feel-guilty-about night of passion. A night only he could give her. Because she trusted him.

"Friends," he said as if testing the word out.

"Yeah. I've missed you in my life. I don't want to give you up again."

Tiny lines etched at the corners of his eyes as he held her stare. "Do you feel like you can go forward from here without this—" he waved a slow hand between them "—getting in the way?"

She knew she could. She'd done it for years before Nate walked out of her life. "I can if you can. Even if you can't tell if you've got a virgin in your bed."

Brows arching high as he let out a sharp laugh, Nate rocked back, pulling Payton over with him. "Be a while before I live that down, will it?"

She squinted at him from her perch atop his chest. "Probably."

"Then I better steer this little chat back toward the ego feeding." Settling against the pillow to get comfortable, he prompted, "So tell me how it is I score bedpost-notch status."

Payton readjusted around him and let her gaze run the length of his pure masculine perfection, complete with one heavily muscled leg thrown over the sheet, and wondered how he could even ask.

"It's just it was so…intense without being…serious. It wasn't candlelight and promises of love everlasting."

"You don't like those things?" he asked, running a finger down the curve of her shoulder.

Guiltily she glanced away, then forced her gaze back. "No, I do. I'm sure I would—" If she ever actually felt that forever kind of glow, she would probably love it. If Nate had wanted to give her those things…

Only he didn't and she knew it. The only thing everlasting

in their future was the schoolgirl crush she expected would never quite go away. And a friendship if she was lucky. "What I mean is this was so...*hot* and it's never been like that for me before. Impulsive. Exciting." She felt the blush creeping into her cheeks—held Nate's gaze anyway, needing him to understand. "No strings. No expectations."

"Hell, if I'd known that I wouldn't have worked so hard."

She let out her own laugh then, swatting harmlessly at his chest. "You know what kind of expectations I'm talking about. The long-term kind." It would be impossible to go to bed with Nate without some kind of expectation. His name was practically scrawled on the ladies' lounge wall next to the words "for a good time". "It's never been so much...fun. So...free. My other experience wasn't like this."

This time it was Nate's turn to pull back. "Your 'other experience'? As in singular? I mean, I knew your experience was limited, but that idiot was your first?"

"Nate! Can't you at least pretend you don't know who I'm talking about? And he isn't an idiot." Clint wasn't perfect. Far from it. What she'd had with him was polite. It was pleasant. But it hadn't been deep and it hadn't been passionate. It hadn't been *real*. How could it have been when one of the people in the relationship hadn't actually existed? Not that Clint ever noticed or cared. But even so, it hardly seemed fair to discuss his lack of creativity and vigor with a man so completely out of his league.

"I can't believe you gave it up to *Clint*."

Payton bristled. Some long-ago disappointment—frustrated and immature—reared its head, lashing out. "Well, you didn't take it," she snapped. "I had to give it to someone."

Nate coughed, his brows crashing down. "Thankfully you never offered."

Yes, probably a good thing since he'd vanished from her life a few days after she'd decided she wanted him to be the one. She'd finally been ready to screw up the courage and tell him how she felt. Only it was too late. The friendship between them had become a casualty of the fallout with Brandt.

Nate's finger caught under her chin, urging her focus back to his face. "I think it might have killed me to say no. But I would have had to. You were sixteen."

"You were only eighteen."

"Yeah, but there's a big difference between those ages, Payton. Besides, I was leaving for school and I didn't ever want to come back."

Because of people like her brother and his friends. Nate knew plenty about being on the wrong side of the talk, just as she did. And right now, she didn't want either of them to have to think about it.

"Well, I suppose you might have been worth waiting for."

Propping an arm behind his head, he cocked a wry smile at her. "So glad you enjoyed yourself."

"The way my life has been going, well, I needed this— you." She blinked up at him, those soft brown eyes tugging at his heart just as they always had. "You really are quite a lot of fun."

Leaning in, he caught her lips with his own. His arm tightened across her back, holding her close through this soft, lingering last kiss. Slowly they parted and Payton let out a sigh that feathered over his jaw and neck as she drew away. It was a sweet, quietly satisfied sound that, coupled with the soft press of her breast against his abdomen, the smooth skin of her thigh crossed over his, and the bare heat of her against him, had him fighting the urge to pull her back.

She felt good and he wanted her again. Wanted more fun. More intensity. He wanted to give her more of what she'd never had before. Except he didn't want to give her any kind of false promise or misconception about the potential for a relationship. And something in those big brown eyes staring up at him said he needed to tread carefully. Payton's heart was a responsibility he didn't want to bear.

"I get what you're saying. And I had a good time, too."

"Had" being the operative word.

"Thanks, Nate." Her grin spread wide and she closed her eyes indulging in one long, languorous stretch that moved her in a slow slide of flesh as she rolled away from him. His gut tensed as she arched back, rotating her hips in a decadent extension of feminine musculature and pretty pink skin. He should look away. Turn his head. Get the hell out of the bed before he did something stupid, but already his heart was turning over, getting ready to rev with thoughts of consequence quickly dissipating.

Maybe just one more—

And then she was climbing out of bed—dragging the sheet he'd barely had a corner of with her as she cast an impish wink back and darted for the bathroom.

His fingers tingled where he'd almost gotten hold of her. Damn, it was a good thing they were taking this off a physical level. He liked control. After the past six months, he needed it. And Payton, all naked and soft, had an unnerving ability to threaten his.

He glared at the closed bathroom door. He wasn't following her in there.

The shower sounded, then the quiet thud of the sliding glass door as it closed.

He wasn't going to take her against the tile wall. Bury himself inside her again. No. Because if he gave in, one more time wouldn't be enough. It would be again and again. Finding new and creative ways to get Payton's petite form wrapped tight around him. In his arms. In his bed. But that was all he'd have to offer her. Sex. And right now, the friendship they both needed was more important than that.

So, no. Definitely not. He wouldn't follow.

CHAPTER SIX

PAYTON stood beneath the hot spray, her body tender from sensual satisfaction, her mind whirling a mile a minute as she began to compartmentalize everything that had happened with Nate. Everything that would happen. She needed to be cool, to make sure he understood she didn't have expectations about a future together. Or at least a romantic future. Because while last night had been incredible—exciting in a way she hadn't believed possible and would never regret—it was the going forward that mattered.

Going forward as friends.

Tipping her face beneath the water, she pushed back the sodden curls, wringing the heavy mass clean.

These past hours with Nate had been a taste of what she'd missed so much over the years. Someone who could see her as she truly was. Accept her without recrimination. He hadn't balked at her attraction—her interest in a single night of insanity. He'd helped her embrace it.

She needed that kind of freedom and acceptance as she edged out of the mold of perfect daughter to a man no longer there to maintain it for. She needed to be real.

Brandt wouldn't approve of this business with Nate, and her mother—well, she was already worried out of her mind about the changes Payton had made with her career, her apartment, Clint. Most of all Clint. Nate would be just one more thing.

But it was time she stopped living her life to someone else's expectations.

Turning the brass tap fixtures to "off", she stepped from the shower and knotted a thick terry bath sheet between her breasts. Stared into the mirror seeing the foggy image of a woman no one knew.

She'd been alone for too long. Surrounded by so many people—all the right people with their picture-perfect smiles and placid conversation—yet none of them knew her. What she really thought. Who she was.

And at the first sign she might be more than they believed, the talk had started. Concerned talk. Catty talk. The kind of talk she'd never been interested in and didn't care to listen to now. She'd rather be alone. Only eventually loneliness wore on a person and they started to search for someone—a friend—to take them as they were.

A breath eased from her chest. A smile curved her lips.

She'd found Nate. And he'd asked her to be the friend he needed. When she needed one most. So this would work.

She opened the bathroom door and stepped into the now sun drenched suite, scanning the floor for her panties and bra. And her dress! She didn't want to put that thing on again, but unless she planned to sprint for Nate's limo in a robe it was the only option.

They'd started by the wall, but the floor was clear. Then the bed—

Her lips parted in silent awe.

Nate sat reclined against the headboard in his black trousers and bare feet, hair a spiky mess and tuxedo shirt hanging open down his chest. His attention fixed on *The Wall Street Journal* in his hands.

The look was all sin and seduction and wild bad-boy. This was the shot the magazine should have run next to his most-wanted bachelor bio. He wouldn't be able to beat the women off with a stick.

Forcing her gaze away before he needed the stick for her, she noticed the pink lounge pants, zip jacket and shirt neatly folded at the foot of the bed. An accompanying set of lacey panties and bra lay beside them. "When— How?"

Without looking up, he yawned, "While you were in the shower."

She checked the tags. This man had practice purchasing women's clothing. "Quite an impressive skill set you have going on—your ability to guess sizes so accurately."

A wry smile tugged at his lips. "I've got my limitations. I'd've had a tough time eyeballing you for a fitting. But I know exactly what fills my palm."

"You're bad," she muttered, running a fingertip over the soft fabric.

"Yeah, but, as we've already established..." he folded the paper and tossed it beside him "...you like it." Rising from the bed, he cast a lazy glance her way—and stopped. His eyes riveted to her.

"What?" Her hands went to her hair, seeking out some pile of suds she'd missed. Then, tucking her chin, she looked down. Everything packed away where it was supposed to be, and yet Nate's halted posture—his unsettled reaction—was clearly in response to her. "Is something wrong?"

And then she saw it, in the last second before he gave an abrupt shake of the head and turned his back to her.

Heat. Desire. Ruthlessly shut down. She understood they weren't continuing a physical relationship, but his almost hostile reaction—

"Nate?" she asked, crossing her arms over her chest to stave off the cool chill running through her heart.

"Nothing. Just realized I forgot a file at the office," he

answered abruptly. "Go on and get dressed and we'll get out of here."

Payton took a step back. "Sure. Of course." Just as well. She'd been looking at Nate like too much of a temptation anyway and that wasn't going to work. Not for either of them. Gathering the loungewear he'd gotten for her, she went back to the bathroom. The sooner they got out of this suite and back onto solid friendship ground, the better.

A few minutes later she returned to find a hastily scrawled note atop the bed.

Had to rush out. My driver is waiting for you downstairs. I'll get your address and stop over this afternoon.

Payton stared down at the note in blatant disbelief. She'd been on the other side of the door, a few panels of wood between then, and he'd left a note? The nerve!

No—this was something other than nerve. Nate would never intentionally hurt her. He might cat around, but he wasn't cruel and he wasn't callous. Her mind played back the minutes before he'd left, slowing to that last glimpse of desire and then anger. He hadn't wanted to see her that way. Hadn't wanted the attraction.

So be it. She'd look at this as the clean break they needed.

When she saw him again, it would be as friends.

And then her *friend* could explain what kind of a mess he'd gotten himself into that he needed a pretend affair to cover it up.

Nate raked his fingers through his hair, balling them at the base of his skull before letting go with a grunt. His dogged strides ate up the sidewalk, taking him fast from the scene of the crime. He was a jackass of the most contemptible variety.

But seeing her there, wrapped in that towel, wet tendrils of hair snaking over her bare shoulders, tiny beads of water sprinkled across the swells of her freshly scrubbed skin—it was like being thrown back in time. To a place he didn't want to revisit.

To a time when he was still mere potential and promise. Trying to exist within the confines of an environment that wanted to squelch the pride and drive out of him. Teach him a lesson. Show him he wasn't good enough. That nothing he did could change it.

When all the frustrations and inequities of his youth came to a head—all driven by one inadvertent mistake. One look. One girl.

And like that, the years folded over and his feet were pounding up the stairs at the Liss house as he went for the textbook he'd left on Brandt's floor the night before. Breaking the landing, he'd looked up, and through the open door of Payton's bedroom, there she was. Brandt's little sister emerging from her bathroom—fresh from the shower. Totally unaware.

He stopped breathing. Stood, mouth agape, stunned. Payton, his little shadow—always bundled in those conservative sweaters, jackets and formless clothing, her hair restrained, her legs covered—stood wrapped in a towel, her curls wet and wild, her curves unmistakable, her legs bare and pink and looking so soft. He jerked his gaze away. Snapped his jaw shut and forced his fists into his pockets.

God help him, she was beautiful. Hell, he'd known she was beautiful. Sweet and funny. But he'd never wanted her until that very minute and it caught him like a sock to the gut.

For too many reasons he had to get out of there. Couldn't risk that he'd look again.

Turning, he opened his eyes to the enraged red of Brandt's face. And in that instant the façade of forced civility between them crumbled and the cold truth glared back at him.

Hatred.

Nate had always been aware of the barely contained aggression simmering beneath the surface with Brandt. It wound the kid off to no end to be dependent on a guy he considered his inferior for the tutoring that put the Ivy League school so necessary to his elitist identity within reach. There'd always been a cool distance. The laughingly misplaced attitude Brandt was the one doing Nate a favor, rather than the other way around. Yeah, Nate had gotten paid—he sure as hell hadn't spent four afternoons a week for three years waiting on Brandt to get off the phone or bother to show up out of friendship. But still, he hadn't expected the depth of loathing he now saw.

"Take it easy. It's not what you think—"

"Bull! You were staring at her." A hand shot out, shoving hard at Nate's shoulder. "I saw your damn face, man. You aren't good enough for her. Not even to look!"

Nate didn't take to being pushed around. Not by anybody, but Payton was Brandt's little sister. So, rather than knocking the guy's head back with the punch gathering in his fist, he reached out and hauled him down the stairs and out to the front yard. Away from Payton. "You're off base. I was leaving."

"Damn straight you are," Brandt sneered. "And you're nuts if you think you're ever coming back here."

"Fine, whatever." Let the Lisses deal with the fallout. The school year was nearly over anyway. He'd get another job, something to last through the summer until he got out of this inbred cesspool and into U of I. "Look, I was going for my Calc book upstairs. If you get it for me, I'll take off."

Brandt let out a snort, rocking back on his heels to look down his nose at Nate. "Yeah, I'll get right on that."

He looked up to the house. He needed that book and, after this, going to Payton wasn't an option either.

*Brandt followed his eyes and let out a disgusted grunt.
"What'd you think, with summer a few weeks off you needed
another ticket onto the gravy train? That sniffing around my
sister would get you back by the poolside?"*

Screw him.

*"Forget it, Evans, Payton's not like the rest of your
dates. The girls who go out with trash to get back at their
daddies."*

*Nate's blood, already hot, began to boil beneath the rise
of a deep-seated pride held too long in check. It was absurd
and he knew it. But still something in the jab stung. Hit a little
too close to an insecurity he didn't want to acknowledge. A
sense of alienation he couldn't quite get past. "Go to hell."*

*"After you. And here." Brandt went for his wallet and
pulled out a stack of crisp bills. More money than Nate earned
in a month. "For the cost of your book."*

*Extracting a fifty, Brandt dropped the bill to the dirt and
ground it in with his heel. "Go ahead. Pick it up. You know
you can't afford to replace it on your own."*

*Nate's muscles bunched, his knuckles whitened at his side
as the world closed in around him. He had to get out of there.
Forcing his legs to move, he turned. Took a step to leave.*

It didn't matter. Brandt didn't matter.

*But the kid wouldn't give it up and grabbed for him. "Hey,
I'm not done with you yet."*

*"Don't be stupid, Liss," he warned, easily shaking the
other boy off, determined to walk away.*

*"You calling me stupid?" Brandt grabbed again...cocking
his arm as he spun Nate back.*

*Mistake. One too many...and then the blood was flowing
fast and red before Nate even realized he'd thrown. Brandt
staggered back a step, fell on his ass with a howl before finding his feet and running toward the house. "You're going to
pay for that, Evans!"*

Damn it, where was his control? Nate's heart slammed within his chest as the repercussions of his actions sped through his mind. Arrest, expulsion, college, his escape from a life he'd almost been free of. His dad could end up paying for this mistake. What the hell had he done?

The door to the Liss house flew open and Payton, now dressed in jeans and a turtleneck, rushed onto the lawn. Eyes wide with hurt disbelief, she stared down at Nate's knuckles and the smear of her brother's blood streaking them.

"I'm sorry." His voice was rough with emotion, shame and disgust. He should have known better. He'd been so close to escaping this place without giving into his own sense of injustice. And now this.

In the end, he hadn't been arrested. Hadn't paid any price beyond his own personal shame at allowing Brandt Liss to goad him into losing control. But that price had been enough.

Hell, it was crazy. One glimpse of Payton wrapped in her towel back in the suite and all the insults and accusations had sliced through time, cutting fresh into his mind. Stupid prejudices. Words he couldn't believe he'd let bother him.

So why had his gut tightened, as though controlled by un-pleasant muscle memory? Why had his body instantly wound tight, setting for a fight? And why, beneath it all, was he still tied up by that single forbidden memory of Payton and the taunt of a guy whose significance to Nate's life barely registered?

Not good enough...not even to look...

Maybe. No, definitely. But sure as hell not for the reasons Brandt believed.

CHAPTER SEVEN

IT WAS close to two when the bell rang. Payton had spent the better part of the morning—what was left of it once she'd been dropped home—doing her best not to think about Nate and what would happen when they saw each other. How exactly one transitioned from lover to friend, and what it would take for her mind to stop playing out scenarios where she ended up back in his arms, beneath his kiss.

That was thinking she couldn't afford. So she'd done as little of it as possible.

But now her avoidance was at an end. Nate was downstairs. At her door. And all the thoughts she'd so effectively ignored were bombarding her at once.

Thoughts like spending the night together had been reckless. Careless. And might have irrevocably changed his feelings for her. Jeopardized their friendship by putting her on par with some nameless "double D" he'd picked up at a club.

Her anxiety rose with each step she descended until she swung open the security door, took in the vision of him—big and broad, dressed casually in weathered jeans, untucked oxford and a lightweight, ash V-neck sweater—and lost her breath to the enormous bouquet of yellow roses he held out in offering.

She fell back against the door, a hand going to her throat where emotion threatened to choke her. He'd brought her friendship flowers. The perfect transition from last night to today. A tender reassurance of the caring between them.

"Oh, you're good," she said, shaking her head in awe.

"What kind of greeting is that for your secret lover?" Nate asked, a smug smile on his face. "Shouldn't you be suspiciously glancing around and then dragging me inside before someone catches sight of us out here?"

"So back to the charade, then?" Trying to curb the grin that spread to her lips when she'd opened the door, she crossed her arms. "You're enjoying this way too much."

He cocked his head as if considering, then shrugged. "You might be right, but, the way I see it, it's a pretty good way to feed my fantasies. Just play like there's a crowd watching and I get a beautiful woman to heed my every command."

He thought she was *beautiful*. "Your every command, huh?"

"Mmm-hmm. Very kinky. The whole control thing. Sorry we didn't get around to it, but there's a limit to even my abilities within one night."

She couldn't help but laugh, wondering how it was that the world at large believed Nate Evans so frightening. She'd never met anyone who took *themselves* less seriously—while at the same time being so seriously driven to success. "So you've gone mad with power, have you?"

"Seems I have."

"Well, in that case…" She made an exaggerated show of peering down the sidewalk and street, first one way and then the other, before grabbing for Nate's shirt and towing him in through the security door. Then, casting him an impish wink, she asked, "Was it good for you? Because it was definitely good for me."

Nate's jaw set to the side as he shook his head. "Sassy thing." Then after a beat, "Are you really okay with this?"

If he led the way…yes. "I am. But before we tempt fate with another hallway, let's get upstairs."

Nate nodded, and then as he glanced around his brow furrowed. She saw the moment his surroundings registered. No flash, no glitter. Just aging tile flooring. A worn banister leading up a simple staircase.

"I figured you for a skyrise penthouse or something. With a fleet of round-the-clock security guards, closed-circuit monitored elevator. This place isn't what I expected."

She headed up the first flight, acting as though his observation hadn't struck a nerve. It was okay. He wasn't entirely off-base, just about twelve months too late.

"I moved in last year." A few weeks after her father passed away. She couldn't stand to live in the apartment he'd been renting for her—let alone afford it. And when she'd found this…well, it suited her.

Catching up, Nate grunted something unintelligible and she decided not to ask. She'd been hoping he'd see the building and understand she was supporting herself. Maybe respect her autonomy. But it didn't matter. He'd see soon enough she'd made herself a home.

Nate rounded the third landing working through the reasons why Payton Liss would live in an apartment like this. Real estate speculation? She'd bought the building and was living-in while she worked a refurb of some sort. But where was the telltale smell of construction? And why the third floor apartment and the hallway reeking of ethnic cuisine. "Something on the stove?"

She shook her head, drawing in a deep breath. "No, that's the Craines on two. I get hungry every time I walk past."

The single door on the third floor stood ajar, left open from when she'd run down to let him in, and two things struck him at once. The first, single women should never leave their apartment doors open. And the second, what the hell had she been running down to the first floor for—where was the security box to screen and admit her guests? Before he could ask, she swung the door open and, smiling wide, walked in.

To a shoe box.

Not even as big as the place he'd lived with his dad.

"What is this?" he demanded, hostility welling inexplicably within him.

"This is my apartment, Nate. And stop scowling at it like it's something you need to scrape off your shoe."

"But what are *you* doing living in it?" She had money, security. It didn't make sense.

She rounded on him with an open-mouthed expression of disbelief and maybe something worse.

He didn't care. "Where's the security intercom?"

"What?"

"It's not safe to leave your apartment and come down to check the security door. How do you even know who's out there? Someone could be waiting in the hall for you to open the door." She was so slight, so petite, she'd never stand a chance against an attacker. His aggravation flared.

Crossing to the front windows, he checked the latches and tested the frame. Secure enough, but—

"For your information, Nate, I like it. It's affordable, close to the school, the 'L' and the lakefront."

A glimpse out the window confirmed what he already suspected: a trip to the lakefront entailed taking the pedestrian underpass below Lake Shore Drive. He turned on her. "Tell me you don't walk over there by yourself."

She looked as though he'd slapped her, but if she didn't have sense enough to look out for herself, then she was going to have to put up with some pointed questions from him.

"Does Brandt even know about this?" Where the hell was her brother's protective instinct now? Her father was gone and that prick Clint had bailed. She needed someone looking out for her now more than ever.

"Yes. Brandt knows. I've had him to dinner once. Though, like you, he found it lacking and he prefers to take me out."

Found it lacking. That was for damn sure. So why hadn't he set her up somewhere more suitable? He knew for a fact Brandt just bought some office building downtown. There was money, so why was Payton living like a pauper? Maybe dropping in on Brandt at work would shed some light on it. He could put the priority of Payton's security into perspective for the guy.

No, forget it. Bad idea. He'd handle the situation himself. He didn't have time to be worrying about her safety.

"You can't live here. We'll find another apartment this afternoon."

Payton's back stiffened, and those earthy warm eyes that had been looking up at him as if he were the only man in the world mere hours ago took on a glare that said he was just another jerk. "What?"

The decision made, he pulled his phone from his pocket to call up a realtor he knew. "Don't worry about the rent."

But then Payton was in his face, her finger jabbing into his chest. "Have you lost your mind?" she snapped. "Of all the controlling, overbearing— I'm not moving out. I chose this place so I could have my *independence. I love it here.*"

He stared at her, comprehension dawning, but not quickly enough to stop the next barb. "When did you become such a damn snob, Nate?"

So she was paying her own way. He knew all too well about independence. The need for it having driven him to finish school early while working a job at the same time. Anything to get far enough ahead he wouldn't have to go back. But if she wasn't safe, it wasn't acceptable. "The intercom—"

"Is being replaced on Monday. And, not that it's any of your business, but I jog at the lakefront every morning and always carry pepper spray and an emergency air horn. The crime rate in the neighborhood is particularly low, my landlord's security precautions are high, and I don't appreciate your steamrolling one bit." Her arms were crossed, her breath coming fast with her frustration. But her eyes—beneath that sparking hostility he caught the glimpse of hurt and disappointment.

What was he doing?

This place was important to her and he'd stormed in and treated it like garbage. What was the matter with him? He'd taken one look, decided it didn't fit his idea of what Payton's life should be like and flown off the handle in what he could only explain as an overprotective, testosterone-driven mania.

"I'm being an ass. There's nothing wrong with your apartment." In fact, as he adjusted his perspective, he couldn't see anything wrong with it at all. It wasn't brand-new or extravagant, but it was clean. Neat. Cozy. The view was attractive, the light good. The design was old Chicago, with attractive molding and high ceilings throughout. Crystal-knob fixtures and etched-glass transoms. A brick hearth. Hardwood floors. The apartment was attractive. The furniture tasteful and conservative. Homey.

He simply hadn't expected to find Payton Liss living here. And for some reason, it irritated him that she did.

Arms still crossed, she shifted her weight from one hip to the other. Blew out a breath that sent a stray curl momentarily adrift, and then moved over to the couch and plopped down into the cushions. "You weren't much worse than Brandt. So, I suppose I'll have to forgive you."

Wow, not much worse than Brandt. He needed to spend more time with his dad if he'd become that much of a snob.

Nate glanced over to where she'd leaned into the cushioned armrest. An open paperback lay atop the coffee table beside her and a cup of tea that looked as though it had gone cool some time ago. He dropped into the opposite corner. It was comfortable. Good to be sitting with her. Only... He reached across and pulled Payton into him, tucking her under his shoulder, adjusting her just so as she laughed, not bothering to protest at all.

"Oh, yeah, that's it." Nice.

How many times had they sat like this as kids, watching TV, talking, joking around? How many times had he thought about it while wondering why another woman didn't fit quite as well? Payton was small boned and delicate, with all those sweet soft spots that made her fit just right.

After a minute of enjoying the familiarity, he rubbed a hand over her shoulder and leaned back to look at her. "I'm not trying to be insulting, but I've got to ask. What about your father's estate? I mean, the Lisses are wealthy."

She plucked a bit at the hem of her shirt before answering. "Honestly, my family is very generous and my mother would probably love to finance my every expenditure, but that kind of dependence comes with too many strings. I earn my own salary and...now that my father is gone, I prefer to pay my own way."

Ah-h-h. There it was. The mention of her father with the accompanying wince to go along. The visible twinge of guilt as though the admission that she was going against his wishes still pained her.

And yet she was doing it anyway. Changing her life.

With no rescue necessary, all he had to offer was the gentle squeeze of his hand over her shoulder. The quiet communication that he understood. And maybe a confidence of his own.

"We've got a date Tuesday night to stir up more press and gossip, but today's beautiful. What do you say we take a ride somewhere and talk?" Payton deserved to know what had spurred this whole fiasco. "Head down to the Dunes? We can work out the game plan for the month. Pace it out. And maybe just catch up some, too."

Her smile lit up the room. "Let me grab a sweater."

CHAPTER EIGHT

BENEATH the late September sky, Nate cut through the side streets, heading for Lake Shore Drive. Payton sat snuggled beside him in the sleek silver convertible, face tipped to catch the warm sunshine washing the city in an amber glow. The cold snap of a few days before coupled with the strong winds had blown half the autumn leaves from their trees in one quick drop. The result was a glorious quilt of toasted hues, alive with the wind, surging in swells and chasing the car in spirals of rusts and golds.

It was beautiful.

Nate grinned beside her. "Fall still your favorite time of year?"

"Yes. Though it isn't quite the same living in the city as it was back at the house."

"You miss raking?"

She glanced over. "Yeah, I do."

Brandt had thought she was nuts. She remembered his disdainful stare as he watched her sweeping the rake back and forth across the yard, pulling the accumulated leaves into mass, ignoring the burn in her shoulders until she had the pile as wide and tall as she was.

And then the surprise of strong hands grabbing her from behind, that wicked laugh coming a second before she was tossed into the pile.

"You always helped me."

He let out a short laugh. "Wasn't like Brandt would."

No. Nor her father. And Mom, she was more of Brandt's mind. Confused why her daughter would even look at a rake when the landscapers would mow, blow and pluck every fallen leaf from the yard each Friday.

They hadn't gotten it. But Nate had.

Payton closed her eyes, giving into the rush of open air around them as Nate blew south on the Drive headed for the Skyway. Her mind played in shadowed memories of leaf piles, Nate laughing at her side…and then as she drifted, lulled by the smooth hum of the engine, the memories became something else. A mix of then and now. A cross of memory and imagining blurred into one. The tastes and touches she'd only just learned coupling with their bodies rolling in a tangled embrace. The heavy weight of Nate pressing her down into a bed of crisp russet and plum foliage, the scent of woods and earth surrounding them.

His name broke her lips on a sigh. "Nate…"

"Yeah, babe?"

Payton jerked in her seat, the heat of embarrassment burning her cheeks even as another heat lingered deeper in her body. Her hands waved in the air as she cast about for some satisfactory explanation other than she'd fallen asleep and begun dreaming about *him*.

"I—I'm—how long do you think until we get there?"

"Forty minutes maybe?" he offered casually. "Plenty of time if you want to grab a little shut-eye."

Stiffening, she managed one word. "What?"

"A nap. There's time." Dark lenses shielded his eyes from her scrutiny, but his mouth sat at that casual tilt so typical of him. He looked relaxed. Comfortable. Not at all as if he'd just busted her moaning his name in her sleep. Maybe she'd merely sounded drowsy.

That was it. Because he'd suggested a nap.

Easing down into the soft leather of the seats, she breathed deeply, trying to let go of the tension snapping through her body at the thought she'd given too much away. After a few moments, her limbs relaxed and her eyes drifted closed. And as fatigue overtook her, a low chuckle sounded from across the distance of her consciousness.

"Pleasant dreams, Payton."

Once parked, Payton roused herself from what she only hoped was a quiet sleep and met Nate around the back of the car.

"Warm enough?" he asked, pulling an old blanket from the trunk.

The wind whipped at her hair, but the sun was still bright. Pulling her sweater tight around her, she nodded, peering up at the steep rise of the dunes before them. "I just need to wake up. And if I remember correctly, the hike up'll get my blood pumping."

"Needed that nap, huh?" Nate brushed a thumb beneath her right eye. "Puffy. Cute."

Pulling back, she instinctively raised a hand to check. Puffy? Wonderful.

Clearing his throat, he stretched his arms out, rotating one shoulder and then the other. "Someone must have done a decent job of wearing you out last night."

Only Nate would find a way to turn sleep-swollen eyes into a means of stroking his own ego.

It was a call to trash-talk if ever she heard one. "Not really. Pretty sure I slept through most of it."

He laughed, already making his way up the rise. "You mean you were rendered unconscious. My attentions have been known to overwhelm."

Payton struggled up beside him. "No." Not to be outdone, she feigned a weary sigh. "I drift off when I'm bored." Then fighting a gloating snicker, she added, "Can't say for sure—I barely remember."

She'd take that point.

Yes, sir.

With a swish of her hips and spring in her step, she pushed up the sandy incline, oblivious to Nate's narrowing eyes or the calculating set to his jaw. In a motion too fast to defend against, he reached for her, one powerful arm pulling her into his chest while the other caught her knee to his hip.

Her breath was gone, her mouth agape. All misconceptions about scoring points swept away by the feral gleam in the blue eyes above her.

Straining for air, she gasped, "What are you doing?"

"Reminding you." The gruff threat was her only warning before his lips descended in a brutal crush. The hand at her back snaked up to wind in the mass of her hair and pull her head back, opening her to the thrust of his tongue. Once. Twice. And her body was alive, pulsing with the need for more—

Except it was over and firm hands were setting her a step away.

A single brow rose in question, the seductive threat radiating off him in waves. "Now what were you saying about last night?"

Too stunned to even contemplate a quick-witted barb or smart-mouthed response, she gave him what he demanded. The truth. "It was incredible, and I'll never forget it."

"Good." He winked, sweeping up the discarded blanket with one hand as he started up again. "No more reminders necessary."

Payton stared in shocked disbelief at Nate's retreating form, her indignation on the rise. "I thought we said one night!"

"We did," he called back, barely bothering to turn his head

to respond. "But if one night's all I get, then, babe, you better believe I'm going to make sure you remember it."

By the time they'd skidded down the beach side of the dune, Payton had her outrage, heart-rate and unwilling smile under control. The kiss had completely blindsided her, serving as an effective warning about going for the last word with a man whose drive to win apparently knew no limits of decency. But it also relieved her anxiety about Nate's ability to handle the lovers-to-friends transition.

That was the kiss of a man unconcerned about his ability to turn it on or off. Which suited Payton fine. After so many years of watching every word, she didn't want to censor herself now.

As they hit the damp packed sand, Nate offered a spot beneath his arm. She stepped into the warmth of his hold and they walked in companionable silence.

Gulls soared overhead, and children sprinted through the sand in the distance.

Nate pulled off his glasses and, tucking them into the V of his sweater, turned to her. The normal vibrancy of his eyes had gone brittle beneath the strain of his burden. She knew what was coming. An explanation for this cloak and dagger game with the press, the pretend affair that all too briefly turned real. He didn't want to talk about it, but he would.

"One of the women I dated last year came to me pregnant."

Her heart stalled in her chest as she imagined a child, a golden-haired, blue-eyed bit of Nate, new to the world. And a woman she couldn't even fathom? "My God, Nate..."

What could she say? Congratulations? It hardly seemed as though joyous celebration were the theme of his disclosure considering the lengths to which he was going to shake the press off the scent of his secret. And yet, offering her sympathy seemed equally inappropriate. Questions rose fast and urgent within her, each more desperate to claw free than the one before, but she willed herself silent, waiting for him to go on.

"I was fairly sure she'd been with someone else after we'd ended things, but the timing she described... It was possible. She wanted to get married. Swore up and down the baby was mine. Only, I knew it wasn't. Hell, I suspected." He let out a heavy sigh, ducked and scooped up a handful of sand. Let the grains sift through his fingers. "Maybe I just wished."

Eyes to the darkening waters of Lake Michigan, he straightened. "Whatever the case, I wouldn't marry her. Not until I had a blood test to confirm her claim. She kept pushing. Didn't want her child born a bastard. Didn't want the risk of a prebirth DNA sample." He shook his head, his jaw set off to one side.

Payton waited, her heart in her throat. Her mind blanked beyond anything but the words coming painfully from Nate's mouth.

"In the end, she was born healthy. Not mine. Not that I'd had much doubt at that point."

"Nate, I'm so sorry. That must have been terrible to wait through."

He cast her a quick smile. "Yeah, well. It's been a tough six months. And honestly, the last thing I need is to have the press getting things stirred up again."

She could only imagine what it had been like for him. Of course he didn't want the gory details rehashed for public consumption.

But what she couldn't understand was how a woman who'd actually dated Nate would ever think she'd get away with a ploy like that. "What happened to them?"

"They live in a small town outside of Stuttgart. They're both doing well."

"You keep track of them?"

"Annegret needed help." His tone didn't convey pity, pain or any other depth of feeling. It was matter-of-fact as he stared out over the turbulent waters. "I don't like what happened. Honestly, I don't like her. But she didn't know how to take care of herself. Her father cut her off. The baby's father was married. And I'd been a part of the picture recently enough…" He let out a heavy sigh. "She was desperate and thought she'd found a solution through me."

Perhaps not so ruthless after all…and maybe that was what he didn't want broadcast around the globe.

"I found her a small house. I cover her bills. But the arrangement is she can't talk. If she tries to profit from this in any way, the funding is off. So there's a reason I don't want the press getting a hold of her."

She could see that quite clearly. He'd financed the woman who tried to trap him into marriage with a false paternity claim. It was a risky precedent to set. So why had he done it?

Slanting a glance his way, she asked, "Did you love her?"

Nate's head snapped around, the strangest expression of shock on his face. "No. No, I didn't."

"But you set her up?"

He waved her off. "She was without resources."

"So are a lot of women. Do you have a charitable foundation in place to help them all?" Though, now that she thought about it, he'd tried to do the very same thing with her that afternoon. Was it some kind of white-knight syndrome or was Nate simply the kind of man who couldn't sit idly by when he was capable of making a difference?

"There was a part of me that wouldn't let myself hate her. I knew on some level it was possible the child was mine. And if it turned out to be true, that baby couldn't be born to a father who loathed her. Do you see what I'm saying?"

Payton didn't trust herself to speak. Didn't trust herself to touch him for fear she wouldn't be able to stop. He'd developed an attachment to a child he hadn't believed was his. Forced himself to care—maybe even to love—on the chance it was.

Pushing beyond her own heartbreak, she reached for his hand. "When you found out?"

His head tilted back, eyes fixing on the sky. "I care about Bella. But I can't drop in and out of her life or be her daddy just because she doesn't have one. It would never work with her mother. So I made sure she was taken care of and I let her go."

That kind of emotional toll was unfathomable.

He seemed to have followed her train of thought. "I'd never planned on having a family. I didn't want one thrust upon me. So in that regard it was a relief."

"Because if she'd been yours?"

He met her gaze, steady and unwavering. "I would have married her mother and played the hand life dealt me."

A nervous alarm sounded deep within her. It had been too close. He would have given everything up and she never would have had him back in her life. "Even though you didn't love her?"

"It wouldn't have mattered. If Bella was mine, I would have made us a family. I would have made it work. No issue. But that's the only way I'd make a trek down the aisle."

It wasn't the first time he'd said he didn't want to marry. Though this time she sensed more distaste behind his words. "Pretty adamant about that, huh?"

Nate caught her sidelong glance. "Yeah."

"Was it always like that with you?" She never would have guessed it from the way he'd been in high school; of course, she wouldn't have wanted to see something that didn't support her fantasy that someday he'd marry her!

"I didn't think a lot about it, but probably. My parents' marriage—" He shook his head, squinting off into the distance before letting the rest drop as though it didn't merit voicing. "In college and after, I was working so hard there wasn't time for much more than a quick— There wasn't time for anything involved."

He caught himself in time, though the crinkling around his eyes and a tilt to his lips told her it had been a close thing.

"So kind of you to look out for my delicate sensibilities," she teased.

"Don't be disappointed. I'll slip up another time. Anyway, the romance thing didn't really become an issue until I'd started making a name for myself. And suddenly I couldn't buy a woman a drink without some jerk sticking a mic in my face to ask when the wedding was. It bugged the hell out of me."

She remembered what it was like when his name hit the papers. The constant speculation about how long he'd be able to dodge the gold band. Nate was so good-looking. So charming and charismatic. His success and wealth growing exponentially, it seemed. The press was forever trying to marry him off, practically placing bets as each new female graced his arm.

"I'm sure your dates loved that. It must have been very awkward." It certainly had been when she and Clint faced similar speculation.

"Some of them got the wrong idea." He laughed at the sky and then turned a wry smile on her. "Some had the wrong idea from the start. Honestly, that kind of constant speculation…" He let out a grunt. "It's not like I had a mind for love and marriage before all that, so it didn't take much to turn me off completely."

"But…the right girl?"

"Payton, there are a million 'right' girls. Right for right now. But it doesn't last with me."

"And you still would have married Annegret? You could have lived like that?" She shook her head, fighting the urge to press her hand against the center of his chest. "Without love?"

Nate let out a short laugh. "It's called responsibility. It's not always fun. But it's necessary. Besides, I've lived without falling in 'love' this long," he said, making the taboo emotion sound like something toxic. "I don't want it."

That much was clear. Even so, she couldn't help but wonder… How many women before her had inadvertently given Nate Evans their heart? And had any of them gotten it back?

CHAPTER NINE

THE temperature had dropped with the afternoon sun, and Nate stood at the rear of his car shaking out the sand from the blanket while Payton sat bundled in the front seat. The roof was up and the heater on. Still, she was chilled and he'd wrapped her into a spare fleece he kept in the trunk. She'd looked fragile tucked into the expanse of his oversized pullover. Like something to shelter. Take into his arms and hold.

Which was nuts. Closing the trunk, he rounded to the driver's side door and levered into his seat.

Payton smiled over at him, then nodded back at the darkening sky. "Beautiful, isn't it?"

Her curls were wild with wind-blown abandon. Her cheeks alive with the pink flush of exertion. "Yes. Breathtaking."

Her gaze dropped to her lap, to where only the tips of her fingers peeked from the ends of cuffed sleeves. A sure sign of the nerves he really shouldn't take such satisfaction in stirring.

"Thank you for bringing me out here."

"It was my pleasure. Been a long time since I was here myself. I guess being around you's making me sort of nostalgic."

She smiled, still not meeting his eyes. "Me, too."

The parking lot was deserted. The interior of the car cozy

and intimate. He didn't want to admit just how nostalgic he'd become for things from his high-school past—like long wet kisses and getting naked in the back seat by the beach. Didn't want to admit even to himself how tempting the idea of slipping his fingers into those soft curls and pulling her over him had become.

But making out was a bad idea, and for more reasons than he was six foot five and this was a stick shift convertible with a back seat too small to accommodate a dog. Payton wasn't the kind of woman Nate normally dated. His relationships were short-term and emotionally barren—the women he indulged in them with all too quickly forgotten. And while the sex from the night before had definitely been of the no-strings variety, Payton would never go for something so shallow on an ongoing basis. Hell, he wouldn't want her to. One night, sure. There'd been an attraction and they both understood the parameters, but that kind of mutual attraction would be dangerous to exploit. He couldn't give her serious and she didn't deserve anything less.

And what was more, she was right about there being friendship between them. A bond unique to her. Something he'd missed over the years without exactly understanding why. But now that they had it back, he wouldn't take it lightly.

And Payton was of a similar mind.

Mostly.

He'd seen the way her gaze drifted to his mouth periodically throughout the day. And he'd seen the way she wrenched it away. The quick shake of her head and even quicker redirect to topics of a non-sexually charged nature. She was on board with the plan. The friends plan.

And yet, even knowing sex wasn't how he wanted the relationship to go, the dark fringe of her lashes, the pout of her bottom lip, even the way her bare feet were tucked beneath her—all of those details had somehow slipped under his skin, calling to a part of him that wasn't platonic.

Maybe it was the environment. He'd brought dates here a time or two. Set up a tent and lost himself in their willing bodies.

Only he wasn't thinking about the dates whose names he could barely remember. He was thinking about Payton. About the sound of her sigh at his ear as he pushed inside her. The clutch of her fingers in his hair as he took her against the wall. The way she cried out when he gave her his mouth—

Not where his mind ought to be going.

Not when Payton had felt his gaze on her and turned those soft brown eyes to meet his. Not when the music of the crashing surf was playing for them and the just-one-night they'd agreed to in a moment of more defined clarity than this had come and gone.

Damn it. Until Payton, friendship and sex had always been mutually exclusive. There'd never been a blurring of the line between the two, so he didn't have any experience with the complication she presented now.

Nate gave himself a firm mental shake. One thing he did know. Friends used their mouths for *talking*. So, fingers wrapped around the steering wheel, he forced his gaze to the road and talked. "Tuesday, the charity event."

Payton shifted around until her knees tucked up and her back half pressed against the passenger door. "We'll arrive separately. Maintain a decent distance throughout."

"Though you find it impossible to keep your eyes off me," he amended, just for kicks.

She snickered. "Is that so?"

"Absolutely. I'm temptation incarnate," he answered, heading for the highway, doing his best to ignore the temptation he wanted no part of in the seat beside him.

* * *

By the time they arrived back at Payton's apartment the tension that filled the car when they'd once again found themselves in close proximity had dissipated. They'd made their plans for Tuesday night and fallen into an easy discussion for the remainder of the ride.

Laughing, talking, catching up on the years that had passed them by.

Nate was interested in her teaching. In her plans. Curious about how she'd gotten into the field of special education and not the least bit concerned about the pay or prestige of the school. He simply made her feel good about her choices and, being the only one, it made all the difference.

She unbuckled as he jogged around the car. A steady rain had begun to fall, and though she'd been more than willing to dash into her apartment alone, Nate wouldn't have it.

So without benefit of umbrella, he let her out and ran up the walk beside her.

Rushing to the security door, she tried the key, fumbled and tried again, giving into a frustrated growl as her clumsiness got the both of them a soak. The chill that settled in at the beach was back in full force, making her fingers stiff and useless.

"Here, let me." A warm hand closed around hers and the blanket of wide male torso covered her back as he created a haven for her with his body.

He felt good. Strong and right. Close. Hot.

Oh, God. She'd been so confident. So sure of her ability to handle her emotions where Nate was concerned. *She'd handled them for years!* But now it didn't take more than one touch and her mind and body began their fast descent into bedroom territory. *Wall* territory.

Of course, what she'd been handling ten years ago had been the infatuation of a high-school girl—passionate and dramatic, yes, but ultimately only as deep as the girl herself. Which, at sixteen…

And then there was the little matter of ignorance versus experience. Now that she'd spent a night in his arms, she knew exactly what there was to miss. The heat of his hands, the taste of his skin, the touch of his mouth. Knowing he was more than she'd ever fantasized he would be.

The lock tumbled and Nate pushed the door open and then, following her into the relative warmth of the stairwell, he rubbed her shoulders in a few rough strokes.

"You're soaked."

"Me? What about you?" Rainwater beaded across the light cashmere covering his shoulders and back. Darkened the gold of his hair, weighing it down against his brow to give him a sort of Superman curl that begged to be twisted around her finger.

He waved her off with one hand, taking her elbow in the other. "Let's get you upstairs before you freeze."

Payton stalled. "I can manage. You should get home, though."

Nate's lips curved into a wry twist. "I'll walk you up. Security, remember?"

She did remember. Only the last thing she wanted was Nate back in her apartment. They'd had an incredible afternoon together, but the underlying sizzle of attraction she'd nearly doused had begun to flame again. She didn't want to acknowledge it. Not after the way they'd talked and laughed. She didn't want anything threatening the easy camaraderie.

Still, what could she say? Nate had a way of getting what he wanted. And he wanted to make sure she got into her apartment safely. But he couldn't come in. No matter what. Because if he did, she'd be offering him a drink while he warmed up. Offering to dry his shirt. Offering to help him take if off. Offering everything she had and was. No, he couldn't come in.

She led the way, their quiet tread upon the stairs screaming volumes in the silence. Finally, reaching the landing, she closed her eyes and took a bracing breath. Opened them and turned to Nate. He stood, hands in his pockets, one shoulder propped against the wall.

"Don't worry. I'm not coming in."

"What? I wasn't—"

He shook his head, cutting her off. "Yeah, I think you were."

Her lips parted in protest, but quickly closed again.

He took a deep breath and shifted his weight, glancing down the empty stairwell. "We were together last night, Payton. It's a safe bet we're looking at more than twelve hours to kick whatever residual attraction there is between us back into something safe and platonic. Look, I know what happened between us was different for you. And for what it's worth, it was different for me, too. So maybe we shouldn't worry about a few rogue emotions or whatever we've got going on. If we give it some time the attraction'll die off."

She wanted to believe him. Only she knew from experience that some attractions had staying power for *years*. "What if it doesn't?"

His lips twisted into a wry smile. "Well, then, I guess we'll cross that bridge when we come to it."

She shook her head. She needed this. "I want us to be friends."

"Yeah." He let out a low chuckle as if somehow surprised to find it so. "I do, too. Now get inside before I back you in there myself and ruin this whole buddy-buddy plan we've got going on. I'll see you Tuesday."

CHAPTER TEN

GLASSES clinked, laughter rose and the poignant melody of "Unforgettable" wound around her like a soothing embrace. Inspired by the classic song and its apt description of her past week, Payton swayed with each step on her way to the bar. She could feel the looks. Sense the questions multiplying around her. Heard one woman's sharp, "What?" rise above the din.

She'd been identified—through process of elimination and then conspicuous absence—as Nate's bridesmaid from the back hall, and word had been spreading like whispered wildfire for days. Already she'd faced the most brazen of her social set, descending upon her arrival with horrified expressions and ghastly rumors.

Of course *they* wouldn't believe such nonsense about Payton, but she deserved to know what people were saying…

She responded with the appropriate denials and a flicker of nerves to feed suspicions, then beat a hasty exit, not trusting herself to fight the obnoxious grin threatening to take over her face. Now all she had to do was follow the plan, drop enough subtle hints with Nate to confirm what her reputation was leading people to reject—and Nate's secret would be safe, buried beneath the rubble of Perfect Payton's good-girl reputation.

"What'll you have, miss?"

The bar was stocked with all the top-shelf labels and an

assortment of excellent vintages including a nice Italian white she kept at home. "The Pinot, please."

A glass was in her hand within seconds and, moving to a quiet corner a few feet off, she sipped, her mind bent to the task of fueling the frenzy of gossip already buzzing around her. The wine was cool and refreshing with a hint of fruity sweetness. A perfect complement to the spice of scandal.

Only then a nervous sense of anticipation swirled through her belly, spreading out until it licked over her skin.

Nate.

Lifting her gaze, she found him in an instant, dressed in an immaculately cut white dinner jacket, exchanging greetings with the owner of a bank a few feet from the main entrance. A flash of brilliant blue locked on her, held her rapt, inciting a sudden panic at the betraying heat flaring to life from one look alone.

She stood arrested beneath Nate's considering scrutiny until a feral gleam lit his eyes and the corner of his mouth curved into a dark smile that touched her from clear across the room. Made her shudder.

Not platonic. Not by a long shot. But not for the crowd or the press or protecting a secret either.

What a mess.

She *needed* his friendship. Was desperate for it. But the pull of this attraction between them was playing with her body and mind, and it hadn't died off in the slightest.

To go on as friends after a single night together was one thing, but if that single night turned into a string of nights, a week, a month—something finite, because she knew without question Nate wasn't interested in forever—what would she be left with when it was done?

The press having a field day splashing her face across the rags. Speculating on why she couldn't hold a man like him. Comparing her to whatever bit of glitz he picked up next.

Dredging up Clint and then demanding to know what she'd been thinking.

Who was she kidding?

That was exactly what she'd signed on for the moment she'd given into Nate's kiss, agreeing to go along with the pretense of this affair. Only in the original scenario, she'd have known in her heart it was all a farce. And as it stood now, she was looking at certain heartbreak... *If she gave in.*

Her eyes closed as the weight of the moment settled around her.

Nate wanted her. She wanted friendship.

She didn't stand a chance. Because deep in her heart she wanted way more than that.

Blinking open, she found the tilt to Nate's lips evened, the brilliant blue of his stare gone flat and focused behind her. Her stomach tensed—

"What the hell's going on, Payton?" The question came quiet and accusing from the one person she hadn't considered through all of this.

"Clint." She spun to face him, heat prickling her cheeks as she faced the man she'd nearly married. Tall, with a lean but healthy build, Clint was typically a well-ordered man. Tucked in. Buttoned down. Only this evening, all of that perfection seemed to have slipped the slightest degree. "I didn't know you'd be here tonight. I thought—"

He cut her off with the wave of a hand. "We finished in New York early so I'm back in town." Through with the pleasantries, he glared down at her. "Do you know what people are saying?"

She bristled at his tone of affront and the disapproving glint in his eyes. He had no right. They'd ended the relationship six months before and she knew for a fact he hadn't been sitting home alone that whole time. "People are always saying something. It doesn't matter."

"It matters to me, Payton. What they say about *you* definitely matters to me."

More to the point, it *reflected* on him. That was what this was about. What everything was about.

His hands went to his jacket, where he adjusted the hang, checked the button. All the while, his gaze tracked over her head, scanning the room behind her. "What are you even doing with Nate Evans?"

Her fingers tightened around the stem of her glass. "Nate and I are friends."

Clint's eyes narrowed. The lines at his mouth pulling down. "No, you aren't. Brandt hates him, and in the years we've been together I can't remember you exchanging more than a passing hello."

She opted to let the answer sit. The seconds ticked past as each waited for the other to back down. It wouldn't be her.

His chin jerked back, his brow furrowed and he reached for her arm. "You can't be serious."

"I'm sorry. I should have called you so you didn't find out this way."

"What are you trying to prove, Payton?" Anger flashed in his eyes as the grip at her elbow tightened; she winced, trying to pull free. "He's a player. A *predator*. The last thing you are to Nate Evans is his friend. Mark my words," he hissed, "you're nothing more than a f—"

Tension snapped through the air and a wall of solid muscle closed in behind her. "That's enough, Clint," Nate cut in, his voice deadly low and serious.

Clint's hand released her, his eyes widening as she rubbed her arm then seeking hers apologetically for the unrecognized force of his hold. Taking a step back, he smoothed his jacket as a flush of pink tinged his cheekbones.

"Evans, this is a matter I need to settle with Payton. I'd appreciate it if you gave us a few minutes."

Nate leveled him with an unyielding stare, pulling Payton into his side. "No."

Clint seemed to gauge the moment, notice the growing attention surrounding them, and shook his head. "Payton, this is a mistake."

If she gave in, he would be right. Her heart would pay for her body's wants. But regardless of her personal indecision, publicly she was committed. "It's my mistake to make."

He held her stare a moment. His features hardening as he acknowledged with a terse nod.

And then he was gone. Retreating through the crowd, offering arm claps and boisterous laughter by way of damage control as he went. Stopping for only one furtive glance back.

"You okay?" Nate asked, a single vein throbbing in his neck as he ran his big hands gently over the place where Clint had bruised her.

Payton placed her palm at the center of his chest, felt the violent punch of his heart beneath. The tight rein on his fury as he fought for control. "I'm fine. Clint wouldn't hurt me."

She took a deep breath as Nate's arm crossed her back, his hand settling possessively at the flare of her hip. It was obvious and so good and not at all what they'd discussed. "I thought the plan was to keep some distance. Play hard to get with the press?"

Nate peered down at her tucked beneath his arm. Wide brown eyes met his and he felt the pull of them straight through the center of his body. A little too far north of his belt for his comfort, truth be told, but it was there nonetheless. "The plan changed."

Yeah, like the second that jerk touched her. But in all honesty, things were pretty shaky before that. "Clint just gave us the perfect opportunity to bring this to a head… Tell me to get the hell away from you."

She jerked out of his hold. "You're pretend breaking up with me?"

As furious as Clint had made him, he couldn't help but smile at the indignation in her expression and tone. "No, princess. I'm not pretend breaking up with you. To the contrary, we're going to have our first public spat. And then I'm hauling you out of here to pretend make up with you."

The corner of her mouth twitched with the amusement overtaking the tension of a moment ago. "What exactly is involved in pretending to make up?"

He leaned that much closer, absorbing the rising heat from her skin. "Tell me to walk away and you'll find out." Her eyes widened, pooling dark at his proximity. Giving into the pull of her so close, Nate brushed his knuckles across her shoulder, over the tiny strap of her black dress. "Tell me to keep my hands to myself before someone realizes what's going on."

Her arms crossed as she gave him her shoulder and spoke toward the crowd using one of those hushed tones that sounded convincing but still managed to carry. "You need to stop. Walk away, Nate."

"Do I?" He let out a gruff laugh followed by a deep sigh, close enough to her ear to stir the fine hairs around it. "Why?"

She shivered. "Someone will notice."

It was exactly what was happening. More eyes turned their way with every passing second. "Mmm, notice how close I'm standing? How long we've been talking? The rapid rise and fall of your chest? Your heightened color suggesting an escalated pulse? Are they going to notice that I want you... or that you want me?"

She spun back to him, face flushed, lips parted with a frustrated plea that flickered between hostility and desire. "Nate..."

He caught her chin in his palm, lowering his face to within an inch of hers. "Let them see. I'm done playing games."

Turning her cheek into his hand, she peered up at him and countered, "You never stop playing games."

CHAPTER ELEVEN

WRAPPED in Nate's dinner jacket, Payton stood before the vast expanse of glass staring out at the light bright cityscape surrounding the penthouse apartment. Waiting.

They'd left the event together, fingers twined, allowing a photographer the opportunity to snap a picture as they darted for the car, knowing a counterpart would be staked out at Nate's building as well. Her heart had been racing, her stomach in tumult as she'd waited for him to make his move. But as the scenery blurred past the windows, Nate kept his distance, content to discuss the success of the night. He was confident there'd be a stack of messages from reporters the next morning looking for the scoop on the relationship with Payton Liss. She'd nodded and agreed, all the while contemplating the two roads before her. One smart. One reckless. One right. One wrong. There shouldn't have been any question at all. Only as she'd watched Nate fall into that wide-legged, masculine sprawl, one arm draped across the leather seatback, all she could think was how tempting it would be to climb into his lap. Run her lips across the faint scrub of his jaw. His neck. His mouth…

Now they were back at his apartment, Nate stepped into the reflection in the dark glass as his hands settled over the slope of her shoulders. "What are you thinking?"

That she was crazy and he was dangerous, and if she wasn't

very careful she'd end up exactly where she wanted to be. "That your secret's safe."

"I think it is. In large part thanks to Clint."

She stiffened. Looked past his image into the night where streetlights illuminated spots of scenery and the red streaks of taillights disappeared around the corner two blocks down. "I should have thought about how he'd react. Warned him. But I didn't think of him at all."

He squeezed gently over her muscles, drawing the tension out with slow strokes. "He's jealous." Not a question. "Wants you back."

"Maybe. Yes." At least he thought he did. Clint wanted the woman she'd pretended to be.

"Not quite the idiot I thought, then. But you don't want him, do you?"

She shook her head. "No. I really don't."

"Good." His breath came close to her ear. "Then that's out of the way."

A warning skittered over her skin and she turned out of his hold. Stepped back. Swallowed. "I should go. Tomorrow's a school day. We both have to work."

Nate dismissed her protest with a flick of his hand.

Nonsense. Inconsequential.

"I wouldn't stop you if marrying Clint was what you wanted." His gaze drifted to her mouth, to where she'd anxiously set her teeth into her lip. "Or maybe I would."

He was flirting, playing as he always did.

Yeah, sure he was.

A nervous laugh escaped her and he took a step forward, one golden brow arched in question. "You think I wouldn't?"

Okay, this was it. Her chance to talk sense. She shook her head and took another step back. Slowly. She wouldn't stand a chance if this turned into a game of chase. "You might be cutthroat and relentless and everything else they say about you, but you're also honest and honorable. You've been that way your whole life—it's just not quite as obvious the way the papers paint you now."

"You're a Pollyanna," he countered with that mischievous glint in his eyes. "But I like it. Did I mention I had a bridge to sell you?"

"No way, Nate," she scoffed, her confidence returning with their banter. "You do the right thing. I trust you. It's why you—your friendship means so much to me." One of the reasons anyway.

He took another step forward. "I'm glad to hear honesty is important to you, because about that friendship thing—"

"Stop." Before it was too late and she ended up losing everything because she couldn't resist the sound of his voice and lure of his words. "Let's think about this for a minute."

"I've already thought about it," he answered flatly.

"Listen," she pleaded. "Imagine we have two roads before us. Friendship is like an interstate highway."

Nate's chin pulled back, amusement battling with distaste. "Remind me not to hire you for any marketing jobs."

Ignoring the little boy who didn't want anyone to make the rules but him, she went on. "The highway is long and constant. Scenic. Pleasant. We could travel it for years."

Arms crossed, he nodded once. "Right."

"Sex is like a blind path through a lush jungle." At his slow-spreading grin, she cleared her throat and stared at her shoes. "Sure, it's hot and wet and exciting—"

"You're trying to talk me out of this?"

"—right up to where the ground falls away in a sheer drop and all the fun is over." And her heart lay a hundred feet below, battered and crushed on some rocky riverbank.

"So what you're saying is…you've got some kind of Tarzan fantasy you want to act out."

The corners of her mouth twitched even as she tried to glower at him. "Nate!"

Unrepentant, he went on. "Because I've got one of those rainforest shower things in my bathroom. You could wear a ratty bikini with a few strategically placed rips. I'll wear a shredded shirt and cargo shorts."

She scrunched her eyes, trying hard not to let her imagination follow where his dirty mouth led...

"I'll invite you back to my room. Show off my *vine*."

She burst out laughing, the tension that threatened to overwhelm her dissipating under Nate's juvenile antics.

He was joking. Well over the line of ridiculous—so why was she suddenly burning with the need to touch him? Tear the sleeves off his shirt and make him beat his chest and roar.

Darn it! He was working around her defenses. But she had more to fight for than a good time. She needed him. In the few days since they'd reconnected she'd discovered how incredible it was to have someone who really saw her. Let her laugh and joke. Have an opinion that didn't follow everyday convention. Someone to talk with. She didn't want to give it up. Couldn't go back to the lonely isolation that had been so much a part of her life for too many years now. It didn't matter the number of people surrounding her, there was only one who actually saw her.

"Nate, this is serious." Her lips pressed together in a firm line as she sought for a means to make him understand. "I don't have a lot of friends—"

"I do. I'll share. And if they aren't enough, we'll start trolling the social clubs together."

"You're making jokes," she shot back. "But the idea of risking something this important isn't funny to me. You pick up pretty, shiny playthings at every turn, have your fun and toss them aside without a backward glance once you've lost interest. I don't want to be another discarded toy in your wake."

A muscle in Nate's jaw ticked, his posture taking a subtle shift. "It wouldn't be like that."

"No? Why not? Is the press really so far off in what they say about you?"

"I don't know, Payton, how accurate are they about you? Could they have predicted it would be like this between us?" He broke off and shoved a hand through his hair. Blew out a harsh breath and then seemed to pull inward for a count. And then he was back in control. Cool. Steady. Reasonable.

"It's not that I *don't want* to be friends, Payton. It's that *I don't think we can be*. Not with what's between us.... I *know* you feel it, too."

She bowed her head with a stubborn shake, hiding the conflict warring in her eyes. Unwilling to reveal the power of his effect on her. How right he was.

She felt it. The connection that messed with her head and threw off her equilibrium, made her dizzy and hot and wanting to justify all kinds of things she knew she shouldn't. Made her want a man more controlling than all the other men in her life put together. Insanity.

"You're going to deny it?" he drawled, low and rough, ominously seductive. The change in tone and tack alerting her to the coming danger.

Clint had been right. Nate was a predator. And she was prey.

She swallowed hard and, shaking her fuddled head, answered, "Yes."

"Hmm. You seem confused. Conflicted." He leaned closer so the heat of him scorched her skin. "I can help with that."

Panic burst to life. Her eyes bulged at her body's betrayal and her own stupidity. He overwhelmed her. Dominated her senses in the realm of desire.

Get it together!

"No." Some rebuke, all breathy and weak.

"Convincing," he taunted, eyes gleaming. "So which is it, Payton? Yes. No. Do you even know yourself?"

"This isn't fair, Nate."

He leveled her with his gaze. "I think it is." Then after a moment that cocky grin broke out across his lips. Trouble. "Here, how's this for fair? We'll put it to a test. I'll kiss you."

Her chin tucked, but he waved off her concern. "Don't worry, in the interest of accuracy, I'll give it my all. And when I'm done, you tell me if you still think we can be friends."

This time her mouth and body worked in unison, her steps carrying her back in quick repetition as her hands flew up to ward him off. "No. That's a very bad idea. You said the attraction would die off. It's only Tuesday. A few days! We haven't given it enough time."

He closed in on her again, confident and sure. Overwhelming in ways beyond his powerful build. "Has it? Only been a few days for you?"

God, that look in his eyes. He knew. A few days plus thirteen years.

This was a disaster. "Nate, we're talking about more than just this next moment—"

"Damn straight we are. I thought I'd proved I could last more than a minute Saturday night."

Suddenly the wall rose up behind her, ending her retreat. Heat burst out over her chest, neck and cheeks. "You know what I mean. I want us to be friends."

His gaze turned serious and for an instant she thought he might walk away, but then he shook his head in response to the hope lighting her eyes. "I do, too, Payton. But it's not going to happen if we can't handle the attraction. Put it in its place."

"We can!" She flicked her hands out in a frantic motion to

sweep him away. "We start by putting some distance between us, that's all, and we'll handle this fine."

But instead of stepping back, Nate braced one hand at the wall above her head and caught her wrist in the other. "You seem so sure. But what happens if we touch...accidentally?"

There was nothing accidental about the stroke of his thumb across the sensitive skin of her wrist or the way he leaned close enough that the air around her went thick and a current of need coursed through her.

His grip was loose, the barricade of his powerful arm limited to one side. She could have pulled away, should have fled, but even when he released his hold to draw the tip of one finger down the length of her neck, the only escape she could manage was to shut her eyes.

"Are you going to go up in flames at the DVD store? Melt all the ice cream in the frozen-food aisle when we hit the market some night?" His breath at her ear sent a jolt through her nervous system, accelerating her pulse and pushing heat to lick at the surface of her skin.

"You know I want you," she whispered on a shaky breath. "But I want something else more."

"Are you sure?"

"Yes." The single word hitched free, begging for something more than what she claimed.

He was so close she could almost feel the light rasp of his jaw, the strength of his body against her, the too-confident smile at his lips. "Then put your money where your mouth is and show me."

"What's a kiss going to prove?" she asked, wanting to kick herself for the husky quality of her question. Only if she dared move her leg an inch, she had no doubt she'd find it wrapped around Nate's hip and all her resistance would be for naught.

Nate straightened, taking the warmth and promise of his body away. "Simple. If we can stop, then we've got a shot at being friends."

It was all too easy to let herself believe the kiss was inevitable. That Nate had decided this was the way to handle the dilemma of their attraction…and so it would be done. But she knew it wasn't true. Somewhere along his line of reasoning the pure masculine scent of him had slipped beneath her skin, making her ache and want. Wonder. Was he right? Was it even possible to have the friendship knowing the fuel of desire burned so hot between them?

Her body trembled. Maybe she had to know, too.

She searched his eyes for understanding, for mercy. "And if we can't stop?"

Nate's features pulled taut, his nostrils flaring with a forced intake of breath. The arm he'd braced against the wall gave at the elbow, slowly bringing him into her space. "Then we don't."

It was one kiss. And all she had to do was stop there. Her gaze fixed on his mouth as memories of what he'd done with it only a few nights before bombarded her.

Her vision hazed. Lips parted.

Simple. As he said. Just stop after one. "Okay. A test."

Bowing his head close, he brushed his lips against her ear so she shivered with delicious chills. "You know what used to drive your brother absolutely *insane*?"

Brandt? The fog of rising lust thinned as she wondered what in the world—and then her breath caught at the memory of a long-ago afternoon. Her brother storming through the door bellowing about his exam—and how Nate Evans *always* blew the curve.

Her eyes flew wide as Nate murmured his final warning. "I test *very* well."

CHAPTER TWELVE

HE COULDN'T just kiss her. Not Nate. No. He had to make a point as he did it. Eyes locked with Payton's—forcing her to watch as he whittled the distance between them, covered her mouth with his and sank into his task with a slow, deliberate pressure. She couldn't close her eyes or look away. But even as panic licked amongst the flames engulfing her, she held strong. Stoically taking what he gave her, she told herself to enjoy it—that it would be the last. If she could maintain her control here, then she'd have had her cake and eaten it, too— one night with Nate and a lifetime of friendship to follow.

She watched him, watching her.

Gentle suction pulled at her restraint. The back and forth rub of firm masculine lips wore at her resolve. God, he was good. Patient and skilled and, if memory served, just getting started. Her pulse skittered faster, a needy ache throbbed low in her belly. Twisting tight.

Be strong.

Even if holding back nearly killed her, no one actually died from denial.

She could do it. She could outlast this one pleasured assault and walk away from the temptation of more. Secure the friendship she didn't want to let go.

Keep Nate forever…

And never again feel the stroke of his tongue skimming the

tight seam of her lips, pushing her molten core past containment, spilling liquid fire through her veins.

Oh, God, she couldn't—shouldn't.

His fingers threaded through the hair at the nape of her neck, wound and pulled with a tension so deliciously forbidden there was nothing to do but open on a trembling gasp. And then he was sliding into her mouth—hot and wet—in a slow, measured thrust and retreat that wiped her mind of anything beyond *more*. Having as much of this kiss as she could for as long as he gave it.

His mouth angled, taking them deeper. Taking more. Taking everything.

She could still stop. Still have the security. Have what they'd had all those years before. Memories rose to fight each decadent thrust of his tongue: Nate with his arm around her as they watched TV on the couch; raking the yard with her; leaning over her shoulder to help with her homework; laughing, with his head back and eyes shut over some dumb joke.

Friendly memories. Warm.

Only there was a constant through each and every one she hadn't wanted to acknowledge until now. As she'd laughed alongside him or taken his assistance with a grateful smile, through it all she'd been fantasizing about—aching for—a moment like the one she resisted now. Where Nate wanted more.

And in that instant she realized if she did the "right thing", took the safe path, she'd be doing exactly what she'd sworn she wouldn't. Living a lie. Pretending to be a friend when she wanted to be a lover. Forcing herself into a mold that didn't fit.

She blinked, once, twice. Gave into the heavy weight of her lids and closed her eyes. Gave up her fight against an inevitable hurt and loss in the future and stopped resisting the want and need that was now.

Her eyes closed and her body went lax in his arms. It was as though she'd simply given up and Nate felt the loss of her fight like a blow to the gut.

He shouldn't care. He never cared. Relationships and whatever came of them were simply what they were. Enjoyable until they weren't. Always on his terms.

But not this time. This time it was out of his control and driving him nuts.

Didn't she understand he couldn't *make* himself see her in a platonic light? It wasn't *choice* firing his blood at the sight of her alone?

Damn, he had to let go, get his head around the fact that he couldn't have her.

His arms loosened their hold. His marauding mouth eased from its plunder as he drew back to break the kiss—the kiss that wouldn't break because the lips he'd poured his every skill and desire into had followed his retreat.

His pulse jacked.

Slight hands balled against his chest, released, crept higher and balled again.

Was he reading this right?

He tried to pull back—to see her face—but those slim arms were wrapped around his neck, clutching and clinging tight as her fragile plea shattered against his lips. "Don't stop."

His breath rushed out on a groan that was relief and desire and victory all in one, and in a combination so potent it nearly took him to his knees. And then she was alive in his arms, opening wide beneath the crush of his kiss, taking everything he gave and demanding more. Meeting the thrust of his tongue with the stroke of her own so they mingled in a sensual dance that was hot and wet and urgent.

Rhythmic. Erotic.

And not nearly enough. Nothing was enough. No matter how he touched her, how she moaned against his lips, pushed and pulled at his clothing until it hung half free of his limbs, begged with quiet sobs as he worked past her panties, teasing one finger and then two through her slippery arousal, it wasn't enough. He had to be inside her. Had to have her. Completely.

His body vibrated with need beyond control. Banding his arms across her back, he lifted her from her feet.

"Say it again," he demanded, his mouth rough against her throat as he moved to the couch.

"Don't stop," she panted, her hands grasping at his shoulders. Her knees settling into the leather at either side of him so her skirt rode up her thighs. Opening her to him.

Damn, he could feel her, soft and hot, through the damp swatch of her silk panties.

Pushing violently at his half-open fly, he freed himself, giving into the temptation of that fragile silk barrier. He palmed her bottom and guided her to the bare skin of his shaft. Had to grip the base of the couch when her hands clenched, her body tensing as she slid against the length of him.

"Don't stop…" she breathed again, her words taking on a desperation that only fed the madness burning within his veins. Her hair hung wild and loose around her face, her breasts swayed half exposed from when they'd wrestled with the straps of her dress. Her eyes were dark, heavy lidded and pleading as she moved over the straining ridge of his erection. "I can't stop."

Too. Much.

Not. Enough.

Reason and restraint snapped. He had her beneath him, her lips parted in a silent cry of pleasure that tore through his very soul as he pushed inside.

Wet friction embraced him. Took hold of his sanity and tossed it aside as he drew back and drove deep again, setting a relentless rhythm of triumph and possession.

He had her. Writhing beneath him. Coming apart around him. The clutch of her slick walls urging him to follow. She felt so good…too good…too good…

Nate froze.

Too good.

She felt too good because he wasn't wearing a condom. Buried inside her, a hair's breadth from release with the receding waves of Payton's orgasm pulsing around him, he didn't dare move.

Control. Where was his control?

His teeth ground together with a series of audible pops as he slowly withdrew. Images of the past six months sliding through his mind, gripping him like icy talons. What the hell was wrong with him?

"Nate?" Her hands smoothed down his chest, her eyes searching. Taunting him with a welcome he couldn't accept. Yet.

"Condom, Payton," he managed on a hoarse growl as he found the foil packet he'd never forgotten before.

"Thank God you remembered." She shook her head, watching him as if he'd managed something remarkable. Well, he'd stopped in time. That was pretty damn remarkable. But the fact that he'd been inside her at all—

Never before. He'd never lost it like that. Never come so close to losing everything.

Never again.

Covering himself, he reached for her. "Now where were we?"

An hour later, they lay sprawled across Nate's bed, naked beneath a blanket of moonlight. Payton traced patterns across his skin, circling this way and that. Her touch was light. Sweetly exploratory. And arousing all too soon after they'd collapsed together mere minutes before.

This was the point where he typically employed some trusty exit or eject strategy, but tonight the foundation of caring and history he had with Payton was throwing him off. Nothing within his arsenal of disentanglement techniques suitably handled the unprecedented situation with a woman whom was both lover and friend and who he had no intention of letting go. At least not any time soon.

Tucking his chin, he watched her fingertips walk the steps of his ribs, climb higher and then smooth across the center of his chest.

Maybe there wasn't anything to handle at all. So long as he used his head and a measure of restraint, no one would get hurt.

Yes, he wanted her. Had nearly lost it when he thought he couldn't have her. But even so, he knew himself—the kind of love that led to marriage and family wasn't part of his makeup, and this wouldn't last forever.

As though reading his mind, Payton turned her eyes, soft and vulnerable, to his. "What are we doing?" she asked quietly. "You didn't want a relationship. You told me. So what is this?" Her question held no accusation, challenge or demand, just a need to know something he didn't have the understanding to explain.

"No, I didn't. But nothing turns out the way I expect with you. I think I know how something's going to play and then suddenly I'm staring open-mouthed at a scenario I couldn't have predicted. This, what's between us—" he shook his head "—it's not common in my life."

"Mine either. But since neither of us seemed able to ignore it, let's just enjoy it for as long as this lasts." She leaned in to kiss him, and he saw the flicker of sadness—remorse maybe—that crept into her eyes. He wanted to make it go away. Only he couldn't lie to her. Promise something they both knew wouldn't happen.

What he could offer was the possibility of a scenario he very much hoped would become reality. He ran a finger along her jaw and tipped her face to his. "You know, just because we're detouring through the jungle now, it doesn't mean there won't be a chance to veer back onto the main drag later."

The fact that it hadn't happened before didn't guarantee it never would. This was Payton, after all, and the power of her optimistic determination knew no bounds.

She blinked up at him, her big brown eyes so wide with trust, once again taking him back through the years to a time when she was the only one who saw the potential in him—to her limitless faith.

He didn't want to let her down. He'd almost done it tonight. Almost let them both down.

"I don't know what's going to happen, Payton, but I'll always care for you."

She nodded, letting her smile spread. "Then how about we forget about what might happen? Let the future take care of itself and, for now, we'll have fun."

She deserved better.

He couldn't give it to her but neither could he let her go. So he shoved the bitter knowledge aside, focusing instead on the now. Payton in his bed. Smiling. Sexy and bare.

CHAPTER THIRTEEN

SATURDAY morning Payton emerged from Nate's bedroom bleary-eyed and desperate for caffeine. Waking alone, she'd managed to locate her panties and Nate's discarded tee shirt from the night before, but after minutes of fruitless searching for her jeans she abandoned the quest. Bare-legged, she padded down the hall following the fresh-brewed scent of dark roast coffee.

They'd been to a wine bar for dinner the night before and, though delicious, that third glass was wreaking havoc on her head this morning. Halfway through their first small plate of chorizo-stuffed dates, a couple of Nate's friends had turned up and joined them bar-side. Not the society crowd Payton was so keen to get away from, just a wonderfully funny and intelligent couple Nate had known for years.

The tone of the evening had been set when Nate introduced her as his girlfriend and she'd choked on her drink and then flushed so red that no one could ignore it. Soon they'd all found themselves laughing about the label, swapping stories about Nate at various ages and overall having such a great time her shaky tolerance was the last thing on her mind.

After, Nate had brought her back to his apartment and proceeded to make love to her until the wee hours of the morning—which invariably had as much to do with the drag in her step as that last glass.

She turned into the kitchen, rubbed a lazy hand at her eye hoping Nate still found 'puffy' cute, and poured some coffee.

Nate's voice sounded from the front room in a low rumble. Probably taking care of some business while she'd been dead to the world in his bed. But noting more rasp than usual, she wondered if perhaps he'd had a glass too many as well. Not likely. Nate didn't get caught up in excess.

She took a steaming swallow, then cradled the mug at her chest to absorb the warmth both inside and out.

"So it's true?" The demand filtered down the hall, sounding almost accusatory, and she considered returning to the bedroom. Maybe taking a shower while he wrapped things up.

Then… "Look, it just sort of happened. We haven't talked since high school, but once we started…you remember what a cool girl she was. Fun, you know?"

She set the mug down on the counter harder than she'd intended, tried to steady it with clumsy hands. This conversation was about *her*. She stepped back to the hall. She definitely shouldn't be listening in.

"Is it serious?" Her brow puckered at the croaked question and she slowed her steps. Visualizing Nate's considering expression. What could he say? It had only been a week since their first night together. And yet they knew each other.

Nate's exasperated sigh propelled her forward. Toward the conversation rather than away from it. She was in the apartment and he was talking about her. Better to let him know she was awake, before this became something uncomfortable between them. Only it wasn't until she turned into the front room and encountered Nate's clear blue eyes—on a face twenty-five years older than the one she went to bed with— that understanding came.

Nate's father. *Mr. Evans*, seemingly paralyzed as he gaped

with what she could only describe as open-mouthed appreciation at the region where her tee shirt ended and bare legs began.

Nate muttered a particularly colorful obscenity, stepping from behind his dad. "Morning, Payton."

Before she could reply, the Evans elder regained use of his faculties, brows slamming down in an all too familiar scowl. He crossed his arms, turning to the younger version of himself, a man who left tycoons cowering, and demanded, "You couldn't tell me she was *here*?"

Nate shrugged—*shrugged!*—and covered his stubbled jaw with one wide hand in a blatant effort to hide his growing smile. "I thought I could get you out before you caught us."

"Uh-uh-umm-I—" She broke off, shaking her head, at a total loss for words as she stumbled back a few steps. Now she understood the dialog she'd overheard, and it was definitely a conversation she didn't want to be a part of.

"Relax, Payton. He's not going to call your mother."

Thanks for that, Nate.

"Why don't you get showered? Dad and I are going to run out and pick up a little breakfast. Wishbone sound good, Dad?"

The older man grunted. "That'll do."

Not for her it wouldn't. "Uh, Nate, I actually need to…" She waved a hand around, casting about for a good excuse to get the heck out of there. Sitting around with Nate's friends was one thing, but Mr. Evans? After he'd given her a B- in World Economics and busted her shacked up with his son? No, thank you. "I need to take care of *that thing* I told you I had to do today."

Mr. Evans wasn't impressed. And Nate simply shook his head with an expression that said, "Fat chance."

"Give me a second with my dad here and I'll be right back."

"Sure," she managed, still on the brink of hyperventilating.

Time to flee. Be gone. Vamoose!

She'd finally tasted the mortification of being caught in a compromising position—something most people probably experienced back in high school—and she had no idea how she would survive it.

Nothing could be worse.

Desperate to make her exit, she hastily spun away—square into the jutting leg of the sideboard. Pain shot through her foot as she tripped forward with a sharp cry.

Sadly, not enough pain to block the two voices following in quick report.

"Oh, God in heaven."

"Dad, turn around!" Nate begged, laughter lacing his plea.

Her eyes bugged and then pinched shut as her crouched position and the cool breeze across her backside registered. She grabbed for the hem of the tee shirt, tugging it down to cover the bit of hot pink lace she'd picked up to entertain Nate.

A peek out of one squinched eye at both Evans men doubled over ensured they were highly entertained. "This is not funny!"

At least his father had the good grace to look away, but Nate simply straightened, hands on his hips, his gaze fixed on her butt. "Oh, Payton. I'm sorry, honey, but yes it is." Then ducking low, he wrapped an arm around her and pulled her up and against him. "Is your foot okay?" he asked, one palm warming her hip.

She looked at her second and third toes, both red and throbbing angrily, and sighed. "Just stubbed. I'm fine." Really it was her pride suffering more than anything else right then.

Nate glanced back over his shoulder. "Close your eyes, old

man, or I'm putting you in a home. You've had enough cheap thrills for one morning."

A dismissive, "Yeah, yeah," came from behind them, and with that she was swept up into the cradle of Nate's arms for the princess-style escort back to his room. Too bad her scantily clad bum was hanging out, ruining the effect.

When Nate deposited her at the door to the master bath, she touched his arm and looked up at him imploringly. "Uh, Nate, how about I let you catch up with your dad? I'll see you—"

His hand closed over hers with a telling squeeze. "No. I'm giving you thirty minutes and then you'll sit there with us enjoying breakfast and making small talk. That's what good *girlfriends* do."

"Are you afraid of your dad?" She raised a mocking brow and met one in return.

"Aren't you?"

"Well, yes." Everyone had been. He'd been the toughest teacher at school. "But he's *your* dad."

"Yeah, who drove all the way into the city to slap a paper with our picture in it against the side of my head."

The image that conjured had her near giggles, only what was behind it wasn't very funny. "He seems upset."

Acknowledging with the barest nod, Nate extracted the weapon in question from where he'd tucked it under his arm and flipped through until he found their page. "Here we go."

Setting it on the granite countertop, he leaned close so the heat of his chest warmed her back as they read. Payton's brows drew down as she scanned the column. There was more information than she would have expected them to find. Particularly since she'd been ignoring the reporters' calls herself.

"Did you do this?" she asked.

"Some." He pointed to the line about being seen around town since the relationship had been publicly outed earlier that week. "I had my assistant Deborah drop the hint that we'd been keeping it under wraps. Hey, they hit the school where you work, too."

An involuntary groan slipped out and Nate chuckled above her. "What, it can't be the first time the press showed up there."

"No. Not the first time." There'd been a few months following her father's death where the interest in her had peaked and reporters seemed to lurk around every corner, waiting for the opportunity to pump her fellow teachers for information.

How was she holding up? Was a wedding in the works? Could the romance sustain through the tragedy? Would she be leaving the school to take a seat at Liss Industries?

It hadn't won her any friends at the new school back then, but over the past year the alienation she'd experienced had died down along with the press's interest. Still, every time she'd found herself pictured in the paper she'd sensed a subtle backlash. She wasn't looking forward to the reaction come Monday.

"It's pretty much what I'd expected." Nate knocked the paper aside with a knuckled fist and stepped back. "Deborah's got a few more nuggets to dole out over the next weeks, so I'd say we're in good shape."

"Mission accomplished."

Rubbing a wide palm over the scrub of his jaw, he nodded. "As for my dad—I don't really talk to him about the women I'm dating, but I should have told him about us. Things are different with you."

"Different?" Hope lit through her veins, pushing into her heart with welcoming ease.

"Yeah." He met her with a blind stare. "He knows you. Probably feels as protective of you from those high-school days as I do."

Nate shook his head, thankfully too wrapped up in the

situation with his father to notice the falter of her smile as her most vital organ hollowed out. It was stupid. She knew what she'd signed on for and the surest way to ruin it or any chance of maintaining a friendship after would be to spend every minute they were together imagining more meaning into Nate's words than they deserved.

"I'm a big girl," she said, as much a reminder to herself as to him. "He doesn't need to worry about me."

This brought a low chuckle as his gaze raked down the length of her. "Okay, *big girl*. You were all over this whole girlfriend business last night. Rolling around in the title like you owned it. Time to start paying those dues."

She let out a cough. "Dues? Come on—"

"Payton, I'm not asking you to see him through his retirement years." He raked a hand through the thick mess of sandy blond spikes. "Just to hang out for an hour or two and show my dad I'm not treating you like some floozy or pulling the wool over your poor innocent eyes."

And suddenly she realized he was serious. "You're worried about what he thinks."

"That surprises you?"

It shouldn't have. But after having spent a lifetime worrying—obsessing—about how her every action would be interpreted by her own father, she'd never really thought of Nate, who always came across so fun and carefree, as having the same issues. "I guess you never seemed…concerned."

"Yeah, well, my mom took off when I was young, so it was just my dad and me. And, you know him, he's not a halfway kind of guy. Since raising me fell wholly on his shoulders, he took the job seriously. Made a lot of sacrifices and spent a lot of years making sure I knew right from wrong, worked hard and did the right thing. Honestly, he couldn't care less about the financial kudos or bank account I've built. He measures my success—and his—by the kind of man I've made. So, yes. It matters to me that he knows he did a good job."

Her heart rolled over with a little sigh for this man who loved his father and had his priorities so well aligned. If only there were room in his heart for more. "He did a very good job. Go get me some grub while I get dressed and I'll tell him so."

It was early afternoon by the time they'd said their good-byes and the elevator doors slid shut with a quiet whoosh. Nate leaned a shoulder against the brushed-steel interior and watched his father. Waiting.

Payton had recovered from her initial embarrassment by the time they'd returned with breakfast. He'd expected the quiet poise and well-mannered reserve she was known for, but she'd been relaxed and comfortable, charming his old man with her bright smile and fresh take on the adventures of academia.

She'd been perfect. Too perfect. Too comfortable. Too right a fit between what had always been just the two of them. God only knew what his dad was thinking now—but he didn't have long to wait to find out.

Solemn eyes that had been shining with merriment half an hour before turned on him. "What are you doing with her?"

Or, more to the point, what was a nice girl like Payton Liss doing with a guy like him? "We're just having some fun, Dad. It's not serious so don't start knitting any booties."

A beat of silence and then, "Does she know that?"

Staring at the numbers as each floor illuminated and went dark, he offered a single nod. "Give me some credit. We wouldn't have gotten anywhere near a bed if she didn't."

"She's not like the others."

Nate fought back a grin. His father hadn't had a say in his sex life since he'd slapped a box of condoms in his hand in high school and sat him down for a man-to-man. "What do you know about the others?"

"I know you haven't introduced me to a date since you were seventeen."

"You already knew Payton. And it wasn't like I brought her home for dinner. She walked in before I could get rid of you."

His dad let out a derisive snort. "I know you're linked to one woman after another, but it never lasts more than a couple weeks because there's no connection."

Yeah, he supposed if anyone had the skill set to recognize something like that it was his dad. Hindsight and all. "You've been spending too much time with your nose in the tabloids."

"I saw you laughing with her. The way she looked at you." His dad stared him straight in the eye. "This one's not going to let go so easily."

Nate shook his head. "Yes, she will."

When the time came, she'd have to. And until then, she wouldn't get too close.

He wouldn't let her.

CHAPTER FOURTEEN

THEY'D spent the evening enjoying dinner, drinks, and non-stop laughter at the Gold Coast home of Diane and Garry Ortiz. Nate tried to warn her ahead of time about his former Marketing VP's larger-than-life personality trapped in a pixie-sized body—but it wasn't until Payton found herself gasping for breath within the enthusiastic squeeze of Diane's shockingly strong arms that she fully grasped his meaning. Stunned, she took a step back, laughing as Nate steadied her with a hand at her hip.

"Diane, I think you broke my date," he joked, dodging to avoid the swat of her arm.

"Oh, stuff it, Nate." She took a deep breath that seemed to fill her entire body, nearly bringing her to her toes, and then let it out in a huge rush. "It's just so wonderful to have finally met you, Payton. I can't believe the nerve of this guy in keeping you a secret for so long."

"Thank you. Tonight was so much fun."

Diane cast a mocking scowl Nate's way. "See? She likes us. No reason to keep her holed up the way you did."

It was hardly the case. As absurd as the suggestion had been, Nate hadn't been kidding about sharing his friends. In their few short weeks together, he'd been steadily circulating her through the various groups he socialized with, encouraging relationships outside himself. Keeping up his end of the bargain while maintaining the ruse around the timing of their reunion for the sake of a child half a world away.

Cocking his signature grin, he winked. "Guess I just wanted her all to myself."

Diane waved him off, pulling Payton into another suffocating embrace, and then set her back with a satisfied smile. "About time you found one worth hanging onto, Evans."

"Definitely." He looked casual, utterly at ease with the implication they had a future together. But Payton knew the truth.

With Nate romancing her several nights a week, filling her days with unexpected surprises, texts and phone calls—it should have been heaven. But their romance was running on borrowed time.

Nate had ways of reminding her. Nothing overt or hostile. Just a subtle distancing when he sensed she was getting ahead of herself. The problem was, she didn't want the distance or to hold back, and more than that she didn't want Nate holding back either. What they had wasn't going to last and, no matter how she sliced it, when the romance ended her heart would break. There was no defense against it. So until that happened, she was going after everything she could get.

Sunshine poured clear and bright from the October sky, the lingering Indian summer giving the city as a whole a reason to smile. Payton, clipping down the sidewalk in her favorite flowing skirt and calf-hugging, heeled leather boots, was no exception. It was an off day from seeing Nate, and thanks to a field trip her afternoon classes were cancelled—which left her free to catch up on a few overdue errands. Only as she rounded the corner of her block, she caught sight of Nate—dangerously appealing in Aviators and dark jeans—pushing off the rough brick pillar at the end of her walk.

"What are you doing here?" she called, rushing forward. "I thought you had meetings all afternoon?"

"Being the boss has its benefits." Nate stretched out his arms, gesturing around him. "Too nice a day to be cooped up indoors. Let's drop your stuff and take a ride."

Payton frowned down the street. "I'd love to, but I've made appointments around town. Papers to sign at the lawyers. Stuff I've been putting off too long."

Nate slipped his fingers beneath the lapels of her jacket and tugged her gently into him, his cajoling smile running at full strength. "So reschedule. Lawyers do it all the time."

"No, I shouldn't—"

"Sure you should."

She sighed, bristling slightly at Nate's domineering attitude. But then he tucked her beneath his jaw and it felt so good in his arms. So right.

"Tell your lawyer it's a crime against nature to waste a day like this one and you'll see him next week." His fingers sifted through the curls at her back, the touch sending a shiver of pleasure skirting her spine.

It would be easy enough to reschedule. But Nate simply expecting she drop everything to accommodate his whim didn't exactly sit right. Even if she had been thinking about him all day, she didn't want to be treated like just another one of his beck-and-call girls.

No, she was making too much of it. The man wanted to see her so he'd dropped by. Big deal. It was a nice thing.

And it wouldn't last forever.

"Come on. We'll play hooky. It'll be fun."

"Hooky?" she scoffed, giving in with a slow caress of her hands down his chest. "What are we going to do? Go to the mall? Catch a movie? Hide out under the bleachers?"

Nate's smile was pure mischief, his tone pure seduction. "Is that what you did?"

"Please. Like I've ever ditched."

He'd moved into leering territory now, his blue-eyed gaze running the length of her. "But I bet you wanted to."

"I did," she replied, her answer escaping on a wistful sigh.

"Yeah," he answered, face tilting toward the sky. "Me, too. But I couldn't exactly get away with it when Dad was teaching two doors down from my homeroom."

"I guess not."

"But no one from the office would dare call him now."

She let out a conspiratorial laugh. "And your secret is safe with me."

Grinning, Nate pulled his phone from his pocket and handed it over. "Reschedule."

Five minutes later Nate threw his leg over the black bike parked at the curb, watching with satisfaction as Payton's eyes went wide and her lips parted on a small intake of breath.

He brought the bike off its center stand and held out the spare helmet. "Hope you like to go fast."

Payton's eyes shot from the bike to the helmet and back to him. "I've never been on one before. I don't know how."

"Really?"

"I always wanted to." She smiled, her eyes seeming to focus on some distant point from the past. "You used to ride that big bike around. I thought it looked so cool. Like such fun."

He remembered. It had been his cousin's. On loan for the summer while Nate worked a job the next county over. He'd seen her walking in town one sunny day and offered a ride. She'd wanted it, her expression reflecting pure desire, but she'd turned him down anyway. Looked guiltily behind her, as if she'd been afraid someone might have seen.

Someone with a heart condition she didn't want to worry.

He hadn't realized at the time. But that was what it had been. He couldn't help but wonder how many desires, big and small, she'd pushed aside to keep from upsetting her father. Or how devastating the loss of him must have been after sacrificing for so long—even if she'd known that, ultimately, the loss was inevitable.

Payton would have her fun now.

His blood pumped faster as he gave into the urge to play. Catching her wrist, he pulled her close. "So I'll be your *first*."

A coy look from beneath the fringe of her lashes. "You will. Be gentle?"

Damn, he had fun with this woman.

"Don't worry. I'll start slow," he promised with a nip at her bottom lip before pulling the helmet over her head. "And if you get scared, just hold on tighter."

The pink tip of her tongue smoothed over his love bite, leaving a moist trail he wanted to follow with a lick of his own, but days like this one didn't last forever. So settling for a too-brief kiss instead, he winked and patted the seat behind him. "Let's hit it."

As it turned out, taking it slow wasn't an issue. Not in the slightest.

He'd expected Payton to be scared. To be holding on for dear life. Exhilarated by the experience, perhaps, but still maintaining some semblance of reserve. A healthy respect for her safety.

He had *not* expected the little minx in the leather jacket and flowing hippy skirt tucked around her thighs to be shamelessly feeling him up with one hand flat against his abdomen, the other snaking over the rise of his thigh. To nearly drive him over the edge with the breathy sounds of her pure, unadulterated delight as she begged him not to stop…to go faster…*yes, yes, yes, like that…*

Damn, how did she keep surprising him like this?

Taking everything he gave her and turning it into something beyond what he'd expected it to be.

He'd been after a quick spin down by the lake—the wind in his face with Payton's legs hugging his hips. That had been three hours ago.

One night. That had been over three weeks ago—

—and with no end in sight.

His back tensed beneath the press of her breasts.

Things were going too far. And he was *letting* it happen.

Even when he held back, she didn't... And the way Payton had fun—her enjoyment amplifying his own—made the willing surrender of his control an all too easy temptation to give into. But falling over the line in the sand he'd drawn—again and again, just because it felt good—was going to land him in a place where he didn't want to be. A place he'd have to walk away from. And that wasn't how he wanted it to go.

Daring fingers flexed and splayed over his thigh, moved ever closer to the hard ridge they'd provoked, forcing a strangled groan from Nate's throat as he throttled down the road toward his place.

Time for a reminder about who was in the driver's seat.

Time to take back control and set some limits. And if boundaries were going to be tested, it would happen the way he liked—on his terms. It was time to push *Payton* to extremes—make her pay for that wandering hand and finally get *her* to say "when".

CHAPTER FIFTEEN

MINUTES later they were rounding the top level of the parking garage in Nate's building. The sun burned low in the sky, casting the stark concrete supports in gilded rays.

"That was incredible!"

He barely heard her over the roar of the engine echoing through the structure and waited until he'd pulled to a stop and cut the engine to respond. Pushing the machine up on its stand, he grinned. "Yeah? Glad you had fun."

"I'm not sure fun even begins to describe it."

He stripped off his helmet and then turned to help her with hers. Damn, that smile was enough to drive a man to distraction.

And about that...he had some payback to attend to.

"Come here." He slipped one hand under her thigh and, the other around her back and, ignoring her squeak of surprise, pulled her around to straddle his lap. The gauzy fabric of her skirt bunched between them. Her heeled leather boots—looking decidedly bad-girl when paired with his bike—tucked behind her as she settled warm and soft against the hard-on he'd been battling for hours.

She stroked his jaw, brushing over the day's growth of stubble with a silky smile that had him responding even as he willed himself to heel. He shook his head, his gaze searching her face, trailing down her neck and body, and then returning to her eyes as he nuzzled into her palm, kissed the hollow and then ramped past "sweet" bringing a scrape of teeth into the action. He wanted her to know where this was going.

Payton's heart skittered to a halt as instant heat surged through her, twisting into a needy ache that left no part of her unaffected. Her breasts, her belly, her fingers and toes. Every fine hair that covered her body took notice, bowed beneath the desire born of his touch.

His tongue licked out as his blue eyes pierced her with his intent. Her breath sucked in. Her body coiled tight. And then he licked again, trailing a cool, wet path of erotic sensation in a circle around the first.

"We should go inside," she murmured, more than ready to let Nate take the exhilaration of the ride to the next level. This was a man who made her want everything. A man who, when merged with her, made her feel invincible. Unstoppable and completely alive.

One large hand snaked around her waist, while the other went to her nape, guiding her closer until their lips met in a soft brush, a teasing introduction after too long apart. Her fingers curled against his thighs, and he angled his head, taking the kiss deeper.

Willing and eager, she opened to him. Moaned against the claiming thrust of his tongue as he filled her mouth. So good but she wanted more than a taste. She wanted him everywhere and all at once. Everything he had. Everything he was.

Something was happening within her, something she knew better than to give into but couldn't seem to stop.

Take me. Make me yours.

The forbidden wish rose unbidden from the dark shadows of her mind.

Hold me. Forever.

When Nate let go of all his careful restraint, he gave her what she'd never had before. Showed her what she didn't know existed. It was incredible. Addictive. It was more than the physical. More than the mind-blowing sensation spearing through her at his slightest touch and deepest penetration.

But it wasn't what they'd agreed to. It wouldn't last. Only when he held her in his arms and stopped holding back, she felt as if, maybe, just maybe…it could.

Soft and wild. That was Payton. It was the sound of the cry that escaped when he caught her lip between his teeth, held and tugged the slightest bit. The sultry moan when he gripped her bottom, dragged her closer and drove his tongue deep into her mouth. Rocked harder as the muscles of her lean thighs bracketed him, flexing and tensing to the rhythm he'd set—until their breath came in fevered bursts between them. Desperate draws cut short by their need for more contact—deeper contact.

"Please…please…oh, God."

That's right. Just like that.

His hands fisted at her hips, seizing the delicate waistband of the panties that kept him from where he wanted to be. Sweet perfection tangled with his tongue, curling around, licking over him, sucking every bit of restraint from a mind that hadn't had much to begin with.

Control. That was what he was after. But her kiss stroked like a match-head over rough stone, igniting Nate in a flash flame. And there was no controlling the combustible desire when she opened to him, invited him in.

Tearing back from the kiss, he sucked air, tried to get a hold of himself. But all he could see were those soft wild curls swaying from side to side as Payton's mouth devoured his neck, his ears, his jaw, and then more when her fingers got in on the game—working the buttons of his shirt, with her lips following down his chest. Each heated kiss punctuated by her breathy pleas and silky declarations, "Nate, oh, Nate. What you do to me…want you…need you…don't stop…"

He couldn't stop. Didn't want to stop.

Don't ever stop.

His eyes opened. Had she said that? Or was it simply where his mind had taken him following his train of thought?

And then, somehow, she'd opened enough of the buttons to get the bulk of his chest free, and the little demon was licking at his nipple again. Her teeth grazing around it and then sucking with enough force the sensation pulled straight from his groin—where her deft fingers tugged at his straining fly and he was once again left panting through gritted teeth as he raced to keep up with her.

He was supposed to be holding the reins! It was Payton's turn to say "when".

"No." Hands clamped on her shoulders, he set her back against the fuel tank.

Her brows pulled together in pained confusion. "Why?"

"No condom." It was true, though only occurred to him as he'd grasped for an excuse to modify their positioning.

"I need to get on the pill," she groaned. Her heartrending cry of distress over their predicament would have been comical if his groin hadn't tightened to the point of pain at the forbidden memory of skin on silky smooth, wet skin. If he weren't totally caught up in her parted, kiss-swollen lips and the warm pants escaping them at a rate that damn near matched his speeding pulse.

"Upstairs," she urged, trying to sit up from her reclined position at the head of his bike.

Nate stopped her by running his hands up her splayed legs, still wrapped around him, and issuing a gruff, "Not yet."

He had a point to make and then, once she got it, he'd take her to the privacy of his apartment and spend the next twelve hours making her scream. But first, he took her hands and then brought them up to the handlebars at either side of her head. "Hold on."

Her eyes went wide and he waited for it, tasting the satisfaction of a success sure to come. This was where she told him "no". Where common sense and self-preservation prevailed and she realized she needed to slow down. Be more careful. Only her knees didn't pull closed, she didn't put a hand out to stop him.

She did as he'd commanded. She held on.

A part of him let out a cheer at the opportunity to take this fantasy come to life a step further. She'd break soon enough, but for now…

Backing down the seat to make his intent perfectly clear, he fingered a bit of her skirt and then flipped it back to expose her panties.

Turquoise. Lace.

Damp.

"Nate," she gasped.

Oh, yeah. Here it comes. "We should stop." Only then, nothing but the anxious shifting of her thighs, the soft musk of her arousal driving him past sanity.

Fine. Desperate times called for desperate measures. "Don't worry," he growled. "There isn't much traffic up here. I doubt anyone will catch us."

No way he could meet her eyes after that one—no one came up to his private garage level, ever—but he was all about pressing the advantage, so, eyes on those racy panties that should have come with a warning, he slid his arms beneath her legs.

This would do it.

He draped first one supple leg and then the other over his shoulders until he had her so erotically laid out he didn't know if he could last. But it wouldn't take much more. It couldn't.

He was taking back control. Showing her who was in charge— Except then he felt it, the slight dig of those killer-heeled boots at his back. Pulling him in.

Payton, Payton.

His hands tightened around her thighs and, slipping the damp scrap of her panties aside, he sank into her sweetness, tasted her cry and the pulse of her body's ready desire. It was insane and irrational, and yet—those stunned breathy gasps of pleasure, the widening of those deep brown eyes he couldn't stop watching—suddenly, he didn't want her to do anything but go with it.

She was desire mixed with an eager curiosity and sense of adventure that left him panting, straining, and demanded he step up to the challenge and make every damn minute they had before this ended the most exciting she'd ever experienced. He wanted her to let him take her as far as he possibly could.

He licked and kissed, circling outward until he felt her writhe beneath him and then working back in until he earned it again. Plumbing with deep thrusts of his tongue and nibbling with the softest graze of his teeth. He closed his mouth over that little bead and drew against her, tasting her cry on his tongue, increasing the strength of his pull with her escalating pleasure until her voice broke, her body quaked and spasmed and she came apart for him with the gift of her total abandon.

When she'd finished, he gathered her close. Ignoring the strain of his erection, he wound his fingers in the back of her hair. The hair that completely betrayed the wild woman inside. Hair that defied conformity, rebelling against every method of restraint imposed upon it. Escaping every bind. Sexy, beautiful, vibrant hair.

He unclasped the barrette she'd secured it with at the nape of her neck, releasing all that wild, soft rebellion into his hands. Sifting through the curls with his fingers as his tongue delved into the wet haven of her mouth.

So he couldn't control everything.

So what. Maybe he didn't want to. Maybe giving into

Payton for a while was just what he needed. Holding back only made him want her more, and at the rate they were going, it would be years before he got her out of his system enough to give her up.

CHAPTER SIXTEEN

NATE pulled a suit from his closet and laid it over the end of the bed where Payton lazed beneath the blankets. "I'll be back Wednesday evening. We can have a late dinner."

A pair of shorts, track pants, tee shirts and socks were stacked haphazardly within his case. Straightening the lot, he caught the languid stretch of a pale arm by the headboard, the shifting of a slender leg. Considered shoving the whole packing mess to the floor and using the bed for the purpose it was intended.

"How is it I've gotten spoiled on you in only one month?" came the quiet purr from amid the sheets. "Five days is so long."

Nate chuckled, taking her pout for the stroke to his ego it was. She'd miss him. They'd fallen into a habit of seeing each other every other day or so and this would be the longest they'd gone apart since their first night together. In all honesty, the break was probably overdue.

As good as being with Payton felt, something about all that rightness—the ease with which she fit into too many areas of his life—was making his skin itch. Making him tug at his tie and rebel against a confine without physical properties. He needed some space. As she'd said, it had been over a month.

His motions slowed and he stood, frozen, holding a boxed shirt suspended above his case.

More than twenty-eight days.

He shot a glance at Payton, searching for an answer to a question he didn't like.

He'd have known if she started her period.

No. No. He was being paranoid. She wasn't pregnant. Couldn't be. How many times had he heard some television or radio commercial touting on about each woman's body being different. They just hadn't been together long enough for him to know what kind of different to expect from hers.

Only suddenly he wanted to pilfer through her diary in search of those little circled numbers. Figure out exactly where she kept that critical information and make a note of it. Reassure himself he hadn't somehow made the most monumental mistake of his life and then play a quiet game of keep away during those most fertile times of the month.

There was no way. A matter of days would confirm it. Only he'd be gone for the next five.

"Nate?" Payton pushed to her elbows and the sheet slipped low across the swell of her breast.

He shoved his hands into his pockets, balled his fists and tried for casual. "Why don't you come with me?"

He'd wanted the space, and at that moment was nearly gasping for breathing room, but the idea of not knowing, not being sure—it was intolerable. He'd set up another trip in a week or two.

She sat straighter. "What?"

"I'm going to be busy with work. Meetings. Drinks and dinners. But eventually I'll have to sleep. And if I have a woman back in my room, they won't try taking me out to some seedy strip club this time. Besides, the shopping is supposed to be top-notch."

Silence rang through the room, bouncing around the slate walls, allowing his agitation to grow.

"Um, that's nice, and I wish I could," she offered at last, "but I take vacations over school breaks."

His jaw set, his focus narrowed. "Call in sick."

She began smoothing one corner of the sheet between her fingers. "I've got plans with my family."

"You could see them anytime."

Her gaze slid away, the turn of her head shutting him out. She looked uncomfortable. As if whatever she was thinking wasn't something she wanted to share. And he was hanging every hope on it being some neurotic hang-up about discussing her menstrual cycle.

"I—well—"

This was ridiculous. He was railroading her into a trip he didn't want her to come on rather than just asking. Man up. "Your period?"

"What?"

"Are you expecting it? Is that why you don't want to come?"

Shifting to sit akimbo, Payton cocked her head in a way where Nate could almost see her calculating dates. Whatever excuse she'd been ready to offer, that wasn't it. Just as well she had a reason to stay behind, particularly since he'd broached the subject and had her on the right track now.

"Actually, yes. In the next few days." Then she squinted an eye at him. "Awfully intuitive. Do you have any hang-ups at all?"

He laughed as if she'd made some great joke, covering the relief that washed through him with tsunami force. "Not about that kind of thing. It's a period. Big deal. Women get them."

It was when they didn't get them, you had something to worry about.

She wrinkled her nose. "But you grew up in a house with just your father. No sisters. And yet, you're miles beyond what Brandt or Clint could handle."

Nate shrugged, feeling lighter than he had in days. "It's probably as much to do with my dad as anything else. Being the educator, he wasn't really one to shy away from a topic because it happened to apply more specifically to the other gender. And because my mom wasn't around to give the female perspective, he invariably felt an obligation to be as forthright as possible. The man was a chronic over-compensator."

Payton laughed and held out her hand. "Tee shirt?"

Nate pulled one from his bag and handed it over.

"You know, you've never really told me about your mom. She was gone by the time we met. But beyond that…"

And here he thought things were turning around. "What do you want to know?"

She had a right to ask. It wasn't any big deal, just not his favorite topic.

"What happened to her?"

"She took off when I was five. Life with Dad and me wasn't right for her. She wanted something different, I guess. Hell, I don't know, something else."

A little line crinkled between her brows, suggesting she didn't like where the story was going. But she needn't have worried, there wasn't much more than what he'd already said.

Leaning across the bed, he dropped a kiss on her knee. "It wasn't too bad. She'd checked out long before she actually left, so it wasn't like we'd suddenly lost something we didn't know how to live without."

"But what did she do? Where did she go?" He could all but see the unspoken question painted across her face. *"How could she leave you?"*

"I don't know where she ended up. Dad did, for a while at least—he made sure she was okay. You know how he is. But for me, once she left, that was it."

"But she's your mother. She knew you. Loved you."

A vision of a pretty smile and distracted eyes slipped through his memory. Soft hair and a nice smell. Remote. Unavailable. Watching her stare out the window, the door… down the road.

Nate zipped the bag and hefted it to the floor before meeting Payton's waiting eyes. She hurt for him. He could see it there, but she didn't need to. "Payton, some people aren't cut out to have a family. I don't think my mom was a bad person, I think she just didn't understand the way she was until it was too late." Deficient. Same as him.

Payton couldn't imagine it. Giving a child five years of attachment and then ripping it away. What did that do to a little boy? What did it do to the man he became? "Is that why you don't—?"

"Does it really matter?"

Maybe it did. Her lips parted to press the question, but the quick shake of Nate's head and hardening of his eyes told her not to.

Ignoring the pinch in her heart, she pushed a smile to lips rebelling against it and tried for the make-light conversation that always smoothed over those sticky moments. "So you've got everything you need for the trip? Razor, toothbrush, stack of singles for the strip club?"

Nate barked out a laugh, his head hang-dog low. "What kind of man do you think I am?" Then, turning that impish blue glint of mischief on her, he grabbed her ankle and pulled her to him. "It's a stack of fives, baby."

"So bad," she murmured, pulling him down to her mouth for a kiss. And like that they were fine. Casual and easy. "And, I know, I like it." She loved it. As she knew she loved him, even though she wasn't supposed to.

Two nights later, Payton curled into the corner of the sofa, phone held to her ear as Nate recounted his botched attempt to evade the strip club the evening before. Eyes closed, she listened to his voice, missing the feel of his arms around her. "I told you what would happen if you didn't come with me."

She sighed. "Poor Nate. The things you suffer for the love of your business."

"She mocks."

"She does. But only a little." She smiled at Nate's low chuckle. "I miss you."

"You, too. When's dinner with your mom and Brandt?"

"Tomorrow night. I'll drive out after school." She pulled the throw higher and tucked her legs beneath her. "It's still strange going home, knowing my father won't be there. You'd think after a year I'd be used to it."

"I think it's perfectly normal. You grew up in that house with him. In your heart, he's a part of it. I'm sorry it hurts, though."

She nodded, simply wishing Nate could be there with her before she thought better of it. Brandt would love that, particularly since this would be the first time she actually had to face him since her relationship began. She took a deep breath, knowing it was time for the call to come to an end. She was getting wistful and both of them needed to get up early the next morning. "Well," she sighed, stretching across the cushions where she'd gone lax under the spell of his voice. "I better let you go."

"Hey, Payton, one more thing?"

"Mmm-hmm?" God, she missed him.

"What we were talking about the other morning," he began, the soothing tone of his voice taking on an efficient business-like edge. "Your period—did you get it?"

She blinked, mildly surprised by his question. "Um, yes, I did. Today actually."

"Good." A long breath filtered through the line, and she pulled the phone from her ear, staring at the receiver. A moment of insecurity touched her with the nagging sensation that last question had been the purpose of the whole call. But then she thought of the circumstances that had brought them together. A pregnancy. A child. Six months of the cruelest uncertainty.

She couldn't blame him for being concerned and suddenly felt immensely grateful this wasn't one of those months she simply missed her period altogether.

"Don't worry, Nate. Everything's fine."

"Have some ice cream or binge on something disgusting or whatever you women do. I'll see you in a few days."

CHAPTER SEVENTEEN

"Mom, Brandt's pulling up," Payton called, watching from the front window as the black Escalade pulled into the circular drive. It had been weeks since she'd seen Brandt and, aside from the one brusque call she'd received about the folly of getting involved with a man like Nate, he'd been unusually quiet as of late, burying himself deep in the running of Liss Industries. Doing well. Her father would have been proud.

Heading to the foyer, she heard the thud of a car door and then stalled mid-step at the sound of another.

A moment later the front door swung open wide and her brother strode in, a cavalier grin on his face and Clint on his heels.

Payton's back straightened, her jaw setting hard.

"Hey, Payton," Brandt offered with a jut of his chin by way of greeting as he crossed to take her in quick hug. "Hope you don't mind, I've brought Clint along for dinner."

She raised a cool brow at her brother as betrayal shot hot through her veins. "I see." She did mind. Very much, in fact, but when had anything as trivial as her opinion ever stopped her brother before?

Clint crossed to her and dropped a chaste kiss to her cheek. "Don't blame Brandt. I asked him to arrange this. Things didn't go the way I'd intended the last time we spoke—" He broke off, letting out a strained breath before turning back to her. "And my behavior was unacceptable. But I'm asking you for a chance to talk. Privately."

She looked from Clint to Brandt and then to her mother, who was descending the wide staircase. "I'm here to have dinner with my family."

"Nonsense," her mother interjected, urging her to understand with her eyes. "There's time enough for everyone. Brandt's taking me over to the store to pick up something to go with the lamb. It'll give you two a chance to talk and then we'll have dinner after we get back."

Brandt crossed his arms over his chest. "Don't be difficult about this, Payton. I think it's the least you can do considering the way these last weeks have played out. In fact, I'd say you owe it to Clint here."

Payton swallowed, looking past her overbearing brother to the door she wished she'd never ventured through this evening. Releasing a short breath, she nodded, taking a step back from Clint even as she agreed to speak with him. She didn't want any misread signals. Any misunderstandings. But she did feel bad about the way she'd handled the Nate situation with him.

Clint acknowledged with a pained twist of his lips and a resigned nod. Extending one arm toward the living room, he gave her the space to pass. Then turned to Brandt and her mother. "I appreciate this."

Payton crossed the ancient oriental and perched at the edge of a wingback chair, ankles crossed, hands folded neatly in her lap. Clint followed her into the room and, catching sight of her there, paused, a small smile touching his lips. "You look beautiful."

"Thank you, but—"

He held up a hand and walked over to the chair opposite her. "Merely stating the facts." Then after a pause, "How did we get here, Payton? So far from where we're supposed to be."

He looked up at her. "I've given you time, but this business with Nate Evans has gone too far."

Payton shook her head. "What's happening with Nate is none of your business—"

"Fine." He leaned forward. "Forget him. He's not important anyway. Not for our future. All I care about is us. You and me. Going forward. I know after your father passed away you had a tough time. You needed…space…to adjust. And I gave it to you."

They'd broken up. She'd told him it was over. Not that she needed space. But Clint wouldn't see it that way. He'd chalked her behavior up to a reaction to her father's death. And maybe it had been, but that didn't change the fact that she'd made the right choice in leaving him.

"I don't love you, Clint."

He shook his head, not willing to hear. Or maybe not caring. "We were good together. Right."

She felt the familiar stab of frustration, bit back the hot denial that rushed to her lips, knowing it would be dismissed as irrational. Pulling her composure around her, she met his stare. "No. We were never that good or that right together. Only you couldn't see it and I didn't want to admit it. But I knew. Even before Daddy… A part of me wouldn't let us go forward, wouldn't talk about marriage when you brought it up… I wanted to be happy about what we had. I wanted to see what everyone else saw. How perfect we were together. But I wasn't being honest with myself or you. I'm so sorry, Clint."

"You realize what you're giving up here?"

She nodded. A life where she felt trapped by a man who, though decent enough, didn't really care to know her.

"I do."

* * *

Knock, knock knock, knock... "Payton, open up."

Brandt. He must have hopped in his car the minute he got back to the house and discovered she'd left.

The last thing she wanted was to continue this little intervention here at home. She'd do about anything to dodge her big brother coming down on her with all his disappointment and bullying. Maybe if she didn't answer he'd just go.

"Don't bother hiding. I know you're in there." Of course he did. Her car was parked outside and she was the sole occupant of the third floor, with every light in the apartment shining down on the street below.

Returning the paperback she'd just picked up to the To Be Read pile beside her couch, she pushed to her feet and walked to the door in time to hear the lock tumble as Brandt made use of the keys she sorely regretted giving him.

"Unless you've got a bolt cutter in there, just give me a second." She slipped the chain and stepped back, arms crossed, ready to face him down. "You can't let yourself in here any time you want."

Brandt swung the door open and met her determined stare, raising it with a measure of disappointment only their mother could rival. "You've done it now. Clint's through."

"I wasn't trying to hurt him, Brandt. But I'm glad he finally believes me."

"You're throwing away your future for some...fling. You know that's what it is, right? Mr. Bachelor of the year...bad-boy billionaire Nate Evans. Are you stupid? You know how he gets those names, right? By pricking around."

"Shut up, Brandt. You don't know what's between Nate and I—"

"Yeah, and I don't want to know, except that, with Dad gone, I'm the one looking out for you."

She let out a harsh breath. "I don't need anyone looking out for me. Especially someone who can't understand the choices I'm making in my life."

She mumbled under her breath, walking away.

"Did you just call me a 'stupid jerk'?"

She had. Heat splashed her cheeks, but, unwilling to back down, she spun on him. "If the shoe fits…"

Only then the absurdity of her muttered insult hit them both. The tension and starch seemed to slip from her brother's shoulders and he leaned back into the wall behind him. Pressing the heels of his palms into his brows, he let out a heavy breath. "I know how you feel, Payton. About Dad. About trying to be perfect for so long. It wears on you and all that pressure makes you resentful. Only you know you can't get angry at him. The weak heart wasn't something he could help. So you keep trying to do the right thing. Take care of him. Be good. Try harder… Except, after all that effort, he goes and dies anyway. It was a raw deal. I know that."

Tears bit at the backs of her eyes as her bully-big-brother voiced what her heart had been sobbing for a year. "It's like everything I did, all the right choices I made were for nothing."

"So now you want to be bad for a while? Is that what this is with Nate? With the apartment? Clint? Every major decision you've made in the last year has been the sort of thing Dad would have hated. Are you trying to get even with him? Show him what happens when he doesn't hold up his end of the bargain and live?"

Her throat was so dry, she didn't think she could speak. She shook her head, blinking away the welling tears. "No. It's about being true to myself. Living my own life. Mine. Not his. The job I want. The apartment I can afford." *The man I love*.

Brandt scanned her apartment, as though doubting her word. Then pushed off the wall and stuffed his hands deep into his pockets. "You know, on the way over to Mom's, Clint and I were talking about when you two started dating. Apparently he'd asked you what you wanted out of a relationship."

Her breath pulled in with a slow ache. She knew where this was going.

"You said, 'Family and security, trust and partnership.' I think he figured out he wanted to marry you that night."

She'd known it, too. Looked at Clint and thought he was exactly the right sort of man to make a life with. And yet every time he'd brought up marriage, she'd shied away.

As if following her thoughts, Brandt offered, "Even if Clint wasn't the one. You gave him an honest answer, didn't you? You still want those things?"

When she didn't answer, Brandt's scowl deepened and the understanding man who might have been her friend a moment ago transformed back into the brother frustrated with the mess his little sister was making of her life. "What does Nate Evans think about those wants? I'm assuming he knows. Or did this 'honest life' you're so keen on living not include being honest with him?"

"It's not like that with Nate. Neither one of us is interested in marriage or forever right now."

Brandt let out a short laugh. "Right. Who are you lying to now, Payton?"

Her mouth burst open in denial, but already he'd gone on. "Have you been honest with that guy for one minute since you started whatever the hell it is you're doing together? Does he have any idea how long you've been pining for him? I'd be willing to bet a sizable chunk of Liss shares that he doesn't. Just like I'd bet he doesn't know how showing up in the papers has affected your work environment—the flak you take for it."

"Things have been better at work lately—"

"I'm glad to hear it, but *come on*, *Payton*, the last time we talked about this you were hell-bent on getting out of the media spotlight. Swearing up and down that wedding you and Evans were caught at would be the last high-profile event. You were desperate. And yet, I think I've seen your name or face in the news more times over the last month than I have in the last year."

"It's different now."

"Why?" he challenged. "Because you're in love?"

"Things are good with Nate. We both knew what we were getting into with this relationship and we're both fine with it."

He took a deep breath and shoved off the wall. Stopping at the door, he turned to her. "Payton, if you have to lie to me, that's one thing. You want to lie to Nate Evans?" He touched the single bump at the bridge of his nose. "Be my guest. Just do me a favor and don't lie to yourself."

The door swung closed with a thud. The lock tumbled and then even the muffled fall of his steps left her. Alone, she faced the uneasy revelation that perhaps Brandt had seen her more clearly than she'd ever given him credit for.

CHAPTER EIGHTEEN

SOMETHING was wrong with Payton.

Nate stood by the exit watching the dinner crowd. The up-scale Mexican restaurant was one of his favorites and Payton had mentioned it as one of hers as well, but tonight she'd barely had a bite of her food and her glass of wine sat all but untouched on the table.

He'd gone to her place straight from O'Hare, ready to pick up where they'd left off almost a week before. The trip had been a success and he was in the mood for a celebration. But even before they'd made it to the car he'd sensed something *off*. They'd talked easily enough, laughed and caught up, but every few minutes her attention would drift, leaving him to wonder where she'd gone.

By the time he closed out the bill his frustration had met its limit and he was ready for answers.

Hitting the sidewalk, Payton looked back at him apologetically. "I'm sorry. I just—" Breaking off with a shake of her head, she stared down the street.

A quiet alarm began to sound in the back of his mind. Obviously something happened while he'd been gone, and whatever it was had her anxious and refusing to meet his eyes. He didn't want to think it, but if he didn't know her better he'd say her behavior smacked of guilt. "What's going on?"

Hugging her arms around her waist, she shivered. "Can we walk a minute?"

He tucked her under his arm, guiding her around the Friday-night pedestrian traffic. As he slowed his stride to match hers his mind ran through the little he knew. She'd been fine when he spoke to her the other night. Laughing and easy. No halting exchanges or strained silence. But that had been three days ago and he hadn't spoken to her since. He should have called again, checked in, but he'd gotten busy, caught up in the workings of a new deal— And he'd wanted the space. The distance.

But just for the few days. Now that he was back he wanted Payton laughing and sexy and giving him everything that threatened to be too much. And she wasn't.

Halfway down the block she turned to him. "I'm being stupid. It's nerves is all—I don't want—" She took a deep breath and shook her head. "The other night I was supposed to have dinner with my family, only we didn't actually make it that far. Brandt decided to bring Clint with him—"

Clint. Tension wrapped tight around his chest, making it difficult to breathe. The guy who'd wanted to marry her. The guy who'd grabbed her in the middle of a charity reception.

"So you left?" he prompted, knowing she hadn't.

"No. My mother and Brandt left, so Clint and I could talk."

"They left you alone with him." Heat crawled up his throat and face as he let loose a violent curse. Immediately he was pushing up her sleeves, trying to see the skin on her arms through the wash of red nearly blinding him. "If he hurt you—" If that was the reason, what she was afraid to tell him—

"No, he didn't touch me. Nate, please." She caught his hand in hers. "I'm fine."

"You are not fine," he growled, barely managing to contain

himself from bellowing. "You're worrying over something, refusing to look me in the eye. And I can't tell if it's because you've done something you think is going to hurt me or because someone else has done something and you think I'm going to hurt them. So *tell me what happened*."

Her chin jerked back in surprise, but quickly she answered. "I was upset, but Clint obviously needed some closure, which I believe he finally got. And when we were through talking, I didn't want to wait around for Mom and Brandt to start in on me again. So I left. Only Brandt followed me home."

"What the hell is that guy's problem?" he roared in frustration, glaring at the sky.

Silence answered, drew out for a moment, and then, "He thinks I'm not being honest about what's going on between us. About what being with you means to me." She took a steadying breath before meeting his eyes again. "And…maybe he's right."

With that the red haze receded, leaving him with an understanding of what was behind Payton's distress. No one had hurt her. At least not yet.

"Because you want…more." Marriage. A family. More than a good time for as long as it held up.

"I do."

He should have seen it coming. Hell, he'd known from the start what her priorities were, that long term they didn't mesh with his. Damn it, he didn't want this now. He just wanted Payton back in his arms after days apart. He wanted her laughing and giving him her smart mouth and her soft body. He wanted the good time. The easy ride.

But the easy ride was over.

She was quiet beside him, her head pressed into her palms. Smoothing a hand down her curls, he pulled her into his chest. "There's nothing wrong with wanting those things, Payton." He looked up at the black night, took a breath of the bracing air and forced himself to say the rest. "So long as you aren't waiting to find them with me."

It was only the barest of movements. No more than the slightest stiffening of her body. But he felt it. He closed his eyes, knowing what he had to say next.

Clearing his throat, he took a step back.

Those brown eyes stared up at him, waiting. Wounded. She knew what was coming. Knew they'd agreed to stop before things got serious. Stupid. As if it hadn't been serious with Payton from the start.

Her lips parted and she whispered a single word. "Don't."

He didn't want to do this.

"Do you think maybe it's time to stop?" he asked, taking her hand in his. She was shaking her head no, but it hadn't really been a question. He caught her cheek in his hand, slid his fingers into that wild hair. "I don't want to hurt you."

Too late.

"Then don't." Her hands covered his chest as though it would be enough to keep him there. Hell. She didn't understand that the organ beneath her hands didn't work the way she needed it to.

"Payton—"

"Aren't you having fun?" Her big brown eyes turned to liquid pools, that kissable bottom lip of hers beginning to tremble. "Hasn't it been good?"

"You know I am. That it has." Damn it, he didn't want to see her cry—didn't want to be the reason for her tears.

"Because, I'm having fun with you. Like I've never had before." Her words coupled with the glitter of wet tears on her lashes would have been laughable, except for the pain behind them. Cutting through him, she wiped at her eye with the back of a wrist. "All I need is the chance that maybe—"

"I care about you. More than I've cared about anyone else."

Only that didn't change the fact that love didn't happen for him. He'd told her about his mother, but what he should have spelled out was he was just like her. His inability to connect completely in the romantic arena was more than a habit born from defense or disgust at being the center of media speculation. More than a convenience too comfortable to investigate, though, in all honesty, it had been that, too. Why bother trying to overcome something that worked just fine for him? He hadn't cared until now.

"Isn't that something? Isn't it enough to wait and see? Yes, I want marriage…someday. But I've been so careful about everything for so long, I'm willing to take a risk for you. I would wait."

He knew she would. If he gave her any hope at all, she'd spend years waiting for something that, in all likelihood, he would never be able to give her. She might be willing to take that risk, but he wasn't. Not with her heart. Her life. Her happiness.

She wanted the white picket fence and the pram around the park. And he wanted her to have it. Even if it meant letting her go so someone else could give it to her.

"I'm sorry, sweetheart." And that was when the first camera flashed and the shutters began snapping.

CHAPTER NINETEEN

PAYTON's gown crinkled, gaping in falls of stiff, creased blue paper as she sat atop the padded exam table, legs crossed with as much lady-like decorum as she could muster given the circumstances. She was crabby. Sick and depressed. Fighting what had become a perpetual state of lethargy for weeks. But she wouldn't give in to it—surrender to the call of her bed simply because she'd been dumped.

It happened. To everyone, she was told.

Though usually not with the media there to witness the critical moment. But what did she really care if they'd splashed the portrait of her heartbreak across the newsstands? Or if Nate was pictured almost daily looking every bit the modern-day rake the papers made him out to be. The only thing that mattered was the affair was over and her life had to go on.

So she kept busy. Waited for the heartrending pain to pass. For her lip to finally stiffen up. For that promised time when another fish from the sea of men might actually appeal to her. She had a job she was passionate about and new friends who wouldn't let her breakup come between them. And even her fellow teachers had reached out to her in spite of the reporters trolling the block. So she got up every day and went to work and kept her appointments.

Like this one she'd scheduled weeks ago.

Dr. Thoms breezed into the room, pumped a handful of

sanitizer into her palm and rubbed it in as she scanned the electronic chart on her worktable. "So this is a regular check up today, and I see you'd called about beginning an oral contraceptive."

Payton's knuckles whitened as she gripped the table's edge, tears threatening again. Please, God, not in the gynecologist's office. They'd be writing her a referral to another kind of doctor altogether if she started sobbing here. "Um, yes, but…"

"Were you thinking primarily about birth control or to regulate your periods?"

Her ears pricked up. Of course she'd known the pill could do both, but she'd never really been inconvenienced enough to consider it. Only now, after weeks of bouncing all over the place emotionally, physically feeling the signs of an impending cycle then barely having one at all… This could be the answer to at least one of her problems. Albeit the most minor.

"Regulating my periods." Since she couldn't imagine ever having sex again. At least with anyone other than Nate…and she was doing her very best not to imagine that.

Thankfully, Dr. Thoms seemed oblivious to her inner turmoil and, focused on the task at hand, continued on. "Okay, then. So how are you feeling overall?"

Sad. Lonely. Stunned beyond belief that Nate could walk away from what they'd had so easily. Stunned even more by the physical toll their breakup was taking on her. "A little run-down, but it's not—no. I'm fine."

"Run-down? Any fever, runny nose, sore throat, upset stomach?"

"My stomach's been off, but I think it's more nerves than anything. And I'm beat." Then going for a little levity, she added, "Just sick and tired of being sick and tired."

Only it fell as flat as everything else.

Ignoring the weak joke, Dr. Thoms stared at her with that placid smile in place. "And when was your last period?"

"I had it for about a day, two and a half weeks ago."

Cool eyes met hers over the top of the chart. "Just a day? Was it heavy? Light?"

The temperature in the room dropped.

Payton didn't like the look she was getting. Her hand went to her stomach again, and those eyes narrowed ever so slightly, following the motion.

"Light." And then she hastily added, "But it's not that unusual. My cycle isn't exactly like clockwork. And we were using protection, so I really don't think you need to worry."

"Mmm-hmm." The doctor typed in a few notes. "Any dizzy spells, unusual tenderness in your breasts, mood swings, cravings or loss of appetite?"

The questions hit her like rapid-fire artillery. Each punching a bigger hole through her façade of calm.

Yes…yes…yes…

Oh, God, it couldn't be. "Doctor, I see where you're going with this, but I can't be—" She broke off, unwilling to even say the words. Desperately trying not to even think them.

Failing.

Pregnant.

Pregnant with a tiny, little piece of Nate growing inside her.

Her eyes pinched shut as she sucked air, willing the precious image away. She couldn't want it to be true, shouldn't be hoping it into existence. But something instinctual stirred to life within her, and on the deepest level she knew it was too late for hopes or wishes to make any difference at all.

"What am I going to do?"

Responding to a question far more encompassing than it had been interpreted, Dr. Thoms answered simply, "You're going to start by taking a pregnancy test."

* * *

Two hours later, the results had been confirmed and an ultrasound done to determine gestation. Payton walked the downtown streets in a daze, barely registering the blare of midday traffic, screeching tires and shouts for taxis as each step brought her closer to a conversation she'd never anticipated having. Explaining to Nate that his biggest fear—his worst nightmare and the horrific scenario he'd so recently escaped—had once again become a reality.

How would he react to the news?

She knew he'd be doing the math, same as she. Wondering if they'd ever had a chance or if their fate had been sealed from that very first night. He'd wonder if the fun and games had been worth it.

Know they hadn't.

The clap of thunder broke through her reverie, pulling her eyes to the gunmetal-gray sky and the steel and glass tower slicing into it. Nate's building.

Wrapping her arms around her waist, she tried to stave off the numbing cold seeping beneath her skin.

Would he hate her?

"Payton, is that you?"

She turned toward the lilting voice and found herself face to face with Nate's longtime assistant.

"Deborah, how are you?" she asked, embarrassed to be caught standing this way by the fifty-ish woman with a soft heart and mind too sharp to chalk her presence there up to coincidence.

"Are you headed up to see Nate?"

She opened her mouth, then simply shut it again. Was she? She'd come here to tell him about the baby, but now that she stood so close to her destination, she couldn't do it. Not like this. Nate deserved better than to have the news dropped in his lap between afternoon meetings. He'd always tried to do right by her, and she owed him, at least, a reasonable conversation in private. The news would devastate him—shatter the life he'd worked so hard to protect. The life he'd sacrificed her to preserve.

Finally, she forced enough air from her lungs to form words. "No. I thought I'd stop in, but I…" she held up her left arm, without looking to see she wasn't wearing a watch "…I don't have time after all."

Compassion shone in the older woman's eyes as she reached out and squeezed Payton's numb hand. "You're shivering, sweetheart." Then turning up her own collar against the wind and chill, she nodded toward the building behind her. "Wouldn't you like to come inside for a coffee?"

The seconds passed as Payton stared at the lobby doors, followed the lines of the architectural mammoth dominating the landscape around it. "No, thank you. I'm going home. Don't worry."

With a reluctant nod, Deborah turned down the sidewalk and went on her way.

Payton smoothed a hand over the still-flat plane of her belly and, eyes fixed on the building that so reflected its owner, the dizzying truth of what would happen when Nate found out she was pregnant hit her full in the face. If she didn't have a rock-solid plan for her future in place before she told him the news, Nate Evans would take over and make one for her.

CHAPTER TWENTY

THE piercing whistle of steam escaping the kettle was broken by the repetitive buzz of her security intercom. She turned off the gas and dashed down the hall. "Hello?"

"It's Nate. Let me up."

She stared blankly at the little white box mounted on her wall. Too soon. She was supposed to have hours more. He couldn't be here already.

Then brain function kicked in and she pushed the "entry" button and swung open the front door. Nate, taking the stairs two at a time, rounded her landing in a matter of seconds. He looked tired and impatient and more handsome than any man had a right to be as he strode to her door, taking in the length of her in a sweeping head-to-toe scan that nearly rocked her back with its intensity. For one precious heartbeat, she thought he'd come for them. That he'd realized he loved her, too. That he missed her enough he couldn't stay away—

"What's wrong?" he demanded, pushing into her apartment.

She stepped aside, closing her eyes before Nate could catch the disappointment there. Obviously, Deborah had spoken to him. She'd suspected it would happen and even turned the phone to voice mail in anticipation of a call, but she hadn't expected him to show up at her door in less than an hour's time. She wasn't prepared to face him yet, only Nate caught her arm, his hold gentle but firm as he forced her to meet his stare. "What's wrong?" he asked more urgently.

I'm pregnant.

It was the simple answer. And yet she couldn't make herself say the words. Not yet.

This much she'd decided.

"I'm sorry, I was going to call. You didn't need to rush over—"

Nate's brows drew down. His mouth pinching flat for a beat. "Deborah told me you'd been standing outside the building…crying. I cancelled my afternoon to come over here so don't give me the runaround."

Wincing at the cut of his sharp tone, she took a bracing breath. "I was thinking about us."

She half expected him to check his watch, see if he could make it back to the office to finish up one of those meetings after all. But he held steady, if not somewhat wary. "Us?"

Us. The two of them. The way it had been when they were together, creating the one who would make three. "I miss you."

Nate raked a hand through his hair, rubbed the back of his head with the rough strokes of a man trying to make sense of something exasperating beyond explanation. "I miss you, too, sweetheart. But we talked about this and decided if there was any chance for us to end up friends down the road…we need to give each other time apart now."

She knew all that. As the she knew the answer to her next question, too—the only question that mattered, the one that would decide everything—but had to ask it anyway. Had to hear him say the words aloud.

She swallowed and then, aching with a desperate heartfelt need, forced the words past her lips. "Do you love me?"

Her breath held, painful and hope-swollen within her chest

as she watched his eyes widen, felt the lingering caress of his gaze as it stroked over her cheeks, lips and eyes.

Please, she begged with every part of her heart, body and soul.

And when he didn't answer, she couldn't stop herself from saying more. Adding to her plea, her heartbreak and humiliation. "What we had was good." He couldn't have forgotten. "I miss it. I miss you." Maybe all he needed was to know. "And I thought after you've had some time away." She had to try. "Some space." Give him every chance. "That you might—"

"Payton, stop. Don't do this to yourself." It was blunt and cruel. But he couldn't stand the idea of prolonging her questions or suffering any longer. "Nothing's changed. And it won't."

Payton banded her arms over her slim waist and nodded. Stiff. "Okay," she whispered on a catch of breath that left him wrecked. She shook her head, the slight motion freeing a solitary tear to escape down the delicate slope of her cheek. "That's what I needed to know."

Damn it, this wasn't how he wanted it to go.

He wanted the fantasy they'd talked about those few months ago. The scenario where the passion between them died a natural death, going peacefully in its sleep some night, months and months from now. The deal where they woke to the friendship that had always been there.

Where, when he saw her crying, reaching out to touch her wouldn't just make it worse for both of them.

Her head fell forward into the cradle of her palm and she let out a shuddering breath he felt through his entire being. His fists clenched, once. Twice, before he physically couldn't stand to let her suffer there alone and reached for her—

"I'm pregnant."

His hand dropped to his side as the air left his lungs in a painful whoosh.

Time stood still and, paralyzed, helpless to stop it, he felt the foundation of his world begin to slide beneath his feet.

No.

This couldn't be happening. Not again. It was impossible—except the defeated set to Payton's shoulders told him it wasn't.

She turned her head in profile, not quite meeting his eyes, and whispered, "I'm so sorry."

Quietly she walked from the room, leaving him to absorb the truth of the situation. She was pregnant.

Alone, Nate walked to the window, stared at the rain beating down on the glass and wondered how after so little time he'd found himself brought full circle. And with the very woman he'd thought would help him leave the nightmare behind.

Ironic.

Fate's little way of giving him the finger, he supposed.

The suspicions that had plagued him from the first minutes following Annegret's teary pregnancy confession lurked in the shadows of his memory, daring him to revisit them. But to all those dark scenarios came the same resounding, "No." This wasn't some mercenary fortune hunter coming to him pregnant. It was Payton. So good even when she wanted to be bad, Payton. If she said there was a baby, there was. And without question it was his.

He shook his head, stunned. How could the entire world change in less than an hour? That was all it had been since Deborah called his direct line from her lunch break. She'd found Payton shaking in the cold outside his building, her red-rimmed eyes looking lost and scared. He'd raced to her apartment, unable to maintain the distance they'd discussed for fear something had happened.

But she'd looked fine when he arrived and he'd been angry

he'd had to see her. Had to see the hurt in her eyes when he didn't want to think about her hurting at all.

He'd wanted her to go away. Find someone else. Forget about him.

Only she hadn't been as fine as he'd thought, and now her going away was no longer an option. She'd never find the life she deserved and he was angry all over again.

How the hell could it have happened? The way he'd been going through condoms while they were together, he should have bought stock in the company. He'd been in charge of the protection and they'd used it every time—except that once.

His gut clenched, guilt working its way up his throat like bile.

He'd stopped before he'd come, found a condom and then returned to finish what he'd started. But unprotected penetration of any kind could result in pregnancy. And he'd been so damn careless. Even after everything he'd been through. Even knowing better.

He'd done this to them.

Eyes fixed on the gray-washed day beyond the glass, he pulled his phone from his pocket and brushed a thumb across the screen to bring up Deborah.

"I need you to get Arnie on the line for me. And then see what it takes to get married in Illinois."

CHAPTER TWENTY-ONE

PAYTON sat at the kitchen table, her gaze fixed on the cooling mug of tea between her palms. She'd left Nate in the living room nearly a half-hour before. After a time, she'd heard the baritone clip of his voice as he began making calls. Then a moment ago silence resumed.

The hardwood groaned its quiet protest under the weight of his approach and then Nate's dark form filled the doorway. Arms braced against the frame like a looming threat, he pressed into the room without entering.

"I found out this morning at my doctor's," she volunteered, figuring it as good a place to start as any.

Concern furrowed his brow. "Are you okay?"

It didn't surprise her; there'd never been a question of caring. Only of degree.

"Yes. It was time for my annual and I'd mentioned getting on the pill when I booked the appointment. One thing led to another and then…I knew." She picked up the mug and took a lukewarm sip, wishing for the soothing relief the picture on the box promised. "It happened within that first week or two."

Nate shouldered through the door and dropped into the seat across the table, meeting her eyes for the first time since she'd told him she was pregnant. The cold acceptance in his gaze should have hurt, but the pain was gone—replaced by a hollow kind of numb that had taken hold after she'd ripped her soul open, exposing the most tender, vulnerable part of herself to him. Begging him to love her. The blissful void of emotion wouldn't last, but she'd savor every moment while it did.

He reached across the table and wrapped his fingers around hers in a hold that felt stiff, uncomfortably dutiful. "Do you have a doctor? An OB for the pregnancy?"

She shook her head. Noted the lines deepening across his forehead and around his mouth.

His voice lowered, taking on a hard edge she could hear him fighting. "But you *are* getting one."

Then she understood what he was asking—if she planned to keep their child. "I've known about the baby for less than one day, Nate. The fact that I haven't gotten a doctor yet doesn't mean anything except that I need to do some research before selecting one."

His eyes cleared with relief. "I'm sorry, I just—" He shook his head and blew out a strained breath. "It's important. I have to ask certain things."

She nodded, her neck sore from the tension that had gripped her hours ago.

"I'm meeting with Arnie tomorrow about changing my will and drawing up a prenuptial agreement for us."

Payton fought an empty smile, noting his subtle pairing of death and marriage. Her mouth opened to set him straight, but he had his hand out, ready to cut her off.

"You know I'm going to be fair. The details are flexible, but I'm non-negotiable on the point of the agreement itself."

She couldn't care less about a prenuptial agreement. Because they wouldn't need one.

"I'm not marrying you." No satisfaction came from the words, only the bone-deep certainty that they were true.

"Don't be like this, Payton. It's important. An agreement will protect us both."

"Nate, it's not about the prenup. *I'm not marrying you.*"

His eyes narrowed on her. "What are you talking about? You're pregnant. Of course you are."

"No."

She saw the moment it clicked for him. When the pieces fell into place and a dark shadow fell across his hardening features. "The questions. You weren't worrying about me stepping up. It was a test. A trap. Making me tell you—" His eyes pinched shut, a vein popping to life along his temple. "Damn it, Payton."

"I needed to make sure. Before you knew about the baby."

"Why? So you could back yourself into a corner you can't get out of? Well, forget it. Forget what I said and forget about not marrying me. Everything's different now."

"Not everything." Their eyes clashed, held. Hers telling him she wouldn't back down. His begging to differ.

"You aren't thinking straight," he said levelly, his body language conveying all the confidence in the world that she'd see it his way. But she was onto his manipulative tactics.

Fat chance.

"You're a smart woman. All you need is some rest and a little perspective in the morning. We'll get you something to eat. Do you have any cravings? I'll have anything you want here inside thirty minutes."

"Nate, stop—"

"*No.* We'll get you some dinner and we'll go to bed. With you in my arms…and our baby inside you."

Her breath caught as a wave of emotion crashed through her, so intense her throat seized and her vision swam. And like that, the bliss of numb was torn away, leaving her raw and trembling. "I said stop!"

"I'm not stopping!" he snapped, those blue eyes she'd once been foolish enough to call arctic blazing at her. "Not until you see reason on this."

"Reason?" She was on her feet then, glaring at him across the table. "Give me a break. You go from assuring me there's *no chance* for a future with us to offering up the rest of your life—complete with a gold band and handy prenup—within the span of thirty minutes. Who's not being reasonable?"

"We're going to have a baby. A child between us. It changes things. I'm adapting."

"Then you better find another way to do it, Nate, because I'm not marrying you. There's no love—no emotion behind your proposal and I don't want to live the rest of my life as an obligation."

"That's not how it would be." A harsh breath followed as he threw one hand up in question. "I don't see why you're fighting this. *You're getting what you wanted.*"

"Like hell I am!" How could he even think that?

He watched her. Waited a beat as though assessing the situation before replying. Slowly, so she wouldn't miss even one word. "*Like hell you won't.* I'll make you happy. You know I can." The muscle in his jaw jumped. "You said it yourself—we get along great together. We have fun."

"I want more than fun, Nate."

Exasperation shot up his brows. "And I'm offering it."

Not even close. "Can you deny that an hour ago the idea of this future you're asking me to share with you didn't have you running in the other direction?"

"An hour ago I thought I had a choice!"

Mistake. Payton's frame shook as though he'd struck her. Too late, he saw his error. Damn it, he was blowing this, but she wasn't giving in!

"I'm sorry." Rounding the table, he pulled her into his arms and shifted them both back into the chair so she rested in his lap. "That's not what I meant."

"Yes, it is," she whispered, pressing her face into his chest so her soft curls spilled over him.

His arms tightened over shoulders that had never seemed so slight before. The hammering in his chest eased and for a moment they sat quietly together. And then she drew back, peering up at him, with those big brown eyes, liquid and pleading. "Nate, can't you understand that I don't want to take a lifetime of choices from you? That maybe I don't want you to take them from me?"

He understood it, all right. And was more sorry than he could have imagined possible. He knew what she was going through. Knew the feeling of betrayal that had to be welling inside of her. He'd tasted that bitterness, knew firsthand the threat of someone taking the life he'd planned. Only this time, Nate's carelessness had been the culprit to take Payton's choices and no test six months from now could set her free.

Damn it, he hadn't wanted to take anything away from her. It was the reason he ended things between them. He'd wanted her to be able to move on and find the man who would care for her the way she needed, wholly, without reservation. Only with those two uttered words, "I'm pregnant," that man became him.

Unlike with Annegret, there wasn't a single doubt in his mind. This baby was his—which meant so was Payton. And getting her to accept that was the first priority.

Fundamentally, he understood the problem. Payton had had a mere handful of hours to come to terms with the fact her life had changed immediately and irrevocably. Whereas, he'd been through this before—had months to contemplate his sense of priorities and values as they applied to a child entering his life. He'd known then what he would do, as he knew now.

He'd make a family. Make them whole.

"I understand, Payton. I do. But everything is different now that there's a baby. We're bound together for the rest of our lives through the child inside you."

"I'm not arguing that, but it doesn't mean we have to get married. You know I would never keep you from seeing him."

Him. She thought it would be a boy. He closed his eyes, pushing back the images that one word conjured. Visions he wasn't yet ready to face. "No. You won't. Because we'll be together. All of us."

She tried to stand, but he held her in place. Close to him, where she belonged.

"Nate, what you're suggesting is—"

"Important."

"Impossible. There are all kinds of families. People with situations much more convoluted than ours make it work without being married."

He shook his head, cupped her chin in his palm. "It won't work for me if I miss out on half of my child's life because I don't live with him."

Payton wanted to shove against his chest and scream her frustration, but the stress of the day had taken its toll and sapped the little energy she'd begun with. Now all she could do was whisper her protest. "I can't."

"I know you're scared, sweetheart. But I swear you don't have to be. We'll work this out. It doesn't have to happen tonight."

"No. It doesn't." They both needed some time to get used to the idea. Figure out how they really felt. What they wanted.

Nate would see.

"Have you told anyone yet?"

She shook her head. "No. Not yet."

"I'd appreciate it if you didn't. Not for a while."

She pulled back, searching his face for some sign of why, but all she saw was a man closed down and unavailable to her.

A sudden anxiety rose within her. Had he started to see someone else? Her stomach hollowed. Was there a woman he needed to tell? To give up—

"My dad. After what happened with Annegret—all the uncertainty. I'd rather wait to tell him about the pregnancy until we've sorted more of the details out ourselves."

His father. She should have realized.

"Of course. I won't say anything," she promised, the threat of tears leaving her voice unsteady.

Why couldn't he just love her? Why couldn't he have told her there was a chance for them? That walking away from what they'd had was tearing him apart? Given her *anything* to pin her hopes on so now she could take his reassurances and promises and wrap herself tight in them. Why did she have to know that an hour ago he still hadn't wanted her?

To that last, she reminded herself the answer was simple. She'd made him tell her. Because signing on to a loveless marriage wasn't something she could live with. Or perhaps it was. But a marriage where *she loved Nate* and he didn't love her? No. That would be a daily heartbreak she couldn't endure. So she'd demanded the truth.

Nate's wide hand gathered her hair at the nape of her neck, stroked over the mass of it as he pulled her close. "We'll work it out, sweetheart. I promise."

Too weary to do anything else, she gave into the comfort of a hold she'd never wanted to give up—from a man who didn't love her.

CHAPTER TWENTY-TWO

How in the hell was he supposed to make this work when Payton wouldn't give a damn inch?

"I'm not giving up my job!" Her cheeks were flush, her eyes overbright with shadows beneath as she planted hands on hips and glared at him from across the distance of his living room.

"People work because they need the money," he answered steadily, unwilling to be baited into a shouting match with this stubborn little demon woman carrying his child. "*You* don't need the money." He was the calm one. The reasonable one. Casually sprawled in his chair, smiling his most patient, unfazed smile—his hand, all the while, discreetly flexing the tension from his body behind the arm of the wingback.

They'd been going round like this for an hour now. And engaging in some variation of it for a month. He'd make a suggestion. She'd take offense. He'd clarify, take a different tack. She'd glower and throw whatever he'd offered back in his face. It didn't matter what merit his idea held. If the suggestion came from him, she didn't trust it, assuming it tied into his grand scheme to get her married to him.

She was right.

"Really, Nate? How do you feel about charity? How did you feel about it back when you weren't the one offering?"

He took a steadying breath. "Payton, this isn't charity.

There are laws in place to ensure that fathers provide for their children. I'm providing."

Her eyes flashed accusation. "You're trying to make me dependent on you."

"That isn't true. While the idea of taking care of you appeals to me a great deal, stealing your independence is not my goal here." He pushed up from the chair and paced between the fireplace and the bank of windows fronting the apartment. Blazing to bleak and back again. There was no good place to be.

"Hell, Payton, I'm not a villain. I want to make sure you and our baby have everything. I don't want you to work when you're tired. I don't want you to have to leave our child with a nanny because you can't afford not to. Can't you see I want to help here?" *And help my cause by offering assistance as I remind you of the practicalities surrounding a single mother's life.*

"I don't want any help." But even as she said the words the glitter of coming tears filled her eyes. She was scared and, though he'd been there every step of the way, he knew she felt alone. Because every step of the way, he'd been coming at her, working his own agenda. Trying to break her down enough that she'd let him pick her up.

A tremble touched her lips.

Why wouldn't she just *give*?

He was sick of the adversarial tango between them. He could barely remember what it had been like between them before they'd found out about the baby— No. That wasn't true. It would be easier if he could forget because he missed what they'd had. Missed the laughter and softness. The thoughtful exchanges. The hot rush that surged through him when that wild smile burst across her lips. He missed her body. Her heart. The show of too much emotion shining in her eyes when she was beneath him—that had been damn near impossible to give up. He wanted it back. Wanted to grab her shoulders and shake until she saw sense, stopped being so bullheaded and took the life he was offering her.

Watching him with wary eyes, she let out a defeated sigh and turned, giving him her back.

Screw this.

He had months before the baby came—before he *had* to get his shackle around her ring finger. Yes, he wanted resolution sooner. Like last week. But today he wasn't getting anywhere. Payton needed comfort, and he'd be damned if he wasn't going to lend her some.

Ignoring the aching memory of her eager acceptance of his hold—that perfect fit—he pulled Payton's tension-stiff frame into his arms and didn't let go. He stroked a hand down her back, bent his head to hers, and whispered into her hair. "Payton, stop fighting me. I know you're upset and we don't see eye to eye on…most anything these days. But this is new for us both. We're going to figure it out together. Okay?"

Her body shuddered once, and then she gave in. Softening against him as the tension sapped from her frame. "I'm going crazy, Nate. I'm so upset. And I—I—"

"Shh. I'll be there for you," he promised. "Both of you. No matter what."

Her head bowed forward, the crown rubbing against the center of his chest as she succumbed to a quiet sob.

Ducking to the side, he caught her against him, sweeping an arm beneath her knees. She didn't fight him as he carried her to the corner of the couch closest to the fire and held her in his lap as her tears soaked his shirt.

He'd take care of her. Whether she wanted him to or not, he'd make her happy. She just had to stop fighting him first.

She'd fallen asleep. It was a mistake, but curled in the strength of Nate's arms she'd felt so safe and calm and she'd been so tired…and then she'd let go. Let fatigue take her. Only now she wasn't tired. But she was still folded into his lap, enveloped in his clean masculine scent, closer than she'd been to him in a month, compounding her mistake with each breath drawn and every passing second she lingered.

Tilting her head, she peered up to his sleeping face. The lines of strain around his eyes, recently etched so deep, were softened and smoothed. His mouth relaxed into the near-smile that was its natural state.

A heavy breath filled the chest beneath her, followed by the rough growl of Nate waking. God, she loved that sound.

He was offering her a lifetime of hearing it. A lifetime of mornings waking to the hard-hewn planes of his face, the security of his arms.

He surveyed her through half-lidded eyes, a slow curve touching his lips before his focus sharpened on her. Heated.

She knew what that steam-rising, jungle gaze meant. *Trouble.*

She tried to pull back, but couldn't—literally.

"Oh!" Her hair tugged against the buttons of the oxford she'd been crashed out on.

Nate shifted up, only minimally pulling at the caught hair. "Hold on, sweetheart. Let me—"

"Ouch!"

"Sorry, whoa, stop squirming."

Keenly aware of her positioning, Payton stilled, her fingers attempting to pull the loose strands from the caught batch. But Nate brushed her hand away.

"Just give me a second." He reached to his back and pulled the shirt over his head, careful to keep the snagged buttons in one place. And then she was free. Sort of. Free from being physically attached to Nate's chest. Only her hair, falling in a tangled curtain in front of her eyes, was still wound up in his buttons. And she was still sitting in his lap.

"Okay, I see it here."

Good. She couldn't see a thing.

Long fingers sifted through the heavy mass, sending shivers of pleasure coursing over her skin.

Not good.

"I can get it." She reached out a staying hand, only to retract it with a jerk when she encountered warm, hard flesh. Nate. Bare-chested and less than six inches away.

"Probably not without scissors. I can see what I'm doing, just hold still."

Another gentle tug and the shirt partially fell away. "That's one."

"What?" she squeaked.

"You're snagged on two here. Probably that little nuzzling thing you do when you're asleep. I guess I must've been shirtless all the other times."

Her mouth went dry. As he was shirtless now. She let out a slow breath and closed her eyes, only to find the stimulus of his touch intensified—his hand sifting gently through her hair, readjusting, gathering, gripping tight and then gentling again—

The shirt came free and she thought she'd been spared, except when Nate tossed it aside she could see what had been opposite that soft button-down— Bare skin and hard-packed muscle. The perfect tight discs of his nipples. The fine line of hair bisecting his torso, trailing into his pants and flaring wide across his pecs. All of it flickering golden in the dying firelight.

She swallowed, raising her eyes to meet the blue of Nate's— steadily fixed on her. A muscle twitched in his jaw.

"Thank you," she whispered, backing off his lap, her gaze dropping to his chest once more as she stepped free.

He didn't answer, just sat there, brows drawn down, watching as she silently collected her things. At the door she turned to him, seeing the man she'd fallen in love with staring back at her for the first time in a month. No antagonism. No calculating manipulation. Just Nate. Wanting her.

She pushed a tremulous smile to her lips. "I'll talk to you tomorrow." And then she fled.

At the snick of the door closing, Nate shoved off the couch with a violent curse.

How the hell could he have been so blind? So stupid!

He'd been going about this all wrong. Wasting precious time respecting Payton's boundaries. Believing the physical interaction—always so easy between them—had become a necessary casualty in his pursuit of her hand. Like an idiot, he'd kept his distance, waiting for her to realize that marrying him was her best option before revisiting the sexual chemistry between them. But that had been backwards thinking, and all it had won him was a month of frustrated nights and the woman he wanted getting too damn comfortable with an arm's length space-cushion.

What he'd just seen—that smolder of lust banked not quite well enough—told him he didn't need space or understanding. He needed seduction. Dirty, down-low seduction that would get Payton writhing, naked beneath him.

The sex had always been more emotional than she'd wanted to admit. He'd known it from the start. Even that first night, he'd seen it in her eyes. She couldn't leave her heart out of anything she did, least of all making love.

So he needed to get her back into his bed. Use his body to batter down her defenses. Unlock the emotions and wants she'd tried to banish. And once he got her there, made her moan and gasp and look up at him with those eyes that gave too much away, he'd hold on and wouldn't let go. He'd make her feel so good she wouldn't think twice when they hopped on a plane to Vegas.

And that was how it was going to have to go. Fast. No time

for second thoughts or backtracking. The only problem was actually getting her beneath him.

If she saw him coming, she'd shut him down a mile away.

So the trick would be to exploit her weakness without letting on what he was doing. Based on the way their proximity and his state of undress affected her tonight, he had a good idea of where to start.

It wasn't fair play, but playing fair hadn't gotten him where he needed to go. He wanted her back. Wanted this whole matter resolved. Payton in his bed. His ring on her finger. Their baby between them.

And now he had a plan.

CHAPTER TWENTY-THREE

PAYTON stood before the closed door to her apartment, hand hovering above the knob as she mentally shored up her defenses. Nate was on his way up. Invariably looking like a new page in some man-by-month calendar, and too dangerously good for her peace of mind. He always looked good. And she'd generally been able to handle it. Register the attraction, tamp it down, sweep it aside. Right up until the night a week ago when she'd gotten her hair stuck in his shirt. Ever since she'd been fighting a losing battle against temptation.

It was unsettling. And what made matters worse, Nate had stopped berating her with the merits of marriage. Oh, she wanted to believe he'd suddenly come to terms with the impossibility of that scenario for her, but this was *Nate*. Relentless. Ruthless. Single-minded in his unwavering determination to make the world bend to his will, Nate. Now that she'd been on the receiving end of all that intensive focus, she didn't believe for one minute he'd actually given up the fight.

Which meant he'd be coming at her in some new devious manner. Unless of course the hormones had made her paranoid in addition to everything else: Hungry, sick, weepy, tired, irritable, sentimental…the list went on and on.

"Hey, Payton, you planning to let me in?"

Startled, she grabbed for the knob, shaking off her suspicion in the hopes of spending a pleasant morning with the father of her child. Whether his change in attitude was legitimate or not, she couldn't deny that Nate in "friend" mode was far superior to Nate as "adversary".

Swinging the door open, an apology poised on her lips, she stared in stunned disbelief…at her high-school fantasy come to life.

Nate Evans dressed in black soccer shorts, jersey, guards and cleats, a ball tucked under his arm and a sport bag slung over his shoulder.

Oh…my…

"I know we'd talked about looking into those Lamaze classes, but Rafe needed a fill-in for this morning's game." One shoulder propped against the doorjamb, not really in or out, he cocked his head toward the hall. "Wondered if you'd like to put the research off until afternoon and get out for some fresh air now?"

She swallowed, trying to loosen her throat enough to spit out a simple, smart, "No, thank you". Only she truly loved soccer. It had been ages since she'd seen a game and, as she remembered it, there wasn't much better than watching Nate play. Besides, he was right, it was a beautiful day—crisp and sunny, in the low fifties. She'd been planning a walk down at the lakefront anyway so it didn't make sense not to go just because her libido had all but rolled over to beg at the sight of Nate outfitted in soccer gear.

God help her, what was she going to do?

Forty minutes later, Payton was comfortably situated in a folding chair Nate had dragged out of the trunk of his car. She had a bottle of water, an organic green apple and a clear view of the players warming up before the game. Nate juggled the ball a few times, causing her gaze to drift down to his legs, the heavy muscles of his thighs flexing and bunching as he deftly passed the ball from knee to knee and then caught it in his hands and brought it back to his chest.

Those legs. Her mouth watered…

What was she doing? The days of pining were over. She wasn't waiting for her favorite player to notice her anymore. He'd noticed. Knocked her up and thrown her over already. Now the only game she could afford to play was keep away. And mooning over the silky caress of his shorts as he limbered up his legs was a definite violation of the rules.

So why then, minutes later, when he scored his first goal and shot her one of those victorious smiles that never ceased to devastate her heart, was she jumping from her seat cheering with the unrestrained enthusiasm of a fourteen-year-old girl dreaming of love and happily-ever-after?

Two things not on offer.

With that in mind, she tempered her reaction and returned to her seat. Forced the cool reserve she'd long ago perfected and watched Nate tear down the field. Held steady when she caught the flinty shift in his eyes.

He was assessing. Calculating. Strategizing for a tactical advantage in a game that had nothing to do with landing a ball in the goal.

He was playing her.

Driving forward, circling back and taking shot after shot until he found a way to outmaneuver her defense. He wanted the win. Her and the baby under his roof and in his care. He wanted to do the "right thing", only he couldn't seem to grasp how *not right* living that life would be for any of them.

Nate said he didn't want their child to miss out on the full-time love and attention living with both of its parents would afford. But what he wasn't considering were the implications of growing up in an environment of pretend. Children knew. Though they might not be able to discern the complexities of why, they sensed when something in their home was off. Like an imbalance of power or detachment of emotion.

Nate had never wanted to marry her. He'd never wanted

a child. And though he said all the right things, talked such a good game about raising their baby, she'd yet to see any indication from him that the child growing inside of her was more than something to claim. He knew it was there. He knew how fathers were *supposed* to feel. What they were supposed to do. But he didn't actually have those feelings himself. And no matter how he might want to provide a perfect life, no one could convincingly fake an attachment they didn't feel forever, something Nate knew from firsthand experience.

Add to that a mother's heartbreak made new through each passing day of make-believe affection—what kind of life would that be for their child?

The kind she didn't want to imagine and wouldn't allow to come to pass. She couldn't make Nate feel. She couldn't make him love. But she could ensure that her child always had a safe haven to return to. A place where the love was unconditional and abundant and the emotional stability wouldn't waiver.

She could do it. So long as she remembered that marrying Nate was not an option.

The game had been fast paced and exciting. The teams evenly matched, exactly the kind of challenge Nate thrived on. But the thrill of the win was dampened by the loss of ground he couldn't explain, except to say, one minute he'd had Payton looking at him as she had all those years before. And the next she'd closed down. Shuttered her emotions and put all that distance back between them.

Unwilling to concede any form of defeat, he jogged over to where she stood at the sidelines, blanket and chair clutched in her arms like a shield—against him.

Going to take more than that, sweetheart.

Giving her his grin, he grabbed her load and tucked it under one arm.

She blinked, looking just nervous enough to truly whet his appetite.

Go ahead and run. Try it.

"So congratulations," she said with a timid wave toward the field behind them.

"Yeah, good game, wasn't it?" He wiped the sweat from his brow with a sweep of his forearm, and caught the hungry drift of her gaze following his motions.

"You were terrific."

"It felt good to get on the field again." Have an outlet for some of the tension accumulated over the last month. Though as outlets went, he had a better one in mind. One he intended to make use of before the day's end.

Suddenly he couldn't wait to get back to Payton's place and put his plan into action. He ducked down to grab his athletic bag, straightened and then froze as the dark brown eyes he always thought of as soft and vulnerable bore straight into him—cold and hard.

He didn't like it. She was thinking too much.

But he knew exactly how to make her stop.

Looking away, he hiked the bag over a shoulder. "Let's get out of here."

The ride back into the city took longer than he'd liked. Too much time for Payton to sit quietly, contemplating her defensive strategies. He'd kept up the conversation, but her head hadn't been in it and eventually he'd left her to her thoughts.

At the apartment she'd predictably tried to put him off about the afternoon, but he had the Lamaze research as his passport and easily gained entry. From there, it was just a matter of chipping away her defenses…one garment at a time. He wished he'd had a camera for the way her jaw dropped when he jerked his jersey over his head—outwardly oblivious to the impact of his actions, inwardly gloating over her reaction to his unsubtle striptease.

And how could she argue when he suggested they look over the different schedules and programs…after he'd cleaned up in the shower? By the time he'd headed off to her bathroom, she'd been shaking, unable to even look at him.

Perfect. And that was just the warm up.

This was the main event. Nate glared into the fogged mirror. It was go time.

"Hey, babe?" Nate called from down the hall.

Payton looked up from the magazine she'd been blindly staring at for the last ten minutes while futilely attempting to keep her mind out of the shower where all that lathering was taking place. Talk about wasted effort. Try as she might to stop them, images of slow-running suds slipping over hard-packed muscles, tight nipples and more flitted one after the next through her mind. Memories of the salty taste of his skin… Not good.

With a shake of her head, she stood, calling back, "Wha—?" but that was as far as she got.

"Did I leave my bag out here?" Nate stood in the hall, a white towel hanging precariously low on his hips. He smiled crookedly her way while he used another towel to rub his hair dry.

The air in her lungs leaked out in a slow hiss, leaving her empty and weak, stunned and lightheaded, hungry and horrified as she fell back into her seat.

The crooked smile vanished, pulling into a hard frown as he dropped to a knee at her side. Concern furrowed his brow. Concern and something else she couldn't quite—

"Payton, sweetheart, are you okay?"

"Yes—no," she stammered in confusion, her chin tucking back. "I'm fine…" But then he was right there. So close she could feel the damp heat rising off his skin, see the water beaded across his chest and shoulders, his eyelashes clinging together in darkened points that made the blue of his eyes stand out bright in vivid contrast.

"You're pale." His voice was a low rumble at her ear, rough and midnight dark in the middle of the day. And then his big hands were moving over her, checking, gently probing... touching her in a way she knew she should stop but couldn't summon the strength to do so. "No swollen glands."

"Nate." Her voice was weak, thready. Something even she wouldn't listen to.

Long fingers skimmed up her neck, teasing through the hairs at her nape... "Chills." They curled over her jaw, brushed her cheeks, and then moved in a slow caress to her forehead. "Flushed, but not feverish."

His thumb swept a gentle arc across her cheekbone as his gaze locked with hers, pulling in slow strokes at that secret place where all her dreams dwelled.

Tell me. Tell me you love me. Give me something. Anything.

"Your pupils are dilated," he murmured. But there was nothing wrong with her. Nothing beyond the fact that temptation had just taken her a step closer to ruin. Making her pulse race and the air go thin and her body begin its achy plea for more of the touch she'd gone too long without.

She wanted him. Needed him. And if it were only her—but it wasn't.

She swallowed. Closed her eyes and thought about her baby before opening them again. "My eyes are fine, Nate." She'd be fine if he stopped touching her.

"Then what is it?" he challenged, meeting her gaze head-on, the heat of it stoking her to smolder.

Tell him. Only if she said the words, let him know how seeing him like this affected her, then he'd use it against—

Wait. The bag in the hall? He couldn't. The shower. The striptease complete with the stretching-out of all those muscles. He wouldn't dare! Only, this was Nate and he'd decided what he wanted. To hell with everyone else.

The soccer game! How long? This week for sure. Her stomach sank with dread.

Heat flamed her skin, only it had nothing to do with attraction and everything to do with outrage.

So he thought he could play her by using his body? Well, she knew a thing about that game. She knew what he liked, knew what sent him past the brink of control. And he'd just given her a lesson in how to achieve it without investing any actual emotion. Thank you, Nate. She could do that, too.

Time for Nate Evans to get a taste of his own medicine.

CHAPTER TWENTY-FOUR

HE WAS losing her.

He'd been so close. She'd been there, he knew it. He'd seen her weaken, start to melt. Felt the hot lick of her eyes over his skin, the current charging the air between them. And then, just that quickly, it changed.

The temperature dropped. The static grounded. And a swarm of angry bees manifested beneath his skin, buzzing in his head, making him itch and sting and want to roar in painful frustration.

Why wouldn't she damned well *give*?

Fighting the vise around his chest, he surged to his feet. Wasn't surprised when Payton rose with him. She leaned into his space, looking up at him with eyes that were flat and bleak, devoid of emotion and speared through his soul like a blade.

"Maybe I don't feel so well after all." Her hand settled cold at the center of his chest.

No. He saw what she was offering him—nothing—and he wouldn't take it.

He wouldn't let her look at him like that. As if somehow the lively, soulful woman who'd lived in this body had been obliterated, leaving an empty husk behind. No, not empty. Just unavailable to him. He couldn't stand it. Wouldn't allow it. Wouldn't let her shut him out and look through him as if he weren't even there.

With too much testosterone burning through his veins like acid, his hands moved possessively to Payton's hips. His thumbs rubbing deliberately over the delicate bones there.

He knew her and no matter how she wanted to close down and bury herself away from him, she couldn't do it completely. But if he wanted her, alive and hot and angry in his arms, he had to find the spot where she was most vulnerable and—even if it meant he was going straight to hell for it—cut deep.

Gaze fixed on the opaque waters of her eyes, he skimmed a hand beneath the hem of her shirt at her hip. Took a gulp of air and braced every muscle in his body as he pressed his palm to the one spot he hadn't touched—hadn't wanted to touch—in all the weeks since he'd learned about the pregnancy.

Payton flinched, her eyes going wide and sparking with all the emotion she'd wanted to cloak. Rage and hurt flashed beneath the surface. And then something stronger than them both swirled in the liquid brown depths below. Hope. The sight of it was so powerfully alluring after the bleakness he'd witnessed only seconds ago, he didn't know if he could ever break free from its spell.

If he ever wanted to.

But then Payton's hands covered his own where they lay flat against her belly—and the world tilted off its axis as they held their child together for the very first time.

There was a soft rise to the belly that had been a flat plane the last time he'd laid his hand to it. A gentle mound protecting the tiny body within. His child. The mergence of two souls into one. *Their child.*

He swallowed, unable to speak. And suddenly he was on his knees, pushing her shirt at both sides so he could see. So he could feel.

His thumbs brushed the smooth skin around her navel.

And then he pressed his forehead against the softness there, turned his ear to rest against her. Wondering if he could hear the sound of her body building its precious shelter. If his baby could hear him.

"Hello?" he whispered against her skin, unable to stop himself.

Slight fingers stroked his hair, teasing through the strands with that familiar touch that after too long without had become foreign.

He turned into her belly and kissed. Drew in the sweet perfume of her skin and kissed again, opening his mouth against her as he prayed she wouldn't push him away. Wouldn't close herself off to him. Again and again, he kissed across the feminine terrain until Payton's fingers tightened in his hair, holding him close.

One thought repeating through his mind. A primal claim, sounding to the rhythm of his pounding heart.

Mine. Mine. Mine.

They both were. And in a way he never could have predicted. Straight through to his soul.

It terrified him. Made his pulse race faster and his hands clutch at the woman he hadn't known how to hold.

Except she was letting him hold her now. Giving him the gift of her body, if only for this one time.

He couldn't think about that. Couldn't think about the void in her eyes when she'd uncovered his latest manipulation. He never wanted to see that look again. Didn't want to think about what it meant that after all the years, he had been the one to put it there. Didn't want to think about what it would take to ensure it never happened again.

Payton knew better. Knew she was headed for heartbreak, but still couldn't back away. A moment before she'd been at the brink of resisting, and then she'd seen it. The instant Nate's universe changed, taking the man she loved to his knees. The look in his eyes when his hand touched her belly. The sense of marvel. Wonder. He'd cradled their child in the palm of his hand. Kissed the place where it grew within her.

The tenderness of that kiss would stay with her for the rest of her life.

There was no more fight. No more will. Only want and the desperate need to give in. Give herself over.

He didn't love her. Maybe he couldn't. But he loved their baby and she didn't have to worry for her child's sake. In that instant she'd seen Nate's father in his eyes. The love and devotion apparent to anyone who crossed their paths. And she knew with sudden vivid clarity that she couldn't deny them a single moment together.

It would be enough for her. More than enough.

Her fingers trembled as they touched his jaw in silent inquiry. He turned up to her, the stark need and depth of emotion in his eyes taking her breath away.

"Let me have you."

She nodded, unable to voice even the most simple word of acceptance.

Nate rose then, so tall and powerful before her. His muscles standing out as though each and every one had gone taut beneath the strain of the last hour.

She reached for the towel at his waist, her fingers trembling as she loosened the cinch. Let it fall away and then grasped the hem of her own shirt.

Nate watched with hungry eyes as she pulled the stretchy cotton overhead and then opened the front catch to her newly too-tight bra. Her breasts spilled free, and she saw that single telling vein pop to life, betraying the expense of his restraint. Restraint she understood was meant to show her he would not take. This time he would wait for her to give.

Her thumbs slipped into the waist of her yoga pants and panties. She pushed them down her hips. Let them pile at her feet before she stepped free, as naked and exposed as the man who waited for her with a single outstretched arm.

He took her into his embrace, wrapping his long arms around her in a hold so flawless it made her ache. She didn't know how long he would have held her that way, but he was thick and hard against her belly, his perfect beaded nipple a scant distance from her mouth, close enough to touch with the barest flick of her tongue. She couldn't help herself.

And all that tightly reined restraint snapped.

Nate swept her into his arms, a gruff sound grating from his throat as she opened beneath the fall of his kiss. Took the thrust of his tongue and twisted in his arms to press her breasts against the harsh rise and fall of his chest.

In her bedroom, Nate propped a knee at the mattress, setting her back with a careful precision—so different from the times he'd tossed her to his bed and followed her down, laughing and growling as he crawled up her body to claim her. This wasn't playful. It wasn't fun.

It was undiluted desperation to join as one.

Mouths fused, tongues mating, sliding over and around each other as their bodies aligned in all the right places. Nate poised at the opening of her body, held back, gritting his teeth against his need to sink deep. Take. Claim. Keep.

Payton peered up at him, her eyes smoked with a need that matched his own, and yet she, too, paused. Her hand cupped his cheek. "I can't fight anymore."

"No more." His voice was a broken rasp. "I promise." He'd glimpsed what it would look like to destroy the only thing he had worth fighting for, and he wouldn't risk it again.

Her body arched against him, wet and too inviting to resist. "Nate, please. Now."

He pushed inside then, groaning as he sank full length into her tight hold. Gritting his teeth through the pure skin-to-skin friction.

Heaven.

To be so close.

To be let in.

To be *together*.

It was physical pleasure, but so much more than that and he never wanted it to end.

He arched back, sank deep again, drawing out each long stroke as far as it would go. Savoring the hug of Payton's legs around his hips, her fingers in his hair holding him close. The breathy pants of her rising desire. The clutch of her body when she took the kiss of his groin against hers. The escalating cries and pleas for more. He wanted to give her more. Give her everything. All he had and all he was. Anything she asked so he never lost this again.

And when her lips parted on a silent cry, her body seized around him, and she stared up at him with those soulful brown eyes that begged him to hold her…longer…harder…just like that…daring him to make it last forever—the world shifted again and he knew it would never be the same.

Braced on strong arms above her, Nate searched her eyes, his deep blue stare more penetrating than the hard body that rocked within her own. He carried her through the crashing waves of orgasm, followed the receding tide, and then urged her into the surf again. Not once looking away.

Let him see.

I love you.

He knew already.

Always you.

There was nothing left to hide.

Forever you.

He drove hard inside her. She arched against him, reveling in the stretch and give of her body as he filled her again and again, taking her fast toward the peak from which she'd just returned.

"Don't stop, please," she gasped, clutching tight at his shoulders. "Please."

He gathered her closer, slid an arm beneath her hips and held her to him as his voice rasped over her soul. "Just let me love you."

She cried out, her body pushed to release. Her heart torn in two. The world shattering around them as Nate followed her over the edge, her name on his lips.

Then gasping ragged breaths, he rolled to her side keeping one arm slung across her waist as he pulled her into the warmth of his body. She buried her face in his chest, letting the moments pass until Nate slipped into an oblivion beyond her grasp.

"Just let me love you."

They were beautiful words of passion to describe the physical act. So beautiful she could almost pretend…

CHAPTER TWENTY-FIVE

NATE sat at the edge of the bed, feet on the floor, forearms propped over his knees, jaw painfully set.

This wasn't going to work.

He looked over his shoulder at Payton's sleeping form, quietly curled into herself, a tiny furrow pulled between her delicate brows.

She didn't want what he was offering. Not really. They'd been in the same book, but on different pages from the start. He'd tried not to hurt her, but he'd been an idiot and in the end that was all he'd managed to do. Even today, when suddenly all the pieces of his life seemed to be falling into place, one jagged edge didn't fit and he'd felt it cut through Payton's vulnerable heart.

Just let me love you.

He shouldn't have said the words like that. What the hell had he been thinking?

Dropping his head into his hands, he let out a frustrated growl. A small noise of protest sounded from behind him as Payton clutched the corner of the sheet closer to her. She needed to rest. Needed a break. Needed a hell of a lot better than what he'd been giving her.

He knew what he had to do.

He pushed to his feet and found the comforter on the floor at the far corner of the bed. Covered her with it and quietly left.

* * *

The afternoon light was dying, leaving puddles of amber and burnt sienna across the western sky. Payton stood by the window, her forehead pressed to the glass, Nate's note in hand. She'd found it on the kitchen table after waking to an empty bed and quiet apartment a half-hour before. Had stalled in her steps at the sight of the single sheet propped against the bud-vase—inexplicably terrified. But the note had been no more than to tell her he'd had a few things to take care of and would be back later. Nothing earth-shattering or cryptic or telling. A few lines about some errands.

She needed to stop being so dramatic.

At the sound of the lock tumbling from down the hall, she straightened. Set the note on the counter and headed toward the door where Nate had just walked in, burdened with an overflowing grocery bag.

Food, she realized with a smile. The man was forever trying to take care of her. Tonight he wanted to make sure she ate a healthy meal.

"Sorry I was gone so long," he apologized, dropping a kiss at her temple before carrying the groceries through to the kitchen. "I stopped to pick up some dinner on the way back."

On the way back? "Were you at the office?"

He set the bag on the counter and turned to her, those too-blue eyes so beautiful they made her weak. "I drove out to my dad's."

"Did you tell him…about the baby?" About them? He'd been waiting to tell his father, she knew, until he'd gotten a marriage commitment from her.

Nate nodded.

So he'd read her decision in her eyes. Just as well. No need to make a big production of telling him he'd won.

No. That wasn't right. It stopped being a game the moment

she'd seen his eyes fill with love for their child. No more fighting. No winners. No losers.

Abandoning the food, he took her into his arms. He smelled so good and felt so strong around her. She'd have this for the rest of her life.

"I told him you were pregnant. And that we weren't getting married."

It took a moment for the words to make sense. She pushed back and looked up into his eyes, stunned. Shocked. And scared.

Her throat was tight and her knees loose. "What— why—?"

She didn't understand. Couldn't form the words to ask for clarification, explanation.

Nate's head dropped, his mouth pulling into a pained grimace. "I've been such a bastard. I never wanted to hurt you. But I've been doing it for so long now I can't remember a time when I wasn't."

She remembered. Her hand pressed flat to his chest, resting over the heavy thump, thump of his heart. "Things have been hard over the last months. Everything changed in the blink of an eye and we've both been reacting emotionally."

"No. That's just it. I haven't been. If I'd been in touch with anything beyond my need to control the situation, I would have realized that forcing you into a loveless marriage wouldn't be fair to either of us."

The words stung, sliced through her, cutting deep. He was giving her what she'd wanted. Wasn't he? Suddenly it didn't feel like it. It felt as if the ground were giving way beneath her feet and she were losing everything.

Forcing herself to nod, she pushed the barest smile to her lips. "How did your father take the news?"

Nate let out a self-deprecating laugh. "He was annoyed I'd waited this long to tell him."

"I bet." She'd known it was hard on him to keep the secret. But he hadn't been ready.

"He was happy to hear I was making him a grandfather, even if I wasn't making an honest woman of you." He shoved a hand through the short waves of his hair, ran it over the muscles of his neck. "But he agreed that after the horse's ass I've been, I was going to lose you forever if I kept pushing you to marry me."

She blinked up at him, to find those blue, blue eyes fixed intently on her. "What are you saying?"

"Payton, I've been such an idiot. I pushed you away, thinking you deserved more than I could give. It was the hardest thing I'd ever done, but I wanted you to have everything—love, marriage, family—all the things I didn't believe I was capable of sharing with you. And then I found out you were pregnant. Without having to examine why I needed it so badly, I suddenly had my justification to hold onto you forever. Only I was so intent on tying you down and fitting us into this perfect box, I didn't realize I'd been backing you into a prison."

Her mouth opened and then snapped closed at the realization she had no idea what to say to him. He finally understood, but how could she explain that when he knocked down the walls and took away the lock, that prison became paradise—the only place she wanted to live.

"I want us to be a family, Payton. But not because it's something I have to do. Not because it's a duty I feel honor bound to uphold. And sure as hell not for some paper certificate. I want it because I want you."

Tears of joy flooded her eyes. He hadn't offered her love, but he'd given her everything else she could ever want. It was enough. More than enough. "I want you, too. More than anything."

And then she was in his arms, held so hard against him. Safe and warm and basking in the promise of their future when the words she'd never thought to hear came gruff against the tumble of her curls. "I love you."

Payton pushed back from his hold, panic that she'd heard wrong or suddenly started hallucinating gripped her. Nate took a step back, letting her see him. The honesty of his words etched across the features of his beautiful face. Her heart tripped in her chest, and the room around her tilted and dimmed at the edges. She reached out grasping at air—found Nate's hand there to support her. She barely had the breath to ask, "You love me?"

"I really do. I didn't think I knew how. It was so foreign to me, so unfamiliar, I didn't recognize it even when it was shaking me to the core. Scaring the hell out of me." Those blue eyes stared steadily back at her, open, windows to a soul… brimming with hope. "I love you. And if you're willing to take a chance on me, I'll spend the rest of my life proving it to you."

Extracting a small black box from his back pocket, Nate went down on one knee. He flipped open the lid revealing an eternity band of glittering diamonds and held it out to her. "Payton Liss. I love you. Will you make me the happiest man alive by agreeing to live unwed with me for the duration of our lives? By allowing me to care for you, provide you with everything your heart desires, and love you and our baby forever?"

Her heart sped and helpless laughter bubbled free. He loved her!

She went to the floor beside him and, arms linking around his neck, answered, "No."

His head jerked up, a harsh bark of laughter escaping him. Amusement lit his eyes. That crazy confidence shining bright.

This man knew her. He really knew her.

"So after all that," he asked, voice thick with emotion he wouldn't hide, "now you want me to marry you, hmm?"

She peered up at him, letting him see everything her heart held. All the love. All the hope. Everything she knew he would cherish and protect. "I really do."

The corner of his mouth kicked into the grin she'd loved her whole life. "When?"

Pulling his head down to hers, she brushed her lips against his. Reveled in his tightening hold. "How fast can you make it happen?"

Before she could blink she'd been pulled into the cradle of his thighs, that gorgeous ring sparkled on her finger, and Nate was issuing orders into his phone.

"I want a plane for Vegas, ready to take off in one hour."

Nate pulled her closer and, holding the phone from his ear, stared deep into her eyes.

With one look, she told him everything he needed to know.

The muscle in his jaw jumped as his gaze went dark. "You're right. We better make it two."

Tossing the phone aside, he slid his fingers into the curls at her nape and captured her mouth with a kiss that touched her soul and tasted like forever.

Cupping her cheek in his palm, he brought his brow to hers. "Tell me. I need to hear the words."

"Forever, Nate. From so long ago and with everything I am. I love you. Always."

DO NOT DISTURB

BY
ANNA CLEARY

As a child, **Anna Cleary** loved reading so much that during the midnight hours she was forced to read with a torch under the bedcovers, to lull the suspicions of her sleep-obsessed parents. From an early age she dreamed of writing her own books. She saw herself in a stone cottage by the sea, wearing a velvet smoking jacket and sipping sherry, like Somerset Maugham.

In real life she became a school teacher, where her greatest pleasure was teaching children to write beautiful stories.

A little while ago, she and one of her friends made a pact to each write the first chapter of a romance novel in their holidays. From writing her very first line Anna was hooked, and she gave up teaching to become a full-time writer. She now lives in Queensland with a deeply sensitive and intelligent cat. She prefers champagne to sherry, and loves music, books, four-legged people, trees, movies and restaurants.

For my lovely niece, Linda.

CHAPTER ONE

THE tall, dark-haired guy in the suit strode into the meeting room of Martin Place Investments, and the hum of conversation faded into silence.

Mirandi Summers sat straight in her chair, her pulse-rate a little elevated. Everyone else was in black or shades of grey. She hoped her violet dress wasn't too pretty for the office.

'Morning,' Joe Sinclair said without bothering to glance at his assembled market analysts, too concerned with checking the hardware for his presentation.

'Morning, Joe.' The responses came from around the room, some bright and eager to please, others more subdued.

This morning Joe looked authoritative and slightly on edge, something in his manner creating more than the usual tension. How he'd changed in ten years. Hard to imagine him burning up the bitumen on his bike now.

'Ah, here we go.' The boyish grin that had the temps drooling made a brief appearance on his lean, tanned face, then vanished.

A brilliant, multi-coloured graph illuminated the screen. On it a number of spiky criss-crossing lines curved upwards, shooting towards infinity.

'There now. Look at that.' Joe's cool blue eyes grew sharp and focused, a line creasing the space between his brows. 'You see before you the future. Looks good, doesn't it?' He sent a commanding glance around at his employees and Mirandi joined the chorus of assent. 'And it *will* be good, people, I think I can promise you that. It will, but only if we are willing to learn from the mistakes of the past.'

He frowned and pulled a face. 'Tomorrow, as you know, I'll be flying off to this conference in Europe. Before I leave I want to know everyone has a clear view of the factors influencing MPI's current direction.'

He touched the button again and another graph lit the screen, this one's projections not quite so sunny. He swept the faces of listeners. 'I'm keen to hear your ideas. Can anyone suggest—'

Suddenly he stopped in mid-sentence. His frown deepening, he swung around until his acute blue glance lighted on Mirandi at the end of the row.

'Oh—er...Miss Summers. *You're* here. Are you—intending to stay?'

Mirandi felt something grab in her insides. Under the weight of her red hair her nape grew uncomfortably warm. 'Well, yes. Of course.' She glanced about her. All the other market analysts were assembled, their laptops at the ready. 'This is the future projections meeting, isn't it?'

Joe Sinclair gave his ear a meditative rub. 'Yes, it is. Just that I was under the impression—Ryan had mentioned something he wanted you to do this morning. Didn't I hear you say that, Ryan?'

Beside Mirandi Ryan Patterson stirred himself to attention. 'Oh, did I? Yeah. Yeah, that's right, Joe. Sorry, Mirandi. I forgot to mention the Trevor file.'

Mirandi gave a small, gurgling laugh. 'Oh, the *Trevor* file. Now that's a mistake from the past if ever there was one.' Everyone joined in her light-hearted laugh, including Ryan Patterson. Everyone except Joe Sinclair, that was. His black lashes were lowered, as it it pained him to look at her.

Smarting, Mirandi changed position slightly and crossed

her legs. 'As it happens, Joe, I've reconciled the Trevor file. It's all finished and accounted for.'

There was a moment of stunned silence, then the other analysts burst into a round of surprised applause and congratulations. Mirandi couldn't help but feel gratified. The Trevor file was notorious and had been around for a long time. Perfect material for a new MA to cut her teeth on. Especially if the boss needed something to keep her occupied whilst keeping her at a distance.

Joe smiled too, though Mirandi felt his quick smouldering glance leave a trail of sparks down her legs. 'Have you, now? Slick work. But have you written the letters to old Trevor and his sons to let them know the outcome?'

Mirandi's flush climbed higher, but she said in dulcet tones, 'Well, as you know, Joe, Ryan's assistant will be back next week and I suspect *she'd* like to have that pleasure.'

Beneath his lashes, Joe's half-lidded glance lasered Mirandi from across the room, though he said with silky gentleness, 'I don't think you understand quite how we operate here, Miss Summers. Until those letters are in the mail the file is incomplete. I'm sure you don't want to leave unfinished business for others to deal with.'

Mirandi felt a savage jump in her blood pressure, though she controlled it, surrendering to the command and rising from her chair with cool grace. 'Unfinished business?' She threw him a mocking smile. 'Heaven forbid. What would you know about that, Joe?'

She made a point of giving Ryan and the others a cheeky grin and a wave, then swept from the room, feeling a visceral flash from Joe's eyes sear through the fabric of her dress.

As she strode back to her desk along the corridor his voice drifted after her. 'Are you free to give us your attention *now*, Ryan?'

It took her a couple of hours to get over the latest clash, but she cooled down in time. She was determined not to go home with tears in her eyes this night. In fact, she might have managed to forget all about it by the end of the day if Ryan Patterson hadn't found something else for her to do. *Might*.

But he had, and ironically here she was, in the middle of the afternoon, approaching no-woman's land. Joseph Sinclair's private residence.

Twenty-second floor. Apartment four.

Leave the folders on the table in the foyer where Joe can easily find them, and hotfoot it straight back to work in time for the three o'clock credit review, were Ryan's spoken instructions. Unspoken, but lurking under the surface like crocodiles, was his more crucial advice. Don't linger there hoping for a chance to flirt, sweetheart. Forget leaving any traces of yourself behind to intrigue him. No strands of your flaming red hair or whiffs of your perfume, strategically squirted here and there. He's no good for the likes of you. He'd use you up without a second thought and break you in the process.

As if Mirandi didn't know that already. She had personal experience. If eyes were the windows to the soul, the colour of Joe Sinclair's was a liar. That heavenly blue had already lured her in once only to leave her floundering, and she wasn't a kid of eighteen any more, naive and willing to be enchanted by a charming young rebel with nothing to lose and everything to prove.

She couldn't have been persuaded to set foot in Joe's posh apartment building if her entire floor hadn't been overstretched with preparations for his big junket to France, and no one else available.

2204. Mirandi paused before the imposing door. Funny how even with a legitimate card key in her hand she felt that prickle of intruder's guilt. Noiselessly, the lock flashed green, she walked in and…

Whoosh.

Oh, wow. The light. The space. And through those double doors into the spacious sitting room—the views.

So this was who he was now. Of course, if an outlaw's natural brilliance had skyrocketed him up the corporate ladder to the highest echelon in an investment firm, why wouldn't he live in a palace at eye level with the top of the Sydney Harbour Bridge?

Hypnotised by the grandeur, she stepped through the double doors, still clutching the folders, and tiptoed the couple of miles across Joe Sinclair's satin hardwood floor to gaze out through the glass. Sydney looked like the postcards from this height, all blue sea, sparkling rooftops and scrapers under a bright azure sky.

She turned and cast an awed eye over the joint, inhaling deeply to soak in the atmosphere. It smelled rich. The furnishings were spare, but tasteful. Mahogany and leather, a richly-hued oriental rug, a couple of paintings...

This glossy apartment was a million miles from that two-roomed flat, their favourite trysting place all those long ago summer afternoons where Joe had initiated her into the delights of passion.

Her eye fell on a photo, frozen in time inside a glass prism. It showed a decrepit motorbike leaning against a wall. It was Joe's old motorbike, before he'd rescued it from rust and made it shine. His pride and joy.

Regret for that long ago summer welled up in her, and, like the sentimental fool she was, even while she smiled in remembrance tears misted her eyes. For a minute she was back in the magic time, the summer she turned eighteen.

It had been late spring, for the jacarandas were in flower, purple carpets underfoot all over Lavender Bay. As sweet and glowing in her mind as if it had been yesterday she was there, standing under the spreading boughs of the jacaranda in the churchyard after morning service, fresh out of school and in love after one brief, world-shaking encounter. There she was, dreamily listening to Auntie Mim chat with friends while her father, who was Captain of the Lavender Bay chapter of the Christian Army, was still engaged in farewelling his flock at the church door.

She could still see her old love-struck self. Nodding, smiling, pretending to listen, holding her secret clutched to her heart until her romantic radar, newly alert, pricked up its ears at the approach of a motorcycle.

A wild hope bloomed inside her, and she swung around just as the big bike roared into the paved entrance and skidded to a halt, its racket idling down to a low, predatory growl.

Astride the mean machine was Jake Sinclair's wayward son, Joe, looking long, lean and darkly satanic as his cool blue gaze combed the little clusters of friends and families in their Sunday uniforms and pastels. Black jeans outlined his powerful thighs, while a black leather vest left his bronzed, sinewy arms bare and highlighted the glossy raven black of his hair and two-day beard.

'What's *he* doing here?' Auntie Mim frowned. 'What could he be wanting?'

Though Mirandi had often noticed him about—who among the females of Lavender Bay hadn't?—she'd only spoken to him for the first time the day before when he'd helped her retrieve her books from a puddle outside the library.

After years of steeping herself in romantic sagas and grand passions played out on the Yorkshire moors, Mirandi knew instinctively what he wanted. *Who.* And to her intense and terrified joy, his bold blue gaze lit on her with an electric summons that sizzled across the paved churchyard and straight to her ovaries.

She was gripped with the purest excitement she'd ever experienced. For a second she vacillated. On the one hand there were her friends, her father, Auntie Mim, the entire church gathering, and on the other the bad boy on the big bike.

Then Joe Sinclair cocked his handsome head at her and

grinned. A primitive urge as deep and irresistible as a cosmic force blazed to life inside her. She took a step in his direction, faltered, took another step, then, thrusting her hymnal into Auntie Mim's grasp, so as not to worry the innocent woman, breathed, 'Auntie, I think I can guess. He's in search of salvation.'

Then she walked across the yard.

'Well, hello, Joe,' she said, every inch the pastor's gracious daughter, though her excited pulse was effervescing through her veins like raspberry fizz. 'Why don't you come in and join us?'

Joe Sinclair flicked a glance across the goggling congregation, then his black lashes made a sleepy descent over his smiling gaze. 'Or you could come for a ride.'

This was only the second time she'd had a chance to dwell on his face up close for any length of time, and she couldn't take her eyes off him. He had a strong straight nose, sexy, chiselled mouth and jaw and gorgeous cheekbones. He was all lean, hard and angular, except for his black lashes. They were amazingly long and luxuriant, but in a masculine way that caught at her lungs and melted her very bone marrow.

'Oh…' she faltered, plunged into a dilemma '…I don't think… Well, my friends are all… And there's—there's my auntie…'

He broke into a grin then that illuminated his lean face and made him so handsome her insides curled over. 'I haven't come for your auntie.'

She didn't hesitate very much longer. With a hasty, placatory wave at Mim, she climbed onto the passenger seat, tucked her skirt primly around her knees, let her fingers sink into his lean ribs and was swept away on the most exhilarating ride of her life.

Oh, it had been thrilling. Clinging to Joe on the bike was the closest intimate contact she'd ever had with a raw, vibrant man.

And, unbelievably for a lanky girl with red hair and no boyfriend experience—hardly even a first kiss to boast of, unless she counted Stewart Beale and a clumsy pash at the school dance—he'd taken her back to his flat and kissed her until her insides melted like dark chocolate and her brain turned to mush.

Then he'd gently but firmly unbuttoned her modest little blouse with his beautiful lean hands and stroked her breasts until she trembled with a delicious fever. And *then* he'd unzipped her Sunday skirt, and with artful, virile skill had demonstrated things to her about riding she'd only ever read about in trashy magazines.

Oh, it had been a golden time. Joe was cynical and mocking about serious things like church, but tender and affectionate with her. He didn't mock her when she tootled her recorder on Saturday mornings in the mall with the church band, though she felt so self-conscious she frowned the whole time so as not to be tempted to laugh.

Every day with him was an adventure. He made her listen to songs, *really* listen, and in between his university studies and part-time work introduced her to writers and ideas she'd never before encountered.

He was passionate about music, rock especially, and animals, and could be so enchanted by the beauty of a wren or a honey-eater he would make her stand still for minutes so as not to scare it.

She could still hear his voice, urging her to take her time. 'Look,' he'd say. 'Look *properly*.' Joe's mother was a painter, he'd once told her, and had taught him how to really look at birds and natural things from when he was a tiny little boy. And he was an artist himself of a sort. Once in the flat she stumbled on some poems he'd composed. Vivid little pictures painted in just a few bright words.

She was supposed to be enrolling in uni, but how could she concentrate on such mundane stuff as her future when she was intoxicated with love? So she deferred her enrolment, and told Auntie Mim and her father she needed a gap year to experience life.

Mim was unimpressed. 'He'll never amount to anything. He's nothing but trouble, that lad. Why can't you find some nice, steady boy from the church?' She'd have been surprised to learn he could find beauty in simple things. That often when Mirandi was in danger of pushing the limits of recklessness too far, it was Joe's steadying hand that restrained her.

When he wasn't fixing up motors he took Mirandi fishing in his father's old dinghy in the little estuary at the head of the bay. How she remembered those lazy afternoons, drifting in the boat, dreaming about the future. Joe in his ancient blue tee shirt that reeked faintly of machine oil no matter how often it was washed.

And she'd loved him. Oh, how she'd loved him.

Shame it had all had to end so miserably. But she'd learned from it. As the song said, life was a bittersweet symphony. And after she'd lost him, once she was over the heartbreak, she'd come to the realisation her happiness depended on herself and not another person. Every woman was a goddess in her own right and was honour bound to walk like one.

She cast a wry glance around at the glossy apartment. Did that mocking, irreverent, irreligious Joe Sinclair still exist somewhere, deep down under the layers of his Italian suits and the corporate skin he now inhabited? Or was this new sophisticated Joe the animal he'd truly been all along?

She paused at an antique sideboard, where a crystal decanter stood among a selection of lethal-looking bottles. A few familiar labels. Whisky, gin, and there was the vodka, her old favourite and first acquaintance with the evil stuff. She could have laughed to think of herself then. How easily she'd succumbed in the name of sophistication. Anything to impress her lover, who'd been so worldly-wise in her naive eyes. Older by a whole six years, though way older in the hard lessons of grief and loss.

She could imagine what her father would think of it all. After a lifetime of caring for the homeless and manning the city soup kitchens, he wouldn't be any more impressed than he'd been ten years ago when he'd scraped Joe's father off the pavement and driven him home because he'd gambled his last dollar and couldn't afford the bus.

It popped into her head that if Joe knew she was here now, invading his private domain, he'd have every right to be furious.

She was conscious then of a vague sensation she hadn't experienced since a time in her childhood when her father had inadvertently left her alone in the house while he rushed to tend some distressed person. A reckless, almost irresistible desire to make the most of her freedom and do something wicked, like raid the freezer for ice cream.

Not, of course, that she'd do anything like that *now*.

However, with Joe ensconced in meetings with the board for the rest of the afternoon, along with Stella, his EA, surely there was time for a little tour of appreciation?

CHAPTER TWO

JOE SINCLAIR directed his long stride back towards his chief executive office, then on an impulse made a left swerve and took the lift down, loosening his tie. Would the day never end?

Something was wrong with him.

If it wasn't weird enough to have been tossing and turning in his sleep these past weeks like a criminal with a conscience, now he had developed the disease most fatal to bankers.

Astonishing this could happen to *him*, a guy with a gift for finance, but in the last couple of months—ever since the casino development had been floated, in fact—board meetings had become excruciating. When had the musical chink of money flowing into the coffers of Martin Place Investment started to fall so flat?

He nearly had to pinch himself. Wasn't he the guy who'd pursued his career with such single-minded zeal his colleagues called him the Money Machine? Nothing ever interfered with his core business. No distraction, no interest, no woman. All of his passions lived in their separate compartments and life was a velvet ride. No collisions, no dramas.

Down in the street, he breathed the open air and lifted his face to the afternoon sun. His first time AWOL in years, he considered how best to make the most of his stolen afternoon. In the absence of a helicopter to lift him out of the business world and drop him somewhere clean and pure, like

Antarctica—or what remained of it—he tossed up between a gym and a bar, and the bar won.

Not for the alcohol, per se, so much as the possibility of finding some luscious lovely decorating the venue with a view to entertainment.

One who didn't want to buy him. He tried not to think of Kirsty, his sometime lover. Way back then those first few weeks had been amusing, but now…

Now, a familiar feeling of ennui lurked around the edges of her carefully groomed image. He could tell, the signs had been there for weeks, an unpleasant crunch was looming. Her father's offer of the house in Vaucluse and an honorary directorship had been the clincher. Every one of his instincts was shouting at him to run like hell before the prison gates clanged shut.

Ironic, wasn't it, that these days society guys wanted to buy him for their daughters? *Him*. Jake Sinclair's son. One-time rebel and seducer of innocent virgins. Did he really come across now as the sort of guy who would trade his soul for connections?

Between them they'd tried every trick in the book. Kirsty had even attempted to make him jealous, flaunting some silver-tailed Romeo in front of his eyes to make him care. What she didn't know—what each of his women had to learn—was that Joe Sinclair didn't have a jealous bone in his body.

He paused at the entrance to the Bamboo Bar, then strolled into its dim, cool refuge and ordered a Scotch. The lunch crowd had diminished. A couple of leggy women perched on barstools glanced his way, but instead of welcoming the signals he was swept with a wave of weariness.

Suddenly it all seemed so predictable, the conquest dance. He'd advance, they'd retreat. He'd advance a little further, they'd take a flirty step in his direction. He'd play it cool, they'd come on strong… It was all too easy.

But, God, he *loved* meeting women. What was wrong with him? He must be sick.

He should be feeling upbeat. Here he was at the top of his game, the world his own personal pomegranate. Tomorrow he'd be flying to the south of France. A change of scene, the possibility of picking up some new contacts, useful information from some of the masters of the game before he decided whether or not the firm should risk its shirt on the Darling Point casino project.

So why should his heart sink at the prospect? Good old reliable Stella would be along to smooth the way and attend to all the little details of his comfort. Well, most of them. And Stella was—well, she was risk free.

Unlike some.

An apparition reared in his mind, one that burned in his thoughts a time too often, in fact, for a highly disciplined CEO with responsibilities.

Was it a whole five weeks since HR had floated her name before him as the potential candidate for the new Market Analyst position the firm was creating? His first reaction had been incredulity. A more unlikely MA he couldn't imagine. Why had she applied? Was she hoping to glean some advantage from their past acquaintance? Had she forgotten how things had played out?

Mirandi Summers, his one-time squeeze. His first instinct was to give her the thumbs down. Last thing he ever wanted was to revisit that final scene where betrayal hung acrid in the air like smoke after a massacre. So why hadn't he blocked her application?

It wasn't guilt, exactly. He'd done the right thing in the end, hadn't he? The *only* thing. He could hardly believe he was still wasting his time even thinking about it.

All right, so these days she wasn't quite the shy, sweet little honey who'd tied his guts in knots. She'd grown up. Her green eyes had acquired the glitter of experience. Where once they'd reflected every passing emotion with honest fervour, these days they were guarded. Wary. But in the competitive jungle of office politics—a girl like her...

The bad taste this morning's meeting had left returned to him with full force. Why the hell was she so keen to swim with the sharks? If only she knew it, he was trying his best to protect her. Given half a chance some of those others would cut her to shreds.

He ran a finger round the inside of his collar. How could he ever be expected to concentrate with her in the room like a woman-sized pack of dynamite?

It had been the same since the day she started. That first morning when he'd strolled down to the coffee room and she'd wafted into view his lungs had gone into cardiac arrest.

Old memories, old guilts had rushed to the surface, and for a guy as fit as himself his blood pressure had made a surprising leap. He'd had to close his eyes a second to reorient himself.

She still radiated the same animal vigour that had sucked him in and driven him wild in his twenties, but now her leggy, coltish beauty had matured into sensuous, smooth-flowing curves and long, silken limbs that had rocked through him like a warm, sultry samba. Limbs he'd once enjoyed to the utmost draped around his neck.

Her bright hair showed none of its old tendency to curl. Now it hung smooth and silky down her back. But surely that purple dress she'd worn today was a little snug? He could see what other guys would make of her. *Hot*.

He was seized with a maniacal desire to rush across the room and drag some covering around her.

As usual, just thinking of the womanly handful she'd become lit a dangerous simmer in his blood. Clearly, hiring her had been a mistake. He'd arranged for her to be tucked under Ryan Patterson's wing for a few weeks while Patterson's EA was on leave, just so she could at least find her feet before she was thrown in with the pack, but it didn't help Joe Sinclair's problem one bit. She was a burr in his imagination. In the end, unless he could work her out of his system, nothing else for it, he'd have to sack her.

Not that he gave a damn about her now, one way or the other. Although, all right, he had taken the time to check out her personnel file just for interest's sake.

She still lived in Lavender Bay not far from the old neighbourhood, and still not married, apparently. Surprising really, considering the course her old man had mapped out for her.

His mouth tightened in a grimace, though the insult had long since ceased to sting. Hell, if he'd been her father he'd probably have done the same thing. She'd been so soft, so tender and giving. Malleable. Too malleable to be at the mercy of a villain like himself. He should probably thank the old guy. It was probably the insulting lack of faith in all things Sinclair that had spurred him on to show the captain and the rest of Lavender Bay that he could rise to any height he set his mind on.

But as for Mirandi in this world…he still couldn't get over it. Did she have any idea of some of the cutthroat decisions she'd have to make? Perfectly good, useful projects she'd have to reject in favour of other, more lucrative investments? The hearts she'd have to break? She was as suitable for the job as a baby. Hell, with her upbringing, if she had any idea of what the board was contemplating at this very minute her tender conscience would send her running in the other direction.

Once or twice he'd been unable to resist an impulse to stroll by Patterson's office. Just to check she was settling in. He'd caught a few glimpses of her, once frowning in concentration at her desk, another time chatting on the phone. To a client, he hoped. She looked perfectly relaxed and confident, though sometimes people had no idea they were struggling and in need of help.

The last time he'd given into that impulse he'd caught her

laughing at something Ryan Patterson said, and she'd glanced around and spotted *him* strolling by. Instantly her laugh had died and her face had assumed that cool, mysterious façade that could drive a man crazy.

He was used to his employees behaving with caution when he was around, it came with the territory, but sometimes he couldn't help wishing he'd gone easier with her on her first day.

He'd resisted checking on her after that, but knowing she was there, her honeyed temptation fragrancing the air along there—the same air breathed by *Patterson*—flavoured every minute of his every day. In fact, he wondered now if it had been such a good idea awarding Patterson the pleasure of easing her in.

He'd chosen the guy because Patterson was mild and well liked, but the choice might have backfired.

If only the bloke would stop raving about her abilities as if she were his own personal discovery. It wasn't beyond the bounds of probability he was in *lust* with her, if a pale, blond milksop of a guy could conjure up enough red blood cells to experience anything so turbulent.

Joe was no stranger to turbulence. Even during his recent bout of disturbed nights, those times when he was torn from his sleep in a cold sweat, as if in search of further punishment his mind had immediately turned to her. How she looked, her expression on her first day in the job when he'd been forced to show her her place.

There'd been something in her face. Ridiculously, it brought back to him with violent force the stricken look he'd seen in her eyes that last time she'd come to his flat. How vulnerable she'd been back then. He'd seen something like that look again this morning.

He tried to suppress a familiar twinge in his guts. It wasn't guilt, exactly, it was just…

He *must* be sick.

His phone buzzed, and he saw it was Stella. He considered letting it ring through to the recorded message, then his conscience got the better of him.

'Stella?' As crisp as ever. Mrs Efficiency would never guess he was standing in a bar room, Scotch in hand, contemplating bolting to the ends of the earth.

Unusually for her she sounded agitated. 'Oh, Joe, I'm on my way to the hospital. It's Mike, my youngest. He's been in a bike accident and they've put him in intensive care. I'm sorry, but I have to be there.'

Bloody hell. *All* he needed. But he said, 'Of course, Stella. Take all the time you need.'

'They're talking about operating. I'm afraid I won't be able to accompany you to Monaco, after all. I'm so sorry.'

'Forget about it,' he said, wincing. 'It can't be helped. Stay with your son. That's where you're needed most.'

'Oh, thank you, Joe. Thanks for being so understanding. And don't worry about your airport transfers. Those have all been taken care of. When you land in Zurich all you have to do is…' Instructions, instructions, instructions. 'And I've left the hotel confirmation on your desk. Don't forget to…' More instructions, more tedious details. It was a wonder she didn't offer to pack for him. A further round of abject apologies and medical details, then the anxious mother disconnected.

Despite his annoyance he felt a surge of approval towards his executive assistant. She'd been touchingly excited about the trip, in her restrained way. A woman prepared to make such a sacrifice for the sake of a son old enough to fend for himself was admirable. Rare, in his experience.

His mood darkened. As if it weren't already a bore, now it would be ten times worse. The long flight by himself, airport queues. Delays. Fights over taxis. Crowded beaches. French food, French people. Days of being locked inside conference rooms with hundreds of eager delegates from around the globe all blathering on about the fabulous weather. As if there weren't enough weather right here in Sydney.

He'd have to dredge up his rusty French. Why the hell couldn't they have held the thing somewhere cold, like Switzerland or Helsinki? Investment bankers could discuss the casino industry quite as well in those places as on the Côte d'Azur.

The very thought of the place sent a wave of distaste through him. He gave himself a mental shake. This was so unlike Joe Sinclair, mover and shaker in high finance, he had to wonder if he was coming down with flu.

Sighing, he flicked open his phone and dialled the office number. No use fighting it. He was a prisoner of his own success and there was no escape.

'Get me Tonia in HR.' He waited. 'Ah, Tonia—Joe. Look, Tonia, take a look through the lists and see if you can find someone who can be spared to fill in for Stella on the trip, will you?' She chatted for a moment, then he slid the phone into his jacket pocket.

Someone pleasant, he should have added. Someone interesting who could keep his mind off the dark places. With a fatalistic shrug he tossed off his Scotch and set down his glass, then, ignoring the lovelies at the bar, walked out into the street.

He reminded himself he was a lucky guy. Someone would turn up.

Mirandi began to relax a little on her prowl around Joe Sinclair's apartment, though she restricted herself to merely glancing into most of the rooms for fear of shedding DNA.

Curiously, there were no other photos. Not a sign of attachment to a single living soul, though she knew he'd never keep any pictures of his family. Joe had always been tight-lipped about them, but Auntie Mim knew the story. His mother had walked out when Joe was a boy of nine or ten, and his father, who'd been a talented architect, had spiralled into an addiction and gambled away all his assets, including the house, over his son's head. The very home he'd designed and built with his own hands.

Joe had never liked being reminded of those times even when she knew him, so what had she expected to see here in his new life? That late-afternoon shot of him and her at the beach, grinning into the camera as though their hearts beat as one? Or any one of that string of girls she'd seen clinging to the back of the old Ducati?

Afterwards. When he was grinding her into the dust with his indifference. Lucky the violence of her youthful passions had been burned out of her.

Through a partly open doorway she glimpsed what must be a bedroom, and hesitated. She shouldn't. She really shouldn't. Though maybe it would help her develop some deeper understanding of how her old love was travelling now.

Her old love. Listen to herself. The truth about that had come out, plain for all to see, so why waste her time peering down that shady lane? She doubted she'd have taken this job at all if she'd realised at the interview that the Joseph Sinclair, CEO of Martin Place Investments, was in fact her old boyfriend, Joe. That final parting had been—so cruel.

Still, she had to be fair and remind herself Joe never knew what it was she'd come to tell him that day. Remembering the moment no longer had the power to make her flinch with anguish, but it was burned into her bone marrow.

His blue eyes, bright with that strangely fierce intensity. 'It's over,' he'd said, his voice hoarse. '*We're* over.' And when in her total shock and devastation she'd whimpered a question, his savage, 'Go home, little girl. Run back to your daddy.'

As break-ups went, it had topped the memorable list and left track marks on her soul. And while time might have cauterised the wound, running into him her first morning in the coffee room had done more than just shake her up. At first glimpse of him, even after ten years the things he'd said had come hissing back and aroused echoes of the old emotions.

The instant she'd caught sight of him a violent upheaval had rearranged her insides, though *he* hadn't seemed similarly affected. His long, lithe stride had checked for less than a heartbeat, and he'd strolled across to her with all the cool, confident composure of the boss man.

She had to remind herself she was no one special. Just someone he'd met along the way. A chick from the past.

His blue gaze flicked over her, veiled, appraising. 'Well, well. Mirandi. Hi.'

So cool. While she was all at sea. His eyes, his deep voice, and her lungs paralysed. No oxygen, no floor under her feet. And straight away, the scent of him. Some woodsy cologne evoking cleanliness and masculinity in the old familiar rush.

As she took in the immediacy of his dark, lean sexiness her gap year came spinning back and she was that giddy girl again, thrilled and half-terrified to be singled out by the bad boy with the wild reputation. Held breathless once again in his heart-stopping blue gaze, she had to restrain an impulse to touch him.

A thousand impressions assaulted her. He was just as devastating in his city suit as he'd been in denim and leather, though at thirty-five his handsomeness had settled into harsher lines.

Sterner. More defined. Every inch the high-powered executive. She wondered how many people here besides herself knew that underneath his designer and beautifully laundered fine white cotton shirt a heavy-duty tattoo rippled down his arm. Even thinking about those arms could still bring her out in a sweat.

Was it so surprising then that her heart, her flesh, her emotions all surged in joyful remembrance? When she saw him her heart was thundering so loudly she could barely hear herself speak.

'*Joe*. Hello.' Straight up, that husky little catch in her voice. 'How are you? I—got such a surprise when I found out you were the CEO here.'

His expressive black brows twitched as if he didn't quite believe her. 'You didn't know?'

'Oh, well, I mean, I knew it was *a* Joseph Sinclair, but I didn't know it was *m*—the Joe Sinclair I once knew.'

His eyes veiled and their last goodbye opened between them like a wound. But he shrugged and gave that faintly mocking smile she knew so well. Used to know.

'Hard to believe?'

'Gosh no, of course not. But—with no photo of you on the website, for some reason—I visualised a much older person. You know the type. Bald, plump...' She made a roundish outline with her hands. 'Toadish. Cigar in breast pocket.' She gave a nervous laugh, aware she was talking too much, and her desperate phrases grew jerky. 'Not the...person I used to know. It was only that I—knew the name it seemed like a—a sign, you know. An omen. Fate, or something.'

Heaven help her, *finally* she managed to draw breath.

'Well, that explains it,' he said smoothly.

She flushed, realising with chagrin how deeply she'd exposed her insecurity. Surely after ten years the past should have lost its sting. But she couldn't help herself, because all the while things she'd once known so well about him were striking her afresh, sucking her in in the same old way.

He didn't often make direct eye contact, and just like before she found herself waiting, breathless, for every glance he flashed her from beneath his black brows. And like before, those blue glances had the power to sear through her entrails and leave a powerful impression, like some rare piercing glimpse of a kingfisher's wing.

He'd pierced her with one of them right then. But it was an

ironic glance, one that revealed nothing of the warmth he'd
once shown her. Before the break-up, that was. Before she'd
wrecked things by offering her eternal love.

'Would you have started here if you'd known?' he said.

'I—of course I would,' she lied. 'Why not?' She'd managed an artificial smile then to conceal her pulse. But though
she'd kept her voice steady, she knew her redhead's skin was
betraying her as always, lighting her up like the Macquarie
beacon with every minuscule fluctuation in her emotions.

'Why not indeed?' There was a faintly sardonic inflection
in his tone that recalled the rejection as if it were yesterday.

She retreated from that horror, hurrying into a safer direction. 'Oh, and, er, do you know how long it will take before my
own office is ready? At the interview I had the impression that
the position was all ready to go. I appreciate Ryan mentoring
me for a few days, of course, but I'm pretty keen to get started
on my real work. Forge my own direction, so to speak.'

She gave a small laugh but he didn't join in. In fact, his
brows drew together in disapproval. 'I think you'll find that
working with Ryan will show you the ropes twice as fast as
you could learn them on your own.'

'Oh, I'm sure. Though I am quite a fast learner.'

His black lashes flickered infinitesimally. 'I remember.'

A silence fell. Nerve-racking seconds ticked by that grew
excruciating.

Why had she said that? She racked her brains for something
warm to say that would ease the tension. 'You know, Joe, I've
often thought of you—since… Wondered—how you were.'
She smiled, nearly put out her hand to touch him, but, jarred
by the flicker in his cool blue gaze, controlled the impulse.

There was a definite warning in that glinting glance. *Don't
go there*, it read, as stern and uncompromising as if it had been
emblazoned in official lettering.

What a fool she was. Of course he didn't want to be reminded of his past, not here in this austere place surrounded

by his employees. Realising she'd opened herself up to another rejection, she flushed outright then and her speech died, hanging her out to dry at the critical moment.

He stood frowning while her discomfort mounted, then he said, 'Look, Mirandi. You're here on probation, same as any new employee. I hope you understand that any personal history between us is of no relevance. All that matters here is how well you perform your job.'

Her insides jolted as if she'd stumbled blindly into a rock face. In a wave of mortification it occurred to her he might think she had hopes of him again. That she might have taken the job with a view to reviving their old connection.

Perhaps he read her embarrassment, for his tone softened a little. 'To be brutally honest, I'm surprised to see you here. Investment banking is a tough world to survive in. I'm not sure this work will suit someone of your temperament.'

'My—temperament?' came from her dry throat.

'Well…' He hesitated, then scratching his ear, said, 'I think you'll find that in finance an excess of emotion and, er, sensibility are luxuries we can't afford.'

She bristled all over. Sensibility indeed. Did he think she was still that gormless idiot who'd broken her heart over him a thousand years ago?

Lucky she was of a proud disposition and could think on her feet while being eviscerated.

'Oh,' she said, 'please don't worry about me, Joe. I've toughened up. Every night I sleep on a bed of nails.' She spread her arms. 'Go on. Dish it out. I can take it.'

A muscle twitched in his gorgeous jaw, then he said drily, 'Very dramatic. I suggest you pour all that *passion* into your work.' There was slight inflection in the way he said the word that reminded her he was no stranger to its various applications.

For a minute or perhaps an hour or two his blue gaze

seemed to burn through her face, then he snapped out of it and looked at his watch. Brisk, unemotional Joe Sinclair, CEO.

'Right. Ryan Patterson will be reporting on how you perform, so since we keep strict hours here you'd better drink your coffee. Oh, and, er…good luck.'

With a curt gesture he walked away.

So brusque. So—unwelcoming.

Indignation threatened to overcome her. So she had an emotional side. She was human, wasn't she? He hadn't seemed to object to her passionate nature ten years ago. She stared after him, striding through the department like an autocrat. She could hardly recognise the guy. If he hadn't still been oozing hotness she'd have wondered if she'd been talking to his twin. Anyone would think he'd been born with a briefcase in his hand.

She smarted for minutes over the implication that she was too soft for the business world. Too *weak*. On what had he based that assessment?

Her credentials were all there in her CV. Her years in the bank, the promotions she'd earned. Just as soon as her office was ready and she could start her own work, she'd show him how efficient she could be.

She could have done with a few private moments to give her galloping pulse time to settle, but she noticed Patterson's curious gaze follow Joe then shift to her, and she knew she had to glide on like a goddess and act as though nothing had happened.

Standing here now in his apartment, searching for some lingering essence of the lazy, laughing, teasing Joe she used to know, she wondered how she could still be so affected by him. Time should have done its work by now. She was a mature woman, hardly that green girl who'd worshipped him and been his adoring slave.

She supposed running into him again had dragged it all up again in her mind. The truth was, she'd never experienced anything like the intensity of the passion she'd had for him. Although at the time, during all the months of grieving, Auntie Mim had made the observation that Joe wouldn't have given her up so abruptly if it hadn't been purely about the sex.

Mim had been right about some of it. There was no denying she'd been followed by a string of wild little hussies, as Mim had termed Joe's other girlfriends. Hot chicks. Even so, she could never regret her wild time with him. Joining the chicks. How could she, when it had been the most exciting time of her life? The time she'd felt most alive.

Perhaps that was why gazing into his bedroom now exerted a violent fascination, though her conscience was telling her loud and clear that a man's bedroom—especially a boss's—an *ex-lover's*—was his fortress. Or should be.

Sadly, while her scruples tried to assert themselves, her feet in their four inch heels were itching to push that door wide and cross the forbidden threshold, and before she was half aware of it she was *in*, staring at a rather severe four-poster heaped with pillows and richly draped in luxurious brocaded fabrics.

Oh, yes. The master suite.

Somehow Joe's bed made her awash with sensations, not all of them positive. Its decadent appeal was amplified by its reflections in several long mirrors.

How would it feel to lie in there at night with him? Her pulse quickened as she imagined his handsome dark head on those champagne satin pillows. They looked soft enough, but looks could be so deceiving where pillows were concerned. For herself, she preferred hers *very* soft, though as she recalled the younger Joe had never worried about anything so domestic.

A simple mattress on the floor, those green patterned sheets—that had been their passion bed, the candle shedding its glow into the small hours on their entwined bodies Joe's concession to romance.

She stared at the four-poster, then, on an impulse, sat on the edge and slipped off her shoes. She dragged a pillow into position, then gingerly lay her head on it. After a moment she lifted her feet onto the bed, then stretched out and, involuntarily relaxing, released a long and languorous sigh.

Ah-h-h. She let herself sink into the bed's soft, sensuous and at the same time buoyant embrace, her head cradled by one of the softest, most delicious pillows she'd ever experienced.

Oh, the comfort. Fearful at first of letting herself go, she lay still a moment, imagining herself floating on a cloud. Perhaps it was inevitable, given her experiences with Joe Sinclair, but her thoughts started to drift down a certain illicit alleyway. One she'd fought and struggled to avoid ever since the coffee-room encounter.

Imagine, for example, it was midnight. Suppose Joe arrived home unexpectedly and found her here?

Her blood warmed to the scenario. For all his powerful six-three Joe was a quiet guy. He never raised his voice when gutting someone with a few well chosen words, and he seemed capable of walking as silently as a cat when prowling the corridors at work. It wasn't impossible to imagine he might walk in and catch her unawares.

Almost unconsciously, she changed position to arrange herself more voluptuously, like Goya's painting of 'The Naked Maja', though of course she didn't take her clothes off. Her little fantastical indulgence was only for a second. She closed her eyes, picturing the scene.

He'd come in, find her here, and be overcome with the old desire. He'd take off his tie and slowly unbutton his shirt…

How well she remembered his beautiful chest and hard, muscled abdomen. Even in his Armani suit it was clear he still looked after his athletic frame. Perhaps he worked out in a gym. There was probably one in this very building.

Although… Shouldn't they start with a kiss? After so long she wouldn't enjoy being rushed.

She banished the undressing scene and started afresh. He'd come in and catch her here, and be so overwhelmed by desire he'd swoop onto the bed beside her, take her in his arms and kiss her with deep, romantic passion. Forget that it was a bit like the Sleeping Beauty or Goldilocks, or whoever. Those babes wouldn't have known how to savour the kiss, anyway, whereas *she*…

Her lids sprang open. Was that sound from inside the apartment, or something next door? The pipes, perhaps? She strained her ears for seconds, then, hearing only silence, relaxed back into the fantasy.

The kiss. No, it was annoying, but before she could really enjoy kissing him she would need some sort of discussion about what had happened. Why he'd suddenly become so cold and unapproachable at the time she'd most needed him.

Why he'd changed overnight from her tender, teasing lover into that grim, distant stranger. Though, on the other hand, recriminations about the past at that exact point could destroy the magic.

So. First he'd kiss her and caress her, and then he'd say…

An instant later a surprised growl jolted her back to earth and she looked up to meet Joe Sinclair's stunned, incredulous gaze. He was standing in the doorway in the lean, solid flesh, staring at her as if she were an hallucination.

CHAPTER THREE

TRANSFIXED INTO A SORT of paralysis, he was holding a phone glued to his ear.

Mirandi scrambled off the bed and made a useless attempt to smooth the coverlet.

'Oh, *Joe*. I didn't expect… I was just…' She noticed the folders on the floor where they'd fallen. She stooped to snatch them up, conscious of the burning tide of sheer mortification rising through her limbs and chest and turning her face red hot.

But she hadn't lived through the past ten years without acquiring a few life skills. Faced with total humiliation, with her back to the wall, Mirandi Summers could schmoozle her way out of a situation as well as the next woman.

Drawing herself up to her full five-seven, she met Joe Sinclair's bemused gaze with resolve. 'I think you should know you have a mouse problem.'

His black brows twitched. A glint lit the deep blue of his irises.

Without taking his gaze off her, he shot a few words down the phone. 'It's no one. I'll talk to you later.' With a deliberate calm, he snapped the phone shut and slipped it inside the jacket of his sleek suit. It buzzed again, but he cut it off and directed the full force of his stunning gaze at her.

'Ah,' he said. 'Mirandi.'

It had always thrilled her that for a guy of such few words, his voice had a deep, rich, almost musical quality. Eighty per cent cocoa, the rest pure cream. But something in the tone of that little exclamation, something smooth and satisfied, as if he'd always suspected she was dying to crawl back into his bed any way she could, and now he was proven *right*, roused an indignant spark in her.

Forget that from her current vantage point he was tall, with his big athletic frame easily able to block a doorway. She'd been towered over by him before, perhaps not with him having the power of life and death over her job, so to speak, but the situation had occurred, as her body seemed vibrantly aware.

She eased into her shoes, grateful for the added inches, then thrust the folders into his hands. 'I was asked to deliver these.'

'To my bedroom?'

'Of course not, Joe. Absolutely not. I intended to put them on the table in the foyer, but when I opened the door and I saw the mouse… I—must have disturbed it. I didn't think you'd want to have to deal with *that* when you got home, so naturally I—took off after it.' She gave an uncertain laugh he didn't join in with, then glanced about her and gave her most convincing shudder. 'It's in here somewhere.'

'In my bed, presumably.'

She felt her flush deepen, especially when she noticed him make a familiar, scorching inventory of her curves. Some things never changed.

His mouth had always been so stirringly expressive. As though sculpted by some sure celestial force, his lips were firm and masculine, the upper one narrow, the lower one fuller, the whole stern ensemble promising the ultimate in sensual pleasure. And delivering, as her body now yearningly recalled.

'Well, it ran—in here, yes. I lost sight of it and… Well, I got scared it might run at *me*. So I'm afraid I—had to jump up on the, er…' A hollow in the pillows was glaringly the size and shape of her head. 'It may not still be in here right *now*, of course.' She tried for her most earnest expression. 'I'm sorry. I didn't have time to think out a strategy.'

'You seem to be doing quite well now, though.'

She evaded his sceptical glance, her face afire just when she needed it to be cool. All right, so her story was thin and he didn't believe a word. He didn't look half as furious as he should be. Warning bells were clanging in her head. It was a situational rerun. Joe, Mirandi, *bed*.

Fantasy may be one thing, reality was definitely another.

'Anyway,' she said, marshalling some faux briskness, 'I have to get back to work.' She made a move to walk past him, nerve-rackingly conscious this was a sackable offence and she'd handed him a platinum-plated advantage in the male/female adversarial stakes.

At the last possible instant he stood aside to allow her through, to her intense relief, though at the moment of passing closest by him the intense masculinity radiating from him singed the skin cells on that side of her body to the third degree.

As she escaped into the hallway and made for the sitting room other phones started ringing, though the sound was cut off almost at once.

'I can't talk *now*, Kirsty,' she heard him say, the merest hint of irritation in his voice. He raised it a little. 'Hold it there, Mirandi. Just a minute.'

He caught up with her just as she was scurrying across an enormous Persian rug towards the front door, faster even than the mouse. If there had truly been a mouse, that was.

'Don't go. Stay a minute. I want to—talk to you.'

He didn't touch her, but it was as if an invisible arm had reached out and grabbed her by the scruff. There was no resisting. She turned to face him, eye to eye, and since he was the one asking her embarrassment over being caught subsided a little. She gave a stiff nod.

'Sit down.' He indicated a handsome chesterfield with

deep cushions. His black lashes flickered. 'Can I get you a drink?'

'No, thanks.' She allowed herself the glimmer of a smile. 'I'm working, aren't I?'

He smiled, raising his eyebrows, and she had a sudden vivid flashback to her vodka afternoon. The first time she'd succumbed and broken her pledge. After that, her solemn childhood promises had fallen thick and fast. Enslaved by her sexual sorcerer, she'd have drunk hemlock if she'd thought it would make her his equal in sophistication.

To her relief he didn't allude to her youthful indiscretions. He strolled over to his drinks sideboard. 'Do you mind…?'

She shook her head, gestured for him to go right ahead. She was the last person to dictate to others after her spectacular fall from grace.

He poured himself a whisky. 'Sit, sit.' He waved his hand in an autocratic gesture, directing her towards the sofa, and she made the wary concession of perching on the edge.

He dropped into a chair across from her, leaning forward a little, his long, lean fingers wrapped idly around his glass. Fingers that had once been familiar with every curve and hollow of her body.

She faced him, her old partner in crime. In passion.

'So…do you feel—settled into the firm?' His glance sank deep, and she could feel the old pull. That magnetic attraction that sparked up her blood and made her heart quicken with excitement. So dangerous, so addictive.

She felt his gaze drift over her, flick to her legs, and her sexual triggers responded with shameless willingness. Even after everything, something inside her switched on to preen and revel in his appreciation.

She shrugged. 'I'm settling in. Everything seems to be going well enough, I suppose, though to be honest I wish I could spend more time on my own work.' She glanced at him from under her lashes. 'I'm really looking forward to my own office.'

'Ah, yes.' His eyes veiled. 'How's it going with Patterson? Helping you find your feet?'

'Oh, yeah.' She nodded, smiling to herself as she thought of Ryan's wry words of advice on everything a girl needed to know on how to survive at Martin Place Investments. 'Ryan's been fantastic. Nothing's too much trouble for him.'

Beneath his black lashes his eyes glinted. 'Fantastic. Tell me about you. How's life?'

Did he mean at work, or personally? She doubted he'd be interested in her father's health situation. Her social life, perhaps? Ah, no. She got it now. None of the above. Long after their year of living dangerously, he wanted to know if she had a partner. A lover.

'Things are fine with me,' she said. 'Splendid.'

'*Splendid?*' He lifted his brows.

'Absolutely.' Well, she was hardly likely to tell him she hadn't been very successful in that regard. That she'd noticed in herself a regrettable tendency not to be able to hold onto a boyfriend. Possibly because she found it quite hard to open up. Her legendary passion must have been letting her down. Curiously, for one of her renowned temperament, they found her too—self-contained. Inhibited, one had complained.

'Anyway, I finished my degree and—'

His eyes glinted. 'Yeah, I'm sure I read that. Well done.'

She flicked him a narrow glance. Was he mocking her? At the time she'd known him he was juggling several part time jobs so he could pursue his ambitions, while she deferred her own education, reluctant to tear herself away from him, greatly to her family's concern.

How they'd stressed over it. The nagging she'd endured.

'Where did you say you studied?'

'Brisbane.'

He lifted his shoulders in sardonic amusement. 'As far away as possible from Joe Sinclair.'

'No, not at all,' she said, flushing, though of course it was true. 'That was the best course of its kind available at the time. Anyway, it was after the…*after* we—broke up.' She mumbled the last few words.

'Not long after, though,' he dropped in, searching her face.

'No.' A nerve jumped deep in her visceral region. He was sailing close to home. Someone should warn him to take care. There were things he wouldn't want to know.

There was a jagged pause, then she said, 'Well, anyway, I decided science as a lead-in to medicine wasn't for me after all and found the job in the bank. It was only ever meant to be temporary, but to my surprise I found I had quite an aptitude for it.'

His brows edged together. 'For finance?'

She nodded, wishing he didn't have to look so dubious.

'What's your plan?' he said. 'Your ultimate goal?'

'Careerwise?'

'Of course. What else?'

She gave him a wry look. What else indeed?

'Oh, well,' she said glibly, as if she weren't a twenty-eight-year-old woman with twenty-eight-year-old eggs in her ovaries. 'I'm aiming for the stars. Managing Director of a firm like this one would seem like a good jumping-off point.'

His sexy mouth twitched and she realised with some irritation he felt amused by her grand, audacious vision. Possibly his masculine ego felt challenged.

'Anyway, as I said,' she finished, 'I'm doing fine, or I will be once I can flex my muscles. What about you, Joe? I can see you've arrived.' She swept an admiring glance around her. 'This is quite—breathtaking. Not bad for a boy who was expelled from two high schools.'

He sipped his Scotch. 'Not quite what your family would have expected, I dare say.'

She put on her bland, non-committal face. Mim certainly hadn't expected him to do well. A solid pillar of the church, she'd made her feelings crystal clear on the subject of that wild heathen Joe Sinclair at every opportunity. Her father hadn't had so much to say, possibly because he was in the dark about her mad love affair, dreamily going about the business of caring for people, never knowing his beloved daughter had plunged in to navigate the treacherous reefs of passion without a compass.

Aware of having pushed her close to a raw edge, Joe lowered his lashes, careful not to glance too long at her breasts, though it was a wrench. His eyes drifted to her mouth. Was she wearing lipstick? Her lips had always been naturally rosy, plump and ripe as cherries, and sweet. Sweet and fresh, like none he'd tasted since.

His mouth watered with a sudden yearning and he realised he was being ridiculous. Of course she'd tasted sweet. She'd been *young*, as the captain was so quick to point out, as he, Joe, had been himself. It was highly unlikely she'd still have that effect on him. Though it would be interesting to find out.

'You *look* very well,' he said, smiling, his pulse quickening with the stir in his blood. 'Still live with your old man?'

Mirandi felt his glance sear her. 'Not for a long time.' Their eyes clashed, then disconnected as if some electrical collision had thrown out sparks.

'Ah,' he said. The chiselled lines of his mouth compressed. He gazed consideringly into his drink, his black lashes screening his eyes, then he said, 'Was it hard to make that break?'

'Everyone has to do it sooner or later. Grow up.'

A silence fell. The air in the room tautened while the wounds between them flared into life.

His eyes scanned her face. 'And have you? Grown up?'

She shrugged. She'd learned enough about love and its

consequences. 'What's there to say? I'm older now. I know better. How about you?'

'Older.'

His mouth edged up at the corners in that sexy way he had and she felt herself slide further towards some cliff's edge. How could someone so bad for her still be so appealing?

He pierced her with one of those glances. 'Do you have someone in your life?'

His tone was casual, as if he didn't care one way or the other. But there was a stillness in him, as if all at once the world turned on her reply.

She relaxed back in the sofa and crossed her legs. 'Is this something bosses need to know about their employees, Joe?'

He smiled at the small challenge. 'Bosses are only human. Isn't it natural to be curious about old lovers?'

She felt an internal flinch at the word, but he'd used it deliberately. *Lovers*. Surely they were people who loved you and wanted to keep you? Especially when you were scared to death?

He continued to taunt her with silken ruthlessness. 'I'd have thought you'd be married by now to some solid citizen in the suburbs. Some pious, clean-living guy who plays the church organ. Mows the grass on Sunday. Takes the kids to the park.'

She felt a sudden upsurge of anger, but controlled it. 'Is that where you're headed, Joe?'

'Me? You've got to be kidding. You know me better than that.'

'Yes,' she said shortly. 'I remember well.' She conquered the emotions unfurling in her chest. After all, it had been ten years. 'Anyway, would that life be so wrong?'

His eyes were mocking, sensual. 'It might be. For you.'

'Oh.' She expelled an exasperated breath, but no doubt his assumption was her own fault. It had been her fatal mistake.

She'd worked so hard to convince him she was super-cool and fearless and ready to fly, when all along she'd been this weak, clinging little girl who'd slipped on the most elementary of rules for conducting an affair with a bad boy. Not any more, though. 'What makes you an authority on what's right for me, Joe?'

He said, deliberately tweaking her tender spots, 'Knowing you in your formative years. Don't tell me you've forgotten your walk on the wild side.'

If only she could. A complex mixture of emotions rose in her, regret and anger uppermost, but she crushed them down and gave a careless shrug, though it pained her to dismiss the enchanted time and its bitter aftermath.

He smiled his devil's smile. 'Remember the time you borrowed your old man's car? How many girls can claim they swam naked at Coogee at midnight, then drove home in their dad's car?' He added softly, 'Still naked?' He broke into a laugh. 'That was some ride. If Captain Summers could have seen his little girl that night.' His voice softened. 'You were—ablaze.'

Straight away her mind flew to the inevitable postscript to that wild, exhilarating ride. His flat. His hard, bronzed beauty in the flickering candlelight, in startling contrast to her own pale nudity. The excitement of being held in those muscled arms. Her passion for him, the intense heat of their coupling...

She met his eyes and knew he was remembering it too. Despite herself she felt the stirrings of desire, tightening the air between them, the sudden sweet possibility of sex. What could be more likely, with the two of them in this otherwise empty apartment? Her breasts swelled with heat and suddenly she was awash with the old bittersweet sensations. The yearning, the helplessness.

How easy it was for a man. No consequences, no griefs to bury.

But she'd already made those mistakes. She said steadily, 'Look, much as I'd love to stay and reminisce, I have to go. I have a job, remember?' She made a move to get up but he put out one lean hand.

'No, don't go. Please. Patterson won't be worried. You can tell him I waylaid you for my own wicked purposes.' He smiled, a sexy smile that crept into her and coiled itself cosily around her insides, as if he shared some secret with her. Some private, *intimate* secret.

The trouble was, he did.

She examined her fingernails. Oh, heavens. Here she went, sliding down the serpent again in the old snake-and-ladders game of life. Was she imagining it, or was the mood seductive? Who else had ever been able to look at her with quite that degree of sexy assurance, as if they knew it was only a matter of time before she fell into his hands like a ripe plum?

She supposed her small test of his pillow had fuelled the flames. Why on earth had she succumbed to such an idiotic impulse? Whatever he was about to suggest, dinner and conversation or an afternoon of dalliance, a glimpse back at all the old pain and humiliation was enough to resolve her.

With a big firm *no* crystallising on her tongue, she looked up again and shouldn't have. He was examining her, one corner of his mouth edged up in a half smile, his stunning eyes gleaming with an amused comprehension that rushed through her like a fizzy drink, stirring her to her entrails.

Was this the time to lose her nerve and turn respectable? No other man had ever been able to look at her like that, as if he knew all the secrets of her sinful heart. Heaven forgive her, but just this once, whatever decadent scenario he suggested, shouldn't she at least listen?

But he surprised her. 'To be honest, I'm glad we have this chance to talk. I guess there are things we both need to acknowledge before we can move on.'

She moistened her lips. Was this how he operated now? He

bamboozled women into his bed? 'Move on? Move on where? I'm not sure I follow…'

His brows edged together. 'Well…' He shook his head, then started again. 'We've come up against each other again, and…' He gestured with his hands. 'It's an opportunity to set the record straight. I know I for one can look back at that time on things I'm not comfortable with. Wouldn't you prefer to operate from a basis of truth?'

If she hadn't been seated she'd have been rocked off her stilettos. What was he doing? Inviting her to be honest? Demanding that all pretences be dropped?

What planet was he on?

The phone rang again. Joe made no move to answer it, instead continuing to search her face with his compelling gaze. He started to speak again, earnestly, sincerely. 'Meeting you again has made me…reevaluate. Some of the things that were said back then… The *way* things happened, have had a—an afterlife.'

He met her eyes with such honesty she felt a deep surge of response. Her heart quickened, suddenly brimming with long-buried emotions. Hope, tenderness, the faint stirring of that all too weakening love. Despite all her protective barriers every cell of her being started urging her to listen to what he was saying.

Maybe there truly was a time when lovers could speak to each other without artifice. Open their hearts. Maybe she should have told him the simple truth that last time they met. Given him his chance to be a hero. Maybe if he understood what had driven her to lower her guard, humiliate herself like that, *beg*…

The phone clicked to answering machine and an urgent female voice flooded the room. 'Joe, I know you're there. *Don't* hang up, please.' Despite an attempt at lightness the voice croaked slightly on the don't. 'We really need to talk.'

He sprang up and grabbed the phone.

'Sorry, Kirsty,' he said in a low voice, 'I'm occupied right now. I'll call you back.' He was about to hang up but something his caller said arrested him and he listened. Even from where she was sitting, Mirandi could hear the agitated female voice, beseeching.

If only the woman had been able to see him she wouldn't have persisted. He was frowning, shaking his head, every line of his body from his chiselled, sensuous mouth to his long, lean limbs set in a steely, definite *no*.

'No. I didn't promise that,' he said coolly. 'I've never said anything *like* that.'

Mirandi's heart started to thump out an unpleasant drum roll. Wasn't this the old familiar scene? How well she knew the female part, having played it herself. The more emotional and extravagant the distressed woman, the cooler, more controlled and inaccessible the man. All that female emotion. So inconvenient.

That impulsive moment when she'd actually flirted with the possibility of opening up her heart to Joe Sinclair died. Thank heavens she hadn't. Embarrassed about intruding any further into his private life, she stood up and started to edge towards the door. But catching sight of her, he held up his hand.

'No, stay there.' His gaze locked with hers and he said quietly, 'Please.' Then he walked away into another room to deal with his call.

She stood there on tenterhooks. Should she stay, or should she go and end this intriguing and unlikely conversation, in which it sounded as if Joe was actually prepared to open up and give his take on their past relationship? Though she could see how risky it would be, with the potential emotional fallout. Still, the temptation to stay and hear what he had to say was tantalising, to say the least.

She truly wasn't straining her ears, but every so often she couldn't help overhearing snatches of his conversation from the study.

'I'm not…why I have to explain…' His voice had taken on an ominous crispness. '*Business*, pure and… As it happens my assistant isn't— Oh? Why's that?' He gave a harsh laugh. 'Certainly I do… Well, I wouldn't expect her to sleep on the street.' After an extended silence, she heard his voice again. 'That's not how I want to play it, Kirsty.' Another silence, then, 'Well, if that's… I think you're probably right… Yep… Yeah…for the best.'

There was something very final in those last few phrases. Mirandi might be an absolute fool at understanding men, but she could tell when one was cutting a woman loose. And she could remember how it felt.

Looked as if poor Kirsty had crossed the line, just as she had ten years ago. Was Kirsty in the same situation? Begging him to know how he felt. *If* he felt.

She felt a wave of disillusionment. For a minute there he'd almost had her convinced. The more things changed…

Inside his study Joe dropped the phone with an angry grimace. The sheer enormity of the woman, attempting to dictate terms to him now about the trip. He wondered, not for the first time, if her father had put her up to it. The fact that the old man had a seat on the MPI board… Could the old manipulator have enlisted his daughter as a means of keeping a check on Joe's meetings in Monaco?

Fuming, he was about to call the devious old devil when the phone rang again. He snatched it up, ready to deliver a few sharp words, but this time it wasn't Kirsty.

'Oh, Joe.' Tonia's voice purred down the phone, and he relaxed and allowed the anger to drain out of him. 'About Stella's replacement—what about that new girl, Mirandi? Her office still hasn't been decided and Ryan's EA comes back next week, anyway.'

'No, no, Tonia. Not possible.' Hell, that *would* open a can of worms.

Although… Would it necessarily?

'Ah-h-h… Leave it with me,' he said quickly. 'I'll think about it and get back to you.'

He replaced the phone very gently in its cradle. No, no, no. He couldn't do it. Out of the question. Though…well, certainly it would provide a neat system solution. He could see the appeal from Tonia's point of view. Business in the office would tick over as usual without anyone being disturbed.

But it was far too dangerous. Fraught with risk. Dynamite in what it could unleash. Possibilities flashed through his mind, some of them quite scintillating, but he thrust those away. No rational man would ever open that door again.

Still…

He felt his pulse quicken.

Why not? Those old issues from the past were over and done with now. He could contain the situation, keep it on an even keel. He'd always been able to control it. Come to think of it…maybe this was the very thing needed to defuse the past and its grip on his imagination.

He flexed his shoulders, then strolled out to the sitting room in time to catch her in the act of sneaking to the door.

'Hey. Now, don't run away,' he said. 'There's something I need to ask you. Oh, and—sorry about that interruption.'

Mirandi surrendered her escape bid and turned to examine him with curiosity. Was she imagining it, or was there an added bounce to his step? His eyes were alight with positivity. She felt a bitter pang. Was this what finishing with a woman did for him? Smiling, brisk Joseph Sinclair, CEO? In charge, his lean, tanned hands clean, with no clinging traces of the woman he'd just dusted off?

He hesitated a second, searching her face.

'Do you have a current passport?' When she nodded his eyes lit with satisfaction.

'Great. I'm needing an assistant for my trip to France and it might as well be you.'

'*Me?*' Stunned, she took a second to collect herself. 'Are you kidding? I mean… Isn't Stella going?'

'She can't come. Her son's been in an accident and she needs to be with him.' He brushed all that aside in a gesture. 'So? I need an assistant. Can you be ready by noon tomorrow?'

She searched his face for signs of derangement. Could he be serious? Had he forgotten who she was?

But no, he was back to behaving like the office Joe, crisp and businesslike, focused and professional. Trouble was, with her emotional deeps still in disturbance, her sexual sensors in a spin from the Joe she'd been with a few minutes earlier, the whole world felt as if it were spinning too fast. What about the cool head she'd sworn to hang onto from now on?

'Well,' she dithered. 'But…but what about Ryan?'

'Ryan? Oh, forget *Ryan*.' He gave the name an inflection, as if there were something wrong with Ryan. 'Leave him to me. I'll fix Ryan. So?' He advanced on her, smiling, his masculine assurance so attractive, persuasive. She caught the scent of him, that faint appealing tang of soap and sandalwood. 'It'll only be a few days on the Riviera.'

While her senses responded to Joe-Sinclair-induced sensations, her giddy head whirled with visions of charming seaside resorts, villages and little bays with fishing boats tied up in their marinas. For an instant visions swayed in her mind of the two of them together, swimming in the Mediterranean, lazing side by side on golden sands.

'Oh, gosh,' she said weakly. 'The Riviera does sound—*lovely*.'

'You think?' To her surprise he gave a small grimace. 'Yeah. Well, I admit the possibilities are improving.' His voice deepened the tiniest fraction, and his glance flickered over her with a sudden mesmeric gleam that made her catch her breath. There'd be the hotel, of course. Her mind shied away from that risky image.

He strode into his study and came back with a thin sheaf of papers and a laptop, murmuring something about flights.

Visions shimmered in her mind. Surely he wouldn't be suggesting she go unless he was planning it as some sort of interlude. Though warning bells clanged from some distant horizon, part of her was warming to the notion of a French fling with her old lover. How thoroughly sophisticated. How *delicious*. And why not? She was an adult, wasn't she? She could handle it.

Temptation trickled along her veins like silky honey. She could see the movie version now. *Rapprochement on the Côte D'Azur*. Nothing so sexy had come her way in years, though of course there were dangers involved.

As she eyed his handsome, assured face frowning into his screen she reminded herself of how weak she'd been with him in the past. Putty in his hands. Her eye fell on the smooth, bronzed, clever hands that had broken her heart.

Could she really betray her younger self like that? All the pain she'd suffered, her sad little loss? The trouble was, gorgeous though he might be, the beloved object of her passionate young heart, Kirsty's call rang fresh in her ears. And what about those other women, the chicks who'd come after her?

Regrettably, reality fastened its grip on her and shook her wandering brain cells back into place. 'I don't think so, Joe.'

He glanced up from his screen. 'What?'

She placed her hand on the door handle, smiling, though she sensed a sudden strain. 'Thank you, but no. Why not ask Kirsty?'

He blinked and sat very still. Then he said, 'Kirsty isn't in my employ.' There was a dangerous quietness in his deep voice.

It occurred to her that this was probably the first time she'd not fallen in with anything he suggested. Ten years ago she'd been the junior partner. So madly, joyously in love. So eager to please.

He got up and strolled towards her, his hands shoved in his pockets. 'What makes you think you have a choice?' He spoke casually enough, but there was an autocratic note in the words that disconcerted her.

'Well... You must see it's not a good idea.'

'In what way isn't it?' His blue eyes narrowed, making an infinitesimal flick to her mouth even in his displeasure. Though cool, relaxed, there was alertness in his stance. 'This is a perfect solution to a glitch in the system. Do you have some commitment that prevents you from travelling?'

She shrugged. 'Not really.'

'Then what's the trouble? Is there something you're afraid of?'

Her heart thumped into its adrenaline rhythm. 'You could say so.' As he tilted his handsome head interrogatively she said, 'We're finished, Joe. Remember? That book is closed.' Adding softly, 'The song has ended, lover.'

For seconds he looked thunderstruck. Then he gave a small, incredulous laugh. 'You're leaping to conclusions, Mirandi. You've misunderstood what I...' A flush darkened his lean cheeks. 'That brief *song* was a lifetime ago, darling. You need to get over it.'

Her anger surged. 'As I recall it lasted a whole year. I wouldn't have called it brief. And I am over it. Well and truly, Joe, though I wonder if you can say the same.' Her treacherous voice wobbled.

He looked amused, though his eyes blazed bright in a way she recognised as signalling he was angry. It was such a rare look with him, the few times she'd seen it she'd been shaken, since there had to have been some major cause to disturb his usual lazy good humour.

But he controlled it, challenging her assertion with an infu- riating crispness. 'On what grounds do you say that? Because I asked you on this trip? The trip is about business, pure and simple. It's an assistant I'm in need of here, not a—a—sleeping partner.'

'All right. If you say so.' She lifted her shoulders. 'I'm sorry. Though I'm not an assistant, am I?' she couldn't resist pointing out. 'I'm a market analyst, though people could be forgiven for not knowing that. Even poor Ryan seems to think I'm there as his assistant.'

Blue sparks flared in his eyes. 'You were never there as his *assistant*, but I'm glad you brought up the subject of Patterson.' His accusatory gaze lasered through her skull. 'Before you fling yourself into his bed you should know the firm doesn't encourage liaisons between personnel.'

She laughed in his face. '*What?* Oh, that's… That's just ridiculous.' Then she stared at him in shocked disbelief as the import of his words sank in. Had she heard aright? 'I don't know what you're even talking about. As if I *would*…'

He rode roughshod over her denial, striding about with an imperious air and flinging his hands about to defend himself.

'My choosing *you* is purely a business decision. As CEO I seek ways of wringing the best from my staff. You seem so— *volatile* whenever we meet…'

'*I* seem volatile?'

He ignored her interruption. 'Taking you on this trip seems like a way to develop a—a working relationship with you. Investment banking can be a soulless world. People feel out of place in it. I was hoping to establish some trust with you, to help you feel—'

She made a smouldering grimace. 'Oh, trust. Have you ever known what that was?'

He spun around to impale her with a glare. She felt the blue flash sear straight through her and knew she'd struck home. Truth to tell, she was feeling a little volatile right then, what with Kirsty and the shot about Ryan and all. Her heart was pounding like a mad thing, and she was trembling, no longer in total control of her tongue.

'On what grounds should I trust you, Joe? I was hired as a market analyst, and I've been sidelined into fetching and carrying for Ryan Patterson for the last month. I'm sure that was a perfect system solution for you, but it's not what I was promised. It's an outrageous breach of—the *law*.'

An angry flush darkened his harsh cheekbones. 'It's perfectly within the law, Mirandi. The—the arrangement was purely for your own benefit. While you work for me you fulfil any role I assign to you.'

A red-hot wave sizzled her face then rushed straight up through the top of her scalp. 'Oh, no, I don't,' she snapped. 'Because, as of this moment, I *quit*.'

He stilled and stared at her, his narrowed eyes glittering. 'You can't be serious. For what good reason?'

'For the good reason that I don't want to work for a man who doesn't keep his word.' Her voice shook with emotion. 'You haven't changed, have you? I don't know why you're so bothered about me refusing to go with you. I bet you've got stacks of reserves you could draw on.'

He froze and his eyes iced over, as chill as an arctic wasteland. After a nerve-racking second he said in a dangerous voice, 'Are you sure it's me you don't trust, sweetheart, or yourself? How long is it since I found you lolling on my bed? A whole thirty minutes?'

She couldn't trust herself to reply coolly, that much was certain. But she did manage to retort in a gravelly voice, 'I'm not your sweetheart, Joe. And that's the point.' Then she walked out and flung the door shut.

CHAPTER FOUR

JOE was running along the familiar pavement, past the garden house with the roses, around the corner house with the stone lions, and into the leafy street winding up to his place, his cricket bag knocking against his hip with every stride.

Someone would be there waiting for him. Home again at last to fill the house with flowers, laughter and her own sweet fragrance. Dinner in the oven. He felt a sudden cold fear that he wouldn't be in time. If he didn't hurry faster she wouldn't be able to wait and she'd be gone. He tried to run faster, but the way was uphill, his bag heavy and his legs wouldn't work properly.

He tried and tried to make them work, until his breath was coming in painful gasps, his lungs ready to burst, his cricket bag a leaden weight on the steep slope. With all his might he fought to gain traction on the cement path, but it was futile, the ascent changing to slippery glass and almost vertical, then just when he thought he must slide backwards he saw the yellow taxi.

It came down the hill fast, the passenger in the rear. It slowed as it approached him, and this time he could see the passenger's face. With a sickening shock he saw it was his mother. He waved at her, then as it drew level he ran shouting into the street, frantic to attract her attention, but though she looked right at him she mustn't have recognised him, because she turned her face away.

He woke with a start and lay there in the dark, bathed in sweat, waiting for the pounding brick in his chest to slow its wild *ker-thunk*. After a while he reached for the light, and the familiar solidity of his room swam into reassuring focus.

He rubbed his eyes. For God's sake, he hadn't dreamed of the yellow taxi in years. After a few minutes of slow, calm breathing he got up and thudded to the kitchen, filled a glass with water, and drank long and deep.

Something had stirred up the old nightmares, and it hardly took Sigmund Freud to work out what it was. *Who.*

In some bizarre way, Mirandi seemed to have become tangled up with his subconscious dramas. The afternoon's scene swam back to him with its astounding conclusion. Probably because of his tension about the trip, he'd felt quite churned up for a minute or two there. Completely out of character for him these days.

Mirandi was like a clover bindi underfoot. Soft, lush and enticing on the surface, with an ability to prick a man where it stung, work her way under his skin and give him everlasting grief.

Something about her had always made him feel twitchy and energised, even after a fight, though this one had ended entirely the wrong way and left him hanging off a cliff.

He set down his glass and sank onto the bed. Why did she have to be so prickly? She'd never been like that before; he remembered her as always being so soft and giving. Hell, today she'd been downright forceful.

For God's sake, the past was gone with all its wounds and it was time to move on. There was hardly a thing a man could say to her that didn't arouse some sort of touchy rejoinder. It wasn't as if he'd been unpleasant to her. Most of his employees would have jumped at the chance to accompany him to Monaco.

He felt a burning sense of injustice. A boss had every right to expect compliance from his employees. He'd only wanted to be generous with her. Why had she taken such a suspicious view of his perfectly appropriate proposition? How dared she challenge his authority. Dammit, who was running the show, he or Mirandi Summers?

He sprang to his feet again and paced the room.

It was clear she was still hooked on the dynamics of the old relationship. He should have made her understand somehow that now he was her boss the old formula could no longer work.

But for a few minutes there today... Guilt crept through him and he was swept with remorse. Now she was out of a job. Wasn't he responsible in some part at least for failing to help her make the transition? He really should have taken more care with her. Talked with her more, shown her how things stood between them now. The Patterson strategy hadn't helped either. She seemed to feel so confident she could hold her own, perhaps he should have just thrown her into the deep-end and let her sink or swim.

The image rose before him of her shapely form lying indolently on that very bed like some dreamy Lorelei. He'd rarely been so ravished. That intriguing glimpse of her private self had delivered the sweetest shock he'd known in years. He couldn't remember feeling so affected. Not since...the old days.

Had her breasts always been so full? Memories of an afternoon in Lavender Bay with her lissom body astride him, her naked breasts, their sweet taut raspberries in tantalising proximity to his mouth, made a sudden alluring appearance in his mind and he felt his blood quicken with sweet, heavy heat.

Strangely, today things had spun out of control. How much had been his fault? All he'd wanted was a little conversation, some civilised attempt at smoothing the way between them for the sake of future intercourse.

He closed his eyes. *Oh, Joe, Joe.* Where had that sprung from? Of all the Freudian slips.

Call it regret or natural concern, but he couldn't bring himself to believe he'd allowed her to walk out so abruptly. Was he to just let her go and make no effort to fix things? Surely masculine honour demanded that when he strolled onto that plane tomorrow, Mirandi Summers should be right there beside him.

Filled with sudden purpose, he strode into his study and picked up his diary to riffle through to the page of last month's board meeting. Here it was, the place where he'd absent-mindedly doodled her address.

3/ 357 Lilac Crescent, Lavender Bay.

At sight of the address a dark claw pinched his gut. The pretty little corner of Sydney he'd sworn never to set foot in again in his life. Nightmare territory.

Mirandi tossed on her bed, trying to find a comfortable position. Had her pillow always been so flat and hard? She tried to punch it into some sort of supportive mound.

Her angry tears had left a damp patch right in the spot where she wanted to rest her cheek. She hadn't felt so awful in years. Her chest hurt as if she'd swallowed something nasty that had failed to sink beyond a certain point. And the worst part was, she knew she deserved it. She'd sunk her own boat.

What sort of fool was she to have taken the job at MPI, anyway? Joe didn't want her there. He'd never wanted to see her again in his life. He'd made that plain ten years ago.

As for letting herself be caught on his *bed*…

She couldn't restrain a moan. How could she have? Was she *insane*?

Hot waves of anguish swept through her every time she thought of the moment he'd appeared in his bedroom doorway, and she couldn't hold back the tears of mortification. To be found like that after he'd *rejected* her. Even a village idiot would have had more control. More self-respect.

No one would be so stupid as to let themselves be caught in that situation after that devastating rejection. No one.

As for walking like a goddess... It was all very well to stride out of his apartment triumphant, crowing to herself over having shown him, but she'd done herself out of a job, after boasting to all her friends about having won it. Her father and Mim had been so proud. Her first proper opportunity to be a straight market analyst. Now what would she tell them?

Why had she let her emotions take over? It was just as Joe had said. She was too emotional for an MA job, any kind of job. She should be locked up somewhere remote with water access only. She'd allowed herself to get all stirred up over that Kirsty as if Joe had still been hers, when...face it. She didn't know a thing about what had gone on between them.

The truth was, admit it, she just couldn't stand to hear of him being in a relationship with *anyone*. No wonder he'd made that humiliating crack at the end. He probably thought—no, he definitely thought—the old fires were still there underneath, blazing away.

She'd exposed so much of herself she could die.

Visions of how sexy he'd looked at the end, all stern and hard and angry while he taunted her about lolling on his bed, came back to haunt her, and against all her pride and principles she couldn't suppress a sick pang of yearning.

For heaven's sake, her evil genius whispered, she could have been on a plane to France with him tomorrow if only it hadn't been for her stupid pride and her wicked temper.

After a long miserable while she realised that she'd have to start job-hunting the next day, and if she didn't act fast she'd have red swollen eyes.

She got up and tiptoed out to the kitchen in an effort not to wake her flatmates, opened the fridge and dug around in the vegetable crisper for a cucumber. Failing to find one, she settled for a courgette. Surely they had antioxidants?

She cut a few slices without much hope, then lay back on her bed and spread them over her face and eyes. Redheads were blotchy enough to start with, and it would take more than a courgette to fix her issues. She couldn't imagine what Joe had ever seen in her in the first place.

Joe's dashboard digital showed 1:58 a.m. He sighed. With a twenty-six-hour flight ahead of him, wouldn't it have been sensible to sleep? Though what was sleep? He hadn't had eight straight hours for weeks, ever since the casino project... *No.* Since Mirandi Summers had sashayed back into his life.

He turned into Lilac Crescent and slowed in an attempt to make out the house numbers. Moonlight washed the sleeping avenue in shadows, making it ideal territory for ghosts, though thankfully no ravaged, broken face of Jake Sinclair lurched out of the dark to greet him. The contours of the street had changed a little, but it was still all nerve-rackingly familiar. He felt suddenly aware of his blood pressure.

In chinks between apartment buildings he could see the city scrapers, the lights from an occasional vessel on the harbour. He supposed it was a desirable address for the innocent. Why did Mirandi still have to cling here, though? Was her father still appointed to the church here?

Indigo Street and the Sinclair house was just over the hill and around the corner, but Joe wasn't tempted. He shut it out of his mind.

The illuminated number on a high brick fence caught his eye. So this was where she'd made her home.

He drew up at the kerb. The enormity of what he was about to do, waking her and probably her flatmates in the dead of night, struck him, and he hesitated, but only for an instant. His father had always said it did no good when negotiating with a woman to start on the back foot. Not that poor Jake had wrung much benefit from his own advice.

The low buzz of the security intercom startled Mirandi from the doze she'd finally drifted into. One of the other tenants, she thought hazily, forgotten their key and mistaking the number. She settled back for sleep.

The buzzer sounded again, this time in a series of imperious staccato bursts.

Oh, for goodness' sake. Did they want to wake the whole street? Groggily, she dragged herself up and staggered out to where the intercom was fixed in the kitchen.

'Who is it?' she snarled when she'd located the button in the dark. 'Are you trying to wake the dead?'

'It's Joe.'

Shock followed fast by adrenaline sent her heart ricocheting around her chest cavity. 'Joe.'

'Yeah. Look, I, er— Sorry, I know it's late but I need to talk to you.'

Her brain made a wobbly spin. *'Now?'*

'That's right. Can I come up?'

She shut her eyes and made an attempt to think. What possible reason could he have unless it was to talk her out of quitting? An energising hope sprang up in her heart. Maybe... maybe she was still in with a chance?

'Mirandi?'

'Oh, well...' She remembered her bare blotchy face. No one should ever see her like this, let alone Joe, and in this extreme situation. 'No,' she breathed. 'Give me a minute and I'll come down.'

It might have taken more than a minute to smooth on a thin layer of make-up, perhaps two, three or even five minutes to achieve the natural look she aspired to, though she hurried as fast as she could for fear of him changing his mind and driving away. Finally she wrapped herself in her robe and flew downstairs to the entrance.

She paused to steady herself, then took a deep breath and opened the heavy door a crack.

Joe was standing on the porch surveying the street, his brows drawn. He was in jeans and a black tee shirt that stretched over his powerful chest and shoulders. His bronzed arms looked so satisfyingly solid that despite everything she felt her heart pound. Even in extremis she wasn't immune to their seduction.

He turned sharply, and she noticed his dark beard devastatingly in evidence. Hot gleams made his eyes burn when he saw her in her robe and slippers. His thorough, all-encompassing survey made her feel intensely female and vulnerable.

Remembering the way his eyes darkened like that under certain stimuli, she drew the robe closer about her. 'This—this is a surprise.'

'Yeah. Well…' He frowned, though that gleam still shone in the darkened depths. 'I've been thinking about this afternoon. I thought—maybe you'd like to talk.'

Hope fluttered in her heart but she barely allowed herself to breathe. 'About what?'

'Your decision. Were you planning to quit before today?' His hot gaze held hers for a dizzying second, then drifted down to her throat and the opening of her robe.

She dropped her lashes and shrugged. 'Well, no. Probably not. I was… I had hopes that…somehow the job might eventually work out.' She drew her fingers through her hair and his sharp glance followed the gesture, fastening on her loose tumbled locks with wolfish intensity.

His voice deepened. 'I'm pleased to hear you say that.' He scrutinised her for a moment, then the shadow of a smile touched his sensuous mouth. 'I think…er…today maybe things got a bit overheated. Things were said that shouldn't have been.'

She gave a stiff nod of admission, and as she moved further into the light his gaze sharpened on her face and she wondered if her make-up was letting her down. She edged back, but a frown entered his dark blue eyes.

'Were you asleep?'

'Of course.'

'Alone?'

She gasped. 'Yes. *Alone*. Though why you should think you can ask—'

He gestured. 'Sorry. I'm sorry, honestly. I don't know why I said that.'

A hot retort rose to her tongue, but she managed to repress it. Despite her natural annoyance at such masculine impertinence, her brain cells perked up. Why would he ask such a question if he wasn't at all interested in her? Why would he even *be* here? Surely…surely this was how the old Joe Sinclair had always operated at the time when he was crazy about her.

He resumed his smooth CEO expression, but she could feel his scorching gaze on her mouth and breasts and sense the hot magnetic current emanating from him. It sparked her nerves and made her feel extremely conscious of her nakedness under her flimsy night things.

He continued, devouring her with his eyes. 'I probably asked because I was needing to ascertain how available you are for—this offer.'

She elevated her brows. 'What offer?'

He didn't smile, but there was a burning intensity in his gaze that seared straight through her robe, her nightie and into her rapidly churning bloodstream. 'I thought you might like your job back. Interested?'

Interested. Such a flood of relief coursed through her she wanted to burst into rapturous smiles, but she knew better than to appear too pathetically grateful. 'Are we talking about my *real* job, Joe, or the job as Ryan's assistant?'

He lowered his eyelids briefly. 'Look, you were never Ryan's *assistant*. But—all right…' He lifted his hands. 'I admit we should have moved faster in setting up your office. That situation will be rectified at once if you still want the job. Okay?'

She nodded, though a joyful pulse started pumping through her veins and she wanted to sing, dance, frolic in the moonlight, maybe even throw her arms around him.

Instead she controlled herself and said with hauteur, 'Since you ask, I dare say I could—reconsider. I haven't taken on anything else yet, so…'

'Good.' His lashes flickered down but not before she saw his gleam of satisfaction. Almost imperceptibly he moved closer to her. His chest wasn't too far from her breasts. She could feel the heat from his big lean body sear her, teasing her erotic zones into an electric arousal she had no right to be feeling.

Short of breath, she edged back out of range. Heavens, how could she be so affected? So he smelled good and looked hot. Just because they were alone out here in the dark did she have to be at the mercy of her senses?

He inclined his head towards her. 'Where's that rose fragrance coming from? Is it perfume?'

She felt herself flush all over, though in a pleasant way. 'Bath oil, if you must know.'

'Oh, the old bath oil. Right.' His sensuous mouth quivered and the depths of his eyes burned brighter. 'Good. Oh, and, er—there's a condition.'

Right. With a pang of misgiving, she folded her arms under her breasts and braced for it. 'I might have known.'

Without blinking he said, 'I need you to come with me on the trip to Provence.'

An irrepressible, weakening thrill shot through her, but though the temptation to cave in was overwhelming she couldn't let go of her pride altogether. She drew herself up to stand straight and tall. 'I thought I had made it clear—'

'You did. You made it clear. But this is the condition. Take it or leave it.' His tone didn't waver while his unequivocal gaze compelled hers with mesmerising power.

She had no doubt he'd drive the bargain to the limit and walk away if she refused. Questions reeled through her head. What about the dangers? The possibilities she hardly dared even contemplate?

'Why, Joe?' she hedged. 'Why me?'

'Isn't it obvious? I need a market analyst along.'

'Oh, *right*.' She gave a disbelieving laugh, though she was excited. So excited. 'That's not what you said this afternoon. So really. Tell me what this is about.'

He hesitated. His black lashes swept down, then he pierced her with one of those glances. 'Well... I guess...it's a long trip. I'm not exactly looking forward to it and...' He exhaled in a long sigh and spread his hands. 'Somehow it would feel *right* to have you—someone I know, I mean,' he added hastily, 'along.'

Frowning, she searched his face, the involuntary leap in her heartrate warring with some warning bells that were suddenly jangling an urgent message. A message she wasn't so keen to hear. 'I don't know...'

'Do you want your job back?' A silky seductiveness had entered his voice, and he lifted one brow, assured, persuasive.

She bit her lip, hesitating, then shrugged. 'You know I do.'

'Fine. It's yours.' He smiled and warmth of a different sort, the sort of intimate, friendly warmth she used to see in the old Joe, flooded his eyes and rayed like the sun into her arteries.

For a breathless moment she almost expected him to kiss her or touch her at the very least, but he did neither. Instead he reverted to his brisk boss demeanour.

'All right, you'd better get some sleep. Check-in's at noon.'
He drew his brows in admonition. 'And for once in your life
don't be late.' He waited for her obedient nod, then, lifting a
casual hand, turned for the porch steps.

She pulled herself together. 'Wait. Wait, Joe.'

He paused and glanced back. 'Something worrying
you?'

'Yes, there is.' She braced. 'All right, I'll come, but I have
a condition of my own.'

His brows went up interrogatively.

She looked steadily at him. 'You don't try to use this as an
opportunity to seduce me.'

His brows flew higher still and a laugh sprang into his eyes,
then he put his hand over his heart. 'Mirandi. What sort of
guy do you think I am?'

'You forget,' she said without smiling. 'I know exactly what
sort of guy you are.'

Her words were soft on the night air, but they must have
reached their target for the lines of his face froze. Fleetingly,
but perceptibly, then a muscle moved in his lean cheek and
he shrugged. 'You *think* you know. But, all right, I'll accept
your condition. So long as you agree to it.'

She lifted her brows. '*I* agree?'

'Of course.' Amusement tinged his lean face and his gaze
sparked with challenge. '*You* must agree not to try to seduce
me.'

'Oh,' she scoffed, rolling her eyes. 'As if there was ever
any likelihood of that.' She gave a tinkling little laugh, then
his knowing glance met hers, loaded with everything that had
ever happened between them, every clinch, every wild act of
passion, and she felt her face go pink.

'So, then,' he said, backing away, the gleam in his eyes. 'I'll
let you know if there's any problems reserving your place on

the flight. Otherwise… Noon at the International check-in. Oh, and—bring your passport.'

She damped down her mad, joyful desire to whoop down the street. 'Certainly, Joe,' she said. 'Noon.'

CHAPTER FIVE

ONLY an idiot or someone very desperate would have agreed to fly across the world with a man who'd broken her heart. And on such short notice. For a thrilled second last night on the doorstep Mirandi had actually had the sensation she was about to climb back on the Ducati.

Looking back, she suspected she might have gone a little crazy since walking into Joe's apartment yesterday afternoon. Still, a woman needed a job, and at least she'd insisted on her condition, flimsy though it might have been.

The truth was, despite her excitement, when he'd turned and walked to his car last night she'd been in a turmoil. Certainly he'd seemed appreciative of her appearance, but he'd made no move towards her—and she was grateful for that, wasn't she? After everything, especially the volcanic emotions of their afternoon encounter, it was certainly best they avoid complications and stick to their working relationship.

Still, no live woman in proximity to Joe's lips after midnight could be blamed for hungering for them. After she'd bounded upstairs to bed, all churned up and excited by the transaction on the doorstep, she was ashamed to admit she couldn't stop thinking about how sexy he'd looked with the heavy shadow outlining his mouth.

It seemed she could control her will now when it came to Joe, but there was no controlling her body. Everything about him was too deeply embedded in her senses. At least she knew now she must fight the attraction. And she could. As long as he kept his distance she'd be fine, she firmly believed it. Certainly she'd had no power of resistance when she was a green girl. But she wasn't a green girl any more.

As soon as she spotted him in Departures at noon, several things hit her between the eyes at once. He looked like an intriguing mixture of the corporate Joe and the old Joe. With his long, lean frame clad in blue jeans, loafers, and a blue shirt that reflected his eyes and brought out the highlights in his raven hair, he could have slung her over his handlebars and roared away in a second. Just as well for one of her impulsive temperament that he was carrying a casual navy jacket slung over his shoulder and his briefcase. It added that soupçon of discreet elegance the younger Joe had never aspired to.

Another thing, he was leaning against a column, brooding and looking more than a little tired. Hardly surprising, considering his habit of making nocturnal visits, though when she first observed how grim he looked she experienced a pang. Was he regretting the invitation?

He glanced up, saw her and his expression lightened at once. Her heart made a joyous little skip. That first glimpse meant truth. No chance to pretend.

She herself hadn't managed any sleep at all, she'd been so excited, wired about what to pack and doubtful. Wary. *Amazed* Joe was so keen to have her along. And in the blackest night before dawn, filled with misgivings. Warning herself not to be too thrilled. What felt so right about taking her? What had he mean by it, really?

Just take it calmly, don't be a fool, act like an MA, don't fall in love, forget the past... Oh, for goodness' sake. Under no circumstances should she allow herself to forget the past.

As Joe scrutinised her in her own jeans and jacket with a thorough, veiled gaze she enquired, 'Have you fixed the flights? Did you talk to Ryan? Should I phone him myself?'

'Relax. Everything's under control. So far,' he muttered in a grim undertone.

She shot him a quick glance. 'It's not too late to change your mind, Joe. You don't have to go through with it.'

'Of course I have to. It's my job.'

'Taking me, I mean.'

'Oh, that.' He smiled and touched her cheek. 'Oh, but I do. You're the essential ingredient.'

'Yeah?' She tried to look nonchalant, but the truth was, though it might have been a strange thing to say, those words and that careless brush of her cheek sizzled into her capillaries and radiated glowing embers through her bloodstream. It was the first time he'd actually touched her since…all those years ago.

She'd had no idea her skin was so in need of a masculine touch. So deeply in need. 'As your Market Analyst.'

'What else?'

'I hope you haven't forgotten my office.'

He spread his hands. 'In progress as we speak.'

'Good.' She beamed and he acknowledged it with a wry smile. Then his brow corrugated, almost as if he was worried.

On the flight, she threw herself into her MA role with enthusiasm.

'What's the theme of the conference?' she enquired, nestled into her business class seat sipping lemonade through a straw.

Joe frowned ahead into space, seemingly reluctant to answer.

'Making money any way we can,' he growled at last. 'What else?'

'Sounds good. Talk me through the agenda.'

He was lounging back, his eyes nearly closed, but she could see their glint through the dark lashes. His deep voice had a smoky sensuality. 'Do you still have that sexy little vest you used to wear? What was it you called it? You know...' He painted a curvy outline with his hands.

She sent him a repressive glance. 'You may be referring to a bustier. Are you sure it was me who used to wear it, or one of your chicks?'

'It was you. I'm sure it was you. I remember because it was the same bluey green as your eyes.'

She rolled her eyes. 'I doubt if *they* had much to do with it.'

He gave a lazy, reminiscent laugh. 'Oh, I can assure you, baby, they had everything to do with it.'

As the hours flew by he grew increasingly flirty and difficult to pin down about work. She'd brought her laptop, and expected to spend at least part of the flight going through the agenda with him. He should at least brief her about the appointments he'd set up with other delegates. Every time she suggested it he changed the subject.

All right, so he didn't feel like concentrating. She wished he'd tell her more about what to expect, though. How was she to do the job operating in the dark, so to speak?

He'd always been the same, as she recalled. Loath to open up. He was such a private guy, the year they'd been lovers he'd hardly even told her a thing about his family, except a few rare, affectionate allusions he made to his father. Though Jake Sinclair had died a bitter, broken man according to Auntie Mim, who'd even hinted that he'd chosen to abandon his teenage son and die by his own hand, Joe had never seemed to harbour any resentment towards him.

At least, ten hours into the flight he was looking slightly less gloomy. Devastating, in truth, lounging back in his seat, his blue shirt rolled back a little at the cuffs to reveal his sinewy forearms. It was probably safer for her not to look at him, though when she looked elsewhere his image stayed etched on her retina like a solar flare.

His book lay open on his lap but he wasn't reading. She

leaned over and flipped it to the cover. *High Finance and Ethics*. Whew. The guy really liked to relax on a flight.

'Will there be anyone you know at the conference?'

'I sincerely hope not,' he growled.

She lifted her brows in surprise. 'No, really? No old banking friends from the past?'

He looked amused. 'Bankers don't make friends, they just make money.'

She laughed, wincing. 'That's such a bleak outlook. How lonely you make it sound.'

'Well, isn't it?' He smiled, watching her face with curiosity. 'You'll find it out soon enough if you stay in it.' He gave his head a small shake. 'A crusader like *you* in investment. I have to say I was surprised.'

She gazed wonderingly at him. 'It doesn't have to be the way you describe, though, does it? Good things can be done with money. It just takes enough good people to influence an organisation to make a real difference in the world.'

Joe saw the shining conviction in her eyes and felt a pang in his chest. Even now that passion was still bubbling through her like a constant spring. Her enthusiasm for righting the world's wrongs had struck such a resonant chord with him back then. How enchanted he'd been. He realised there'd been no one in his life since with quite that quality.

'I hope you find you can hold onto your ideals,' he said quietly.

She turned an unnervingly perceptive glance on him. 'Is it that hard, Joe?'

Only a constant clench in the gut. But he had to admit it was a relief to talk about it, even so lightly. And he was impressed at her quick understanding. He examined her, trying to reconcile the woman she'd become with the girl he'd known. Maybe this was what he'd been missing. A woman he could talk to.

He yawned and stretched his long frame, then leaned across

and patted her knee. 'Don't worry, I'm sure you'll still find a way to save the world.' He tightened his hand on her knee, savouring its sensual shape against his palm.

Mirandi waited a second, then coolly removed his hand and placed it firmly on his side of the barrier.

He laughed, while her knee felt deprived.

Still, she was pleased to hear him laugh. Since the airport there'd been a tiny, permanent crease between his brows, and now she zeroed in on the grim little lines around his mouth. She guessed it wasn't all champagne and roses being the CEO.

He noticed her gaze and gave his jaw a rub. 'What? My beard still fascinate you?'

She gave his advancing shadow a wry inspection. The black fuzz hadn't even made it to the stubble stage, though it had the tantalising effect of outlining his chiselled mouth and making his lips seem sexier than ever.

'You're overstating, as usual,' she said. 'It has a long way to go before it can rate as a beard. As for whether it *still* fascinates me, that implies it ever did.'

A sensual gleam warmed his eyes and his expressive mouth edged up a little at the corners. 'Admit it.' His deep voice was low and silky. 'It's the best you've ever rubbed up against.'

She lowered her lashes, sipped her lemon squash, took a moment to contemplate an elderly woman's progress down the aisle. Then she turned to meet his sleepy, teasing glance.

'The brashest, maybe. The cockiest. Certainly the most conceited.'

His deep laugh broke out and illuminated his face. 'You've become very sassy along the way, Miss Summers. Don't you know that can get you into trouble?'

His sensuous mouth held the smile for a few extra heart-beats and there was seduction in his eyes.

Mirandi felt her heart lurch with the old dangerous thrill. But it was only banter, wasn't it? A few harmless flirty words were only natural between a man and a woman confined together in a travel situation. It didn't signal anything, or promise that anything might happen between them later.

So, regardless of how sexy he looked, how desirable he was making her feel, she was still on the straight and her conscience was clear. Strangely though, Marilyn Monroe seemed to take over her voice and she became quite breathy, as if his grin had soaked into her bloodstream and taken up the oxygen.

She made an effort to keep her mind on the matters at hand. 'Don't you just love a conference?'

'No.'

'Why not? You get to travel, have a free holiday, meet people...'

He scowled. 'There are people in Sydney.'

'Well,' she said, exasperated, 'if it's such a bore why didn't you send someone else along?'

'Because I have to go myself.' He gestured with some impatience. 'I'm researching a project the board is keen to invest in.'

'What project?'

He hesitated, then with a careful lack of expression, said, 'Investing in the entertainment industry.'

'Really? How exciting. There's big dollars to be made there.'

He searched her face, a frown in his eyes, then gave a shrug. After a while he leaned across and tucked a lock of hair behind her ear.

First her knee, now her hair. And there had been the cheek, though maybe that didn't count. Her ear tingled, and she met his hot, slumberous gaze with the blandest one she could manage, considering her blood was quickening its flow, seething with the old anticipation. She knew what those touches signalled.

Temptation was lurking in the grass and she was faced with a dilemma. A crossroads was approaching.

While she mused on the fraught possibilities, she continued on with the easy chat. 'Why don't you look on the trip as a lovely break? The south of France, of all places. Who wouldn't want to go there?'

He must have suddenly felt tired because he tilted his chair back and closed his eyes. She could tell he was still listening though by the tense way his arms were folded across his belt.

'It must be one of the most charming locations in the world.'

'Charming.'

'But you don't care for it?' After a while he shrugged, and she said, 'How many times have you been there?'

He was silent for an age. She started to repeat her enquiry when he growled, 'Once.'

'For how long?'

He frowned and opened his eyes. 'A weekend. What is this? The inquisition?'

'Must have been a lousy weekend.'

His patience snapped. 'Aren't you tired?'

She settled back into her seat. 'I remember that about you now. You always get grumpy when you're in need of sleep.'

His eyes sparked. 'And I remember things about *you*. One of them is that you're too nosy by half.'

Smiling, she tilted her seat into horizontal position, arranged the pillow, pulled the blanket over her and closed her eyes. Some bell rang in her memory, some distant echo from an old conversation, but when she tried to pin it down it slipped away. But give it time. It would come back.

She let herself drift into a doze.

When the blessed silence had settled for a while, Joe opened his eyes. Sleep was too risky here in a public space. Last thing he wanted was to be bellowing out about yellow taxis in front of several hundred people. He pulled his chair upright and took the opportunity to examine Mirandi Summers' unguarded face.

Something about the honest freshness of it put that twinge back in his chest again. Hell, he'd been through a dozen women since—maybe even a couple of dozen if he was to be honest with himself—but no break-up had been as rugged as that one. Possibly because the fling hadn't run its full course when it hit the wall at top speed. He hadn't had time to get bored, and she'd stayed fresh in his memory. Unspoiled.

He smiled to himself. That effervescent optimism was so infectious.

If this had been his first trip to Provence, he might even have shared it. He felt that wall of distaste again, and crushed it down. Since he *had* to be there, he'd focus his mind squarely on his task, think about the firm's bottom line, and get out as soon as he decently could. This hangover from his recent rash of nightmares would soon dissipate.

It wasn't as if any unwelcome faces would be looming up out of the distant past to confront him. No one he had any remote connection with even knew he was coming, and that was how he wanted it.

It would all be cool. He'd stay well away from Antibes, keep to his end of the coast, and allow the ghosts to moulder undisturbed at theirs.

In the meantime he had the perfect antidote.

Business class meant passable meals and some quite drinkable wine, though his newest MA kept to softer drinks. Without him around to lead her astray, her father's early training had prevailed. No smoking, no drinking, no gambling. No sex with bad men?

'Red wine is good for the heart,' he urged her when the stewardess came by.

'It didn't help mine,' she said, smiling her refusal to the woman.

'What was that pledge you took when you were a little girl?'

She searched his face as if sensing a trap. Seeing her wariness gave him a slight pang of remorse. Perhaps he had been guilty of teasing her in the past for the things her old dad had taught her. Maybe he'd been a bit embarrassed, knowing how often the good honest captain had been the one to drag Jake Sinclair out of the club and bring him home to his hungry kid.

With some reluctance she admitted, 'To do the most good to the most people in the most need.'

He laughed, though the words cut him in a way he didn't care to acknowledge right then. 'I'm so glad you joined MPI.'

During the dark hours, when most people were asleep under their blankets, Joe kept himself awake by reading in the cone of light from overhead. He must have disturbed Mirandi, because she woke and squinted at him.

'Can't you sleep?'

'Shh.'

After a while she pressed the upright button on her seat. 'All right, I give up. I'm too excited now. My mind keeps spinning.'

He put his book aside and suggested they stroll up to the lounge cabin so they could talk without disturbing people. She stood up and stretched, and he caught a glimpse of her breasts outlined against the material of her shirt. It was a pleasure and a torment to walk behind her and watch the supple muscles work, the pull of her jeans, snug against her taut little arse.

Mirandi felt his eyes on her in a turmoil of feelings she didn't care to acknowledge. She could sense his desire and she was affected, there was no denying it. The attraction was still there. Just a few hours in his company and she was savouring every move he made, every nuance. She shouldn't encourage it. She really shouldn't.

But, oh, some yearning part of her cried, it had been so long since she'd been appreciated by a truly sexy man. Shouldn't she just accept the gifts that life offered and bask in this pleasant time out of time?

There were a couple of other non-sleepers enjoying the open space of the lounge cabin. She stood a while, wriggling her toes, inviting her blood to flow to her ankles, conscious of Joe an arm's length away, leaning idly back against the bar. Too conscious. Too aware of the invisible pull. Here, a mile high, time had no meaning, as if the usual rules should be suspended.

Joe moved closer to her to make room for a newcomer at the bar. What was it about green eyes that gave a woman that look of potential mischief? He remembered the sensation he always used to have with her. Whatever they talked about on the surface, he felt that other, mysterious female complications were whirring away in her head.

He leaned her way and caught a trace of her fragrance. 'Do you still sing in the choir?'

'Not for years.' Her passionate mouth curved. 'Do you still sing in the shower?'

'Never seem to now. Funny, that.' The reminder evoked some intimate occasions where she'd been a star participant. 'You were pretty good in the shower yourself. I seem to remember you striking some high notes.'

Her shadowy emerald eyes flickered, then she turned away with a brief laugh. A low, throaty, *sexy* laugh.

'Does your father know where you are?'

She hesitated just a beat, then gave a perfectly serene shrug. 'There wasn't time to tell him, but if I had he wouldn't have been concerned.'

That little hesitation made him wonder how much the old man knew. Had she even told her father she was working for *him* now?

He searched her face. 'Wouldn't he? Even if he knew you were with that wicked Joe Sinclair?'

'Course not. He knows I'm a big girl. Anyway, he's never thought you were wicked.'

'Not even after I stormed the citadel and snatched away his princess?'

Her lips were enticing, curved in a smile. So plump and juicy and edible. 'It wasn't Dad who was so worried. It was poor Auntie Mim.'

Ah, so she still didn't know. Probably just as well, though some insane reckless impulse tempted him to push the boundaries of the subject. Maybe he should tell her, let her know her father's part in their little drama.

'Poor Auntie Mim,' he echoed, remembering the anxious little lady who could be so surprisingly fierce. 'What was she so worried about?'

Something disturbed the tranquil irises. Too late he felt the warning pang slice through him. His heart-rate bumped up a notch.

But her smile didn't waver. 'She was afraid you'd break my heart.'

For a second he wondered if the airbus engines had died and they were about to fall out of the sky. Then he realised it was his lungs that had stopped working.

Knowing she'd struck some momentous note, Mirandi parted her lips to say something to ease the thundering tension, but with a shock of primitive recognition saw his eyes darken.

He inclined his head and kissed her just as the plane gave a shudder, or it might have been herself being rocked to the foundations. His scorching lips touched hers with a blaze of delicious fire. Electricity sizzled through her like a lightning bolt and held her paralysed, while her blood lifted off in a wild erotic surge and swelled her breasts.

She was vaguely aware of a warning ping, a voice issuing

instructions over the tannoy, then the plane vibrated again and they rocked apart.

Hypnotised, she stared at him, her heart thundering in her ears, her breath coming in quick, erratic bursts. The hostess's voice sounded again, urging everyone to return to their seats and fasten their belts until they were through the bout of turbulence, but that brief searing touch of Joe's lips had aroused a flame.

The bar attendant stood by while people filed from the small cabin. Mirandi braced against the vibrations of the plane, under a spell, mesmerised by the fire in Joe's blue eyes, the tingling ache in her parched lips. The attendant watched them all leave, then headed for his own seat. As she and Joe started down their aisle Joe's hand snaked out and grabbed her wrist, and he pulled her back and bundled her into the washroom.

She should have resisted, but her blood was aroused and her brain had gone into a retreat. When had she and Joe *not* snatched every illicit opportunity? Squeezed into the impossibly narrow space, her guilty senses thrilling with forbidden excitement, she felt his strong arms around her, his chest in friction with her breasts, and forgot her resolutions. Distantly she heard the steward's warning voice, but it came from another realm.

In panting accord, their hungry lips met in a cosmic sensual collision. As Joe took hungry possession of her mouth Mirandi was oblivious to the discomfort of hard edges sticking into her, and concentrated on the familiar angles and planes of her hard, lean lover. Electricity was shooting through her flesh from every point of contact, knees, thighs, his angular pelvis, his strong chest pressing her breasts.

He tasted so good, his stern, sensuous mouth demanding her surrender with the same old sexy ruthlessness. Flickers of fire danced along her lips, fanning her hunger to a flame, and her nipples roused to hot aching peaks.

He deepened the kiss and his tongue slid inside her mouth.

Oh, it had been so long. Like a homecoming, the raw animal flavours of the man she'd loved so passionately invaded her senses with a heady rush and made her drunk. Her primal female instincts opened to sheer pleasure, craving to possess every fibre of him.

Hypnotised, in thrall to the irresistible sexual narcotic, she entwined herself around him, desire flaming in her blood like an incendiary. In enthusiastic response he dragged her even closer against his iron-hard frame. Oblivious of where she was, she let her hands rove his powerful shoulders and chest, rediscovering his lean, muscular solidity.

Every part of him felt so satisfying to her touch.

Hungrily she caressed the silky hair in his nape, enjoying the sensation on her fingertips. It was a sensual explosion. Drenched in desire, her breath mingling with his, her yearning nipples and the tender tissues between her thighs burned for his caress.

As if in instinctive understanding he slipped a hand under her shirt and pushed up her bra for an exploration of her breasts. His big warm hand felt so pleasant on her soft skin, so *right*, while his gentle tease of her nipples added fuel to the flames.

His erection prodded her, heightening her arousal. Her craving for his clever hands to roam in a southerly direction raged in her blood like wildfire.

They slid to her bottom, stroking her with a delicious touch. Urgent for contact where it counted, she made an attempt in the cramped space to hook her leg around his calf.

Obligingly, he pulled her pelvis hard against him and rotated his hips in a primitive rhythm she found wildly stimulating. While his hand squeezed one grateful breast, and his tongue tickled the delicate tissues inside her mouth, she felt his hard penis tantalise the yearning delta between her legs.

The friction was erotic, it held the promise of ecstasy, but with so many clothes in the way it wasn't nearly enough.

She reached for his belt buckle, but abruptly, and probably just in time, a sharp tattoo on the door roused her from her escalating sensual trance. Surfacing back to painful awareness of her uncomfortable surroundings, she broke from the kiss.

A glimpse of her face in the mirror acted on her hot fraught body like a douse of cold water. Panting, she pushed vigorously at Joe's chest and slapped at his roving hands.

'Stop this,' she hissed. 'Get out of here. Go on.'

He looked startled. 'Now?' he said hoarsely.

A glance into his dark inflamed eyes threatened to send her under again, but she insisted.

'Go on.' She squeezed away from the door to make space for it to open. With a last burning look at her, he edged past her and left.

She spent some time splashing her face and tidying up, alone and not regretting it, her thoughts on hold until she could bear to look herself in the face. When she emerged, the main cabin lights were back on, people were moving and shuffling around, and all the signals were there that a meal was about to be served.

Somehow she found her seat and settled back into it, fighting to compose herself and will away the sweet, insidious pleasure still mingling in her bloodstream with all the dissatisfied cravings the clinch had aroused.

Guilt washed through her, and a sobering streak of anxiety. How could she have been so weak, so thoughtless? When she had everything to lose, at the very first test of her resolve she'd fallen. She hadn't even made it through the flight without surrendering herself to him. She blenched to think of how quickly she'd succumbed.

All through the night she'd been castigating herself for not having properly ascertained what it was he expected from her on this trip. Was this it?

Shame and disappointment chilled her heart. How did he think of her? That she was his ever-ready pushover? That he could still seduce her, make her love him, then break her heart and walk away?

She tried to struggle out of her attack of conscience with a more positive view. If she'd engaged in a sexy interlude in the washroom with him ten years ago, she wouldn't have ejected him quite so soon. At least now she could congratulate herself for having drawn some sort of line.

It was hard to think clearly all churned up, but she needed to be brutally honest with herself. Had she really expected nothing to happen? Did she really *want* nothing to happen? She'd loved it when he came to her doorstep to negotiate because it had allowed her to cave in and still preserve her pride.

But while that strict little voice in her head was hauling her naked across the burning coals, there was no denying her old wild reckless part was still there, crazy to plunge straight in with him again. It was a dilemma, and it was wrong. *She* was wrong.

Although maybe it was right. Why else did it feel so right?

Oh, she was a weak, weak vessel, and she needed to put a definite distance between herself and Joe Sinclair.

She waited, tense as a wire, but he didn't return for some time. Probably gloating over his easy conquest, she glowered to herself. No doubt knocking back a triumphal Scotch.

When he did come, she had her headphones on and her book open before her. He slipped into his seat silently, with just a sidelong glance at her. She quickly lowered her eyes.

He took his own book from the seat pouch and started to read. It was like a taunt to her, how relaxed he seemed after breaking her condition. His employee, no less. He should have been ashamed.

After a long tense while, in which she hardly took in a

word of what she was reading, he put his book aside, reached across and lifted hers out of her hands.

'Talk to me.'

She lifted an earphone and gazed coldly at him, eyebrows raised. 'Sorry?'

'I don't think you should be regretting that kiss.'

A hot little pulse started up in her head. 'Don't you?' She narrowed her eyes. 'Perhaps what I'm regretting is that you seem to feel you still have the right to kiss me.'

His sleepy, sensual gaze drifted to her mouth. 'Well…it wasn't so much that I feel I have the *right*. Whoever knows he has the right? I think I feel as if I have—the connection.' He smiled, dropped her book in her lap and leaned back in his chair.

She found her page and stared at it for a while, churning. There was truth in what he claimed, of course, but could she just surrender like a weakling? But she must restrain herself from arguing with him. She knew of old that when he mocked her in that flirty way her resistance to his charm crumbled. In no time she found herself melting, smiling like a loon, and before she knew it flirting like some meowing siren. She should never allow herself to look into his eyes.

But by her honour as a woman, could she truly let him have the last word?

She stared into her book a while longer, then snapped it shut and reached across to snag his sleeve. 'You were wrong.'

'Sorry?'

'The connection is dead.'

His black brows shot up. 'Really? You mean you were faking it?' Despite his apparent cool, lounging there in his seat like a relaxed panther, his beard shadow very much in evidence, there was a sly smile in his eyes. It was infuriating. And so damnably attractive.

'You took me by surprise,' she accused, annoyed at herself for being so intensely aware of how sexy he looked. How kissable, how mouth-watering his lips were, outlined by the shadow. She could have climbed up on his lap there and then and…

The truth was, he was *driving* her to lie.

'I'm a civilised person. Naturally I didn't want to make a scene. I may have pretended to co-operate but I was only being polite.'

He smiled. '*Very* polite.'

Despite her guilty knowledge of her own disgraceful compliance, her feminine spirit rose up on its hind legs, and with it the certainty she could trust herself to be a virtuous woman from now on.

'Mock if you like,' she said crushingly, 'but you can be sure neither that kiss nor anything like it will ever happen again. Let me remind you of my condition.'

He was silent a moment, studying her face, his expression grave apart from a curious little gleam in his eyes. Then he said, 'And let me remind you of *my* condition.'

She narrowed her eyes. 'You're not trying to claim *I* started that clinch, are you?'

'Well, you were extremely tempting.' His voice had a deep, sonorous, velvety texture that crept into her bones and made them weak. 'Too tempting to resist, all soft and curvy and luscious.'

She couldn't hold back a hearty laugh, though it came out sounding a little on the silvery side. Not that she wanted to give the impression she was flattered. She wasn't a bit.

'Oh, that's nonsense,' she scoffed. 'That's as ridiculous as if I said I kissed you because you were—' she cast about for some suitable words '—*hard and sexy.*'

He gave a deep, rumbling laugh. 'Yeah. At least one of those was so, so true.' He rubbed his handsome jaw, still laughing, an amused reminiscent gleam in his eye. 'Anyway, does it really matter who succumbed to who? Once that train has left the station it hardly matters who's doing the driving, sweetheart.'

Intoxicating vibrations were weakening her, seducing her, threatening to drag her in, but she said as firmly as she could, 'Be assured, mister, the train *hasn't* left the station.'

He nodded, though that lazy smile was still in his eyes. 'If you say so. Course it hasn't.'

He relapsed into silence after that, but it was an exciting, connected silence, as if invisible wires were attached to them and primitive messages were pinging back and forth, whispering thrilling promises.

As time wore on, though, and Zurich drew closer on the radar, the transmission signals changed. Joe grew serious and more remote, as if some inner dialogue was keeping him preoccupied.

Was it about her? Was he having second thoughts about bringing her?

CHAPTER SIX

DAWN brought them to Switzerland, with a day and a night to fill before their connecting flight to Nice. As the plane circled in the lea of the Alps Mirandi caught her breath at the beauty of mist-shrouded lakes and rivers and the lushest green valleys she'd ever dreamed.

Zurich spread along the shores of a vast lake and its connecting river, a fairy tale city dotted with spires and mediaeval clock towers, magical in the crisp early morning air.

After the long flight it was a relief to check into the Chateau du Lac and relax with a warm shower and a change of clothes. Stella had arranged for an especially early check-in, and Mirandi sent the excellent woman a telepathic thank-you across the world for her efficiency and taste for the good life.

Joe had a meeting with a banker in the Bahnhofstrasse, a boulevard in the heart of the city's commercial centre, and Mirandi took some trouble in her preparations, washing her hair and straightening it dry till it hung sleek and silky down her back. It was only right she should try to look her professional best, surely. The last thing any MA/Assistant should do was to disgrace her boss in a high-level business negotiation. She wasn't trying to make herself especially gorgeous or alluring. If efficiency and grooming happened to appeal to a man… Well, then, let it be. With her conscience perfectly clear, she donned her slimmest navy suit, purple silk cami and heels, walked through a soft air-spray of perfume, then took the lift down to the hotel restaurant.

She found Joe ensconced at a window table overlooking the Zurichsee. A newspaper was spread before him, but he didn't appear to be reading. Instead he was frowning into space.

He looked so grim and preoccupied her heart lurched with anxiety. Was he thinking about her? Regretting re-opening the door to desire?

'Hope you weren't waiting long,' she said, laying her notebook in its slim leather envelope on the table.

He started from his reverie and glanced up at her. His quick smile crinkled the corners of his eyes and she felt such a relief.

'Only two newspapers' worth,' he said. 'You must have rushed.'

He looked so handsome, all freshly shaven and shower clean in his fresh suit and crisp cotton shirt, she felt a deep visceral stir in her insides so sweet and intense as to be almost like pain. She noticed him glance at her laptop, then flick an appraising blue gaze over her.

Appreciation warmed his eyes and the glow inside her intensified. Only another frizzy redhead could truly appreciate her beauty exigencies, and she was reminded that Joe could be a remarkably patient man.

'No, *you* must have dawdled,' she retorted, her pulse quickening as his sensual gaze flickered down her legs to her ankles. 'And *two* newspapers is bunkum. Your hair's still damp.'

He laughed, folded his newspaper out of the way and signalled the waiter to bring coffee and hot chocolate.

But the truth was, every little teasing exchange only increased her turmoil. It was of no use to fall in love with him again. She'd been down that road and heartache was the only destination. So, while savouring croissants with him and watching the pleasure craft on the Zurichsee might have been romantic, she couldn't allow herself to acknowledge her pleasure in his company. The more tempted she felt to sur-render to her yearning instincts and plunge right in, the more her conscience and insecurities worked against her.

In twenty-four hours so many moments had revealed nu-ances of her old lover, still there underneath despite every-thing, yet she needed to remind herself that her old Joe had grown tired of her.

And she could sense a tension in him. Despite his easy-going banter, his gaze was pensive, those grim little creases around his mouth subtly deeper. He'd closed up about work, and had little to say about his plans for the day. Doubt about her professional abilities?

She frowned. She was looking forward to attending that meeting with him, learning more about MPI's operations at the highest level. After the debacle of her start with the firm, the opportunity was important to her. If she could demonstrate something of her skills and competence, Joe would see how far she'd grown beyond the raw teenager he'd once known and she could nip his reservations in the bud.

At the appointed time, she strolled along the leafy Bahnhofstrasse with him, taking pleasure in the foreign sights and smells, the trams rattling up and down the centre of the street, not exactly nervous but on her mettle to do well. The bustling city and centre of international commerce seemed remarkably clean and ordered after Sydney's grimy traffic snarls, its very pavements gleaming.

She couldn't help feeling a little smug when women they passed in the street cast sidelong glances at Joe's tall dark form. In his banker's suit, briefcase in hand, he looked as sleek and prosperous as any of the businessmen hurrying to and fro, though hotter. Far hotter.

'Here we are,' he said, halting with a light hand on her elbow.

She gazed up at the discreet façade of one of the richest banks in the world.

'Good. Now what did you say we're meeting about?'

Joe scrutinised her. The blue of her suit turned her skin to milky satin and deepened the indigo ring around her irises. In this light they were teal, their golden flecks turned amber, and he remembered with an uncomfortable twinge how clear-seeing they could be. It flashed through his mind that if she was still the girl he thought she was, her smile might not be so eager and positive when she learned what he was negotiating.

'Well, er...' He frowned and scratched his ear, evaded her gaze. 'I'm negotiating with the bank about an investment the firm is considering in Sydney. But, look, there's no real need for you to come up. Why don't you do some sight-seeing?'

Mirandi felt an acute stab of disappointment. 'But—wouldn't you like me to come with you? Take notes or something?'

He shot her a keen glance, and she read the comprehension in his eyes.

'I won't need notes.' He knew she was hurt, she could sense it, but though his eyes were rueful his tone remained cool and firm. 'Why don't you stay down here and take a look around the shops? As I recall, this street is a women's shopping paradise. I'll meet you at *that* café...' he pointed across the street at an attractive awning sheltering a mass of tables and chairs, then glanced at his watch '...an hour from now.'

She drew breath to protest, but his expression was implacable. She knew that look. There was no use arguing.

Smarting, she watched him stride away. Why hadn't he wanted her with him? He disappeared into the building and she had nothing left to do but turn and stroll along the street, an alien on the other side of the world. Exciting though it was to be set free in this charming foreign city, she was beginning to feel a bit pointless.

Go shopping, he said. Shopping! What was she, a decoration? Was he as evasive about letting Stella in on his work commitments? Visions rose in her mind's eye of Stella at work making calls, striding along beside him, greeting his clients, emerging from meetings looking secretive and important, and she decided not. No, he'd never tell Stella to *go shopping*.

She slipped her laptop into her bag and threaded her way disconsolately among the shoppers, wondering just what her role was.

There was a startling array of designer boutiques around her, some with end-of-summer sale notices posted in their windows. She stared desultorily into a couple, then conceded she might as well take the opportunity to buy something to wear for evening, since her last-minute packing frenzy hadn't allowed her time to acquire anything special.

After several boutiques she tottered out reeling from the prices. Even the most unassuming shops in this precinct were beyond her humble means. And face it. Shopping required a certain mood an excluded MA couldn't summon. With a shrug she gave up the idea of a dress and wandered along the street until a captivating glimpse of the river lured her down a side-street to the quay.

Some time later she found the Bahnhofstrasse again and hastened back to the rendezvous, scanning for Joe. Her heart skipped when she saw his tall figure, standing quietly by the café. He was leaning against the wall, arms folded across his chest, his brows lowered in brooding contemplation. Had the meeting gone badly?

She hurried up to him.

'There you are.' He straightened up, lifting his brows at her empty hands. 'What? No shopping?'

She shook her head, smiling to cover the smouldering embers of her razed self-esteem. 'Plenty of fruitless looking, though. How did your meeting go?'

For an instant his strong lean face was motionless, then he lifted his shoulders with casual unconcern. 'Probably a bit too well.'

'Oh.' She slanted him a glance. 'So they agreed with your investment in the Sydney thing?'

'Yep,' he said curtly. 'They agreed.'

'Well, that's great, isn't it?'

He shrugged. 'Of course. Great.'

But there was a shadow in his eyes and she felt confused. Of course she was being too intrusive, asking for information he clearly didn't want to discuss. Maybe there were some things an assistant couldn't be privy to, especially one who was a last-minute stand-in. Still, rationalise it as much as she might, her doubts about his attitude towards her began to intensify.

Why bring her along if he didn't trust her?

Perhaps he sensed her hurt, because he made an effort to recapture their friendly mood and suggested they stroll down to the river and see some of the sights. She agreed, grateful for a way to ease the tension. And it worked. Even the gloomiest couple in the world would have found it impossible not to smile at the swans gliding along with majestic unconcern as their anxious cygnets paddled madly to keep up. And an hour or two of wandering through the fascinating old town on the other side of the bridge smoothed over the momentary abyss in communication. Soon Joe charmed her into laughing again, teasing and flirting with her as if she were the most desirable woman in Zurich.

At lunchtime they chose a café on the busy quay, hung with pots of scarlet geraniums to match the chequered table-cloths.

'Oh, I adore Zurich,' she enthused, stretching back in her chair and glancing around her. 'I can't imagine Nice will be any the nicer.'

He smiled at her over the top of his menu, acknowledging her terrible pun. 'You'll probably love it. Millions do.'

Something stirred in her memory then and she narrowed her eyes in recollection. 'Didn't you once tell me your mother lives in Europe somewhere?'

He blinked. His lean face smoothed to become expression-less. 'Did I?'

'I'm sure you did. Didn't you say she's an artist? Does she still paint?'

His blue eyes chilled to impenetrable ice. 'I have no idea.' Frowning, he turned his attention back to his menu. 'Are you ready to order?'

She bit her lip. If that had been a rebuke she deserved it. She should have remembered how reluctant he was to talk about his mother. But after all these years, surely he must have come to terms with his dysfunctional family? Wasn't there a time to face parents as adults? Even she, a certified scarlet sinner in some people's eyes, had managed to find some common ground with her oldies. And according to Mim, who admittedly had strong opinions about everyone she knew, no woman could have put up with Jake Sinclair and the life he'd led.

They lunched on fish caught fresh from the lake, steamed green vegetables and fried potatoes served with Alpine cheese and apple sauce. Mirandi adored every delicious morsel. She battled with her conscience over dessert, but how often would she have the opportunity to taste a bona fide Swiss chocolate torte laced with cherry brandy? In the end, true to form, she gave into temptation.

Joe watched her contemplate the cake set before her with smouldering appreciation. A woman with an unashamedly healthy appetite was a woman of promise, though how she managed to maintain that tiny little waist was a mystery. She was getting to him, there was no denying. His blood quickened as he imagined unwrapping her nakedness, burying himself in her satin heat. A night with her in his arms would surely dispel that sensation he'd been waking to lately of the stone weighing in his chest. Though why wait for night? An after-noon. Hell, an afternoon *and* a night. The next afternoon, the next night…

'Want a taste?'

He watched her ripe lips close over a mouthful, and felt a dangerous stir in his loins. 'Not of the cake,' he said softly.

His burning sensual gaze seared her with unashamed lust and Mirandi felt herself lose motion, like a bird in flight about to fall from the sky, though her blood was thumping fast. The crowds, the noise of the café all receded into the distance.

Still, her heart clamoured for answers.

She lifted her gaze to his. 'I'm confused, Joe,' she said breathlessly. 'What—what am I doing here with you, really?'

He shrugged and his eyes veiled beneath his black lashes. 'I thought I explained. You're here as my—sounding board.' He opened his hands. 'Friend, if you like.'

'I don't think so.' She shook her head. 'Sounding board, MA, *friend*…' The word nearly caught in her throat with all its irony. She added quietly, 'You don't kiss friends. Not like that. I'd just like to know where you think this is going. How about letting me in on the plan?'

His brows shot up. 'There's no *plan*.' He flicked her an oblique glance, then said lightly, 'How about companion? I'm sure you can kiss a companion.'

The emotion roiling away inside her wouldn't allow her to smile. 'I'm serious. We made a condition…'

'A condition we're both guilty of breaking.'

She flushed. 'I know that. The thing is that—after the things that happened with us before, I think you should know I'm not… I have no intention of *ever*—'

He flung up a hand to stop her. 'No, *don't* say that.' His blue gaze was suddenly intent, urgent. 'Never say it. Look…' He closed his eyes an instant. 'Just—listen. How could we not kiss? As soon as I saw you again I realised… That connection with you is still so… You know, I've missed the way I used to feel with you.'

'Oh.' Her heart shook.

Perhaps she should have been more severe with him, but in

all honesty those words struck a deep emotional chord in her, rare as such admissions were from a private guy like Joe. His deep, earnest voice, his intense gaze, his beautiful gesturing hands were sincere, and, foolish or not, she believed him. So, in spite of herself, the massive barrier that had frozen there after his rejection and her bitter aftermath melted a little.

'I see,' she said, lowering her lashes while her pulse thundered in her ears. 'Well, that's really—quite—interesting to know. Only I can't—let you play on my heartstrings again, Joe.'

'*Again,*' he echoed sardonically, a flush darkening his cheeks. Then he added softly, 'That's a two-way street, wouldn't you say, sweetheart?'

A million retorts, questions, reproaches hovered on her tongue and the silence between them pulsed with dangerous vibrations too threatening to voice. She was the one to break it, skittering away from the seismic zone with a husky change of subject.

'So then...' scrambling into safetalk, her pulse still seething, hardly knowing what she was saying, '...at this conference, will it all be just meetings? Is there anything in particular I should be prepared for?'

He studied her with a slight frown in his eyes, then rubbed his cheek and allowed his expressive mouth to relax. A veiled gleam shot into his eyes. 'I think there's some sort of cocktail thing on one night. And maybe a dinner. Or...oh, hell. I probably should have warned you.' She started to speak but he cut in. 'No, let me make amends for—everything. If you'd like to choose something to wear while we're here, the bank will foot the bill.'

She opened her eyes wide. '*What?* Are you serious?'

'Of course.' He reached across and captured her hand. 'Don't look so shocked. I insist. I can't take my loveliest market analyst to the ball unless she's wearing the latest designer creation from Paris.'

'There's no need. I have clothes. And look. Listen, Joe…'

But despite herself, she wavered. It was an olive branch, and kindly meant. And even after her stern warning that strong warm hand clasping hers was a powerful persuader, tuning her in once again to the high-voltage electric current that until yesterday she'd been excluded from for a decade. Oh, how she'd missed it.

Fireworks were lighting her up, confusing her, muffling her self-protective instincts. She was being swept along again on that hot, wild torrent to the place where the rules of the ordinary world didn't apply, just as she had that long ago day in the churchyard.

'What are you doing, Joe?' she said weakly.

He was smiling, a caress in his voice, that desire in his kingfisher-blue eyes so affecting. It was just like the time on the plane. She shouldn't look into his eyes. She *shouldn't*.

He gave her hand a squeeze. 'I'm holding this lovely hand. I'll keep on holding it until you agree.'

Her mind raced, along with her rapid pulse. He was charming her again, undermining her resistance, seducing her. But whether she was a sounding board, MA or friend, allowing him to buy her something as intimate as a dress was against all the rules. She could see where this was headed. Straight into mistress territory.

With an embarrassed glance at the neighbouring tables she tried to tug away, though not very hard. '*Joe.*' Her voice was as croaky as a crow's. 'People are looking at us.'

'Shh. We're shocking these good Swiss. Are you ready to agree, or do we keep holding hands?' He added softly, 'I can feel your electricity shooting up my arm.'

Her heart skittered at that undeniable truth. Her skin welcomed his strong, warm clasp and never wanted to lose it. And wasn't that always the trouble? Despite the imminent dangers, she couldn't prevent her imagination from flying her to the hotel room and envisaging the likely indulgences a mistress might be expected to provide.

Joe adjusted his grip a little, palm to electric palm, watching her eyes, the smiling awareness she couldn't conceal, the desire curving her mouth, warming her neck and cheek. His instincts of imminent victory gathered certainty. For days he'd been remembering how sweet it had been with her. How giving she was. How passionate.

She gave a slightly more determined tug and he released her. Not a moment too soon, if the tightening in his underwear was anything to go by.

'Dresses are what you buy a mistress,' she reproved, but his blood surged at the capitulation in her voice.

He smiled. 'Oh, *mistress*. That's such an old-fashioned concept. It's time it was put to bed.'

'Don't use that sexy tone with me.' Her attempt at sounding stern didn't quite come off. Not with that husky breathless quality in her voice. 'Haven't I made it clear? I'm still an old-fashioned girl and I *haven't* come as your mistress. Or to be put to bed. I'm here as your sounding board, remember? Your MA.'

'And it's as my MA that I'll be escorting you to that cocktail party. And it's as your *boss* that I insist on attiring you in a manner befitting Martin Place Investments.'

'*What?*'

He was startled by the green flash in her eyes.

She leaned forward and said in a low, outraged voice, 'Are you saying—you don't feel confident in the clothes I choose? Are you afraid I'll *embarrass* you?'

Whoa there. His instincts started clanging alarm bells. Careful how you handle this one, victory guy.

'Sweetheart. No, no, sorry—*Mirandi*.' He sighed and spread his hands in rueful appeal. 'You know I think you always look *amazing*.' Words even more dangerous than before flew out before he could call them back. 'When I see you walk by at work looking so—so beautiful and luscious and clever and smart…I just…' Desire threatened to loosen his tongue beyond what was prudent, and he made an adroit sidestep. 'What I'm saying is I—I'm so glad you took the job at MPI. I know you'll be just great there. We need more people like you. And I'll be so proud of my MA at that conference.'

They must have been the right words because he saw her eyes soften and shine. He was shaken by a powerful surge of tenderness towards her, and had to fight an overwhelming impulse to say even more things. Irrevocable things.

If they hadn't been in a public restaurant he could have expressed himself properly without having to resort to words at all.

He restricted himself to saying, 'I just want to give you something—lovely. Something to thank you for coming with me. At least let's wring *some* pleasure from this bloody hell of a trip.'

CHAPTER SEVEN

NATURALLY, Mirandi caved in. Well, her knees had gone weak. Anyway, travelling with a sexy man on a short fuse when she was tired herself required a certain amount of give and take. Joe really did seem to need cheering up.

And truly, when they went strolling through the boutiques and he took her hand with the old easy familiarity, it felt so right. And it was lovely trying on beautiful things she could never have normally dreamed of. Joe was so generous and kind, like her wonderful old Joe, waiting patiently for her to make up her mind, only grinning and giving a shrug when she rejected dress after dress in shop after shop.

In fact, she kept catching him looking at her with a light in his eyes that made her blood effervesce like hot lemonade.

And he could be helpful, as she discovered when she finally tracked down the sort of dress that appealed to her in one highly exclusive couture shop. The manager was a haughty, fortyish Frenchwoman with shrewd black eyes and a tight, narrow smile.

While Mirandi sifted through the beautiful things on the racks, Joe found a wingchair thoughtfully placed outside the fitting room area and settled into it, stretching out his long legs and lounging back with a newspaper over his face.

There was much to choose from, but her final decision was between an ankle-length red satin dress with a plunging neck-line and a split, and a rose-and-peach-coloured silk georgette with narrow straps and a tulip skirt. Each of them was a dream come true, though both were fearfully expensive.

She tried the georgette first. Because of its thin straps she had to remove her bra so as not to spoil the effect of the bodice. The manager hovered outside, ready to dash in at the first opportunity to snatch her sacred merchandise out of harm's way.

Mirandi allowed the woman a glimpse and *madame* was overwhelmed, at the same time as slipping in some sharp observations about how the excellence of the design concealed *mademoiselle's* imperfections. Only see how it created the illusion of breasts, and covered *mademoiselle's* too generous thighs. Such a pretty effect on *mademoiselle* with her unfortunate hair and that pallid complexion was *magnifique*, *parfait*, *incroyable*.

The sound of new customers entering the boutique cut short the stream of superlatives, and the saleswoman bustled away. Though smarting at the slurs on her beauty, it was with some regret that Mirandi carefully peeled off the gorgeous georgette, replaced it on its hanger, then turned to the red satin.

Just her luck, but once she'd poured herself into the fabulous thing and pirouetted a few times to enjoy the sensational effect of its fluid slinkiness front, rear and sideways, the zip stuck fast and she couldn't take it off.

Twisting and turning for a better angle, she struggled to shift it until she felt something give in the fabric.

Oh, *no*. She grew hot. What if she'd torn it? She'd have to call the dragon woman and confess.

She put her head out of the door, but there was a small hallway separating the fitting rooms from the sales floor and the woman was out of sight. Mirandi could hear her voice as she dealt with other customers, and her mind leaped to Joe—who she'd last seen lounging in a chair around the corner.

She poked her head out of the door and called softly to him. He appeared in the hall entrance, looking taken aback.

'I need your help,' she said in a low urgent voice. 'Can you come here a minute?'

His brows lifted, then he sauntered in and stood at the door, quizzical amusement in his eyes. 'Yeah? What seems to be the trouble?'

At the gleam in his eyes she felt misgivings along with a definite charge in her insides. 'Do you mind... Can you help me with this?' She opened the door a tiny bit wider and angled around to show him. 'See, the zip's stuck. I'm afraid I might have damaged it.'

She glanced back at him and a warm shivery sensation shimmied down her spine as his blue eyes swarmed all over her, aglow with searing, sensual admiration.

'Oh, my God, that dress.' His hands flew out, but didn't actually touch her. 'You look—like a *flame*.' His voice deepened on the word.

'All right, all right,' she said tartly, though she couldn't help but be warmed by such overt appreciation. If a woman had to be stuck inside a dress and was forced into calling a man to the rescue, it was as well the dress should be flattering.

'You do know if I've damaged it I'll have to pay for it,' she warned to dampen his enthusiasm. 'And it costs a *fortune*.'

'And worth every red cent,' he exclaimed with heartfelt warmth.

She should have known this would be a mistake. He was loving it. She looked sternly at him and he immediately put on a solemn expression.

'Do you want me to do it out here, or...?' He was trying to sound grave, but his voice had deepened to a revealing huskiness.

A dangerous intuition tingled along her nerve-endings, and her nipples reacted involuntarily, as if his bronzed hands had already brushed her bra-less breasts. This had all the hallmarks of one of those risky occasions. But her options were few.

She cast a quick glance around, then motioned him into the fitting room.

It was only a small room. Perhaps because the walls were shrinking, or because there was a forbidden quality to the situation, what with the strict Frenchwoman close by, she felt a wicked zing ripple through her bloodstream.

She faced him for a breathless second, seared to her entrails by his hot eyes and the raw animal hunger she saw there.

He must have been crazed, because he cradled her face in his hands, scorching her with his devouring gaze, and said hoarsely, 'You're still so gorgeous. You're just—gorgeous.'

Then he kissed her, a sensual tasting of each of her lips while he plundered her mouth tissues with his clever tongue. She didn't care that he was clearly short-sighted and mentally deranged. She supposed she could have interrupted and said, 'It's the *dress*, stupid,' but this wasn't the time to give him a lesson on dresses and what they could do for the female form because she was deeply into the kiss. Her bones were dissolving and she had to cling to him to support herself.

The kiss broke and he stared into her face, his eyes ablaze with two disturbing points of flame she remembered well. An age-old excitement gripped her.

For heaven's sake, some last vestige of reason clanged in her brain, they were in a boutique fitting room. She gave him a small, provocative push away, then turned her back to him and held up her hair.

The move didn't have any dampening effect, it seemed. Now his reflection smouldered before her in the mirror, lust in his eyes.

Against everything her brain knew was wise, her blood surged to the primitive call, rocking into a slow, heavy, sensual beat.

'Have I torn it?' Even to her own ears she sounded huskier than the norm.

'Just a bit.' *His* voice was deeper than a well. 'Looks like a part of the stitching's come away.'

'Shh. Keep your voice down.'

He worked at the zip, frowning in concentration, occasionally brushing her back with his knuckles. Her wanton skin welcomed every tiny contact, and each time it happened his eyes clashed with hers in the mirror and ignited more burning embers in her blood.

At last he murmured, 'There.' She felt him tug at the zip, shift it a little way, then ease it smoothly all the way down to the small of her back. Cooler air played along her spine.

'Great,' she breathed, letting her hair fall. She didn't move, and neither did he move away from her. She grew preternaturally conscious of his closeness, the tense current pulsing between them, her breasts naked under the thin red satin.

The air in the little room grew taut with risk.

His strong hands closed around her upper arms and her heart started to thud. In the mirror she saw him bend towards her. She closed her eyes, quivering as his lips scorched her nape, her flesh leaping in instant response.

He lifted his head, and she waited. She met his darkened gaze in the mirror, and saw that her own eyes were curiously dark and glowing. Her skin prickled as he ran a light finger along the ridge of her spine, igniting little streamlets of fire.

Then he paused. She dared not breathe, teetering on the verge of a tingling suspense, longing for him to touch her again. Her nipples tautened with suspense, aching, yearning to be touched.

Then, to her intense pleasure, he slid his warm hands in under the dress opening, loosening the snug bodice. He drew her against him while he held her breasts, softly squeezing and stroking them, igniting little rivulets of fire under her skin. She panted as her breasts swelled with heat, her nipples tingling as he delicately teased and taunted them with his long, lean fingers.

Fingers that were delicious enough to lick. She burned everywhere, but the wildest thirst burned between her legs, and she was seized by that old reckless sensation he'd always inspired in her and forgot all prudent considerations.

He kissed her neck and put his tongue in her ear, his hot breath tickling and inflaming the sensitive orifice.

Lucky he was supporting her with his big lean frame, because her knees nearly collapsed and she sagged against him. The mingled sensations were so pleasant and arousing, her hidden delta craved and yearned to be caressed.

Her veins seemed to flow with liquid fire as though her body were all at once bursting from its conventional constraints and longing to plunge into a wild explosion of every possible pleasure.

She tried to turn around to him to open up the possibilities but he held her severely before him. Feeling the hard length of his erection pressing into her, she reached behind her in an attempt to encourage him to hurry in their stolen hideaway. But growling something under his breath, he grabbed her hands and held them still.

His face in the mirror was so raw and naked it scorched her mesmerised gaze and she couldn't look away.

She couldn't remember feeling so hot, but still he toyed with her. He slid his hot, urgent hands caressingly over her hips and thighs as if she were some rare and precious figurine he was moulding from clay, then, when she was least expecting it, to her excitement he eased up the dress and exposed her pants and the nude pale skin at the tops of her stockings.

She saw lust flare in his eyes.

Lust was infectious. She stilled, holding her breath, her erotic tissues ignited with a desperate craving. Then fascinated, simmering with fever, she watched the reflection as his lean tanned hand slid across her navel then down beneath the elastic of the flimsy underwear.

She felt a small involuntary rush of moisture.

Panting and trembling, she could feel his hot breath on her neck. As if he understood her most intimate needs, with exquisite softness his smooth fingertips sought the delicate lips, found her sensitive, burning, engorged folds and stroked them. Found her sweetest, most delicate, most explosive spot, and caressed her there.

Ah-h-h. Rapture forced a series of little gasps from her. Then hypnotised, swooning with delight, she watched as he slid those long smooth fingers inside her.

Ecstasy.

Shuddering, her breath coming in hoarse gasps—she might have whimpered—she parted her thighs to give him more access and gave herself up to enjoyment of the forbidden magic. Just when she was climbing to a pitch of the most fantastic, blissful tension, a demanding feminine voice cut through the sultry mists of her pleasure.

'*Mademoiselle. Mam'selle exige-t-il l'aide?*'

She started back to reality and they both froze. 'What?' she mouthed at Joe.

He frowned and shook his head, signalling no.

'No,' she squeaked. 'No, *merci, madame.* I'm fine, and I'm coming. Now. At once.'

If only that had been true. It was the ultimate in anticlimax. Plans she'd been concocting for Joe's pleasure were put on hold as, hot, flustered and aroused, she gave the woman time to swish away, checked the coast was clear, then pushed a reluctant Joe outside.

Hurriedly she dragged off the dress and struggled into her own clothes, hoping she hadn't made too much noise in the exigency of the moment.

The situation didn't give her much time to think, but she managed to fix her hair and face a little before she sashayed from the fitting room with the dresses. She did her best to smooth out the red one, praying the wrinkles where it had been creased didn't shout what had transpired while she was wearing it.

Joe was waiting at the counter with his back to her, and she checked, then braced herself and strolled up to him as coolly as she could. At first she barely had the nerve to look at him. When he turned to her that hot, hungry gleam shot into his eyes and for a second her heart plunged into the mad, pulsing rhythm again, and she knew she was in trouble.

Hot, helpless trouble.

The saleswoman raised her hard, accusing gaze to Mirandi. She smoothed out each dress and examined them minutely.

Flushing, Mirandi bit her lip, careful to avoid Joe's eyes for fear of laughing. Clearly, the fitting room shenanigans had awakened suspicion.

Bracing herself, she launched into what she could at least confess without shame.

'This dress is excellent, *madame*, but I—I had a bit of trouble with the zip on this one.' She indicated the spot where the stitching had failed. 'I found it difficult to close, then I couldn't easily unzip it to take the dress off.' She illustrated as best she could with her hands.

The woman frowned suspiciously at her, examined the zip seam, then her mouth dropped open and she burst into a stream of voluble French, waving her hands in horror.

Dismayed, Mirandi turned to Joe. To her utter astonishment he took charge of the situation, addressing the saleswoman in smooth, fluent, confident French, waving his hands with Gallic expertise as if he'd been born to a chateau on the Loire. After a rapid-fire exchange of arguments, heated on the woman's side, suavely authoritative on Joe's, the woman backed down a little and a reluctant understanding appeared to be in view.

She turned to Mirandi and explained in English that perhaps the *mademoiselle* was not entirely to blame. It was possible, though extremely *unlikely*, that the fault had been with the product, as *monsieur* had pointed out.

'As it is, this dress cannot now be sold,' she declared with sly triumph. 'It must be returned to Paris and resewn.'

Joe produced a credit card and laid it smoothly before her. 'We'll take it.'

'But no, *monsieur*. This dress must not leave the shop.' The cold glint of revenge made her small black eyes harder than ever. 'As *monsieur* has stated, the reputation of our company is at stake here, of our seamstresses, of our very nation. I am afraid we cannot help *mademoiselle*.'

'I think you can, *madame*,' Joe said in a tone that, although smooth, would allow no argument. 'This is the dress we want, and it is the dress we must have. Exactly as it is. In fact, we'll take both dresses.'

Mirandi swivelled around to stare at him. 'What? *Both*?'

'Both,' he stated firmly. 'And we'll also require some matching shoes and purses.' His eyes lit on a lingerie rack in the far corner. 'And some of those lacy things with the suspenders.'

'*What?*' The shocks were coming so quick and fast Mirandi's mouth was formed in a perpetual O.

Madame considered her options for a bristling moment, then caved in. Such a profitable sale was irresistible.

Afterwards, floating along the street carrying some of the boutique's elegant packages while still more dangled from Joe's hand, Mirandi was in a giddy haze.

'Joe. I really don't know what to say—but…thank you. This was so *generous*. I mean, *two* dresses. One would be amazing enough, but *two*. And the *shoes*. And these bags are to die for. I adore them. I just *adore* them.'

He held up his hand. 'It was my pleasure. Every minute of it.' He gave a wicked reminiscent laugh.

She joined in with her own gurgle of laughter. 'All right, but you know…two—*two* dresses. Do you have any idea what those shoes cost? And two bags. I don't ever own more than one and I keep it until it falls apart. *And* those lace knickers.

And the corset with the suspenders…' She cast him a sidelong glance. 'I can't imagine where I'll ever wear that.'

'Can't you?' His eyes shimmered. 'But you are wearing it now, aren't you?' His voice was deeper than midnight.

She smiled acknowledgement. The truth was she'd admired herself in it so much, especially the way the black bustier pushed up her breasts and made them swell at the top, she hadn't been able to bear to take it off and had informed *madame* she would wear it home under her clothes.

'Clever of you to remember,' she teased.

Of course, under *madame's* watchful eye Joe hadn't been privy to the fitting room at the trying-on of the corselet, but overhearing this discussion he'd turned a fascinated gaze on Mirandi, almost as if he were seeing straight through her blue suit to the sexy black lace underneath.

'It's not the sort of thing a man forgets. It's the only thing keeping me awake.'

She laughed. 'Really. Oh, and before I forget. I have to tell you how impressed I am by your magnificent French. I've forgotten most of mine from school. For a guy who only visited France for one weekend, how do you manage it?'

He gave a shrug, and the corner of his mouth curled in a grimace. 'I once knew a Frenchwoman.'

'Oh.' Her heart took a dive. Of course. She should have known. The only question was how many?

She tried not to let it deflate her. She had no claims on him now. A fitting-room clinch didn't mark him as hers. Face it, he'd already evaded her brand of entanglement in the past. He wasn't about to plunge into it again.

Strolling along under the leafy canopy of trees, she stole a look at him and saw his face shadowed with that brooding absorption he'd had earlier, and mentally kicked herself for being a fool. Why spoil a near-perfect day with useless speculation about how many women he'd had? Was currently seeing, despite poor Kirsty having bitten the dust?

'Anyway,' she said, determined to recapture the mood. 'It was so kind and generous of you. *More* than generous, Joe, it was...' She spread her arms wide. 'How can I ever thank you?'

He grabbed her and held her still, smiling into her eyes with tender amusement. 'Don't thank me. I'm the one who should be thanking *you*.'

He put his arms around her, and, as though both driven by the same impulse, their lips collided. His strong arms tightened around her and he deepened the kiss, as far as it was possible in a public boulevard with shoppers milling around them. Straight away, so soon after the last kiss, the desire still lurking between them sprang back to life and sizzled through her like fifty thousand volts of electricity.

She'd noticed before that they were heading in the direction of the hotel and the ferry quay. When they broke apart she felt breathless and a little drunk. 'So...what do you think now? A cruise on Lake Zurich?'

His eyes shimmered. 'Well, as you said, we're jet-lagged.' His voice deepened and his expression grew solemn. 'I think an afternoon rest would do us good, don't you?' His eyes were surprisingly bright for a man contemplating sleep, his voice deep and velvety. 'Give us plenty of energy for tonight.'

'Tonight?' She sent him a quick oblique glance.

His eyes smouldered. 'Well, we don't want to waste it, do we?'

CHAPTER EIGHT

EUPHORIA was a beautiful thing. It carried them up in the lift and along the hotel corridor, punctuated by kisses and giggles from Mirandi and shouts of laughter from Joe whenever they remembered the boutique woman's face.

'We can't really blame her.'

'But at least she was happy in the end with her sale, wasn't she?'

'Though if she'd had a humane bone in her body she could at least have given us another five minutes…'

'Oh, yes, if *only*. I had *such* plans for you, you'll never know. Pity you couldn't have come in with me while I tried on the lingerie.'

Joe's eyes gleamed. 'Ah, yes. The lingerie.'

He took the key from her hand and slid it into the slot. Her room door opened, and he stood back and allowed her to float through first.

Rooms at the Chateau du Lac were airy and opulent, with windows you could open, pretty painted ceilings and a gratifying number of mirrors that gave a woman plenty of angles from which to observe the effect she was making.

She wafted into the centre of hers, twirled, then dropped her packages on the floor and turned to face Joe. Desire electrified the air, whispered along her nerve-endings and teased her erotic zones with pleasant yearning. Joe deposited his parcels on a chair, then caught her at the waist and held her still, his light firm grip searing her through her clothes.

Her breath was trapped in her lungs when she met the fever burning in his eyes like points of flame. It was too late for resolutions.

'This is exactly what we said we wouldn't do,' she said shakily, her heart pounding like a wild thing.

'And what we always knew we *would* do.'

His voice had thickened with the intensity of his lust, instantly reviving her own unassuaged desire until her body trembled to know his embrace and burned.

He reached for the top button of her jacket and she smiled as swiftly and expertly he stripped her of her suit.

His eyes flared when he revealed her in her lacy corselet. He stood back to take in the full effect of her suspenders, the stockings attached and her flimsy little see-through pants, and with a primitive urge to inspire him she slipped the grips on the suspenders and peeled off her stockings with long, caressing, sensual movements, holding each of them high and letting them flutter to the ground.

She held him at bay with a gesture, then she danced a little, provocatively stroking her hips and swaying, fanning her hair out then arching her back to let the silky stuff fall behind her in a mass.

When she straightened he was standing as though riveted, breathing hard, his eyes burning like coals. His tie was hanging loose and she saw the faintest sheen of moisture on his upper lip.

A buoyant sensation she'd nearly forgotten existed shot through her, as if her veins were injected with magic. She felt like a midnight witch, reckless and sexy and aroused. Powerful. Inspired.

Desire whispered along her nerve-endings and pulsed in her blood. Tantalising her masculine captive, she swayed a little more to help him appreciate the treasures on offer, pouted to remind him she had lips in other places, and wiggled her hips to entice him.

It seemed to work. Though she held him in check with her tease, his devouring gaze, a certain tension in the lines of his big lean body, suggested his unaccustomed patience in such a situation was about to explode into action.

She sashayed up to him to unbutton his shirt and he stood even more motionless, but it was brooding stillness like that of a ticking grenade. He watched her face while she slipped the buttons, her trembling hands affected by the powerful heartbeat she could feel beneath the thin fabric. Only his harsh quickened breath revealed the control he was employing to hold the volcano of passion in check.

He undid his cufflinks, then tore off his shirt. Her mouth dried when she saw his broad, bronzed chest again, with his powerful pecs and lean muscled abdomen as stirring as ever before. Greedily her eyes devoured the black whorls of hair arrowing down below his belt.

Sighing, unable to help herself, she pressed her lips to his hard chest and they felt scorched by the heat in his skin. At once his arms snaked around her, then his hands slid to her arms and held them in a purposeful grip. She could feel the hot current of passion flowing through him.

'I can't believe what you're doing to me,' he said, his voice deep and gravelly. 'Come here.'

He dragged her to him and seared her lips with his in masterful possession, plundering her mouth with his tongue, sucking the breath from her lungs till she was giddy, then he broke the sizzling contact to devour her throat and breasts with urgent kisses.

She struggled with the bow of her corselet but the lustful man couldn't wait for her to take it off. He lifted one breast from its cup, licked the tender yearning nipple, then drew on it with his mouth.

Oh, heavenly day. She mewled with pure pleasure, clinging

to him as her bones dissolved in bliss, then, just when she thought her desire couldn't blaze any brighter, he sucked on the other one as well, fanning the flames of her hunger to an inferno.

Fire raged through her blood and in the tender folds between her thighs until her very channel burned with longing to take him inside.

With a small growl he pushed her onto the bed, devouring her semi-nude body with his eyes while he stripped off the rest of his clothes and flung them aside.

When she saw the proud extent of his virility, her blood slowed in her veins like treacle.

'Oh, my,' she purred, moistening her lips.

There was little doubt of his enthusiasm for the task in hand. His magnificent erection jutted free and proud, and she felt her womb melt and juice dampen her between her legs in avid anticipation.

She reached out and touched him, stroking his hot, hard penis, marvelling at the velvet skin encasing the engorged beauty. Closing her hand around the shaft, she felt the roiling surge of intense heat, and, amazingly, felt him harden still further in her grasp.

'Careful,' he bit out, closing his eyes, his voice a shuddering growl.

Smiling, she rolled into the middle of the bed and lolled there with her head on the pillow, slowly parting her legs for him in voluptuous encouragement. He started in surprise, staring with his hot lubricious gaze, then deliberately leaned forward and drew her knickers off.

A shiver of excitement rippled down her spine.

He waited to see if she would resume the same enticing pose without her protective covering, and, challenged, she didn't disappoint him.

He stood smouldering, taking in her nakedness below the bustier, his eyes dark with desire, his powerful chest heaving, then all at once turned to swoop at his clothes and make a frantic search through the pockets.

With an exclamation of satisfaction he produced a foil packet and held it up, grinning.

'Aha.'

As she had so many times before, she watched him roll on the sheath, breathless with excitement for the pleasure to come.

He joined her on the bed and stretched out over her, searching her eyes hungrily at first before taking her lips in a slow tender kiss.

When he drew back she gazed up at him, feeling the fever force thrumming in his virile body, enjoying the familiar, evocative scent of him, the erotic rub of his body hair on her breasts and legs. Precious flesh on flesh, beloved bone on bone. Familiar knee, familiar hip. The old sensation that their bodies had been fashioned to fit.

He gazed at her, frowning, his eyes all at once serious. He said, a curious roughness in his deep voice, 'I can't get over how everything about you is still—with me. You're engrained in my senses.'

Her heart thrilled to hear her sensations reflected.

He added even more hoarsely, his eyes glowing with a fierce sincerity, 'I'm still wild for you. Whatever they told you, that never ended.'

His face contorted with some strong emotion, then his eyes burned with a particular primitive purpose and she tensed with expectation. She wrapped her legs around him and with a strong sure thrust he drove into her.

She let out a gasp, having forgotten how fabulously he filled her with his thick, hard length.

He scanned her face with a mesmeric, heavy-lidded gaze. 'I want to rock you until you forget every other guy in the universe.'

Breathlessly she gasped, 'What other guys?'

He started to move inside her, rocking her in a subtle, sinuous, sexy rhythm that ignited little streamlets of pleasure inside her moist, empty darkness like rays of light. He took her mouth in urgent possession, then as the rhythm grew faster and harder, and his thrusting rod stroked her aroused inner walls, she felt herself open to him. Felt the light expand as their bodies fitted, locked tight in the sexy, satisfying rumba.

She clung to her old lover as if to a lifeline, revelling in the power of him, the erotic friction with his strong chest. At first he watched her face, reading her responses, but as the tempo quickened his eyes closed and she knew he'd been overtaken by his own blissful concentration.

With each escalating thrust her pleasure soared, rising higher and higher up some steep tense slope and she was on a wild high ride to ecstasy.

She felt herself reach the summit, saw his neck sinews ridge with effort as he held back his climax to wait for her. Then just as she teetered on the edge she felt his powerful frame tense for the first spasm of climax. Somehow that violent tension fuelled her own with all the impetus she needed, and her suspense fractured and dissolved into a million exquisite shards and irradiated her entire body.

Afterwards, after she'd recovered her breath and the blood had ceased drumming in her ears, when the sweat had dried on her skin and she was free of her corselet, she turned to examine him.

He'd been up and washed, and now lay with his eyes closed, apparently dozing. The room was bathed in the soft light that preceded dusk.

'You haven't lost your touch,' she murmured.

She saw the edges of his mouth twitch. 'I know. I was inspired.'

She grinned. 'Still so charmingly modest.'

'Thank you.' His eyes opened and he reached out and touched her. '*You* inspired me.'

'Oh. Good. I hoped I was having an effect.'

'When didn't you?' He leaned towards her and kissed her lips.

That reminded her of something he'd said before about never changing, but of course he'd declared it in the heat of the moment. People often said things then. Before their brains cooled.

Still, there was a thrilling atmosphere of togetherness winding around them. He pulled her closer to him and she lay silently, pleasantly entwined, savouring the precious intimacy of afterglow, wishing it would never end.

He'd closed his eyes again, but she could tell his brain was ticking over.

'Do you still write the poems?' she said after a while, softly tracing the outline of his tattoo.

'Nope.' He smiled. 'Sometimes I think of things I might write down, and then something intervenes. You know, work… I'm surprised you remember.'

'I'm starting to remember quite a lot.'

His lips twitched. 'Not too much, I hope.' Then after a while he opened his eyes and said cautiously, 'Did you ever wish we hadn't ended when we did?'

She stilled, then disentangled herself from him and lay back on her pillow, her heart thumping ridiculously, considering it had all happened ten years ago. 'Did you?'

'I guess. Though at the time it seemed—for the best.'

A million questions jostled for answers, not least the ones beginning with 'why' if this idle conversation was intended to convey how much he regretted their crash and burn. Still, she knew how to play the caution card too. In fact, it was the only one she ever dared use these days.

'Who for?' she said, as casual as he, while underneath her façade her adolescent heart was bursting through the layers to demonstrate that all along it had been ticking away alive and well, nursing all its old unresolved violence, just waiting for a trigger, a chance to spill its guts.

His blue eyes met hers, intent, earnest, held them an intense, throat-catching instant, then veiled and slid away.

'Ah…probably both of us,' he said gruffly, retreating onto his pillow. 'It wasn't the sort of dependence either of us could afford at that age, was it?'

Spoken like a chief executive officer.

She couldn't resist some gentle mockery, unable to betray her savage soul altogether. 'You mean there was too much emotion involved? Too much passion?'

He crooked his arm over his eyes while her words floated on the air. After what seemed like for ever, he stirred himself to lean up on his elbow and gaze down at her, pure and thrilling sin brimming from his smiling eyes.

'I think we both know there can never be too much passion.' He reached for her and kissed her swollen lips with the same passionate fervour as the first time.

CHAPTER NINE

IT WAS absurd to hold a grudge, and, truly, those painful emotions had long since cooled. She was an adult now, fast approaching the era of life when her womanly powers would be at their height, so if a man was fun and exciting, charming, wicked and a virile, sensitive lover who could send her over the edge, how crazy would she be to hold it against him that he'd once let her down?

So long as she kept her head and didn't harbour any destructive yearnings for a long-term arrangement, she could enjoy the current fling and walk away with a satisfied grin.

Surely.

So when the plane cruised her over the Alps and into Nice, with a night of the most fantastic and voluptuous love-making still warming her spirit she had nothing to complain of. Unless she counted a slight tenderness in certain delicate areas and a pressing need to sleep. Pity there was a day of conferencing to get through first.

To her surprise they were met at the airport by a uniformed man in a cap marked Hotel Metropole, who bowed. '*Mam'selle et monsieur*, your 'elicopter awaits you.'

'Our helicopter?' she exclaimed to Joe. 'From here into the city?'

'Oh, didn't I mention it? The conference is in Monte Carlo. *Merci*,' he said to the pilot, launching into a stream of fluent French in response to something the man said.

Monte Carlo. Well, one exotic location was as good as another, and who was she to quibble if he didn't inform her of absolutely every minute detail?

And, truly, she'd never experienced anything like that helicopter flight. It was her first time, and gazing down into the dazzling Mediterranean as it foamed up on the shores of a million little bays and inlets was a stunning experience. Marinas thronging with yachts and fishing boats, heart-stopping little villages perched on hillsides, spilling down cliff-faces... Image after charming image unfolded, etching themselves into her thrilled heart for all eternity. And Monte Carlo itself was a fairy tale. Spilling over the hillsides, the pale pink and cream sandstone city descended to a harbour marina where vessels were packed like sardines. A little further out some of the big glossy cruising yachts rode at anchor on the waves.

'You see that chateau on the edge of the sea?' their pilot enthused. 'There is our famous Monte Carlo casino. And here we go down.'

The pretty houses, the turquoise sea... Every view from every angle was breathtaking. How could Joe not be swept away?

He wasn't, though, she could tell when the fantastic ride was over and they strolled into the sumptuous lobby of the Metropole. While she glanced excitedly around her at what looked like a palace, taking in the rich furnishings, the tapestries, the elegant clientele chatting over their coffees, Joe was frowning, the grim lines around his eyes and mouth a reminder of their sleepless night.

'Why didn't you mention the helicopter and Monte Carlo?' she murmured while they were waiting for the desk clerk to attend to them.

'Maybe I don't care for the name.'

She gave him a sharp look and Joe felt a slight twinge of guilt. He supposed he had been less than forthcoming with her about the details of the trip.

'Oh, well.' He spread his hands. 'I said the south of France. There's hardly a great difference.'

'Tell that to the Monacons.'

'The Monegasque,' he corrected gently. 'Or the Monacoians.'

He could hardly blame her feeling ruffled, but the truth was the very name Monte Carlo had an unpleasant ring to him. It conjured up visions of hungry, desperate people poring over roulette wheels. Lost souls with empty eyes and wallets, risking their children's bread on the ride of a pitiless dice. Besides, the place was far too close to Antibes.

Now he was here on the spot, Antibes loomed like a black cloud. With a resurgence of that dread feeling in his gut he tried to remember why he'd allowed himself to be pressured into coming. Why hadn't he just ticked all the boxes and given the casino project the go-ahead? Did he seriously think he'd learn anything here he could use?

His vision—the one where he produced some incontrovertible evidence that changed the minds of his directors—started to look like what it was. An hallucination.

The truth was those guys were all salivating over the potential for obscene profits. Unless he could come up with an angle to quell their greed, they'd never listen.

'Joe.' He felt her tug at his sleeve. 'Which conference is ours?'

The moment of truth. Bracing for trouble, he followed Mirandi's gaze to a placard where the hotel's current conferences had been listed in both French and English.

International Bankers Symposium
Casino Acquisition and Marketing
Capital Investors Roundtable

Though his shirt collar all at once seemed to tighten around his neck like a noose, he met her gaze without flinching. 'The second.'

'Casinos? But…'

'But what?'

Wariness veiled her gaze, though he really hadn't intended that little snap in his voice.

'Well…' She gazed steadily at him. 'I guess when you mentioned entertainment for some reason I thought you meant the music industry.'

'Hardly.' He saw her brows edge together and it made his nerves jangle. 'Is there something you want to say?'

The atmosphere grew prickly. She evaded his eyes and he felt his blood pressure jump a notch. He tried to guess what she was thinking. Remembering his father, the fatal addiction? How could Joe betray his father's suffering like that? Or even worse. Was Joe the *same* as his father?

She glanced around her, extended her hands in wordless acquiescence. 'We're here, aren't we? Would anything I say make a difference?'

Irritation grabbed him. 'Probably not.'

'Then I'll save my breath.'

She flashed him a grin to show there were no hard feelings. But he could feel her slip him one or two shrewd glances. She was thinking plenty, he'd be willing to stake his last dollar on it—if he'd been a gambling man, of course, which he certainly was *not*. He could almost hear the moral judgements ticking over inside her glossy head.

Although she gave no sign of it, considering she was smiling at the desk clerk, making chit-chat with her usual serenity. Perhaps he'd misread her. Paradoxically then he regretted cutting off her queries and wished he knew exactly *what* she was thinking. One thing he could always rely on in the past was her ability to see right into the heart of an issue.

'Your keys, *mam'selle et monsieur*,' the desk clerk beamed, only too eager to assist the *mademoiselle*. 'Your baggage has already been transported to your rooms.'

Mirandi thanked him. Conscious of a need to bridge the jagged chasm suddenly yawning between her and Joe, she turned to him. 'Coffee first?' She indicated the sign pointing outside to the pool bar and café, but he glanced at his watch, frowning.

'Not if we want to unpack before we register for the conference. Don't you want to change?'

'Oh, all right.' Her heart sank. So soon? After that delightful helicopter ride, switching straight back into work mode felt something of an anticlimax, but Joe's demeanour didn't encourage rebellion.

She wished the conference was about the music industry. She wasn't sure she could bear sitting through days of discussing something that clashed with her own values and upbringing in every way. As for Joe... How could he even contemplate it?

The mood had changed. Didn't last night and the things they'd said to each other—those thrilling half-promises, all the demonstrations of rapture in each others' company—didn't they mean anything?

The upper reaches of the hotel were decorated in the same luxurious style as the vestibule, with lovely antique table lamps and paintings in unexpected corners. Whether by accident or design they'd been assigned adjoining rooms. When she reached her door she arranged to meet Joe in thirty minutes, then walked inside, frowning.

Something was wrong. She considered all the casual references Joe had made to the trip. The things he'd said in Zurich. *This bloody hell of a trip.*

Maybe it wasn't the place that was bothering him at all. Maybe it was the conference itself. She guessed that would explain his reluctance to discuss it with her.

Although what was a conference, anyway—a few meetings, a lot of discussion? Despite the topic, it was hardly something to dread. He could walk away in a minute, but he had the look of a man about to undertake some gruelling trial. Was there someone he expected to meet there he didn't want to see? Some old flame?

He had plenty of them, she thought gloomily. It wasn't hard to imagine they might pepper the world. Maybe that would explain his reluctance to share any information with her. Although...

Looking back, she realised he hadn't even been willing to tell her the theme of the conference. That hadn't just been an oversight, she could tell by the tension in his tone downstairs. Face it, it was such an *amazing* theme for Joe of all people to be exploring. Casinos, of all things.

The more she thought of it, the stranger it felt. Whoever he was now, she knew the Joe he'd been and where he'd come from. One thing she remembered all too clearly was his dislike of casinos and all their implications.

And it was understandable, for him. He might not have been brought up as she had by a tough church minister with a tender social conscience, but as a teenager he'd been dealt one of life's cruellest blows.

Joe had put the tragedy behind him, but Jake had been his father, his beloved father, and though Joe never spoke of that terrible time she knew it was woven into the fabric of him, warp and weft. In fact, anyone knowing these things about Joe would assume Monte Carlo to be the last place he'd think of visiting.

So why had he chosen to come?

Worriedly, she turned her attention to locating her suitcase, and for the first time took time to examine her room properly.

Overwhelmed, she stood stock still to drink it all in.

After the luxury of Zurich she knew better than to wonder if Stella had made some mistake with the bookings. This time the thoughtful woman had excelled herself.

The room was charming, opulent and distinctly French. High of ceiling, it boasted an antique writing desk and rose satin drapes framing two sets of French doors that opened to a small balcony.

Unable to resist, Mirandi walked outside and leaned on the stone balustrade, inhaling the heady Mediterranean air, thrilled by the sights and sounds of the fairy-tale city. Below her was a terraced garden with ponds and fountains and beyond that, across the rooftops, the sea.

If only she and Joe were here on a real holiday. She toyed with the idea of distracting him from his purpose. Considerations of how she might achieve it would have made her grin if she hadn't felt such a sense of foreboding. His moods had suddenly become so unpredictable who knew if he'd still want her by nightfall?

With a sigh she turned back inside.

If she had to be confined to a hotel, she was glad it was this one, at any rate.

She strolled around, opening all the doors and investigating the drawers.

The king-sized bed—surely an excess for one person—was attired with a heavy satin counterpane of roses on a cream background, with rose-covered pillows. A vase of the real thing in fragrant, partly unfurled buds of pink and red adorned a side table.

It was a duchess's room. A princess's. She couldn't wait to sink amongst those fluffy pillows on that inviting bed and sleep.

The bathroom was equally grand. Besides vast expanses of marble and a glassed-in shower recess, she was gratified to find a huge old-fashioned tub with detachable shower hose. Beside it, fresh rose petals in a jar waited to float in her bath water.

Perfect. Or it would be, once the conference was finished for the day.

She sighed again, and set about hanging up her clothes. At least Joe had given her the two lovely dresses and she wouldn't be disgracing herself among the glamorous clientele. The minor problem of that tricky zip occurred to her, and, taking up the brochure detailing the hotel facilities, she sprawled as delicately as she could on the rose-covered counterpane and leafed through it.

Aha. As she'd hoped, garment mending was on offer. Taking a chance the person on the other end of the phone had better English than her few words of French, she dialled Housekeeping. In no time a housemaid was at the door to collect her red dress with the promise it would be hanging back in the closet within the hour.

This was the life.

She changed into her suit and was brushing her hair when Joe's crisp tap sounded on the door. Conference time.

Joe had definitely switched into CEO mode, his eyes serious and purposeful, the lines of his face taut. She grimaced. Forget any notions of a holiday. This was business.

Downstairs, they queued at the conference desk among all the other business people with their briefcases and phones. She was frowning into space, trying to remember what else Auntie Mim had told her about Jake Sinclair, when Joe suddenly took her hand and gave it a squeeze.

'Don't look so worried.' He gave her a wry smile. 'It's only the jaws of hell we're walking into.'

She grinned, her heart glowing with relief. He was still there somewhere, her tender, mocking, affectionate Joe.

Once they'd signed in and been issued with ID tags and prospectuses, he suggested they plan their agenda over coffee by the pool. Mirandi needed no persuading.

They waited for their coffees seated in comfortable armchairs on the pool terrace. The pool looked almost too inviting to resist, with its radiant aqua water lapping the tiles at its edge. The sun dappled their table, a sea-scented breeze trifled with her hair, and while she perused the conference agenda she was half aware of the holiday tang of sun lotion, splashes and shouts of laughter from people with nothing to do but play.

There were information sessions planned all that day and the next with a cocktail party to be held at the casino that evening. She read that delegates would have an opportunity to try their luck at the tables, if they so desired. She pursed her lips, frowning.

Delegates. People like her and Joe.

No one would come to Monte Carlo without visiting the casino, at least for a look. Even her father would be interested in visiting the building to view its fabled splendours. So why did she feel so uneasy?

She scoured her conscience, aware of a nasty gnawing sensation in the pit of her stomach. Admit it. She didn't want Joe to go there. Everything about it seemed so—dangerous. What if…? A frightening thought crossed her mind and she crushed it to smithereens.

That wouldn't be Joe. It just wouldn't.

A waiter brought their coffees and placed them on the low table between them.

Though who ever knew they had a weakness until opportunity crossed their path? A sickening thought crept up on her. Maybe the addiction had already claimed him. Wouldn't that explain the entire trip?

'Well, out with it,' Joe said, replacing his wallet after slipping the man a note. 'I'm sure you have an opinion.'

Mirandi glanced up warily from stirring her coffee. 'About what?'

'You know what.'

She raised the cup to her lips and sipped the creamy brew, then glanced across at him. His expression was apparently relaxed, but his black brows were drawn over his alert blue eyes and there was a curious tension in his frame, as if the fate of the world suddenly hung on her reply.

What could she say? Don't risk it, Joe? Turn away from temptation before it sucks you in like quicksand?

She gave a shrug. 'The hotel is fabulous, my room is a

dream. I have a lovely dress to wear tonight and another one tomorrow night. I'm jet-lagged and a little tired and would appreciate a long hot soak in that tub upstairs, but you're the boss. If you say I have to spend my time on the Côte d'Azur in a conference about gaming, then that's what I'll do.'

His mouth tightened. 'I get it. You disapprove, but you're just following orders.'

She blinked, startled. 'What do you want me to say?'

Anger flashed from his eyes. 'Be honest. Say what you think.'

Hot words rushed to her tongue but she bit them back. 'I'm a market analyst for an investment company, remember? Too much sensibility is a handicap for the likes of me.'

'That's no answer and you know it. It's a cop-out.'

The unexpected emotional undertow was dragging her towards saying some things she might regret. But she held her cup tight and kept her voice cool. 'If you're planning on investing in a casino I'm sure it will be very lucrative. I'm not your conscience.'

'Good,' he said curtly, rising to his feet. He pointed a warning finger. 'Just you remember that.'

But...but...what had she said? Her head swirling with bewilderment and annoyance, she followed him back inside.

'Well, anyway,' she said, hurrying to keep up with him as he strode towards the lift. 'Thousands of people go to casinos every day without coming to any harm. Millions. People are free to choose their style of entertainment. If rich people want to play games with their money...'

He halted and turned fiercely on her, grabbing her arm. '*Don't* say that to me. Don't *ever*...' His face twisted and she was shaken by a bolt of utter shock. He must have seen it because he released her arm and brought his momentary loss of cool under control. 'Sorry. I'm sorry. But—*don't* try preaching morality as per the blessed Reverend Summers at me, either. I'm here to make a reasoned decision. *You're* here as an MA, so stay out of it.'

She blinked. 'But what have I said? All I said was… You *asked* me…'

He made a stern silencing gesture.

Fuming, she folded her arms and turned her back on him on the ride up in the lift. Fine, not another word on the subject would cross her lips. If his conscience was so tender, let him deal with it on his own.

Not surprisingly, the conference sessions were an endurance. With Joe so apparently angry with her for no good reason, she felt too resentful to care if he gleaned any useful information from the various speakers with all their videos and graphs and risk projections. She listened to it all on one level and brooded on another.

Every so often she felt his eyes flick to her as if attempting to penetrate her reactions to the topics under discussion. Things about profit. Loss. Public relations. She refused to help him out. If he didn't know what she really thought of it all, then he didn't know Mirandi Summers.

He didn't recover his good humour. During the lunch break, while other delegates took the opportunity to meet each other and engage in civilised conversation on the terrace, he leaned up against the stonework looking like a thundercloud, his arms folded across his chest.

She supposed it didn't help that the roof of the casino was visible through the shrubbery, the dome and spires of the fanciful Belle Epoque extravaganza drawing admiring comments from the gathering. Luring them there.

Joe remained silent. She attempted conversation a few times but he was as impenetrable as a wall and she gave up. She'd have had no one to talk to at all if a pleasant American man hadn't started up a conversation with her when she sashayed over for a refill of her coffee.

He introduced himself as Louis. He was from Chicago.

A lawyer, he told her in his charming American drawl. He looked smooth and clever and had twinkling dark eyes and a way of looking at a woman as if she were the only person in the world. In truth, he seemed quite intrigued by her accent.

Naturally she warmed to him. She might have laughed once or twice at some of the teasing things he said about Aussies, because once she glanced over at Joe and was nearly electrocuted by his forbidding blue glare.

The sheer nerve of the guy. He wouldn't talk to her *himself*, but he didn't want her to chat with anyone else.

It was a relief to meet such an uncomplicated, friendly guy as Louis. She turned her back on Joe Sinclair, though her insides were churning with hurt and resentment at his unreasonable behaviour, and she could feel his eyes boring through the back of her skull.

Louis took out his phone and showed her pictures of himself competing in a swimming race in Lake Michigan. The event was called Big Shoulders, and the photos proved Louis had the shoulders, all right. And the chest. There was nothing wrong with his abs, either.

She was just leaning over to delve further when Joe strode up, brusquely introduced himself, shook Louis's hand in what looked like a crushing grip, then hustled her back inside the hotel.

'We need to go through our notes,' he stated.

'What notes would that be?' she snapped. 'I'm not aware you took any.'

'But you did, surely. Surely I can rely on you for *something*.'

'Well, no, you can't. I'm out of it, remember? Boss's orders.'

He closed his eyes briefly. 'Mirandi...' He made some kind of effort and the rigidity of his shoulders eased. All at once he looked so weary her heart melted with pity for him.

'Look.' He breathed deeply, his hands clenching and

unclenching. 'I'm not really in the mood for games. Try to be less provocative, will you?'

The sheer injustice of the man. She abandoned her sympathy and raised a haughty eyebrow. 'That will be hard for a woman of my renowned temperament, Joe. In fact, at the risk of being provocative, I think you're seriously overtired. If you ask me anything, you should be spending this afternoon sleeping.'

'Then it's as well I'm not asking you, isn't it?' he said in a gentle, maddeningly reasonable voice.

Hostilities didn't improve during the afternoon, although there weren't more actual words spoken. When the last interminable session ended, she and Joe stalked to the lifts to join the small crowd waiting there in stony silence.

At last there was a ping, then one set of lift doors slid open to eject a small party of women. As they emerged into the hall, chattering and laughing, one small elderly lady in the middle of the bunch suddenly stopped and stood stock still, staring.

Her face seemed to stiffen. '*Joseph.*'

Whipping a surprised glance at Joe, Mirandi saw that he seemed to have frozen still. But he was only disconcerted for a moment. Before her eyes his face smoothed into an expressionless mask.

'I'm afraid I don't know you, *madame*,' he said to the small woman, utterly chilling in his politeness. Mirandi became aware then of his grip tightening to steel on her arm and being jostled in to join the crowd in the lift.

Just before the doors closed Mirandi saw the woman halt and turn for another glimpse of them, her eyes huge in her white face.

Mirandi rubbed her arm resentfully. Conscious of the others in the small space with them, she lowered her voice. 'Who was—?'

She broke off when she glanced at Joe.

His posture had taken on a strange rigidity. His jaw was

tight—clenched, his nostrils flaring, while his eyes glittered like ice beneath his black brows. She noted with a small shock a tiny vein throbbing in his temple.

Whatever the small woman represented to Joe Sinclair, it was dynamite.

The lift stopped at their floor and they had to wait their turn to exit. As soon as they were in the hall and out of earshot of other people, she ventured to Joe, 'Are you all right?'

'What do you mean? Of course I'm *all right*.' He didn't sound all right. He reefed his hand distractedly through his hair, then made an apologetic gesture. 'Sorry. What was that you were saying? Oh, and, er…sorry about earlier. I know I've been a bit… It's been a long forty-eight hours. How about you? Are *you* all right?'

Hang on. Was she in some parallel universe? Unless her radar was way out of whack something tumultuous had just happened to Joe, and here he was talking as if she'd enquired about the weather. Though smooth enough, he couldn't disguise the unnaturalness in his tone, or the effort it was taking to produce those normal-sounding words.

Whatever the encounter meant, clearly he wasn't about to discuss it with her. Well, Mirandi Summers could take a hint. Curiosity might be killing her, but she was beginning to guess when not to intrude. Though the way things had gone for her this day she could be wrong.

Following his lead, she acted as though nothing unusual had occurred in the vestibule of the Hotel Metropole, and continued on with the artificial small talk.

Like a tightrope dancer pirouetting on point across Niagara Falls she said, 'Truthfully? I'm shattered. I can't wait to sink into a hot tub. Are you—are you planning on going to the casino tonight?'

He'd stopped to stare fixedly at a painting in the hall. It was an oil, a view of a local fishing village.

When he didn't reply she repeated her question, and

he swung around all at once to laser her with a glittering glance. He said very softly, 'Is there any reason you think I shouldn't?'

With a stab of guilt she struggled to retrieve herself. 'Well, no. Not at all. I just wondered if—since we're both quite tired…' Suddenly everywhere she turned was a no-go zone with an elephant galumphing all over it.

'Don't you want to go?' he demanded.

'Look,' she said, clenching her fists at her sides. 'I'm happy to go if you want to.'

'You really want to?' He narrowed his eyes searchingly at her.

She hesitated. '*If* you want me to.' She smiled in hopeful appeal. 'Or maybe you'd prefer to go another time when we're better rested.'

'No, I wouldn't,' he muttered grimly. 'All right then. Let's do it and get the whole bloody thing over with.' Then he seemed to collect himself a little. 'I mean, this is an important part of the whole event. We need to immerse ourselves in it to get the full picture.'

'Oh, Joe.' She rolled her eyes and couldn't help muttering to herself. 'As if you don't *know* what the full picture is.'

But his gaze had drifted back to the painting and it didn't seem to matter what she muttered, because it was pretty clear he wasn't hearing a word she was saying.

Eventually he stirred himself to move on and they reached her room. She unlocked the door, then turned to him. She cleared her throat.

'Joe, who was that woman in the lobby?'

He closed his eyes. 'No one. You know, Mirandi, you should—never give into jet-lag. It's best to carry on regardless until you drop.' He pushed back his cuff and showed her his watch. 'See? It's barely five.'

She hardly took in the time. All she could focus on was Joe's hand, shaking. Joe, the coolest, strongest, most controlled guy she'd ever met. He must have noticed it at the same time because he drew back his hand and said harshly, 'All right? I'll collect you in two hours.'

Two hours were hardly the time she needed for a decent wallow, a satisfying snooze and time to dress, but somehow she didn't feel like pushing him any further. 'Look, are you sure you're—?'

'What?' he said sharply.

'Oh, nothing. Two hours, then.'

Left to her own devices, she stood chewing her lip, speculating on the woman downstairs. The Frenchwoman.

Joe closed his door behind him and headed straight for the minibar. Thank God for single malt.

He downed a quick Scotch, then another. Somewhere through the third his heartrate slowed down to a gallop and his blood pressure felt as if it was beginning to subside. He made the effort to think.

He'd probably laugh later—much later—at the amazing irony. Of all the traps set by fate, this had to be the most diabolical. Now that the woman had sprung his presence here, she'd seek him out again, that much was certain. She'd hound him and harass him... Just as she had when he was a boy. After the funeral. As if he could ever have borne to lay eyes on her again.

Some dark injustice he was doing her clawed inside his chest but he ignored it. He'd check them out of the hotel tomorrow, first thing. Take the first flight they could catch. Mirandi had seemed enchanted with Zurich, though *anywhere*, anywhere would do. He could explain to her that the conference was too...too...

Oh, bloody hell. The board. His shareholders.

He felt moisture on his hand and looked down in surprise. Somehow the glass had broken and blood mixed with whisky was dripping from his fingers onto the floor. He glanced around for the bathroom and strode for a wash cloth.

Lucky the cut was little more than a scratch. Wrapping his hand in the cloth, he caught sight of himself in the mirror and did a double take. His heart muscle suffered another slam. Was that *him*? He looked like a guy who'd seen a ghost.

Forcing himself to breathe, he acknowledged he had, in a manner of speaking. He was a million miles from the guy in that Zurich mirror early this morning. Anyone seeing him now would think he was falling apart.

His gut clenched. Mirandi would think it. Those green eyes saw too much.

He felt an urgent, almost irresistible yearning to go in there at once, talk to her, be with her, lose himself in her. Chat about ordinary things. Make sexy small talk. Tease her and enjoy the shock in her eyes when he said something wicked. Drown in her smiling gaze. Lay his head on her soft, forgiving breasts and sleep for a hundred years.

He was actually shaking. He recognised with disbelief that he was teetering on the verge of a loss of control. He needed to get a grip. Shock must have momentarily thrown him, that was all.

He took a deep breath and leaned both hands on the vanity to steady himself. Remember your forte, Sinclair, he commanded himself. Compartmentalise. Stuff all the horrors back into their appropriate boxes and batten down the lids.

He wasn't a shell-shocked kid any more and if he could hold the past at bay *then*, he could more than do it now. Amelie Sinclair had no power to affect him. Amelie Sinclair...that little woman...

How small she'd seemed. Could she have shrunk?

He tried to calculate how old she'd be now. She was certainly showing her age. The lines beneath her eyes had deepened and multiplied. She'd looked—harmless.

Of course she was *harmless*, for God's sake. She was merely…merely…

In a determined effort to relax, he loosened his shoulders and breathed out. Concentrate on the good things. A shower, shave, and—he flinched away from thinking about the cocktail function. The casino had to be faced, though, and, admit it, he had some curiosity about the place.

It was more than time he set foot inside a casino and tested his mettle, and why not this one? After all, it was where his father had first contracted his addiction. Surely if he hadn't succumbed by now he never would. People couldn't inherit *all* their parents' genes.

He'd endure it as long as he could, then once that hurdle was past he could relax with Mirandi over dinner, and, if there truly was a God, hold her lusciousness in his arms all night and sink into blessed forgetfulness and release.

Though come to think of it, Mirandi had been astoundingly difficult all day long. Nothing had shocked or shamed her. Anyone would think she *loved* casinos. Of all the people in the world he'd thought he could rely on…

Shouldn't she be trying to talk him out of it?

A man believed he knew a woman, understood her through to her bone marrow, knew where he was with her, knew exactly what to expect from her, then the minute he took his eyes from her for a year or so she morphed into another being altogether.

If only all bathtubs came with padded neck rests. Still, the water was as hot as she could bear it, and Mirandi sank into it by degrees and relaxed.

Ah-h-h. She lay back and closed her eyes, luxuriating, thinking of Joe, running the day's conversations through her mind like a tape. It seemed to her that just about everything she'd said today had irritated him. She couldn't remember ever seeing Joe in this cantankerous mood. The guy was spoiling for a fight.

She closed her eyes, but it was hard to hold onto thoughts

with this tingling warmth permeating her bones all the way up to her chin. The sensual pleasantness lulled her into a dreamy state somewhere between a stupor and sleep until the water began to chill, then suddenly, from out of nowhere, a jarring thought pierced the mists.

Her eyes sprang open and she sat bolt upright.

If a man grew tired of a woman's company, a man suffering the effects of jet-lag and in the grip of a terrible fascination, might it not be difficult for that man to conceal his boredom and irritation? Considering they'd been in close confinement now for more than forty-eight hours, wasn't it almost inevitable that Joe *should* be fed up with her?

Was this simply a case of history repeating itself?

Now that he'd had her and achieved his victory, it wasn't impossible he'd tired of her all over again. With a nasty stab she remembered only too clearly the suddenness of his turn-around in feeling the last time. Loved and desired one day, consigned to the deep freeze the next.

With increasing desperation she scrolled through the day's events. This morning she'd been riding high, floating on a cloud of rose petals buoyed up by the warmth and intimacy of the night in his arms. Then as soon as they checked into this hotel...

Briefly she closed her eyes, then dragged herself out of the tub.

That peach and rose dress was lovely, but was lovely enough? Would that dress cut it? Maybe she needed hot, sexy and exciting.

Whatever it took, she'd glide like a goddess tonight if it killed her.

CHAPTER TEN

MIRANDI'S nerves were strung tight by the time Joe's knock sounded on her door, but she'd done her best with her appearance. At least she'd go down fighting.

She'd twisted her hair into a chignon and hadn't spared either the mascara, the eyeshadow or the ruby-red lipstick. The impossibly high stilettos from the boutique in Zurich lengthened her legs and made her appear tall and magically slender. She didn't have any diamonds, but a pendant on a silver chain drew the eye to her plunging neckline.

If she looked like something of a femme fatale, the long, wordless glance Joe razed her to the floor with when she nervously opened the door to him put at least one of her fears to flight.

In truth, his eyes riveted to her in much the same way as they had the day before in the fitting room. Her other fears weren't vanquished so quickly.

When she surveyed him looking ruggedly handsome in his beautiful dinner suit with the snowy evening shirt and black tie, she had to wonder if he was used to visiting casinos. He would fit in only too perfectly.

At the same instant she realised that despite feeling so troubled she was in deep herself, all over again. Right back where she'd been ten years ago, in the grip of an obsession with Joe Sinclair. Whatever he was, she wanted him. Madly. Absolutely. He smelled so delicious with that appealing tang of fresh, masculine shower essences. In spite of everything, drinking in the smooth kissability of his lean, tanned cheek, she could have eaten him alive on the spot.

As if he felt the current his hot gaze connected with hers, then he grabbed her right there in the doorway and dragged her up against him, searing her lips and every cell in her body in a hot, sexy kiss, tongues and all.

The clinch could have escalated to so much more if people hadn't swished by outside at that exact moment, reminding them of where they were supposed to be going.

They broke apart, and she was left reeling and aroused.

'At least that hasn't changed,' he said, his voice thick and gravelly. He touched a white handkerchief to his mouth. 'You'd better fix your lipstick.'

'Thanks,' she panted quite hoarsely, knowing her pupils were probably as dilated as his. 'I'll do that. You know you— taste of whisky.'

'Do I? *You* taste like nectar.'

Sensing a truce, she smiled and fluttered her lashes. 'And you look like James Bond.'

That might have been a bridge too far. He winced and she tensed, hoping he didn't explode. But he merely continued to scour her with hot sensual appreciation, growling, 'And you look *amazing*.'

On the bright side, whatever had rattled him about the Frenchwoman seemed to have smoothed away, though he carried an air of grim tension about him. His eyes were flint hard and he had a sort of coiled purpose.

As they paused in the queue before the grand entrance to the casino to search for their passes she felt him brace as for an ordeal. When it was their turn, she tucked her hand into the crook of his arm and glided in beside him.

Her first overwhelming impression, apart from the dazzling

chandeliers, was the buzz of the place. Strains of an orchestra reached them and it was impossible not to be infected by a thrilling pulse of excitement in the air.

Cocktails were served in the atrium. 'Oh, Joe,' she exclaimed when they entered the magnificent marble hall. 'Oh, look. It *is* a gilded palace. It really is.'

She spun around to gaze at the glorious ceilings, adorned with gold leaf and frescoed paintings high above a gallery supported by ionic columns. Off to one side of the salon an orchestra played.

Quite a large assembly of delegates to the conference had chosen to attend, and the salon was crowded with people in evening dress. After a short interval one of the conference hosts stepped up onto a dais at one end with a little speech of welcome, inviting them all to enjoy the drinks and the music, dance a little, dine in any of the restaurants and visit any of the public rooms.

In spite of her gnawing anxiety all at once she felt eager to see as much as she could of this jewel of the Belle Epoque.

Joe surveyed the beautiful salon with a serious gaze. 'My father came here as a young man. He was in love with the architecture of the place.' He made a grimace. 'Unfortunately it wasn't the architecture that stayed with him.'

Startled, she looked quickly at him. He'd rarely ever spoken of his father, never of his addiction, and she found this unexpected openness heartening.

A waiter materialised beside them with a tray of drinks. After a moment's hesitation Mirandi accepted a tall flute of champagne. Accepting one himself, Joe turned a surprised gaze on her.

'I'd thought you didn't indulge.'

'I do sometimes.'

'But haven't you made some sort of vow?' He looked almost

disapproving, frowning from her to her guilty glass, and she was aware of a tiny spurt of annoyance.

She smiled tightly. 'Listen to you. You sound like Auntie Mim.'

'I'm shocked, that's all.'

He sipped his own wine, glancing absently about at the guests without apparently noticing his glaring double standard. Then he turned back to her.

'You didn't drink on the plane.'

She shrugged.

'Or in Zurich.'

'I don't enjoy drinking on planes. I didn't feel like wine in Zurich. I was high enough.' She lifted her eyebrows. 'Remember?'

'But…' His jaw hardened and, like a mastiff worrying a bone, he shook his head. 'In the apartment the other afternoon you said…I'm *sure* you said…'

She stared at him in surprise. 'What? That I don't drink during working hours? For goodness' sake, Joe, does it matter?'

'No, no. It's just that…I guess I'm surprised. I keep expecting you to be…'

'What? *Perfect?*' She rolled her eyes, then conscious she might have seemed to be overreacting a tad, pasted on a smile. 'Sorry.' She gave his arm a pat. 'I'm afraid it's too late. I broke my non-alcohol rule years ago. In your presence, if you remember.'

He shook his head. 'Yeah, but…'

But. Always a but.

She laughed, though the truth was her neck was growing hot and she was beginning to feel irritated. So she'd broken her pledge. Millions did it. Face it, in her father's eyes she was a sinner and hellfire awaited her. She had her moments of discomfort about that, but it was her problem. What was *wrong* with the man?

'I'm sure you didn't ever drink very much,' he went on, warming to his theme. 'You couldn't take more than a glass, as I recall.'

'Still can't really. I hope you're not *too* disappointed at how I've turned out.' Like the loose woman she was, she gave her champagne a slurp then ran her tongue-tip provocatively over her top lip. 'I'll try to improve later and be the Miss Goody-Two-Shoes of your imagination.'

She was relieved then to see his eyes gleam with their usual one-track wickedness. He slipped his arm around her and brushed her ear with his lips. 'Not *too* good, I hope. I *like* the way you've turned out.'

Oh, he smelled so fantastically male. Still, it took her a few minutes to quite lose that prickly feeling. She was starting to feel as if she had competition. The Mirandi Summers of ten years ago must have left quite an impression.

Perhaps affected by the dazzle of their legendary surroundings and assisted by French champagne, the dull bankers and business people of the conference had acquired some sparkle to match their pretty jewellery. As the waiters circulated among them with trays laden with drinks and hors d'oeuvres, the conversation rose to a hum and she and Joe found themselves drawn into a circle of bankers and billionaires and their partners.

As she might have expected here of all places, the conversation was mainly about the play. Some of the people were keen to share their experiences at the tables, while others remained silent and watchful.

Joe was one of the silent ones, listening and absorbing, and Mirandi felt her unease increase. This wasn't a good place for Joe, among these people. Too many skeletons were present. Too many seductive influences.

She wished she could just relax, and that she and Joe could be like all those other couples who were here on a night out.

Laughing, dining and dancing, then going home and making love without any anxieties and undercurrents.

She glanced at him, so darkly handsome in his dinner suit, and her entire being clenched with yearning. Why was it that the more barriers she sensed between them, the more she wanted him?

Dancing was under way. A few couples at first, then more as the tempo of the party gathered pace. At one stage she saw Louis from Chicago pushing a statuesque blonde around the dance floor.

'How about it?' she suggested brightly, tilting her head towards the dancers.

Joe made a grimace. 'I'm not really in the mood. Later, maybe?'

Fine. She wasn't desperate to be held in anyone's arms. Other people began to drift towards the salons where the games were under way, so she and Joe followed, strolling from room to room, gazing at the magnificent decor and artwork in each unique space. She couldn't really enjoy it. After the dancing rejection her confidence had started to slip, and she was too burningly aware of the groups riveted by the action at the tables. In some of those grand salons the air fairly crackled with suspense.

If she was so aware of the allure of those tables, how must Joe feel?

They paused at a roulette table and remained there for minutes, mesmerised. The croupier called for a halt to the bids and, as one, the gamblers hunched, poised over the wheel with avid eyes, their adrenaline almost palpable in the air. When the wheel stopped spinning and the ball rolled to its final resting place, all but one set of shoulders slumped a little. A pile of chips was raked towards the flushed, radiant young guy who was the winner, while others at the table watched with hooded gazes, then prepared to place more bids, hunger in their eyes.

She couldn't deny the hypnotic pull of the game and began to feel almost hypersensitive to the tension she'd sensed in Joe ever since their descent into Monte Carlo. Was the fever in this room infecting his blood?

He turned towards her and she could feel him watching her, assessing her reactions. Though he appeared so smooth and controlled, she sensed some subterranean current churning in him, despite his genial responses. She felt a sudden, almost desperate impulse to drag him to some non-threatening place where they could just be natural and open with each other and pretend the past had never happened.

She made an attempt to draw him away, tugging at his sleeve. 'Why don't we…? How about we have dinner some-where in the city? There were some interesting restaurants on the other side of the hotel.'

His eyes glinted. 'Why not here?' Her heart sank as she read the almost sardonic amusement in his gaze. 'Not enough action for you, or too much?' His sudden piercing glance pen-etrated her suspicious soul like a laser beam. 'Are you feeling uncomfortable here, Mirandi?'

She flushed. 'No, not at all. I'm sure *here* would be fantas-tic, though without having booked a table…' She swallowed as she heard the lameness of the excuse. 'Do you think we'd have much chance?' His quizzical brows lifted higher and she hastened to add, 'I mean it would be terrific if we *could*. Heavens—it's so sophisticated. I'm sure every restaurant here must be—wonderful. Everything's—so—so—elegant. The chefs probably have Michelin stars coming out of their ears. I'm sure they're probably booked out every night of the week. People from all over must come here…'

When she finally ran out of assurances he said gently, 'Let's put it to the test, shall we?'

Great. She'd talked him into the very thing she wanted to avoid. And just her luck, a smooth and efficient maître d'hotel found them a table at once in Le Train Bleu, a restaurant atmospherically decorated to resemble a gracious wagon-lit of the thirties.

The food might have been superb, but she failed to do hers justice. Green risotto with chanterelle mushrooms was certainly delicious, whether or not real snails had been sacrificed to create it, but it required a woman with a calm and confident stomach to dig in with gusto, and hers was anything but.

Instead she drank more wine, perhaps a little defiantly. She kept glancing at Joe when she sipped to see how her indulgence in the stuff was affecting him, but though he looked at her from time to time his expression remained impassive.

Somehow the more she worried, the more Joe exuded calm and composure. He tucked into his filet with enthusiasm, and finished up all her leftovers, including the truffled potatoes and the tarte de citron she'd optimistically ordered for dessert.

At the end of the meal when the bill was paid and the coffees nearly empty, she said, 'Shall we go back to the hotel? Have an early night?'

'First I think we should try our luck at the tables.'

Her heart plummeted, and she couldn't restrain herself from bursting out, 'Oh, Joe, *why*?'

'Why not?' He was scrutinising her, a curious light in his eyes. 'Since we're here, it seems silly not to taste the experience.'

She stared at him in appeal, imploring him with everything she could bring to bear. 'But…I can't do that. You know I can't.'

'Why not? Live dangerously. Take a walk on the wild side. Isn't that what you love?'

'Well…' She closed her eyes. '*No*— Look, it probably sounds uncool, but…' The words were dredged out of her. 'Don't mock, but you know I once made a promise. This is the one I *can't* break.' He smiled and started to speak but she hastened on. 'Try to understand.' Visions assailed her of all those sad people her father had brought home in the early hours. Knocks on the door in the dead of night. Broken, desperate people with nowhere else to turn. 'After—after all those years my father worked at the shelter... Then in Lavender Bay... All those poor people he's helped...'

Joe's blue gaze held hers, then he said drily, 'I think you're thinking of *my* father.'

She gazed wordlessly at him, then lowered her eyes. 'Yes.'

A silence fell between them, deeper than the deepest gully on the Mediterranean floor. Then he said in a quiet, level tone, 'I'm not mocking. You see, this is *my* challenge. I don't want you to participate if it hurts you. If you don't want to stay I'll take you back to the hotel.'

Her heart thudded and she squeezed her hands together. 'But, Joe, I... Must you? Do you really have to do it?'

'Believe it.' He regarded her with an intent, shimmering gaze for seconds, then he rose. 'Come on. I'll take you home first and you won't have to watch.'

She stood up and grabbed her purse. '*Oh*, I can see you're already sucked in.' Her throat had thickened and made her voice croakier than a frog's. 'Do you know what? You're a fool, Joe Sinclair.'

She marched out ahead of him, as far as it was possible to march in a skintight dress and very high heels. He attempted to steer her towards the entrance, but she snapped, her eyes swimming all at once, 'No, I'm not leaving. I intend to stay and watch the whole ghastly catastrophe.'

He broke into a grim laugh. 'Now who's talking like Auntie Mim?'

Then, true to his mad intent, ignoring all her pleading and the common sense he was born with, he headed for the salon where he'd already been hypnotised by the roulette wheel.

CHAPTER ELEVEN

MIRANDI only watched for a minute or two after Joe joined the crowd at the roulette table. It was too painful to see him ignore everything she'd said, exchange his precious hard-earned cash for chips, push a stack of them onto a square marked out in the green baize, then concentrate all his brilliance on a spinning wheel.

Instead, she retreated to the bar, commandeered one of the elegant bar stools and focused her blurry gaze on the bartender, whose white dinner jacket set off his Mediterranean tan and flashing dark eyes to perfection. If she tilted her head to the right she could just see Joe's back reflected in the mirror behind the bar, but she couldn't bear to look too often.

She ordered a flirtini with a squirt of pomegranate juice, and anguished. This could be the start of Joe's slide into ruin right here and now, and what good was she? When the chips were down, she could only look on, wailing and gnashing her teeth. What if he was so hooked she couldn't drag him away for days? Weeks even?

It was a disaster, but she couldn't help feeling some indignation towards him. He'd told her he wanted her along as a friend, his sounding board, but the minute she gave him some friendly advice he flung it back in her teeth. Accusing her of sounding like Auntie Mim when all she was trying to do was to save him from himself.

Auntie Mim indeed. She was as far from being like Auntie

Mim as it was possible to get. Ever since they'd arrived in Monte Carlo she'd bent over backwards to go with the flow and not lecture him, when the truth was... When what she secretly ached to do... *Someone* should tell him the truth.

Here she'd been secretly beaming and hugging herself about being back together with him. Admit it, she'd been wishing and hoping as the song said. Praying their relationship would stick this time round. Believing that since they'd grown up they could behave towards each other like adults.

Why did the past always have to dog their footsteps?

She dabbed at her eyes with a tissue, wishing she had the physical strength to march over there, grab Joe by the scruff and haul him out, away from the bitter influences of his past and into the twenty-first century.

The flirtini was honey smooth, and she was halfway through it when someone strolled up and parked on the bar stool second along from hers. She glanced up into the mirror and saw it was Louis.

Without appearing to notice her presence, although how he could have missed her was the biggest mystery since the pyramids, he ordered a whisky. Sporting the traditional evening wear and having allowed his beard to make an interesting stubble, he still wasn't looking quite as chipper as he'd been at the lunch. In truth, he looked a little the worse for wear, and he was frowning into his Scotch as if he had something on his mind.

Perhaps the blonde hadn't worked out. Pity, but everyone in the world had problems. It was a bittersweet symphony, right?

After a while he turned her way and gave a stagey little start as if seeing her there was a complete surprise, then made a long, slow and very comprehensive survey. He took a meditative sip of his drink.

'That's some dress.'

'Thanks.'

He gave his eyebrows a seductive tilt. 'You know, you're a very lovely woman.'

'That's what Joe says.'

On another occasion she might have enjoyed crushing Louis' pretensions with a little robust repartee, but right at this minute, with Joe embarking on a life of misery and decadence, she felt too lacklustre to rise to her usual heights.

Perhaps Louis heard the listlessness in her tone, because he swivelled his stool around until he was facing her. 'Oh, you mean Tough Guy. You know, I noticed you the minute you walked in with him.'

'And I'm sure he noticed you noticing.'

He grinned in acknowledgement of her warning shot, flashing his perfect American teeth. Then he nodded his head and sighed. 'What is it with chicks? They make themselves gorgeous for a guy and all he's interested in is a little ball rolling around a wheel.'

That struck a nerve, but she tried not to show it. Forced herself not to even blink or wring her hands, though she wanted to severely. 'He's just trying it out to see if he likes it.'

'Seems to be loving it, from where I'm sitting. Totally entranced, when he has this beautiful woman sitting here all alone weeping into her beer with her loneliness.'

'Oh, rubbish, I'm not. I'm possibly just a bit jet-lagged, is all.'

He sighed again. 'It's a crying shame, the way good women are neglected.'

'That's not true,' she retorted. For one thing, who could ever call her a good woman? She wasn't even very useful as a sounding board. She was probably no better than she ought to be, as Auntie Mim would say. And no doubt *had*.

Over at the roulette table Joe caught the croupier's eye and pushed some chips onto the red seventeen. As the wheel started to rotate he threw a glance back at the bar and froze as something like a red hot needle skewered straight through his guts.

He couldn't believe his eyes. That American guy was hanging around Mirandi again, smooching up to her with his smooth looks and phony charm.

Was the guy a fool? His persistence was astounding.

Though he had to admit she was irresistible in that dress. Any man seeing her adorning that bar stool with her rich glossy hair and graceful curves, one long leg swinging a little, would desire her. He'd already warned the guy off once. What more would it take?

It flashed through his mind that it had probably been a mistake to leave her alone.

Although she wasn't a child. She could look after herself. And there was no way she would encourage the guy. Surely.

'*Dix-sept rouge*. Red seventeen,' the croupier intoned, dragging Joe's gaze away.

Frowning, he glanced at the table and saw that his small pile of chips had magically enlarged. Looking around, he saw the anonymous strangers at the table staring at him, some with kindness, others envy, in their hungry eyes.

His gaze lit on the young man who'd been there since early on. The boy's glow of success had long since departed. His chips had dwindled to a few, and for an instant Joe glimpsed a desperation in his eyes that brought his father's face before him with such a gut-wrenching immediacy he nearly swayed in his chair.

He shrugged off the image and steeled himself to focus on his task.

'*Nouveau jeu*,' the croupier announced. 'Your bids, *mesdames et messieurs*?'

Making a hasty selection, Joe shoved some chips forward, then edged his chair around so he could get a better view of the bar.

* * *

Mirandi gave her flirtini a desultory swizzle then popped the maraschino cherry into her mouth. It had an unpleasant, chewy texture. A couple approached the bar and Louis made a huge production of making room for them, in the process finding himself forced to shift to the stool next to hers.

Surprise, surprise.

She noticed his cologne. It smelled expensive, like some artfully manufactured designer fragrance. He smiled at her, stroking his designer bristles while he continued his sly interrogation about the shortfalls of her alleged lover.

'I guess *Joe* would have made certain you had some fun too. Did he spin you around the dance floor?' He said Joe's name with a sarcastic inflection she didn't warm to.

'Oh, well, he would have, but…' *Listen* to her, lying through her teeth for a man who'd rather play roulette than spend an hour with her. 'I was tired.'

'You don't look tired.'

Much Louis knew. Her nerves had been so ragged all day she felt exhausted. It was only the adrenaline in the room propping her up. And the knots in her stomach.

'Did you hear the orchestra?' Louis said. 'Not bad for a European outfit.'

He fell silent, swirling the remains of his Scotch musingly around his glass. After a while he glanced at her. 'They have the doors open to the gardens now and people are dancing outside on the terrace.' He lowered his lashes, seduction in his dark eyes, then made a suggestive waggle of his eyebrows. 'Under the moon.'

She had to hand it to Louis for nerve, trying to waltz her off under Joe's very nose. She even contemplated the invitation for a moment. Dancing with Big Shoulders in the moonlight, smelling his classy cologne. He was attractive enough, but everything inside her rose up in revolt.

She glanced across at Joe's broad back. Everything seemed to have gone wrong since they arrived in Monte Carlo. If only she could get him away from this place, think of a way to retrieve that wonderful feeling that was growing between them again in Switzerland, she'd do it, whatever it took.

'Listen, Louis,' she said, 'I'm not in the mood for dancing. If you wouldn't mind, I'd appreciate it if you'd just—'

'Hey now.' He stopped her, shocked at her forthrightness. 'Don't let's be negative. Come on, what are you drinking?' He tossed off the remains of his drink, set down his glass and slid it along to the bartender, adding, 'The lady needs another... what is it? Ah, sure it is. A flirtini.'

He chuckled.

Joe watched the croupier push the pile of chips towards him with a curious sense of impatience. Hundreds, five hundreds, thousands, who cared? Couldn't they hurry it along? He wasn't a possessive guy by any means, but it gnawed at him that after the trip and everything they'd said and hadn't said but had surely meant, not least the night in Zurich, Mirandi would flirt with some guy.

Here he was putting himself through this harrowing ordeal and she was fairly tearing a hole in his chest.

He angled around for another glimpse of her and did a double take. The American had insinuated himself onto the barstool next to her. His body language said it all. And if Joe wasn't mistaken, that drink she was holding was *fresh*.

He sprang to his feet and covered the distance between the roulette table and the bar in less than a click of his fingers. He bore down on Mirandi Summers, a complex mix of outrage, disappointment and pure molten rage boiling in his veins, and snatched the glass from her fingers.

'Joe.' Her startled gaze widened. 'What...?'

He turned on the American guy and snarled, 'Here. Take this with you.' He stuffed the glass into the guy's hand.

Perhaps dreaming of defending himself, the American

set the glass on the bar. 'Now hang on there, buddy. This lady is—'

'She's with *me*,' Joe informed him through gritted teeth.

The American looked about him as if begging Security to come beefing down on them from all directions, then stood up and held up his hands.

'All right, all right, tough guy. Chill.' He made a mock apologetic gesture to Mirandi. 'Sorry, ma'am, if my presence *offended* you.' Then his amused gaze shifted back to Joe. 'Take it easy, man. No offence intended. Mirandi—I mean *your ladyfriend* here—was looking a little blue. I was only cheering her up.'

He grimaced in what was intended as a suave smile, then swivelled on his heel and made as dignified an exit as a guy could, under those circumstances.

His hackles still bristling, Joe swung around to Mirandi and encountered sparkling emerald anger.

'Just where do you think you are?' she snapped in a low voice. 'That could have been the most ghastly and embarrassing scene. Lucky *Louis* is a gentleman.' She collected her purse and slid off her bar stool.

'*Louis* is a gigolo.'

'Oh, what would you know?' she retorted. 'You were too interested in watching some stupid little spinning ball. For all you cared I could have been getting it on with the bartender.'

'Is he your type?' He felt her withering look but it glanced off him like an arrow. Ridiculously, his emotions seemed to be engaged and he said, far too harshly for the size of the offence, 'I don't know how you could even *think* of encouraging that guy.'

As soon as the words were out he wanted to bite them back, but her expression told him it was too late. She started stalking towards the exit, something it wouldn't have been unpleasant to watch in other circumstances with the voluptuous sway of her hips. He wanted to run after her, but was distracted when an attendant in a tuxedo approached and held out a cloth bag.

'Your winnings, *monsieur*. Please exchange them at the bank.' He indicated the teller's cage at the end of the room.

'Look,' Joe said, exasperated. 'I haven't got time for that now. You take them.' He looked around for Mirandi but there was no sign of her.

'But *monsieur*...' The man appeared shocked. 'I cannot... We must not... It is not permitted...'

'Sorry, mate,' Joe said, pushing past the guy. 'You deal with it. There's someone I need to catch up with.'

What the hell was she playing at? He couldn't see her anywhere in the room. With a nasty lurch he wondered if she'd gone after that American. She was mad enough to do something crazy like that. He'd noticed several times lately that this new Mirandi Summers had quite a temper when she was aroused.

His eye was caught by a flash of red in the adjoining salon.

He took off in pursuit, threading his way through knots of people, dodging waiters, questions resurfacing in his mind at her having allowed the American to chat her up in his very sight.

Faster than the speed of light a million thoughts jabbed his brain. Had she changed this much? Was this how seriously she took him now? He couldn't suppose she was attracted to the guy, not after last night, but whoever knew with women? One minute they seemed to be happy with a man, the next they were headed off into the wild blue yonder ready to take up with the first new gun that came along.

With a sickening jolt he realised that, to be true to himself, if he couldn't trust her he'd have to pull the plug on her. Sever all connections.

Although, perhaps he was overreacting and it needn't come

to that. Probably what he'd witnessed had been nothing more
than a conversation. He should, he really should, give her the
benefit of the doubt. He entered the next dazzling chamber
only to see the red flash of her dress disappear down a hallway, and gritted his teeth with frustration as people got in his
way.

Why wouldn't she wait?

He hurried into the hall and had nearly closed the distance
between them only to see that it wasn't Mirandi's red dress he
was following but some other woman's. Where the hell *was*
she?

He glanced about and experienced such a plunge of anxiety
he had to stop to draw a few deep breaths and take stock. For
God's sake, Joe Sinclair did *not* run an emotional overdraft.
Cool it, man. Take a sophisticated view. Nothing had happened. She hadn't gone off with the guy, had she?

As he strode on to the next salon, in an attempt to be rational he fought with the evil genius that had taken over his
brain. Face it, this reaction to a little harmless flirting was
out of character. Hypocritical, even. How many times had he
done the same thing himself? And when had he ever cared
what his girlfriends did on the side? If he found out they were
dishonest he simply cut them off, no emotion involved.

He *knew* that, but a part of his brain was standing back in
bemusement, watching the rest of him get all churned up. It
even occurred to him that perhaps this absurd raw feeling as
if his guts had been chopped into little pieces was merely the
aftermath of the test he'd set himself tonight.

It had been quite confronting, after all. And it had been
a long day. Suddenly the unwonted vision of the shock he'd
encountered that afternoon popped back into his head and he
felt his blood pressure leap to a higher bracket.

His mind shied away from Amelie Sinclair. He'd think
about her later. The one thing he *was* dead set certain about
was this. Of all the women he'd ever known in his life Mirandi

Summers was the one, the *only* one, he'd never expected to have to doubt.

She really had some explaining to do. When he got his hands on her...

He searched the place, striding grimly from room to room, scanning for that splash of red, often forced to check his stride to avoid a whirling crowd. He was swept into one salon that was grand indeed, its panelled wall space dominated by an enormous and sensuous painting of three lovely nudes. Beneath the incredible rococo ceilings were giant windows festooned with hundreds of metres of satin.

The magnificence was lost on him. There was only one beauty he wanted to lay eyes on, and she wasn't there. He couldn't see her anywhere.

From somewhere close by he heard a lush-stringed tango playing and felt a surge of hope. Something about the music suggested a live orchestra. He turned from the crowded salon and followed the strains until he found himself back in the atrium. The reception was well under way, almost the entire room given over to couples dancing.

And she was there. With a lightening in his chest he saw her across the room, her face pale and wan, clinging to the wall, looking about her for someone. With a violent pang in his gut he thought, *Who?* The American?

He stifled the feeling, and, desperate to talk with her, *reason* with her, wove a path through the crowd of dancers. He was beside her before she had a chance to notice his approach.

He touched her shoulder. 'What the bloody hell do you think you're *doing*?'

She turned with a start, and he saw her momentary look of relief change as she registered his tone. Had he actually shouted?

She stiffened a little. 'I was looking for the entrance.'

'You were planning to leave? By *yourself*?'

'Why not? I'm free and over twenty-one.' She folded her arms and angled away from him.

He compressed his lips, knowing he'd provoked that haughty reaction by his damned impatience. Hell, he really needed to tone himself down. Trouble was, the noise and activity in the room was not conducive to the quiet heart-to-heart he needed with her.

He glanced about for some peaceful corner to take her and noticed that the doors to the terrace had been opened. 'Look, let's get away from this racket.'

She scanned him with a small appraising frown, hesitating, then accompanied him outside into the balmy Mediterranean night without any more trouble. A few couples were strolling the terrace, and he could hear giggles coming from the extensive gardens. His gaze was drawn down a never-ending vista of ponds and fountains.

It was atmospheric down there, he supposed, with all the fountains playing in the moonlight. Shadowy pathways led off to either side, lit by glimmering lights, and here and there classical statues peeped from among the shrubbery, coyly covering their private parts. Some sweet summery scent like honeysuckle flavoured the air.

If only things were different and he could have established some bottom line with Mirandi, a stroll in the moonlit garden with her would not have been a bad thing. Or mightn't have been. If only she hadn't…

He felt something raw in his chest, but his life's practice had been to ignore pain, and he carried on with his usual aplomb. Trouble was, his voice came out sounding strangely hoarse.

'We really need to talk,' he rasped.

'Yes, I think we do.' Though she was still rather proud and stiff, out here in the night air her voice had a sweet silvery quality, as if she were made of magic. He had that feeling of being a huge hulking angry brute while she was a fragile, elusive creature, but the situation had to be faced.

She still had the power to gut him.

But could he just let it happen? Sure she'd grown up a lot, he could see that now, but a guy needed to make his expectations clear. As always he would be civilised about it and employ subtle tactics, though this was one time he felt the need to let her see just where she'd gone wrong and what she was doing to him.

He cleared his throat. 'Look, I've got to tell you I felt— disappointed about you flirting with that guy.'

She looked indignantly at him. 'I *wasn't* flirting.' She sounded so firm and unequivocal, he had to admit it had the ring of truth.

'I saw how he was looking at you.'

'But did you see how I was looking at *him*?'

Always so sassy. Always quick with an answer, he could give her that. She was clever, so bright. No wonder she'd always kept him interested. He felt a wave of intense regret at how much he'd miss that.

'He bought you that drink,' he accused.

'He ordered it before I could stop him. After I told him to get *lost*.' Her mouth trembled. 'He forced it on me and I just… You're not listening to me, are you? You never listen. You haven't listened to a word I've said all day. You just went ahead and risked your—your *life*…'

His guts were churning. 'Is that why you did it? You were angry. You wanted to punish me?'

'I wasn't angry. I was—*scared*. Anyway…' her voice wobbled, with all the emotion running high '…since when do you care who I talk to?'

'Since always.' The truth of that statement tightened around his chest like a garotte.

He thought of that awful day when she was just a kid and he'd had to tell her it was over.

She was twisting her hands in front of her, her graceful white arms satin in the moonlight. 'Oh, that's just not true,

Joe. You didn't care about me back then, not the littlest bit, even though I told you… I all but *told* you, how I—I… You wanted to live free and easy. That's what you said. You didn't want to clutter your life with responsibilities.'

He closed his eyes. 'I *had* to say that. It couldn't go anywhere with us, could it?' Something had a stranglehold on his larynx and was putting his voice through a strainer. 'Look, it was ten years ago. We both knew you were too young. Your father said… Even *I* could see he was right. You needed to go to uni. How great a life would it have been with no money coming in?'

Her eyes glistened with tears. 'As if it was ever about money. It never even occurred to you that day, did it, that I might be…? What I'd come to tell you. No, of course it didn't,' she muttered. 'You couldn't have known. And even if you had you'd have run twice as fast.' She made a hopeless little gesture. 'Oh, I'm such a fool. I don't know why I agreed to come. I let myself get sucked in all over again in Zurich, and here we are. So over, how could I even have…?' Her voice choked and she turned sharply away from him.

A gentle breeze messed a few strands of her hair and when she lifted her hand to smooth it he could see that her fingers were trembling. He cast about for something to say but his speech was paralysed. Suddenly an almighty black catastrophe was bearing down on him and he felt helpless to avert it.

'This was such a mistake,' she said, her voice nearly as hoarse as his. She turned for the stairs that led down to the garden. 'I'm going home.'

He watched her step down onto the garden walk, the impassioned phrases they'd hurled at each other rolling around in his head in meaningless clusters, his whole being churned up in a way he scarcely recognised.

She was walking quickly away with her head high, but even from behind he could tell she was crying. He stood there like a clumsy thunderstruck oaf while she rounded a bend in the path, then disappeared from his view, hidden by the shrubbery and the walls of a small folly that had been built to resemble some Roman temple.

All at once the cold reality that she was seriously walking away from him for all eternity slammed into him and a bolt of pure panic galvanised him to action.

He bounded down the steps after her and sprinted to catch her up. 'Wait, Mirandi… *Wait*.' She didn't pause, instead her step quickened and he had a suffocating sense of déjà vu, as if he were back in the dream. At least this was real life and his legs could work, and he swiftly covered the ground between them and came up alongside her.

'What couldn't I have known? What? What did you mean?' Panting, urgent, he grabbed her arms and forced her to stand still. 'What would I have run from?'

She trembled in his hands, her arms cool in the night air. In the dim light she was whiter than he'd ever seen, her lovely face strained and streaked with tears. 'Are you sure you want to know? It's something *sad*, Joe.'

He said roughly, his voice as hoarse as a foghorn, 'Don't you think I might have already known sad things once or twice?'

She lowered her wet lashes. 'Oh, I know. You have, of course.' She moistened her lips. 'All right, then.' She glanced around, making sure no one was nearby to overhear. Then she said in a low voice, 'What I meant to tell you that day, and would have if you'd been more welcoming, was that I was—expecting.'

He felt the blood drain from his heart. '*What?*'

She nodded. 'I'd only just found out.' She broke away from him and made a helpless gesture. 'I was in such a spin I didn't know *what* to do. I thought if I told you, but—well, you know how things went.'

He reeled away from her, flooded by the most appalling guilt and remorse. 'Oh. Oh, my God.' He clutched his forehead, ran his hand through his hair while his wits tried to assemble the facts.

A pregnant girl came to see him, to inform she was with child, *his* child, and he was intent on rejecting her. For her own good.

'Oh, no,' he ground out. 'My poor girl. Mirandi, I—I don't know what to say. I'm so very sorry. If only I'd known. I—I wish I hadn't had to…' He closed his eyes. 'I wish it hadn't been like that.' A jolting thought struck him. 'So where is your—your child?'

His child.

'There isn't one,' she said baldly, dashing sudden tears away with the back of her hand. 'I only managed to keep him inside a couple of months and…something went wrong, I guess. I lost him.'

His guts clenched as though held in a vice. He imagined her rounded and vulnerable, and a groan escaped him as the implications of what she must have gone through lacerated his guilty conscience.

He *had* to ask, though he hardly dared for fear of what her answer might be. 'Sweetheart, did you—did your father *know* you were pregnant that day you came to see me?'

She shook her head and he could feel that measure of relief, at least. At least the captain hadn't begged him to cut his daughter loose knowing she was with child.

With a womanly dignity that impressed him, he saw her make a visible effort to control her emotions.

She said in a low voice, 'I was in Brisbane when it happened. When I—when I lost the baby. That was why I *chose* Brisbane, so I could put some distance between my family and—everyone before I broke the news. I was scared of telling Dad. As it turned out, I never needed to. It was—quite a—a painful time.' Her voice croaked on the word and he felt his heartstrings twist savagely.

'Oh, sweetheart.' He put his arms around her, drew her

against his chest and laid his cheek against her hair. He could feel her soft breasts, her heart beating against his own. He pressed her to him and stroked her, struggling with the old dilemma. Tell her the whole truth and risk turning her against her dad? Hurt her even more?

She angled her face into his neck and even in the exigency of emotion the scent of her rose in his nostrils like an aphrodisiac.

'I should've been there,' he said painfully. 'I should've been *with* you…'

'Oh, Joe.' She sighed and her breath fanned his neck. 'What would have been the use? You were already tired of me. You're tired of me now.'

'I wasn't tired of you. I'm not—I could *never* be tired of you.' He felt some hard inner shell give inside his chest and suddenly he was awash with raw, hot emotion and truth could no longer be contained. 'It *killed* me to break it off,' he said, his voice as rough as if it were being strained through gravel. 'Afterwards I missed you… All those nights I *ached* for you… A hundred times I nearly gave in and texted you.'

'Then why…?'

'Because I knew he was right, your father. It didn't matter how angry I felt, how—rebellious, I s'pose—I knew it was true. You were too young and I had nothing to give you. I wasn't even sure of what direction I wanted to go in. I'm *still* not sure.'

'Oh, Joe, Dad doesn't think like that.'

He held her a little away from him and ruefully scanned her face. How well did she understand her father?

Moisture glistened on her lashes. Her sensuous mouth was so soft and luscious his blood quickened with desire, and whatever else he *should* have said the time for talking was over. Unable to resist, with a groan he took her sweet lips, tenderly at first, then as her soft curves sank against him and he had the taste of her, God help him, he was overtaken with lust and kissed her deeply and hungrily.

The sound of approaching voices made an annoying distraction. But he was as hard as a log, and, trembling with urgency, he drew her off the path and into a shadowy niche between some dense, fragrant shrubs and the stone balustrade of the folly.

As he hid with her there in the secluded shadowy place, all at once the moonlit night seemed to ping with a taut expectation, as if reckless spirits were winging on the vibrant air. Bending to taste her white satin throat, he heard her quickened breath, felt her breasts rise and fall under his hands, and his passion to have her intensified.

For an instant he paused, and it was like the lull before the storm. He sensed her answering excitement as she panted in his arms, aroused by their forbidden location, infected by the honeysuckle-scented magic of the night.

The electric moment intensified, then he took her mouth, kissing her back against the wall while he unzipped his trousers and allowed his straining shaft its grateful freedom. Her fragrance, part perfumed sweetness, part primitive, aroused woman, stormed his senses in an irresistible erotic invasion. With lustful haste he dragged up the red dress. Already her undies were excitingly moist, and he tore them away with hands that shook, inflamed by the exposure of the delicious curls. Positioning her carefully, he supported her bottom with his hands while she clung to his neck and wrapped her legs around his waist, then he thrust into her, evoking a guttural cry from deep in her throat.

He drove and drove again, deeper and harder, while she gripped him with her thighs and met him thrust for thrust, her hot, slick walls blissfully tight around his length. The sweet, painful pressure mounted, but he held himself back from the ultimate ecstasy until he felt her first honeyed spasm grip him like a heavenly vice, then his orgasm broke in a hot, wild release of rushing seed.

As her last rapturous cries melted into silence he held her panting in his arms, tasting the sweet, slightly salt sweat on her neck.

She was *his*, was all he was capable of thinking. He couldn't let her go again. He couldn't.

CHAPTER TWELVE

SOMETHING crept into Mirandi's awareness, strange bird calls, followed some time later by occasional muffled bumps and thuds. Then much later sudden flurries of voices, surprisingly close, and sounds of gushing water that might have come from outside.

Sensing the morning, she swam closer to consciousness. She had an awareness then of a feeling of warmth down the length of her back, a solid, comfortable presence she'd relied on through the night.

She opened her eyes. As she blinked at the light issuing through chinks in the curtains she had the sensation the morning was well advanced. Gradually the mists of sleep dispersed and everything came crowding back.

The casino and her quarrel with Joe. She'd come so close to throwing in the towel again, but somehow the situation had turned about and… Had that *really* happened? Love in the casino gardens, just like their wild old days? She smiled, remembering it all with that intoxicated, laughing, rapturous walk home.

As she turned Joe's words over in her mind about their ancient break-up she almost felt like pinching herself. After all the anguish she'd suffered back then, to discover that he'd broken her heart with the best of intentions evoked some mixed feelings. Had he somehow found out about her family's concerns? She must have let it leak out. She wrinkled her row in the effort to recall. It was all so long ago the sequence of events had blurred in her mind, except of course for her secret grief. She had no doubt that would stay with her for ever, sharp and clear.

But she was so glad she'd told him the truth at last. It was as though her confession had unlocked a door between them. There were still questions she needed to ask, though. Perhaps, when the time was ripe…

The time. Oh, damn. The conference. Her pleasant glow doused, she lifted her head to squint at the bedside clock and saw it had already reached ten-thirty. Too late, surely, though if they hurried up she supposed they could make the middle sessions.

If only Joe weren't such a stickler for work.

Easing around, she saw that he was still deeply asleep. Gingerly she lifted his protective arm from across her body and slid out of the bed. He barely stirred.

She hesitated a moment, then gently replaced the covers over him. In sleep the deep lines around his eyes and mouth had smoothed, and he looked younger, less careworn. This must have been his first real sleep since they left Sydney. Waking him would be such a pity.

She tiptoed to the bathroom. With hunger gnawing at her insides she spent no more than twenty minutes in the shower, restraining a bubbling desire to warble at the top of her voice, then, when she'd dried herself in the big fluffy Metropole towel, she wrapped the robe around her and padded out to rummage through her suitcase for something to wear.

'Come here.'

Startled, she looked around and saw Joe leaning up on his elbow, his jaw dark with stubble, a seductive smile playing on his sensuous lips. With a laugh she sashayed across the room, then dived into his bristly embrace.

'Do you know what the time is?' she panted when she was finally free to breathe, tracing the line of his gorgeous bones

from cheekbone to roughened jaw with one delicate fingertip.
'As your MA, I think I should warn you that you've missed
two conference sessions already.'

His brows edged together as he examined her with a gleaming gaze. 'I think you're taking this MA role too seriously.
Haven't you heard that the Côte d'Azur should be a place to
relax?'

'Yeah,' she said in a dispirited tone, rolling her eyes. 'I've
heard it. If only I could try it.'

He grinned. 'How about we hire one of those spots under
the beach umbrellas and find out how swimming in the
Mediterranean compares with Coogee?'

She bounded upright and squealed. 'Oh, *yes*. Now you're
talking.'

'And since we're here, we might as well have a look around
and see what other fleshpots we can plunge into. But first...'
He planted a light kiss on her swollen lips, then cast the cover
aside and rose magnificently from the bed. 'I could eat a
lion.'

A pavement café with a view of the marina served them a
delicious brunch of omelettes and crusty rolls with a Provençal
salad and coffee. Joe's tension of the day before seemed to
have eased. It was as if he'd walked through some trial of fire
and come safely out on the other side. Today he'd reverted to
his easy-going self, though there were moments of silence
between them when Mirandi still sensed areas of reserve.

She did some thinking of her own. Last night had certainly
indicated that Joe's passion for her continued unabated, but
her dream of an ongoing relationship felt a little shaky. Desire
didn't necessarily mean love, and love as she understood it
meant trust and unconditional honesty.

Though which came first? And how could she demand
the one without first being secure in the other? Maybe she
was wanting too much. Maybe souls were all entitled to their

secrets and she should just be patient and wait for the cards to fall as they would.

She relaxed in her chair under the awning and spread strawberry jam on her roll, enjoying the ocean breeze whispering through her hair.

'Feeling good today?' she ventured.

Joe smiled. 'Much better.' He reached out and took her hand. 'Thanks to you. If you hadn't been with me last night...'

'*Moi?* But you were so angry with me.'

He looked rueful. 'Yeah, I know. I was—I have to admit—a bit jealous. Does that shock you?'

'I don't know. I'd have been jealous of *you* if I'd thought you were chatting up a blonde. As it was, I was jealous of the roulette wheel.'

He smiled. 'No need to be ever again. That was my first and last dance with the spinning witch.'

'Truly?' She looked keenly at him.

'Truly. I find I don't have an aptitude for it.'

She felt such a flood of relief. 'Oh, Joe. That's *such* good news.' After a moment she sent him another sidelong glance. 'Is that why you needed to do it? To find out?'

He nodded. 'Yeah. Funny how I'd built it up in my mind. I guess I was afraid I might get hooked like my old man. It's good to know I can take it or leave it like any ordinary Joe.'

She smiled behind her sunglasses. As if he would ever be ordinary. Not to her, at any rate.

Swimming seemed risky after such a feast, so they bought hats at a boutique, donned their cameras and joined the tourists strolling around the town, delighted by the maze of narrow paved alleyways and sunny courtyards, the overhead balconies dripping with geranium or bougainvillea.

In the shopping boulevards every luxury brand imaginable seemed represented behind the discreet awnings, and classic car shops abounded. After Joe had needed to pause for a close examination of at least his seventh expensive Italian auto parked in the street, Mirandi was grateful for his suggestion that they cool off in the sea.

The Metropole boasted its own private beach just a two minute ride away. By Australian standards it was cramped, with every available centimetre packed with sun worshippers on their hired loungers, but swimming in the sea was as exhilarating as ever.

'This is peaceful, isn't it?' Joe said, lazing beside her under the umbrella, drops of sea water glistening among the black whorls of hair on his bronzed chest. 'You know, I can't remember having a holiday since I was a kid.' He turned his smiling blue gaze to hers. 'How would it feel to stay on a few extra days? Maybe find a place further along the coast, perhaps at Cap Ferrat or Villefranche?'

'Oh, *Joe*, I'd love that.' She beamed at him until reality intruded and her smile faltered a bit. 'Can we do that, though? What about work?'

'I'm sure I can arrange it. CEOs do get to have some time off. I'll make an executive decision. How about it?' He smiled and she could see the tiny lines crinkle at the corners of his eyes under his dark glasses.

She grinned back. 'Do you really need to ask?' After a second she added cautiously, 'But, er...how will you explain me staying on with you?'

'Ah, yes.' His brows edged together. 'That might require some ingenuity. We may have to make it a study tour of Provence, like politicians do.'

She laughed. 'Why not a study tour of Europe? Then we could stay a year.'

Later that afternoon, lounging back in her spa tub at the Metropole among the bubbles and the floating rose petals, she said dreamily, 'And there were you, dreading coming to Provence. You seem to have taken to it very well.'

There was a fine line of beading along Joe's upper lip. 'Well, I am half French.'

Her nerves jumped, though she tried to be nonchalant. 'You've never really mentioned that.'

'Haven't I? No. No, *well…*' He rested his head against the side of the tub and closed his eyes. She felt his hand tighten on her leg.

She waited, then after a while said, 'That was your mother in the lobby, wasn't it?'

He let out a breath. 'I guess.'

'You—haven't seen her for a while?'

'Since I was fourteen.'

'She seemed quite devastated to see you.'

'Did she?'

After quite a long time, when she thought he wouldn't say any more, he said, 'I scarcely know her.'

'Aren't you curious?'

'About what?'

'How she—*who* she is.'

'I can guess,' he growled.

It felt prudent not to pursue the delicate topic any further, and Mirandi gave herself up to days of hedonistic pleasure. Dancing in nightclubs, swimming, though sometimes on the beach she thought of those long, soft, sandy crescents she'd taken for granted at home. They dined every evening on delicious fare prepared by some of the world's finest chefs, then later, were lucky to find a villa to rent on the outskirts of the tiny village of Sancerre-sur-Mer with a rocky path from their garden down to a tiny beach, and settled in for a week of idyllic relaxation.

Joe hired a car and drove them far and wide, to explore hillside villages perched incredibly on the edges of cliffs, with narrow, twisting mediaeval streets. He seemed keen to get in touch with his French side, and visited every little museum and bookshop in the area to delve for local history. They hired bicycles, and on a hot, hot day rode along a hill path, swam in the chill waters of a stream, and in the shade of a dense grove of trees picnicked on cheese, fresh crusty bread from the local *boulangerie*, and a delicious flaky pissaladière tart filled with anchovy and olives washed down with white wine.

'I'll be so fat,' Mirandi said, stretching out on a patch of grass to stare at the cerulean sky. 'All this lovely food.'

'All the better.' Joe was sprawled out with his head cushioned on the canvas picnic-pack. 'I'd love to see you all plump and cuddly.'

'You say that *now*.' She rolled over on her tummy and plucked a blade of grass, then tickled him under his chin with it. 'Aren't you going to see her before we leave?'

He closed his eyes and didn't answer for an age. She began to wonder if he'd even heard her question, then he opened his lids and pierced her with a glinting blue glance.

'It's not as simple as that.'

'Why not? Do you know where she lives?'

'She has a villa in Antibes,' he conceded reluctantly. 'At least she—had one. She lives there with her husband. Or for all I know she could be onto her third, fourth or fifth husband.'

'Oh. What makes you think she's had so many husbands?'

'I don't *know* she has. I'm guessing.' She looked queryingly at him and he let out an exasperated breath. 'Oh, all right. Perhaps she hasn't. She walked out on us when I was nine, or thereabouts.'

'Why did she leave?'

He made a grimace. 'Oh, probably over the gambling. The disease really had him by then.'

'Didn't she want to take you with her?'

He evaded her eyes. When he spoke his voice was so deep and gruff she needed to strain her ears to hear him properly. 'She tried. She moved into a flat over in Ryde, packed up all my clothes, and transported it all there in a taxi. But I—wouldn't stay. I ran away and caught the train home.'

'Oh. Didn't you get on with her?'

He was silent again. Then as if the words were torn from deep inside him he growled, 'I did, in fact. I—loved her. But I couldn't leave Dad.'

'Oh.' The poignant simplicity of the story moved her, and she had to turn her face away so he wouldn't see the tears blurring her eyes. 'Didn't she come to visit you?'

His pain almost tangible, he put his arm over his eyes. 'Yes, she did, often enough, but she'd never stay. Dad—*I*—wanted her to. It was too painful after a while for Dad. She kept begging me to go with her and I got angry one day. I said things, as kids do. She must have given up hope then, I s'pose, because she left Sydney and came back here to her family.' After a small charged silence he said, 'She used to write to me.'

'Did you write back?'

After an eternity he said, 'No. I…well, I never opened the letters.'

'Oh.' She sighed. 'That's such a shame.'

He removed his arm and lifted his head to look at her. 'Well, it would have felt like a betrayal of Dad. You see?'

She shrugged. 'I guess.' A deep silence fell, and in the stillness she could hear insects whirring in some nearby gorse. Every so often the faint breeze carried the scent of lavender from a nearby farm. Joe sank back, his eyes closed.

She said, pursuing the delicate thread, 'But you did come over here at some point. You mentioned being here for that weekend.'

He glanced across at her, curling a corner of his lip. 'Oh, yes. It was after the funeral. She came to Sydney for it and insisted I come back here with her. I was only fourteen and—in a bit of a—black hole, so to speak, after…so I… Well, I was pleased to have somewhere to *go*. And I—liked her. I trusted her, but of course when we arrived here I discovered she had a new man.'

'Oh, Joe.' Her heart welled with pity and she couldn't prevent a rush of tears. She crawled over and lay on top of him with her arms around him. She could feel his big heart thumping against hers through their thin cotton clothes as he held her tight, tolerating her teary kisses.

'Sorry, sorry,' she said after a while, mopping up after Joe was forced to comfort *her*. 'So what happened when you were here?'

'He probably wasn't even such a bad bloke, but you know, I was a boy, and I couldn't live with it. Anyway, after a pretty bleak weekend, I forced them to pay my way back. I'm sure her partner was only too glad to put me on the plane. Then in Sydney I moved in with my cousin Neil until the law said I was old enough to fend for myself. You must remember Neil.' She nodded, and he smiled grimly. 'Yeah. Neil was twenty-one at the time and a bit of a wild lad himself, though you'd never know it now.' His smile warmed in recollection of his wild beginnings. 'I'll always be grateful to Neil.' He shrugged and spread his hands. 'Anyway, the rest is history.'

'But it's not over yet.'

'Isn't it?' He turned lazily to look at her, though his eyes were alert. 'What does that mean, Miss Summers?'

'Well…' She gazed into his eyes. 'You're here. You're an adult now. You can see it all through a man's eyes. I'm sure *she*…your mother…'

'Amelie.'

'Amelie? Oh, that's such a lovely name. Well, I'm sure she'd be open to—talking to you at least.'

'I doubt it. No, no way.' He shook his head with conviction. 'Not after all the times I…rejected her. Anyway, there's no point. What would be the point?'

'The *point*.' She sat up and brushed herself down. 'Well, she's your mother. In my view that's a pretty strong point. Having grown up without one, even though I had Auntie Min and I love the dear old girl despite everything, if I had the chance—just *one* chance to spend an hour with my mother before I die…' Her voice wobbled. 'Even five minutes. *One* minute. I'd fly across the world. I'd shift heaven and earth for that minute.'

He gazed quizzically at her for a moment, then his black lashes screened his eyes. After a minute or two he hauled himself up with his usual athletic grace and stood, stretching out his hand to her. 'Come. Siesta will be over now in the town. Didn't you say you wanted to do some shopping for dinner?'

Joe didn't speak of his mother again that evening, although Mirandi ventured one further question over their ravioli and salad.

'What became of her letters?'

He looked curiously at her. 'Amelie's?' His eyes slid away from her, and he gave an off-hand shrug. 'Oh, they're somewhere, I suppose.'

Somewhere. Then not destroyed. Not torn to shreds or burned to ashes in some backyard bonfire. That suggested they were kept by someone. Someone who cared deep down, perhaps. At least these were Mirandi's musings, though she was careful not to reveal them.

The following day was their last before the precious time ended and they flew back to reality. It started early with a swim before breakfast. The sea was too chilly at that hour for Mirandi to stay long, so she waved to Joe and climbed the rocky steps up to their villa with chattering teeth.

Half an hour later, with coffee brewing, she set orange juice, yoghurt, strawberries and wild raspberries on the terrace table, and waited for Joe to arrive with the basket of warm croissants from the boulangerie.

It wasn't long before they were facing each other over breakfast.

'I was wondering,' Joe said, about to bite into a croissant with his white teeth, 'if you would care to drive into Antibes today?'

Mirandi's ears pricked up, but she concealed her surge of

interest. Silly to leap to conclusions. A drive might be no more than that. She said as calmly as she could, 'I'd love to. Any particular reason?'

'Possibly.' He lifted his shoulders, gruffness in his voice. 'We'll see.'

Since Joe wasn't sure any more of his mother's surname, he used the Internet to search for her telephone number. The last surname he had for her was Bonnard. If a Bonnard still lived at the old address, he would have to assume it was still hers and her husband's. As it turned out, the initial to the Christian name was all that had changed in the directory listing. Now, it seemed, there was only an A. Bonnard.

Finding her number was the easy part. Dialling it was something else. Mirandi left him to make the call in privacy, though she was agog to know the outcome.

'She'll see us at noon,' Joe said, emerging from the bedroom. Though his voice was steady, she sensed a tension in him that hadn't been there for days.

'How did she sound?'

'I don't know.' His voice sounded strained. 'She—she didn't take the call. It was Marie I spoke to. The housekeeper.'

Mirandi crossed her fingers. Oh, for a successful visit.

The drive to Antibes was spectacular, though Joe didn't have too much to say, possibly because he was concentrating on the road. Just possibly. Or perhaps he was feeling as nerve-racked as Mirandi.

They followed the Corniche as far as Nice, and enjoyed breathtaking views of sea and coast, as well as some hair-raising bends. Antibes wasn't a great deal further on from Nice and the hire car's navigation guide helped them find the correct address.

When they drew up at the villa with ivy trailing over the pink stone walls and twining itself around high black ironwork gates, Joe turned off the ignition and sat in silence, his hands clenching the wheel.

Mirandi noticed the tiny pulse throbbing at his temple. 'I'll wait here,' she said after several minutes.

He gave a small start and turned to her. 'Are you sure?'

She smiled and touched his hand. 'It's your meeting.'

He leaned over to kiss her, then got out of the car and straightened his jeans and jacket. In the side vision mirror she watched him brace himself, run a finger around the inside of his shirt collar, then stride up to the gate and ring the bell.

Almost at once the gates opened.

CHAPTER THIRTEEN

JOE walked up the path and climbed the few steps to the small stone portico, conscious of his increased heartrate and moistening palms. The heavy front door was ajar, the same maid standing there in wait as had stood on his previous arrival, albeit with twenty more years of living lining her grave face, and touches of silver at her temples.

'*Bonjour*, Marie,' he said. 'Do you remember me?'

'Of course, M. Joe,' she said, bowing her head. '*Mais bienvenue. Madame* expects you. Please…'

He followed her along a hall, then through some glass doors and across a small walled courtyard cooled partly by an orange tree and partly by Aphrodite, who was rising from the centre of a fountain and projecting a graceful spray through her eternally pursed lips.

He remembered it all with a curious tug in his chest, though it seemed smaller than he'd thought, apart from the tree, which could have done with a prune. Marie led him across the courtyard and into another part of the house. She knocked on a door, then showed him into a long, light room with a glass ceiling at one end.

A strong aroma of paint and turpentine assailed him, and one part of his brain registered numerous canvases stacked against the walls.

His mother was standing by a sturdy work table, wiping her hands with a cloth. She continued to wipe as he approached her, and he saw with a shock that her hands were trembling. Then he realised that all of her diminutive frame was atremble.

He felt such a rush of emotion that for a moment he couldn't speak. He noticed that her soft eyes were moist, or it might have been his own.

'Bonjour, Maman,' he said hoarsely. 'I am sorry... So sorry...'

'Oh,' she said, dropping the cloth and holding out her hands. 'Joey. Here you are.'

Mirandi waited and listened to music for nearly an hour, then got out of the car and strolled up and down the street. After several turns, she heard someone calling and saw a woman beckoning her from Joe's mother's gate.

Smiling uncertainly, she walked back. The woman introduced herself as Marie. 'Madame would like you to visit with us, if you please, mam'selle.'

She beamed. 'That would be lovely, Marie. Thank you.'

Marie showed her through the villa to a small sheltered loggia with two open sides giving magnificent views of the Mediterranean. Joe and his mother were seated at a table charmingly set with three places.

Joe rose when Mirandi stepped out onto the flagged floor of the balcony, and swiftly took her hand. 'Maman, this is Mirandi. Mirandi, may I present Mme Bonnard.'

Joe's mother greeted her warmly and invited her to sit. Throughout the lunch she listened with great attention to everything Mirandi said, though her eyes rested fondly on her son's face more often than not. Joe laughed often, and Mirandi couldn't help but be aware that sometimes both his and his mother's eyes seemed to acquire a moist shimmer.

There was much unspoken emotion in the air, though Amelie still managed to insert some penetrating questions into the conversation vis-à-vis Mirandi's work, her living arrangements in Sydney and her family history, dating back before the invasion.

In some ways the gentle interrogation was so typical of

Mim's whenever Mirandi had taken a friend home for tea, Mirandi felt quite comfortable with it.

There were several points in the conversation when Amelie's gentle glance shifted from Joe to Mirandi and back, and Mirandi knew there was no doubt in the Frenchwoman's mind of her passion for Joe.

After the lunch, Amelie began to wilt a little, and Mirandi remembered siesta was the custom in Provence. Comprehending at the same time, Joe exchanged a glance with Mirandi and they took their leave, each of them shaking hands with Amelie and being kissed on both cheeks.

There was more kissing at the front door, and Amelie held both of Joe's hands and said, 'Come again, my son. Please.'

The plea was heartfelt, and Mirandi understood it was a wrench for them both to part after having found each other again for such a brief time. Perhaps that was why Joe was nearly as silent on the journey back to Sancerre-sur-Mer as he'd been on the journey to Antibes, though this time his silence had a different quality. Often Mirandi felt his gaze drift her way as though she was in his thoughts, and once or twice his hand strayed to touch her.

That evening when she was packing her suitcase and arranging what she needed to wear on the plane, he came into the room with a pensive frown.

'Ah...I've been thinking.' He dragged a hand through his hair. 'You know...one visit with my mother in twenty years doesn't seem very fair to her, does it? Who knows when I'll have the time to come back here?' He shot her a glance, drifted across to the window and gazed out.

'I know,' she said warmly. 'It was so wonderful meeting her. It's a pity we don't have more time.'

'It *is*. Yes, it is,' he agreed with enthusiasm. 'That's why I've been thinking... At least one of us will have to go back or the firm will think we've absconded.' He gave a small laugh.

He turned to face her, his face filled with a light she hadn't seen before, then advanced and took her shoulders in his hands. For some reason her heart started to sink. 'Sweetheart, how confident do you feel about flying back to Sydney on your own?'

'Oh.' Her heart took a definite plunge, but she knew when it was time to put on a bright face. 'I'm fine with it. Course I am. Hey, an intrepid traveller like me?' She grinned to demonstrate her complete lack of concern. 'Why, how—long do you think you might stay?'

'Probably not long. A few days, a week? Two? Just long enough—so I can to know her again. Do you understand?'

'Of course I do, Joe. It's a wonderful idea, and very important.'

'I knew you'd understand.' He looked suddenly twitchy, as if he was somehow all up in the air. 'Are you sure you don't mind? You won't be nervous on your own?'

'Nervous? *Moi*?'

Terrified more like, because she could see where this was heading. His newly discovered French side was taking over and he would never come home.

'Don't you worry about me,' she lied with phony bravado. 'I have nerves of steel. I'm a market analyst now, remember?'

'Yes, yes, of course,' he said heartily. 'And don't you worry. When you go to work next Monday morning Patterson will show you to your new office.'

'Will he?' Suddenly she felt almost faint. Everything was already arranged. He'd been on the phone to Patterson, spoken to people at work. The reality of work was looming and she'd have to face it without Joe.

She might have to face everything without Joe. Life. The future.

It was an emotional farewell at the airport in Nice, on her side at any rate. Joe kept putting his arms around her and kissing her, and she had to fight to hold herself together. What if she never saw him again? Stranger things had happened.

When he kissed her goodbye for the last time, she said, 'You will come home, won't you?'

'You'd better believe it.'

And he laughed. But it was a happy laugh. Not the laugh of a man contemplating a separation from the woman he loved. Whereas she... All she could think of was how would she be without him now? How would she *sleep*?

It could very well mean she *wasn't* the woman he loved.

On the plane she tried to console herself with the reflection that Joe had conquered some demons on this trip and would be much the happier for it. *Happier but in France*, her evil genius chipped in.

She was surprised when she finally landed at Sydney airport to see Ryan Patterson waiting for her. Patterson, of all people. Joe had organised it from France, Patterson told her. To ease her back into her job.

If that wasn't a sign she didn't know what was. If ever there was a man Joe had shown no confidence in whatsoever, Patterson was the man. And now she'd been handed over to him.

It was the old story. There was a new woman in Joe's life, and it wasn't Mirandi Summers.

She visited Mim and her father and told them she'd been to Provence with Joe. They both looked startled over the sponge cake and teacups to hear of Joe's successes, and Mim exclaimed, 'Joe *Sinclair*? Who'd ever believe he'd amount to anything?'

Her father lifted his brows at Mim. 'Joe? No, no, you've got him wrong, Mim. Joe was a bright lad, and good-hearted underneath. He knew how to keep his word.'

Mirandi's ears pricked up. 'What do you mean by that, Dad?'

Her father sent his sister a look and Mim frowned and gave

her head a very slight shake. Not so slight that Mirandi missed it, though.

Her curiosity piqued, she looked from one to the other evasive face. 'What?' she prompted. 'What is it?'

Her father's eyes met Mirandi's then slid away. 'Well...'

Mirandi's heart started to beat really fast. 'Is this...is this something about Joe and me, Dad? Something I don't know about?'

Embarrassed, her father looked down at his teacup. 'Well, it was only ever intended for the best for both of you. Joe needed to establish himself. He had no one else...'

'He had me,' she said quietly, her pulse suddenly booming in her ears.

Her father lifted his rueful gaze to hers. 'You were too young, love, to take on that job. I'm sorry you—went through a bad time, but I acted for the best. I couldn't have—*we* could never have guessed how hard you'd take it.' On the edge of her vision Mirandi noticed Mim dab at her eyes, while the captain went on, 'We thought...we honestly thought you'd get over it in a few weeks at most, once you started at uni.'

Mirandi could feel herself turning white, but she held herself together. 'What did you do? You went to see Joe? You said things to him?'

Her father sighed. His bluff face was so kind, so wise, and sometimes so *wrong*.

'It wasn't like that. I just—pointed out to him how *young* you were. He—saw the force of my argument. And I was right, you know. Look how well you've done. You've *both* done.'

'You hurt him, Dad,' she said hoarsely. 'You hurt him.'

Mim started to weep quietly and Mirandi rose abruptly to her feet. 'I'll have to think about this.'

'But you've found each other again, haven't you?' Mim cried after her when Mirandi was rushing out the front door. 'Isn't that what you came to tell us?'

'I don't *know*,' Mirandi said.

CHAPTER FOURTEEN

HER emotions ran high for days, but when Mirandi had digested the shock she eventually stopped agonising. It was of no use to blame them. At least she understood now so many of those oblique things Joe had said to her. Her father had done it out of love, and who was to know how things would have turned out otherwise? Joe might have dumped her soon enough anyway.

She let them invite her around for Sunday dinner and showed them some of her photos. At least now she was in charge of her life, and she could choose to be with Joe and no one could prevent her. Except for Joe himself, of course. She couldn't repress a pang of fear at the thought.

She had other reasons to be emotional. For one, she was yearning for Joe night and day. She knew she was probably being irrational, but her imagination had been going berserk since that last goodbye. Sometimes at night when she was sprinkling her pillow with tears, she told herself that, after all they'd been through together, in the end the love of her life had relegated her back to being a mere employee.

Her new job could probably be quite interesting once she started concentrating on it properly. Somehow though, without Joe, even the new office had lost its relish. The meetings weren't nearly as intriguing knowing that Joe wasn't lurking about threatening to stride by looking autocratic and dripping with hotness.

As well, a couple of her colleagues who'd thought she was a lowly assistant were quite snotty when they discovered she was a bona fide MA with her own office. At least Ryan was supportive. She thanked him for it one day and he said cheerfully, 'Boss's orders. I've been instructed to look after you.'

What? He'd been *instructed* to be her friend?

She could have burst into tears on the spot. She'd never felt so alone. Though, forcing herself to look on the bright side, she probably could have picked herself up and sashayed around the office like a goddess if only she hadn't always felt so deathly tired. In fact, it wasn't impossible she was coming down with dengue fever. Who knew what a woman could catch in the Mediterranean?

Joe emailed her often, but it wasn't the same. Anything could be said in an email. It wasn't like looking into the person's eyes. To prove her point she emailed back with bright snappy chatter about how fantastic everything was. How absolutely *fine* she felt. How bursting with ideas she was for running the company.

Joe's week had stretched into three the day the bombshell dropped. She was standing in her office reading through some policy files when Ryan Patterson dropped in and told her that Joe had resigned from the firm.

She simply froze. The blow was so extreme she felt unable to speak, just forced a shattered smile for Patterson, then as soon as he left the room she had to rush to the bathroom to throw up.

How could Joe not have told her? He'd emailed her only the day before. To *resign*. Just like that, without warning. Her worst, most maniacal fears were realised to the fullest extent. Provence had crept into his heart and he couldn't tear himself away.

For the rest of the week, bereft of her lover, her faith in humanity destroyed, she walked through the days like an automaton. An automaton that needed to throw up every morning, that was.

On Saturday, grateful for the reprieve from having to put on a cheery office face to confound those witches on the fourteenth floor, she stayed in bed. There was something in the bathroom she didn't want to see.

At least the girls she shared with were away for the weekend, thank goodness. It didn't matter how blotchy and miserable she looked, so she gave herself up to an emotional binge and let the floodgates open wide. Fifty billion megalitres of water exploded over the floodway.

This was why, when the security intercom buzzed, she ignored it. It repeated several times, and then whoever it must have been was either let in by other tenants or had given up and left. Not that she cared. They wouldn't be buzzing for her. No one would ever buzz for her again.

She was dragged from her soggy tissues by the sound of someone brisk hammering on the door of the flat. Someone with a deep, commanding voice.

'Mirandi? Mirandi, are you in there? Sweetheart, are you all right?'

Her heart boomeranged around her chest cavity and she sprang up out of the bed. 'Oh…' She started a wild run for the door, but bumped into an armoire and stubbed her toe on the dressing table. Catching sight of herself in the wing mirrors, she shrieked, 'Oh, no.'

Limping and running, she made it to the front door without bouncing off any other pieces of furniture, and halted there. 'Joe? Is that you?'

'Of course it's me.' He sounded slightly bewildered by the question. 'Who else?'

'Can you give me a minute?'

There was an incredulous silence, then she felt sure she heard him sigh.

'A minute. Fine. All right.'

She turned for the bathroom, remembered she couldn't go in there, and made for the kitchen sink instead. Forget hygiene. This was an emergency. She splashed her face and dried it on a tea towel, then hurried back to the bedroom to do her best with make-up.

Transformed to some degree, a minute or so later she opened the door. Well, all right, it might have been several minutes.

Joe was slouched against the wall in the hallway with his eyes shut.

'Hello,' she said, hoping she didn't still sound bleary. 'Sorry to keep you.'

He opened his eyes and sprang to his feet, and his eyes lit up.

They truly did.

Before another word was spoken he grabbed her and dragged her against his lean sexy bones in the most comprehensive embrace, showering her with kisses and growling things like, 'Oh, I've missed you. Oh, it's been so *hard*. Oh, to feel you. To *hold* you. I've needed this. You'll never *know*.'

Her heart spilling over with joy and relief, she didn't attempt to discourage his flattering words, but when he walked her backwards into the flat and directed her with an unerring instinct towards her bedroom she felt it was time to draw a line in the sand.

'It's good to see you too,' she panted. 'I thought you weren't coming back.'

'I know you thought that,' he said with a hearty laugh. 'Your emails were full of it.'

She raised a brow at that. As far as she knew her emails had been models of restraint. 'Well, but... What did you expect? How did you think I would feel? What's all this about you resigning?'

He made an exasperated, '*Tsk*. Who told you that? I bet it

was Ryan Patterson. It was supposed to be top secret until I had everything tied up.'

'Well, didn't you think I might be *interested*?'

'Of course I did, sweetheart, of course, but…' They'd reached her bedroom by this time, and he steered her towards the only surface where someone might sit, which was the bed. Her rather rumpled bed.

He didn't appear to notice that, though. It seemed he only had eyes for her. He gazed tenderly at her and softened his voice as if she were an invalid. 'Well, sweetheart, I know how you worry and I wanted to tell you face to face. I gathered you were feeling a little down and I thought it might upset you if you heard the news without knowing the full story.'

Hope rose in her heart. 'What *is* the full story?'

He sprang up and started striding about and flinging his arms about as he talked. 'Well, in the first place it was about this *firm*. I haven't always been happy with the direction things were taking.' He halted to look at her, the light of excitement blazing in his eyes. 'I've been feeling restless for some time. You know, some of the things the board are so keen to support aren't really my thing. So I've decided to start my own firm.'

'Wow.' She widened her eyes. 'Well, *that* sounds good.'

Smiling, he sat down beside her. 'I knew you'd be right there with me. *I* feel pretty good about it. I emailed my resignation to give them time to digest it before I came back. Some members of the board have already tried to talk me out of it, but I think this is the right time to make the break. I feel as if everything has come together for me at this point in my life. Do you know that feeling?'

Her heart skipped a massive beat. 'Well…'

He seized her hands in his strong, warm grasp. 'I'm not sure if this change started with my having to go to Monte Carlo, or with finding *you* again, but it's all worked together and it's been the most *special* time. Honestly, my darling girl, I feel as if I'm floating on air. And without you, none of it would have happened.'

He kissed her so deeply and tenderly she nearly swooned. It had been *so long*. And all the time she was thinking—my darling girl? She was still his darling girl? Her heart began to thrill with the most fantastic instinct. Could it be...?

'Oh,' she said at last after she'd gasped in some air. 'Of course it would all have happened. You'd have still gone to Monte Carlo and found out the real truth about who you are. And I know you'd have gone to see Amelie in the end.'

His face became grave. 'Possibly, and all of those things were important, of course. But the most important was *us*. Don't you think?'

She nodded for seconds, unable to prevent herself from beaming, and, after all she'd done to try to reclaim them, her eyes filled up with more tears. 'I do think so. Yes, Joe, I do.'

She noticed then that Joe's eyes had that shimmer she'd only seen once before, the day in Antibes, and her heart surged with love and tenderness for him.

'I wanted to tell you so many times while we were away.' His voice was serious, his stunning eyes alight with a sincere, ardent glow. 'But there always seemed to be so much going on, the moment didn't arrive. So I'll try to say it now. I love you, Mirandi. You're the only one for me. I—love you so much I don't ever want to be without you again.'

She felt as if pure, incandescent joy must shine from her. 'And I love you, my darling Joe,' she breathed. 'I've always loved you.'

'Really?' To her absolute amazement, he got off the bed and onto his knees. She stared at him, fascinated. Then he said, 'Well, then, Mirandi... Will you—will you marry me?'

Her most precious, solemn moment had arrived and she felt composed solely of starbursts and ecstasy and bubbling, hilarious laughter. 'Oh, yes, *yes*! I'll marry you.'

She couldn't help giggling as he got up off the floor, but

he grabbed her to him then with such masculine conviction, kissing her back against the pillows, that she was stirred with nothing but the gravest respect.

She was just settling into position for some fantastic and overdue pre-marital bliss when Joe raised his head and interrupted his passionate appreciation of her. 'Er…excuse me a second. I've only just got off the plane. Customs, you know. And then there was the wait in the hall. Where's the bathroom here?'

She sighed. 'It's just through there and down that hall.'

'Won't be a second.' As he strode off in the direction of the bathroom a shocking thought struck her.

'*Joe.*'

She bounded from the bed and raced to catch up with him. Cutting him off, she darted in front of him in the nick of time and stood with her back to the door.

'Joe, you can't go in there.'

He looked thoroughly bemused. 'I can't? Why not?'

She gazed at him for seconds while a million complex thoughts scrambled to make sense of themselves inside her mushy brain.

His black brows merged together in total perplexity. 'Why not, Mirandi? What is it?' His tone grew demanding. 'What's—*who's* in that bathroom?'

She let out a long breath. 'Well, Joe…my darling Joe.' She smiled and trailed her fingers up his gorgeous arms and clung to them as tightly as she could. 'You see…as it happens… there's something I may have to tell you.'

FORBIDDEN OR
FOR BEDDING?

BY
JULIA JAMES

Julia James lives in England with her family. Mills & Boon® novels were the first "grown-up" books she read as a teenager, alongside Georgette Heyer and Daphne du Maurier, and she's been reading them ever since. Julia adores the English and Celtic countryside, in all its seasons, and is fascinated by all things historical, from castles to cottages. She also has a special love for the Mediterranean—"The most perfect landscape after England!"—and considers both ideal settings for romance stories. In between writing she enjoys walking, gardening, needlework, baking extremely gooey cakes and trying to stay fit!

PROLOGUE

MILD autumnal sunshine was filtering through the kitchen window of Alexa's flat on the borders of Notting Hill, illuminating the pinewood table set for breakfast for two. The simple but elegant pottery creamware and silver-plated cutlery had been acquired painstakingly and piecemeal from antiques shops. Bright flowers adorned the table in a glass vase, and the aroma of freshly made ground coffee hung in the air.

So did a tension that Alexa would have had to be a block of stone not to feel.

She had had no inkling of it until this moment. Until this moment her mood had been languid—sensual, even—for making love upon waking was something that never failed to leave her with a sense of rich well-being that lasted all the day long—even on days like this when, unlike the previous night, she would go to bed alone.

But she was used to that by now. Used to going from a night of sensual overload that left her dazed, swept to shores she had once known nothing of but to which now she was a familiar, oh, so familiar traveler, to abstinance. But as she stood by the table, coffee pot in hand, her slender body concealed by nothing but a pale green silk peignoir, her long, still slightly tousled hair rippling down her back, she felt her throat give a little catch, as though her body—more than her body—remembered with absolute clarity that sense of wonder, almost disbelief, that would sweep her away on a tsunami of emotion.

Not that she ever revealed that emotion. Only the passion with which it was expressed. The emotion itself could never be acknowledged.

For a moment—an endless, empty moment—bleakness showed in her eyes. Then it was gone. She had accepted, had *had* to accept, that all she could have was what she had now. These brief, precious times when she would burn with an intensity that transformed her life, which carried her through the intervening days and nights of celibacy until her phone would ring and everything else became secondary, inconsequential, irrelevant. Her friends, her work, her whole life—all put aside.

And then for one night, perhaps two, perhaps—so rarely—more, when the call summoned her to a private airfield and whisked her away within an hour of the summons to some continental city or—even more rarely, even more blissfully—to some Italian villa, some Alpine ski lodge, some Monagasque penthouse, she would give herself entirely to the moment. However brief, however fleeting.

Was she rash, foolish, intemperate to be so? Of course she was! She knew it—knew it with every last ounce of sense within her. Good sense. Sense that tempered, as it must—should—that volatility of emotion which was the other half of her, that intensity of emotion that fuelled not just her life but her art. Sense that kept her outward persona cool, composed—controlled.

That was what others saw. The persona she deliberately projected. Few of her friends, especially those in the heady and passionate world of art, realised that her outward appearance of dispassionate calm in fact concealed an inner intensity of emotion—emotion that she channelled only into the art that she painted for herself, not for her profession. Others saw a tranquil beauty—a pale, silken-haired English rose—but few recognised the flame that burnt deep, deep within her.

Raised by parents who had led ordered, intellectual lives, Alexa knew that they had been taken aback to discover their only child was as artistically talented as soon became evident during her schooldays. They had not opposed her choice of subject—far from it—but Alexa had always recognised that they found it faintly astonishing that their daughter should have taken so to art which, to their sedate minds, was associated with stormy passions, extreme emotions and, worst of all, a tendency to lead disordered and messy lives.

Was that why—almost as a favour to her parents, perhaps—she had schooled herself to be as unlike a temperamental artist as she could? Why she enjoyed a tranquil, ordered existence, keeping her outward life calm and temperate and restraining her emotionality to her work? Yet she knew that it also came naturally to her to be reserved, dispassionate, self-contained, and once she had graduated from art school she ran her professional life as smoothly as her personal life.

As for men… Drawn by her pale beauty, they had come and gone—but mostly gone, for they had not, Alexa had known, been special to her. So she reserved herself on that score as well, enjoying the company of a select few boyfriends, with whom she mostly enjoyed going to the theatre, to concerts, to art exhibitions. Emotionally, though, she was untouched, and physically none had ever set her afire to explore the sensual promise of the body. No one had succeeded in lighting that flame hidden so deep within her.

No one but the man who stood there now, paused in the

doorway, a man who, every time her eyes rested on him, made the breath catch in her throat, her pulse quicken. Every time.

As it did now.

He stood there, dominating the physical space just as he dominated her mental space, six foot of lean masculinity sheathed in an immaculately hand-made pale grey suit, with an effortless elegance about him that only served to emphasise his maleness while indicating his continental heritage. Guy de Rochement would never be taken for an Englishman, yet his French surname was only a fraction of the complex pan-European inheritance that had made the banking house of Rochement-Lorenz a byword for wealth, prestige and power.

Now, those extraordinary long-lashed eyes that could melt Alexa into quivering jelly by a single glance were resting on her. She felt, as she always did, their power, but now, for the first time, she also felt, deep within her, something different—the tension that seemed to set the air between them vibrating with a fine disturbance of the equilibrium.

She paused, waited, the coffee pot that she had been holding as he'd walked into the sunlit kitchen still in her hand. Suddenly the kitchen seemed less bright, less warmed by the sunshine. Time stretched between them, tangible, tense—it seemed to last for ever, and yet it was only the beat of a single heart.

Then he spoke.

'I have something to tell you.' Guy's accent in English was almost perfect, but not quite, still holding a faint sus-suration of French, Italian, German—any of the half-dozen languages he'd grown up speaking amongst his polyglot relatives. His voice was clipped, and as she heard it Alexa felt the first tremor of emotion deep within her—an emotion she would have given the world not to feel. It was an emotion she would give no name to, would deny completely, because to admit it would be to open within her a door so dangerous it might destroy her. It was a door she must never open—no matter what Guy did, what he said.

Even when it was the words he was saying now. She heard the words, but they came from very far away, from a place she'd dreaded, feared. His clipped, reserved expression told her far more than the words themselves, though each syllable was like a scalpel slicing across her bare flesh.

'I'm getting married,' said Guy de Rochement.

Alexa was standing very still. Almost as if she were a statue, he thought irrelevantly—for his mind was doing strange things to him, despite the self-control he was ruthlessly exerting on himself right now. A statue by one of those absurd and over-inflated contemporary artists with no more talent than an ability to mock greatness, a woman in a kitchen holding a coffee pot as if it were a Greek urn. He, too, seemed frozen. Or at least his mind did. He had walked into the kitchen knowing what he had to say, and knowing the implications of it.

Those implications were clear. Unambiguous. Unavoidable.

Completely obvious to him.

A minute frown shadowed his eyes momentarily.

Were they as obvious to her, though?

He went on studying her for the space of another heartbeat as she stood there, perfectly motionless, as if frozen in time. Nothing seemed to register in those luminous, clear-sighted eyes that had so entranced him from the very

first moment he had seen her. Eyes arrestingly beautiful,
set in a face that even *his* high standards for female allure
could not fault. Her beauty was completed by possession
of a figure of slender perfection that had immediately, irrevocably captured his interest—an interest that he had
pursued with all his customary ruthlessness when it came
to such matters.

Some women, when he had shown an initial speculative interest, had sought to intrigue him further by playing
pointless games—which, he assumed, they believed would
entice him the more, encourage his pursuit or, even more
presumptuously, serve as a means to exert control over
him. But Alexa had, to his satisfaction, shown no such
predilection for futile attempts to manipulate him. From the
first she had shown no disingenuous reluctance, coyness or
coquetry, and even when seduction had been accomplished,
and he had begun his affair with her, she had recognised
implicitly the terms under which it was to be conducted,
and complied with them without demur.

Complied without demur with everything he wanted.
Right from their very first night together…that unforgettable night…

In his mind, memory flickered like a flame in dry un-
dergrowth. He sluiced it instantly. That fire must be put
out—permanently. With all the discipline he habitually
exerted he doused the flickering memory. This was not a
time for memory—it was a time for clarity.

Brutal clarity if need be.

He needed to say it. Not just for her, but for himself as
well. To make it crystal-clear…

She was standing immobile still, and something in her
very stillness made the tension pull at him. Tension he did
not want to feel.

Time to make things clear.

Cool and terse, the words fell into the space between them.

'I shan't be seeing you again, Alexa.'

For the space of another heartbeat time held still. An eternity of time in the briefest span. Then, like a film starting to play again, her body unfroze. With her customary graceful movements she lowered the coffee pot to its slate mat on the table and started to depress the plunger, letting the dark pungent liquid settle, then pouring it carefully out into one of the creamware cups. Gracefully she lifted the cup and saucer, proffering it to the man standing such a short space away from her.

Such an infinite distance now.

'Of course,' she answered. Her voice was serene, untroubled. '*C'est bien entendue*—that's the correct French, isn't it?' Her tone was conversational, unexceptional. 'Are you having coffee before you go?'

There was no emotion in her face as she spoke.

She would permit none.

In her hand, the coffee cup she was rock-steady. Not a tremor. She caught the scent of coffee coiling into the air, the molecules wafting upwards. Her eyes were resting on his face, limpid, untroubled. As if he had merely uttered a pleasantry of no consequence or significance.

He did not take the cup. His face remained closed, unreadable. But then she did not seek to read it. Sought only to hold the cup as steady as a rock, to hold her gaze as steady. It was as though a section of her brain had dissociated itself from the rest of her and was operating in a space all of its own.

For one last heartbeat she held the cup, then slowly—infinitely slowly—lowered it to the table. Her regard went back to him, still showing nothing in her eyes except politeness.

'I hope you will permit me to wish you every happiness in your forthcoming marriage,' she said, her voice as untroubled as her regard.

Smoothly, she moved towards the door, indicating thereby that she recognised he would take his leave now—coffee untouched, affair disposed of. She did not pause to see if he was following her, merely headed unhurriedly, gracefully, the silken length of her peignoir brushing against her bare legs, across the narrow entrance hall of her flat to the front door.

She heard rather than saw him follow her. She slid back the security bolts that were inevitable in London, even on a quiet, tree-lined road such as the one she lived on. She stepped back, holding open the door for him. He came forward, halted one moment, looked at her one moment. His face was still closed, unreadable.

Then... 'Thank you,' he said.

He might have been thanking her for her felicitations, but Alexa knew that he was not. Knew that he was thanking her for something he appreciated far more. Her acceptance.

His eyes still held hers. 'It has been good, *non*?'

Laconic to the last. She, too.

'Yes, it has.'

Briefly, like swansdown, she leant forward to brush with the lightest touch his cheek.

'I wish you well.'

Then she stood back.

'Goodbye, Guy,' she said.

For one last time her eyes held him. Then, with the merest nod of acknowledgement of her farewell, he walked out.

Out of her life.

She did not watch him go. Instead she shut the door. Slowly—very slowly. As if it weighed more than she could bear. Then slowly—very slowly—she leant back against it, staring expressionlessly across the hallway. There was no sound. Not even his footsteps descending the flight of steps.

Guy was gone. The affair was over.

Slowly—very slowly—her fingers curved into the palms of her hand.

Gouging deep.

Guy's car was waiting for him at the kerb. He'd phoned for it as he dressed, knowing that he would want it there for as soon as he'd told Alexa what he must. He had put it off for as long as it was possible. Until it was no longer possible to stay silent. As he walked down the stone steps from the front door of the terraced house of which Alexa's apartment occupied the top floor, his driver got out and came round to open the rear passenger door for him. He got in, barely acknowledging the gesture.

As he sank back into the soft leather seat his face remained expressionless.

Well, it was done. Alexa was out of his life. And she wouldn't be coming back.

Guy reached for the neatly folded copy of the *Financial Times* his driver had placed carefully beside him, and started to read.

There was no expression in his face. His eyes.

He would permit none.

Alexa was cleaning the bathroom. She should have been working, but she couldn't. She'd tried. She'd mixed colours, got herself ready, put up a brand new canvas, dipped her brush in the colours, lifted it to the canvas.

But nothing had happened. She'd hung, frozen, like an aborted computer program, unable to continue.

Jerkily she'd lowered the brush, eased off the surplus paint, and stuck it into turps. Then she'd blinked a few times, stared blankly ahead for a moment, before turning on her heel and walking out of her studio.

She'd walked into the kitchen and put the kettle on. But for some reason she hadn't been able to make a cup of tea. Or coffee. Or even run the tap for a glass of water. After a little while she'd gone into the bathroom.

She'd seen the bath could do with a clean, so she'd set to. That had seemed to work. Then she'd moved on to the basin, then the toilet pedestal, then the rest of the surfaces and walls. She rubbed hard, using elbow grease and a lot of household cleaner foaming on the sponge. It seemed to take a lot of cleaning, and she rubbed hard.

Harder and harder.

And as she rubbed and scrubbed her brain darted, like dragonflies scything across a pond with sharp, knifing movements. She wondered what the dragonflies in her brain were. Then she knew. Knew by their iridescent wings, their flash as they caught the light.

They were memories.

So many memories.

Stabbing and darting through her head. Memory after memory.

As sharp as knives.

Working backwards through time, taking her back, and back, and back.

CHAPTER ONE

Six months earlier....

'DARLING! You'll never *believe* who I've bagged for you!'

Imogen's voice came gushing down the line. Alexa, the receiver crooked under her ear, concentrated on catching the sheen on a petal that was proving tricky.

'Alexa? Are you there? Did you hear what I said? You'll never *believe* who—'

Alexa, who knew that Imogen could no more be halted in full flight than she herself could be dragged to the phone when she was painting by anyone other than her friend and business manager, interrupted.

'Who?' She knew Imogen was dying to be asked, so she could give the dramatic answer she was clearly bursting to give.

'He's absolutely *devastating*!' gushed Imogen. 'A million, zillion miles from *any* of the usual boring old suits.'

An extravagant sigh wafted down the line. Alexa wondered what Imogen was on about, then went back to working on the petal. She was dimly aware that Imogen was still in full flow, but didn't pay attention. Imogen loved to gush, and Alexa let her get on with it while she focussed on what was important at the moment.

Finally there was silence on the line.

'So?' came Imogen's prompt a moment later. 'Are you over the moon or what?'

Alexa frowned absently. 'What?'

An exasperated sign came into her ear. 'Darling, *do* pay attention! Put the paintbrush down and listen for two minutes. Even *you* are going to be impressed, I promise. *Guy de Rochement* phoned. Well,' Imogen temporised, 'not him personally, of course, but his London PA.' She paused. 'So, tell me you're impressed. Tell me—' her voice changed and adopted a husky timbre '—you're quivering all down your insides.'

Alexa, her paintbrush reduced to hovering over the canvas, intensified her slight frown.

'Quivering?' she echoed. 'What for?'

The exasperated sigh came again. 'Oh, really, Alexa, don't do that Little Miss Supercool with me! I'm not a bloke. And don't even *think* you'll be able to get away with it with Guy de Rochement. Not even *you* could do that. He'll have you swooning just like the rest of the female population.'

Alexa's brow furrowed. 'Am I supposed to know who this guy is?'

Imogen gave a trill of laughter. 'Darling—a pun! His name is Guy in English, but of course he's French—well, mostly—so it's pronounced with a long "*ee*". *Guy*.' She gave it a Gallic slant. 'Sounds *so* much sexier…' She gave another gusty sigh.

Alexa cut to the chase. She hadn't a clue what was going on, and didn't want any more of her time wasted.

'Imogen—who is he, why are you being so loopy about it, and what are you trying to tell me anyway?'

Imogen sounded more disbelieving than indignant. 'Don't tell me you've never heard of Guy de Rochement?

He's just all *over* the celeb mags! Only the posh ones, mind you! He's a triple-A-lister. Total class!'

'I don't read magazines like that,' replied Alexa. 'They're all rubbish.'

'Ooh, look at you. Hoity-toity!' shot back Imogen in mock admonition. 'Well, if you *did* sully your pure artistic soul with such guff you'd know who I was talking about— and why. Listen, even at *your* elevated heights I take it you've heard of Rochement-Lorenz?'

Recognition—not strong, but there all the same—was dredged into Alexa's forebrain. 'Mega-rich bankers all over the place and going way back into history?'

'That's them!' Imogen trilled. 'One of the *über*-dynasties across the Channel. Utterly rolling in it. Made pots of money in every country in Europe for the last two hundred years,' she reeled off. 'Just about financed the Industrial Revolution and bankrolled merchant fleets to every far-flung colony. They're so seriously into money and survival they even made it pretty much intact through the last century—both the World Wars, not to mention the Cold War—probably because they had family on every side going. And now they are riding higher than ever, despite the recession. And a *lot* of that is due to Guy de Rochement. He's the whiz-kid that's propelled the bank into the twenty-first century, and the whole vast clan just *slobbers* all over him because he's raking in the loot for them.'

Her voice changed, adopting that husky tone again. 'Mind you, I'd take a punt it's the females in the family that do the most slobbering. Just like the females outside the family! I was practically salivating down the phone, and I was only speaking to his PA.'

Alexa cut to the chase again. Imogen was clearly bowled over by this *Guy* guy, whoever he was, and Alexa had certainly never heard of him.

'So what's the deal, Immie?' she asked.

'The *deal*, darling, is that he's interested in being painted by you!' cooed Imogen dramatically. 'And if he goes for it you'll be *made*, my sweet. No more dull old suits and cigars. You'll be able to take your pick of the A-listers—the really fab ones, up in the stratosphere. They're all as vain as peacocks, and they'll just *snap* you up. You'll be rolling in it!'

Alexa made a wry little face to herself. The whole portraiture kick had been Imogen's idea. When they'd both emerged from art college several years ago, her fellow student and friend had announced straight away that she was never going to be good enough to make anything out of art, and she was going to go into commercial management.

'And you'll be first on my books!' she'd informed Alexa gaily. 'I'll make you *pots* of money, see if I don't. No starving in garrets eating the acrylics for you, I promise!'

'I'm not really very interested in making money out of art,' Alexa had temporised.

'Yes, well,' Imogen had retorted, and Alexa knew there had been a touch of condemnation in her voice, 'not all of us can afford to be so high-minded.'

Then, immediately seeing the flash of pain in Alexa's eyes, she'd backtracked, hugging her friend.

'I'm sorry. My mouth sometimes... Forgive me?'

She'd been contrite, honestly so, and Alexa had nodded, hugging her back.

Imogen's family—large and rambling and open-hearted—had taken Alexa in, literally, during that first terrible term at art school, when Alexa's parents had been killed in a plane crash while coming back from holiday. Imogen and her family had got her through that nightmare time, giving her a refuge in her stricken grief, as well as helping her with all the practical fall-out from their deaths, which had included sorting out the best thing to do with what she had inherited. It was not vast riches by any means, but prudently invested it had provided Alexa with enough to buy a flat, pay her student fees and living expenses, and yield a small but sufficient income that meant she would have the luxury of not having to rely exclusively on her artistic career to live.

Even so, Imogen was dead set on turning her friend into a high-flyer in the art world.

'With your fantastic looks it's a dead cert!' she'd enthused.

'I thought it was whether I was any good or not,' Alexa had replied dryly.

'Yeah, right. That as well, OK. But come on—we know what makes the world go round, and good-looks definitely make it spin in your direction. You're a PR dream!'

But Alexa had been adamant. Something flash and showy and insubstantial in artistic terms was not what she was after. What it was exactly that she wanted, though, she was less sure. She enjoyed most media, most styles, was eclectic in her approach, and got completely absorbed in whatever she was doing. But then she got equally absorbed even if her next project was quite different. There was no clear artistic way forward for her.

Which was why, she knew, she had let Imogen have her head when she'd told her that she had a clear flair for portraiture—Alexa had painted Imogen's family to say thank-you for their kindness to her—and it would be a criminal shame to waste it. So when, out of her myriad contacts, Imogen had wangled a couple of commissions, Alexa had gone along with her friend's ambitions for her. And now, four years later, it had paid off handsomely—at least in financial terms.

It seemed she did indeed have a flair for portraiture,

for she had a generosity of spirit that enabled her to depict her sitters in ways that, whilst truthful, tended to show them in their best light. Considering that as Imogen moved her remorselessly up the fee scale her sitters became increasingly corpulent and middle-aged, that was no mean achievement. Yet, whatever her clients' unprepossessing exterior, Alexa found she enjoyed depicting the incisive intelligence, shrewdness, or sheer force of character that had got them where they were: to the upper reaches of the corporate ladder.

Which was why she was less than impressed at the prospect of having Guy de Rochement as a sitter. From what Imogen said he sounded no better than some kind of flash celebrity playboy, inheriting bucketloads and now merely swanning around the world making yet more. He would, she darkly surmised, be spoilt, conceited and full of himself—just because he was the scion of such a famous banking house.

Her thoughts darkened even more, recalling Imogen's drooling. And just because he happened to have a reputation for being sexy.

Alexa's mouth tightened. Rich, conceited and sexy. Great. He sounded like a royal pain in the proverbial.

Her opinion to that effect was only strengthened some days later when, Imogen having beavered away like crazy to set it up, Alexa's initial appointment with the fabled Guy de Rochemont was cancelled by phone at the last moment. The glacially indifferent PA's dismissive tone clearly told Alexa she was considered something little better than a minion—doubtless one of hundreds who waited on Guy de Rochemont's plutocratic convenience.

Automatically Alexa felt her hackles rise. So, when Imogen phoned her two hours later to ask breathlessly,

'Well, how did it go? Is he even more gorgeous in the flesh than in photos?' Alexa was icy.

'I have no idea. I was cancelled,' she said simply.

Imogen's reaction was immediately to temporise. 'Oh, darling, he's terribly, terribly busy—always flying off at the drop of a hat. And his PA's a cow anyway. So when have you rearranged for?'

'I neither know nor care,' was Alexa's terse reply.

Imogen wailed. 'Honestly, if you just *knew* how hard I'd worked to get you set up there! Hey-ho—I'll just have to suck up to the bovine PA and get another meeting sorted.'

She was back ten minutes later, cock-a-hoop. 'Jackpot! He's dining at Le Mireille tomorrow evening, and has agreed to meet you in the bar at seven forty-five beforehand.' She gave a trill of glee. 'Ooh, it's almost like a *date*!' she gushed. 'I wonder if he'll fall for your gorgeous English rose looks and be smitten in a *coup de foudre*? You must make sure you're looking absolutely *stunning*!'

Fortunately for her friend's blood pressure, Alexa made sure Imogen did not see her before she set off, with deep reluctance, to the ultra-fashionable watering hole the next evening. The moment she walked in she was extremely glad she had chosen to wear what she had. Every female there was in a number that screamed *Look at me!* By contrast, Alexa knew that her grey blouse and grey pencil skirt, with grey low-heeled shoes and matching bag, together with no make-up and hair repressed into a tight, businesslike bun, was designed to minimise her looks.

She gave her name—and that of the man she was due to meet—to the snooty-looking greeter inside the entrance. The woman's eyebrows lifted palpably as Alexa said Guy de Rochemont's name, and cast a sceptical glance over her unassuming appearance. Nevertheless she despatched a minion into the hallowed interior of the premises, where only the select few were permitted. The look of scepticism increased when the minion returned with a nod to indicate that, unlikely as it was, someone as dull looking as Alexa *was* of the slightest interest to such a man as Guy de Rochemont.

'It's a business appointment,' she said crisply, and then wished she hadn't—because why on earth did she care what a snooty greeter in a place like this thought one way or the other?

As she was led into the bar area—already crowded and filled with people noisily sounding off about themselves— her mouth tightened. This was not a place she'd have spent a single penny, even if she'd had the hundreds it required to dine here. It was showy, flash and superficial.

Was that what her prospective sitter was going to be like? Briefly she flicked her eyes around, looking for someone who might look like the way Imogen had so gushingly described him. There were certainly plenty of candidates. If egos had mass, the collective weight of self-regard in the room could have sunk the *Titanic*, Alexa thought waspishly. And doubtless Guy de Rochemont's ego would be a prime contributor. So which one was he? It could be any of them, Alexa acknowledged, for all the men looked sleek, rich, and unswervingly pleased with their own existence.

'M'sieu de Rochemont?'

The minion had halted, and the rest of what he said disappeared into French too fast for Alexa to follow. It was addressed to someone sitting at a low table. She could only see his back, shadowed by the minion's body. As the minion spoke to him he nodded briefly, and the minion beckoned her forward. She walked stiffly up to the unoccupied chair on the far side of the table, and sat down without waiting for either invitation or instruction.

'Good evening,' she said, her voice workmanlike, busying herself setting down her handbag. Then she lifted her eyes to the man seated opposite.

Could you hear the sound of a jaw dropping? she wondered, with some fragment of her brain that still functioned outside the complete fuzz that was suddenly her sole consciousness. Then another thought gelled. *Oh, hell, Imogen was right...*

Because, like it or not, whatever her scepticism had been, one thing was completely and irrefutably incontrovertible about Guy de Rochemont. He really was—well... She flailed about in her brain, trying to find words. Failing. Visual impressions raced through her mind—and more. Guy de Rochemont hit places that were far more than visual.

Visceral.

How—she scrambled for sense—how could a mere arrangement of features common to every human being vary so much in their impact? How was it that a combination of things that everyone else had—eyes, nose, mouth—could be so...so...

Her eyes skittered over him, taking in everything and anything—the sculpted face, the slant of his eyebrows, the thin blade of his nose, the finely shaped mouth, the edged line of his jaw, the sable hair that was perfectly framed around his head. She drank him in, unable to do anything else but succumb to the impact.

Dimly she was aware that he had half-risen at her appearance, but had sat back again as she had already sat down, and was now sitting with a kind of lean grace that—again—she could viscerally register without conscious assessment, one long leg crossed over the other and arms resting on the curving contour of the tub chair, relaxed and completely at ease with himself.

That's the pose, she felt herself think, feeling the familiar leap of conviction when the physical world arranged itself to perfection, ready for her to capture it to canvas.

Her eyes narrowed slightly, her brain still processing what her eyes were conveying to her. There was a rushing feeling going through her, a breathlessness. She was used to getting the buzz of pre-creation, but this was different. Far more intense…

Different.

She knew it was different—so different. She also knew she had never reacted in this way before in her life, but she pushed the knowledge to one side. She would deal with it later. Wonder about it later. Analyse it later. Right now… Right now all she wanted to do, all she *could* do, was simply let her eyes work over that extraordinary face, the incredible arrangement of features that just made her want to gaze and gaze and gaze at them.

Then, as if from far away, consciousness forced its way through. Awareness of what she was doing. Staring wordlessly at the man sitting opposite her.

Who was *letting* her gaze at him.

And even as the consciousness came through she felt, as if in slow motion, a wave of reaction. More than consciousness—self-consciousness. Her jaw tightened, and she stiffened, deliberately blinking to cut off her riveted perusal of him, regain some normality again. But it was hard. All she wanted to do, she knew, was to go right back to gazing at him, working her way over and over his features.

What colour are his eyes?

The question seared across her brain, and she realised she couldn't answer. It sent a thread of panic through her that she didn't know his eye colour yet. Her gaze pulled to get back to his face, to resume its study. She yanked it back. *No!* This was ridiculous, absurd. Embarrassing. She wasn't going to gaze at him gormlessly like a teenager! Or scrutinise him as if he were already sitting for her.

She straightened her spine, as if putting backbone into herself. Forced a polite smile to her mouth that was the right mix of social and business.

'I understand you are considering having your portrait painted?' she said. Her voice sounded, to her relief, crisp and businesslike.

For just a moment Guy de Rochemont did not answer her—almost as if he had not heard her speak. He continued to hold his pose, quite motionless, as if he were still under her scrutiny. He didn't seem to think it odd, she registered dimly, and then wondered just how long—or how—briefly—she'd been gazing at him. Perhaps it hadn't taken more than few seconds—she didn't know, couldn't tell.

Then, with the slightest indentation of his mouth, matching the socially polite smile Alexa had just given, he spoke.

'Yes,' he said. 'I've been persuaded to that ultimate vanity. The portrait will be a gift to my mother. She seems to consider it something she would like.' His voice was dry, and had a trace not just of an accent somewhere in his near perfect pronounciation, but of wry humour too. It also possessed a quality that, to Alexa's dismay, did very strange things to her. Things she busily pushed to one side. She gave a nod, and another polite smile.

'One thing, Mr de Rochemont, that I always warn clients about—should you wish to commission me, of course—is the amount of time that must be set aside for portraiture,' she began. 'Whilst I appreciate that calls on your time will be extensive, nevertheless—'

He held up a hand. It was, she saw, long, narrow, and

with manicured nails that gave the lie to a manicure being an effeminate practice.

'What would you like to drink, Ms Harcourt?'

Alexa stopped in mid-sentence, as if the question had taken her aback. 'Oh, nothing, thank you,' she said. 'I really don't have time for a drink, I'm afraid.'

Guy de Rochemont raised an eyebrow. Alexa felt her eyes go straight there. Felt the same rush of intensity that she had felt when she had first seen him. The simple movement on his part had changed the angles on his face, changed his expression, given him a look that was both questioning and amused.

'*Dommage,*' she heard him murmur. His eyes rested on her a moment.

They're green, she found herself thinking. *Green like deep water in a forest. Deep pools to drown in…*

She was doing it again. Letting herself be sucked into just gazing and gazing at him. She pulled back out again—out of the drowning emerald pool—with another straightening of her spine.

'Completion of the portrait will depend entirely on the number of sittings and the intervals between them. I understand it may well be irksome for you, but—'

Yet again, Guy de Rochemont effortlessly interrupted her determined reversion to the practicalities of immortalising him for his mother on canvas.

'So, tell me, Ms Harcourt, why should I select *you* for this task, in your opinion?'

The quizzical, questioning look was in his eye again. And something more. Something that Alexa found she didn't like. Up till now he had been the subject, she the observer—the riveted observer, unable to tear her eyes away from him. Now, suddenly, the tables were turned.

It was as if a veil had lifted from his eyes.

Emerald jewels...

Guy de Rochemont was looking at her. Straight at her. Unveiled and with full power.

It was heady, intoxicating—made her breathless! The words tumbled through the remains of her conscious mind, even as she felt the air catch in her throat.

Oh, good grief, he really is...

Attempts at analysis, classification, evaporated. They couldn't do anything else, because all she was capable of doing was sitting there, letting Guy de Rochemont look at her.

Assess her.

Because that was what he was doing. It came to her fuzzily, through the daze in her brain from the impact of those incredible green eyes resting on her. He was assessing her.

Rejection tightened through her. It was one thing for her to study *his* appearance—she was supposed to capture it on canvas! But it was quite another thing for him to subject her to the same scrutiny. And she knew just why he was doing it. For the same reason any man would do so. And when the man in question was someone like Guy de Rochemont, with a banking empire in his wallet and the looks of a film star, well—yes, he would think, wouldn't he, that he was entitled to evaluate her to that end?

Her mouth pressed together, and a spark showed in her eye. She suppressed it. She would not show she was reacting to him...to his uninvited scrutiny, she amended mentally. Because of course she was *not* reacting to him—not in any way other than to acknowledge, quite objectively, that his looks were exceptional, and that she needed to study them in order to paint them. That was all. *All.*

Yet again she recovered her composure, stifling her reaction to him, to those extraordinary eyes.

'That isn't a question for me to answer, Monsieur de Rochemont,' she responded. 'The selection of portraitist is entirely your own affair. If you wish to commission me, that is your privilege, and I will see whether my schedule is congruent with yours.'

She met his regard straight on. Her voice had been admirably crisp, which she was pleased about. All right, Guy de Rochemont was... Well, she wasn't about to run through the adjectives again—the evidence was right in front of her eyes! But that didn't mean she had to put up with being on the receiving end of his attention. Not that she had any reason to be concerned, anyway. There was only one outcome from his assessment. He would be seeing a plainly dressed, unadorned woman who was making not the slightest attempt to enhance her looks to please the male gender, and signalling thereby on all frequencies that she was not on any man's menu. Even that of a man who could quite clearly take his pick of the world's most beautiful women.

She wondered whether he would take offence at the way she'd responded to his question. Tough. She didn't need the commission, and if—and it was, she knew, a very big if—she took it and if—and that was probably an even bigger if, because a man like him wouldn't care to be answered off-handedly—he commissioned her anyway, she was most definitely *not* going to pander to the man. Yes, he would doubtless cancel sittings—because all her clients did to some extent or another—and that was understandable given the demands on his time because of his high-powered business life, and it was something she could cope with. But there was no way he was going to get the slightest pandering to, or her begging for the commission, or anything like that, thank you very much! She offered a service, a degree of skill and artistry. If a client wanted to buy it, that was that. If not—well, that was that too.

She met his gaze dispassionately as she finished speaking. For a moment he did not answer. She did not break her gaze, merely held his, looking untroubled and composed. The brilliance of his eyes seemed veiled somehow, as if he were masking something from her.

His reaction, she thought. *I can't tell whether he's annoyed, or indifferent, or what. I can't see into him.*

Again, it wasn't something that was unusual for her, given the calibre of her clients. Powerful men were not transparent to the world, and indeed that air of elusiveness, of restrained power, was something that usually went into her portraits—she knew, with a slight waspishness, that it was a form of flattery by her, to portray them as inscrutable.

But with Guy de Rochement the masking was, she felt, more pronounced. Perhaps it was because his was such a remarkably handsome face, so incredibly, overtly attractive to women. Women—any women—would expect to see some sort of reaction to them in his eyes, even if it were only polite indifference. But with Guy de Rochement nothing at all came through of what he was thinking.

She felt a tug of fascination go through her—the eternal fascination of an enigmatic man—and then, on its heels, a different emotion, a more chilling one.

He keeps apart. He holds back. He shows only what he wants to show, what is appropriate for the moment.

Then, abruptly, he was speaking again, and her attention went to what he was saying. What his face was suddenly showing.

She could see quite plainly what it was.

It was amusement.

Not open, not pronounced, but there all the same—in

the narrowing of his eyes, in the indentation of his sculpted lips. And more than amusement there was something else, just discernible to her. Slight but distinct surprise.

Alexa knew why. *He's not used to being answered like that—and not by a woman.*

She felt a sliver of satisfaction go through her. Then was annoyed with herself for feeling it. Oh, for heaven's sake, what did she care whether this man was or was not used to having someone answer him like that?

'You do not believe in pitching, do you, Ms Harcourt?' The subtly accented voice was dry.

Alexa gave the slightest shrug. 'To what purpose? Either you like my work and wish to engage me, or you do not. It's a very simple matter.'

'Indeed.' The voice was a dry murmur again. One narrow, long-fingered hand reached out to close around the stem of a martini glass and raise it contemplatively to his mouth, before lowering it to the table again. His regard was still impassively on her. Then, as if reaching a decision, he got to his feet.

Alexa did likewise. *OK*, she thought, *that's it. No deal. Well, so what? Imogen will be cross with me, but actually I'm glad he's decided against me.*

She wondered why she felt so certain of that, but knew she did. She'd work out later just what that reason was. Then it came to her.

Because it's simpler. Easier. More straightforward.

Yet even so she felt her mind sheering away. And necessarily so. Now was not the time to analyse why a feeling of relief was going through her *not* to be painting Guy de Rochement's portrait—or why the feeling running just beneath the surface of that relief was something quite, quite different.

Regret...

No! Don't be absurd, she admonished herself sternly. *It's just a commission, that's all. You've done dozens, and you'll do dozens more. Just because unlike all the others this one is young and ludicrously handsome, it means nothing at all. Nothing.*

He was speaking, and she cut short her futile cogitations.

'Well, Ms Harcourt, I think we have reached the end of our necessary exchange, don't you?'

Guy de Rochemont was holding his hand out to her. She made herself take it, ignoring the cool of his touch and dropping it again the moment social convention permitted.

'Quite,' she agreed crisply. She picked up her bag, ready to turn and leave.

'So,' Guy de Rochemont continued, 'I will have my PA phone your representative and arrange my first sitting—should it prove possible within the restraints of our respective diaries.' He paused a moment. Just the fraction of a moment. 'I trust that meets with your approval, Ms Harcourt?'

Was that amusement in his voice again? A deliberate blandness in his gaze? Alexa found her lips pressing together as her thoughts underwent a sudden and complete rearrangement.

'Yes—thank you,' she answered, and her voice, she was glad to hear, was as crisp as ever.

'Good,' said her latest client, as if the word closed the transaction. And then, as if Alexa had just ceased to exist, he looked past her. His expression changed.

'Guy! Darling!'

A woman sailed up to him, ignoring Alexa's presence as if she were invisible. A cloud of heavy scent surrounded the woman even as her slender braceleted arms came around Guy de Rochemont to envelop him. Alexa caught an impression of tightly sheathed black silk, long lush black hair, and a tanned complexion. Moreover, the woman's features were definitely familiar. Who was she? Oh, yes, Carla Crespi—that was it. An Italian *femme fatale* film actress who specialised in sultry roles. Alexa hadn't seen any of her films, as they weren't to her taste, but it would have been hard not to have heard of the woman at all.

She turned to go. It was par for the course that a male of Guy de Rochemont's calibre would have a woman like that in tow. Someone high-profile, high-maintenance, who would, above all, adorn him. A trophy woman for an alpha-plus male.

She heard the woman launch into a stream of rapid Italian, pitched too loud for private conversation and therefore, Alexa assumed, designed for public consumption—drawing attention to herself, to the man she was with. Tucking her handbag firmly under her arm, Alexa left her to it and departed.

She felt strangely disconcerted.

And it annoyed her.

She would have felt even more disconcerted, and certainly more annoyed, had she realised that behind her Guy de Rochemont had disengaged himself from Carla Crespi and was looking after Alexa's departing figure as she threaded her way across the room.

His eyes were very slightly narrowed and their expression was speculative. With just a hint—the barest hint—of amusement in their long-lashed emerald-green depths.

Imogen was, predictably, cock-a-hoop at Alexa's triumph. Not that Alexa saw it in that light at all—not even when Imogen disclosed the fee she had negotiated, which was considerably higher than Alexa had yet commanded.

'Didn't I tell you you'll be made after this?' Imogen demanded. 'You'll be able to name your own price, however stratospheric. It's all fashion—you know that!'

'Thank you,' Alexa said dryly. 'And there was I thinking it was my talent.'

'Yes, yes, yes,' said Imogen. 'But brilliant artists are ten a penny and starving in their garrets surrounded by their masterpieces. Look, Alexa, art is a *market*, remember? And you have to work the market, that's all. Stick with me and one day you'll be worth squillions—and so will I!'

But Alexa only shook her head lightly, and forebore to discuss a subject they would never see eye to eye on. Nor did she discuss her latest client, even though Imogen was ruthless in trying to squeeze every last detail out of her.

'Look, he's just what you said he was, all right? A jaw-droppingly fantastic-looking male, rich as Croesus. So what? What's that got to do with me? I'm painting him, that's all. He'll turn up late to sittings, cancel more than he makes, and somehow or other I'll get the portrait delivered, get my fee paid, and that will be an end of it. He's having the portrait done for his mother, and presumably it will hang in her boudoir, or the ancestral hall, or one of them. I don't know, and I don't care. I'll never see it again and that will be that.'

'Mmm,' said Imogen, ignoring the latter half of Alexa's pronouncement and rolling her eyeballs dreamily. 'All those one-on-ones with him. All that up-close-and-personal as he poses for you. All that—'

'All that cool, composed professional distance,' completed Alexa brusquely.

'Oh, come on, Alexa,' her friend cried exasperatedly. 'Don't tell me you wouldn't swoon if he made a pass at you. Of *course* you would—even you! Mind you...' Her eyes targeted Alexa critically. 'Dressed like that you won't get the chance!'

Precisely, thought Alexa silently. And anyway, not only was a man who had Carla Crespi panting for him never going to look twice at any other female, but—and this was the biggest but in the box—the only thing she was remotely interested in Guy de Rochemont for was whether she could successfully paint him.

The prospect was starting to trouble her. Up till now her main challenge had been not to make her sitters too aware of their physical limitations. With Guy de Rochemont it was a different ballgame. She found she was going over the problem in her head, calling his face into her mind's eye and wondering how she should tackle it. Wondering whether she could catch the full jaw-dropping quality of the man.

Will I be able to do him justice?

Doubts assailed her right from the start. As she had predicted, he missed the first sitting and was ninety minutes late for the next one. Yet when he did arrive his manner was brisk and businesslike, and apart from taking three mobile calls in succession, in as many languages, he let Alexa make her first preliminary sketches without interruption.

'May I see?' he said at the end, and his tone of voice told Alexa that this was not a request, despite the phrasing. Silently she handed across her sketchbook, watching his face as he flicked through her afternoon's work.

Pencil and charcoal were good media for him, she'd realised. They somehow managed to distil him down to his essence. Beginning full-on with oils would make his looks unreal, she feared. No one would believe a man could look that breathtaking. People would think she'd flattered him shamelessly.

But it was impossible to flatter Guy de Rochemont, she

knew. The extraordinary visual impact he'd had on her at her first encounter with him had not lessened an iota. When he'd walked into her studio earlier that afternoon she'd found, to her annoyance—and to quite another emotion she refused to call anything but her artistic instinct—that her gaze was, yet again, completely riveted to him. She simply could not tear her eyes away. She just wanted to drink him in, absorb every feature, every line.

When his mobile had rung, and with only the most cursory 'excuse me' he'd launched into French so fast and idiomatic it was impossible for her to follow a single word, she had actually welcomed the opportunity to resume her scrutiny of him. Unconsciously she'd found herself reaching for her sketchbook and pencil.

Now, as he flicked through her labours' fruits, she was watching him again. He definitely, she thought, had the gift of not showing his reaction. Whether he approved of what she'd done or not, she had no idea. Not that his disapproval would have bothered her in the least.

If he doesn't like what I produce, he can sack me, she thought, with a defiance she had never applied to her other clients.

But then never had she had a client like Guy de Rochemont.

As the sittings proceeded, intermittently and interrupted, as she knew they would—because his diary could alter drastically from day to day as with all such high-flyers who relied on others to accommodate themselves around them—she realised with what at first was nothing more than mild irritation that he started to disturb her. And it disturbed her that he disturbed her.

Even more that it was starting to show.

Oh, not to him. To him she was still able to keep entirely distanced during the sittings, to maintain a brisk, almost taciturn demeanour which, thankfully, mirrored his. He would usually arrive with a PA or an aide, with whom he more often than not maintained a flow of rapid conversation in a language Alexa did not understand, while the PA or aide took dictation or notes. Sometimes he took phone calls, or made them, and once he nodded a cursory apology to her when a second aide arrived with a laptop which he handed to his boss to peruse. After he had done so, Guy snapped it shut and resumed his pose again. Alexa coped with it all, and said nothing. She preferred not to speak to him. Preferred to keep any exchange to the barest functional minimum.

Yet it didn't help. Not in the slightest.

Guy de Rochemont still disturbed her in ways that she just did *not* want to think about.

Unfortunately, Imogen did. Worse—she revelled in it!

'Of *course* he's getting to you!' she trilled triumphantly. 'Otherwise you wouldn't snap when you say his name, or when I do. It's a sure sign.' She gave a gusty sigh. 'It's all totally theoretical, alas. He's all over Carla Crespi. She's preening herself rotten about it. Puts the pair of them in front of every camera she can find. Or buy. Even with your looks—if you bothered to do anything to show them off— you couldn't compete with her.'

Alexa tightened her jaw and refused to rise to the bait.

Besides, she had bigger problems than Imogen winding her up.

The portrait wasn't working.

It had taken her a while to realise it. At first she'd thought it was going well—the initial sketches had worked, the simple line drawing being ideal for catching the angled planes of that incredible face—but as she started to paint in oil, it didn't happen. At first she thought it was the medium, that oil was not the best for such a face. Then, after a while, it started to dawn on her, with a deep chill inside her, that the problem was not the medium. It was her.

I can't catch him. I can't get him down. I can't get the essence of him!

She took to staring, long after he had gone, at her efforts. She could feel frustration welling up in her. More than frustration.

Why can't I make this work? Why? What's going wrong?

But she got no answer. She tried at one point to make a fresh start, on fresh canvas, working from the initial sketches all alone at night in her studio. But her second attempt failed too. She stared, and glared, and then with dawning realisation knew that, however hard she tried, it was simply not going to work. She could not paint Guy de Rochemont.

Not from life, not from sketches, not from memory.

Nor from dreams.

Because that was the most disturbing thing of all. She'd started to dream about him. Dream of painting him. Disturbing, restless dreams that left her with a feeling of frustration and discomfort. At first she had told herself it was nothing more than her brain's natural attempt to come up with a solution that her waking mind and conscious artistry could not achieve. That dreaming of painting Guy de Rochement was simply a means to work through the inexplicable block she was suffering from.

But then, after the third time she'd dreamt of him, and woken herself from sleep with a jolt at the realisation that yet again he'd intruded into the privacy of her mind, she knew she'd have to throw in the towel and admit defeat.

It galled her, though—badly. It went against the grain to give up on a commission. She'd never done it before, and it was totally unprofessional. But it was also unprofessional to turn in substandard work. That broke every rule in her book. So, like it or not—and she didn't—she had no option. She was going to have to admit she couldn't do the portrait, and that was that.

Even so, it took time—and a lot of agonising—to bring herself to the point where she knew she would have to inform Guy de Rochemont of her decision. When to do it? And how? Wait until he turned up—eventually—for his next sitting, and then apologise in front of whichever of his staff were there with him that day? Or, worse, ask him for a word in private and then tell him? One cowardly part of her thought to let Imogen do it—after all, Imogen was her agent. But if there was one thing Alexa knew for sure, it was that Imogen would refuse to let her throw in the towel. No, she would just have to bite the bullet and do it herself, face to face. And it wasn't fair on the man to make him turn up for a sitting he scarcely had time for anyway and then tell him she was resigning the commission.

So she phoned his office instead.

The PA—whose manner had not improved—told her snootily that Mr de Rochemont was out of the country, and an appointment to see him was highly unlikely before the date of the next sitting. So Alexa was surprised when the PA rang back later, to tell her that it would be convenient for Guy to see Alexa in a week's time, at six in the evening. Alexa wanted to say that the time would not be in the least convenient for her, but forebore. This had to be done, and she wanted it over with.

When she turned up at the London headquarters of Rochemont-Lorenz, she was kept waiting in Reception for a good half an hour—not a surprise—and then finally taken up in a bronze-lined lift to the executive floor, some twenty storeys above Reception. Her feet sank into carpet an inch thick, and thence she went through huge mahogany double doors into the chairman's suite.

The setting sun was streaming in through plate glass windows.

Guy de Rochemont got to his feet from behind a desk that was the size of a car and about a tennis court's length from the entrance doors, and came forward.

'Ms Harcourt...'

His voice was smooth, his suit so immaculate that it clung to his lean, elegant body like a glove.

And yet again Alexa found herself gazing at him. Drinking him in. Feeling that incredible breathless rushing in her veins as she watched him cross the deep carpet, his gait lithe, purposeful, like a soft footed leopard.

Prince of the pride...

Thoughts, reactions, tumbled through her head as he came up to her.

This is his natural environment. Here in this penthouse, overlooking the City. With money and power and wealth and privilege. An ivory tower remote from the world. Where he reigns supreme, alone.

He had come right up to her, his long-fingered hand extended. Automatically she took it, wishing she did not have to, did not have to feel the cool strength in his brief social grip before he let her go.

He looked at her, studying her face a moment with a flicker of his eyes. The familiar thought stuttered through her brain.

Green eyes—as rich as emeralds... And lashes, those ridiculously long lashes, and that veiling I can't see through...

'Is there a problem?'

She stared. How had he known? She'd said nothing—nothing at all—of the problems she was having. She scarcely spoke to him during sittings, and thank heavens he had never asked to see her progress—not once she'd started on the oils. Nor had he made any comment at all on the initial pen-and-ink sketches. She'd been glad. She hadn't wanted his comment—hadn't wanted anything to do with him, if truth be told. She had been relieved that he wanted no conversation with her, that he was basically using her studio as an extension of his office. His preoccupation with his work meant she could study him, paint him in full concentration. Hiding completely the fact that she was utterly failing to capture his likeness—his essence—in a portrait.

For a moment she was stymied by his directness. Then, with a stiffening of her back, she answered, moving slightly away from him to increase the distance between them. It felt more comfortable that way.

'I'm afraid so,' she said. Her voice was stiff, but she couldn't help it. She was just about to tell a rich and influential client whose portrait was, as Imogen never failed to remind her, the gateway to unprecedented commercial success, that she was incapable of fulfilling the commission.

He raised a slightly, enquiring eyebrow, but said nothing. His eyes still had that veiling over them.

How's he going to take this? Finding out all that priceless time of his has been wasted, that there's nothing to show for it, and never will be? He's going to be livid!

For the first time she felt apprehensive—not because she was going to have to admit artistic failure, but because it was dawning on her that Guy de Rochemont could ruin her career. All he had to do was say that she was unreliable...

She took a deep breath. She owed him the truth, and could not put it off any longer. He was clearly waiting for her explanation. So she gave it.

'I can't paint you.'

His expression did not change. He merely paused, for a sliver of time so brief she hardly noticed, then said, his eyes resting on her, 'Why is that?'

'Because I can't,' said Alexa. She sounded an idiot, but couldn't help it. Couldn't explain. She took a breath, her voice sounding more clipped than politeness required. 'I can't paint you. I've tried and I've tried, and it's just not working. I'm extremely sorry but I have to resign the commission. I mustn't waste any more of your time.'

She waited for his reaction. It would not be pleasant—and who could blame him? His time was invaluable, and she'd wasted a great deal of it. She felt her shoulders squaring in preparation.

But his reaction was completely *not* what she had steeled herself for. He merely walked back to his desk, gestured to the huge leather executive chair slightly to one side of it, and then lowered himself down into his even huger chair behind the desk.

'Artist's block,' he said dismissively. *'N'inquietez vous.'*

Alexa could only stare.

'No,' she repeated, 'I really can't paint you. I'm extremely sorry.'

He smiled—a brief, social smile that barely indented his mouth. *'Pas de tout.* Please—won't you sit down? May I offer you some coffee? A drink, perhaps, as the sun has very nearly set?'

She didn't move. 'Mr de Rochemont, I really have to emphasise that I have no choice but to resign the commission. I can't paint you. It's impossible! Just impossible!'

She could hear her voice rising, and it dismayed her. She wanted to get out of here, but how could she? Guy de Rochemont was still indicating that she should come and sit down, and without knowing why she found that that was exactly what she was doing. She sat, almost with a bump, clutching her handbag.

'I can't paint you,' she said again.

His eyes were resting on her with that familiar veiled regard that she could not read in the slightest. 'Very well. If that is your decision I respect it entirely. Now, tell me, Ms Harcourt, do you have an engagement this evening?'

Alexa stared. What had *that* got to do with anything?

He took her silence for negation. 'Then I wonder,' he went on, his eyes never leaving her face, 'if it would be agreeable to you to be my guest this evening. I feel sure the event would be of interest to you. It is the private opening of the forthcoming exhibition on Revolution and Romanticism: Art in the Napoleonic Period. Rochemont-Lorenz has the privilege of being one of the key sponsors.'

Alexa went on staring. Then she said the first coherent thing that came into her head. 'I'm not dressed for the evening.'

Once more Guy de Rochemont gave a brief social smile.

'Pas de probleme,' he said.

And it wasn't.

There was, Alexa discovered over the course of the next hour, absolutely no problem at all in transforming her from someone who was wearing the same dull grey blouse and skirt that she'd worn the first time she'd encountered her client to someone who—courtesy of the use of the facilities of a penthouse apartment that seemed to form a substantial portion of the executive floor, plus a stylist who appeared out of nowhere with two sidekicks, hairdresser and make-up artist, and a portable wardrobe of eveningwear—looked astoundingly, shockingly different.

When she emerged, one hectic, extraordinary hour later, and walked into the executive floor reception area, Guy de

Rochemont looked up from where he'd been talking on the phone at the deserted secretarial desk and said only one thing to her.

His eyes—those green, inscrutable eyes—rested on her for only a brief moment. He took in the slender figure in raw silk—burnt sienna, with a high neckline but bare arms—her hair in a crown around her head and her face in full make-up, with eyes as deep as oceans.

Then he walked forward, stopped just in front of her.

'At last.'

That was all he said.

And he didn't mean how long she'd kept him waiting.

Satisfaction ran through Guy as he surveyed the woman in front of him. He had had more than ample time to peruse her attributes during his sittings, and Alexa Harcourt in evening attire was all that he wanted her to be.

Superbe.

The single adjective formed in his mind, and he plucked it from the list of many that he could apply to her and considered it. Yes, *superbe*…

Nothing less would do as a description. He had known from the first moment he'd laid eyes on her that once he'd disposed of the prim schoolteacher image she so amusingly put forward he would reveal for his delectation a beauty well worth his attention. And so it had proved.

His eyes rested on her appreciatively. Yes, *superbe* indeed. Tall, graceful, slender, with that classic English chic—so understated, yet so powerfully alluring for that very reason—she was exactly what he wanted her to be. A wisp of a smile played at his lips as he called to mind the muted, self-effacing persona she had presented up to this point. At first he had assumed it was a ploy, for women went to vast efforts to engage his interest, and she would not have been the first to attempt a pose of indifference to him. But as the sittings had continued he had come to the conclusion—surprising, but for that very reason enticing—that Alexa Harcourt was *not* courting his interest.

Not, of course, that she was not all too aware of him. That had been evident to him from the first, and it had come to be a source of amusement to him, adding a rare piquancy to his pursuit—a pursuit which he had taken considerable enjoyment in extending for far longer than he customarily did when it came to the women he selected for his relaxation. But he had found that it was *fort amusant* to sit, posed like a prince in his Renaissance palace, while his portrait was captured for posterity—or in his case for his fond *maman*—and let his eyes play over her sculpted features. He found pleasure in this casual scrutiny, while she assiduously endeavoured to ignore his regard.

But not without revealing by her very assiduity just how responsive she was increasingly becoming to his presence.

His eyes veiled momentarily. That increasing responsiveness was evidently, the reason why she had come here to make her dramatic announcement that she could not continue with making his portrait. Again, at first for a few moments he had assumed she had done so merely to put to the test whether he was or was not interested in her. But then he had realised, with a sense of relief as well as satisfaction, that his reading of her was unchanged—she was quite genuine in her determination to abandon his portrait.

It was an excellent sign! Excellent that she was not attempting to be *intrigant*, but even more excellent that she was having such problems with the task of capturing his likeness. Because the reason for that was obvious—he was no longer nothing more than a client to her. And most

essential of all, her inability to capture his likeness beto-
kened her increasing frustration at her own attraction to
him. She could not paint him….because she could only
desire him.

And desire was exactly what he felt for her. He had
experienced it the moment he'd realised how much of a
front her austere appearance and repressive manner was.
He had allowed himself the luxury of a slow, enjoyable
cultivation of his desire. Now, as she stood before him in
the rich, lustrous beauty she was finally revealing to him,
his desire rose pleasurably. Anticipation speared within him
for what he knew would be the delights of the evening—the
night—ahead.

Not that she gave any sign yet of realising what was to
happen. She was, he knew, quite unconscious of what lay
ahead with absolute inevitability. How was it, he found
himself wondering with amusement, that she could be so
unaware of it? He knew of no other woman who would not
have realised long before that he was interested in her. But
then, he mused, that was part of her allure.

It would, of course, make her seduction even more
piquant—even more enticing!

And now the evening was about to begin.

'Shall we?' he invited.

He ushered her to the door, and across the now-desert-
ed reception area of the executive floor. She walked with
superb grace, his appreciative eye noted, although there
was the very slightest tension in her shoulders. As if she
were not entirely at her ease.

But of course she would not be. She was still, *évidem-
ment*, quite *bouleversé*, by the unexpectedness of the situation. Yet striving to carry it off all the same—as if she had
quite expected to be gowned and coiffed and taken off to a
gala soirée. It amused him to think it was her oh-so-English

sang-froid that was allowing her to be so matter-of-fact about it.

On their descent to the underground car park lot in his personal elevator, he chatted inconsequentially about the forthcoming event. She made the appropriate responses, civil and unexceptional, and in that manner they gained the waiting limo, its engine purring as they emerged. He guided her into its interior and followed likewise, giving the signal to his chauffeur to proceed.

The journey was a bare fifteen minutes, if that, to the West End, and in the car he continued with his inconsequential chat. But it was sporadic only, and he was pleased. It was good to know that she was not one of those tiresome women who felt impelled to chatter the whole time. Alexa's reserve won his approval, as did her obvious ability to travel without incessant talking. Instead, she seemed perfectly content merely to make whatever appropriate comment was required to answer his remarks, being neither taciturn nor garrulous.

He liked that, he decided. And, moreover, he liked the opportunity it gave him, as she gazed composedly out of the tinted windows at the passing London scene, to let his regard appreciate her fully, her profile averted, and all her graceful figure displayed to him at his leisure.

Yes, she was indeed well worth his time and attention. Pleased with his choice, he relaxed fully into the leather seats and continued his appreciative surveillance. The evening stretched pleasurably ahead of him.

And the night—ah, the night would be exceptional...

Dim daylight was pressing at Alexa's eyelids. Slowly, as if lifting a weight, she opened her eyes. Taking in her surroundings.

It was a hotel bedroom. A hotel whose famous name

alone was synonymous with style, exclusiveness and luxury. A hotel in which she had dined the previous evening, in a suite larger than her apartment, at a dining table resplendent with silver and napery around which had been seated half a dozen couples, all guests at the highly prestigious art gallery earlier in the evening, all of whom, so it appeared, had been invited to dine with Guy de Rochemont. Along with herself.

Precisely how that had come about she had not quite understood—only that Guy de Rochemont had taken her elbow as the reception ended and guided her back into the chauffeured limo. They'd been disgorged a short while later into the lobby of the hotel, and then she'd been swept up with the other arriving dinner guests to the penthouse floor and into this suite.

There had seemed to be no good opportunity to take her leave, and instead she had found herself being seated at the dinner table along with the others. At that point she had acquiesced as composedly as she could, and accepted that her presence at Guy de Rochemont's side must be for the same reason he had taken her to the opening.

And that could only be, Alexa had mused, trying to make sense of his extraordinary behaviour, because his preferred partner—surely the exotic Carla Crespi still?—had for whatever reason not been available, and he must have assumed that the exhibition would be of intrinsic artistic interest to her as a portraitist. Indeed it had been, despite her acute consciousness of the disturbing presence of Guy de Rochemont at her side.

Because disturbing it most definitely was. She had done her best to ignore his presence, but Guy de Rochemont was difficult to ignore at all times, and the sleek dark sheath of a tuxedo made it completely impossible. But her mounting consciousness of him should—*must*! she had thought—be utterly suppressed. Whatever the reason she could not complete his portrait, whatever the reason for her quite inappropriate consciousness of him all evening, the only reaction to him she must show was none at all. She must be cool, she must be composed, she must be an unobtrusive guest and nothing more.

Her dogged composure had held through the meal, even through the ritual of serving coffee and liqueurs in the suite's sitting room, but as the guests had taken their leave she had found it difficult, yet again, to time the moment of announcing her own departure. So, to her consternation, as the last couple had left, she'd been left with Guy de Rochemont *à deux.*

Instantly, without the social conversation of the other guests, the atmosphere had seemed to change—though she'd known it was nothing more than her own resurgent consciousness of him. Definitely time to take her leave and remove herself from what had been a very taxing evening. It had been considerate of her august client not to be annoyed at her resigning his commission, gracious of him to invite her to an exhibition she would be professionally interested in, and courteous of him to include her in his dinner party, despite her having no claim whatsoever to be there. But the dinner party had been over, and it had been time for her to go. Time for her to regain the soothing sanctuary of her flat. Time to put her brief, professionally based acquaintance—nothing more than that!—with Guy de Rochemont behind her.

With that purpose clear, she had taken a breath, put a polite smile on her face

'I really must go,' she said, her voice admirably controlled, she was glad to note. Though she had partaken only frugally of alcohol, champagne had circulated at the exhibition and an array of wines had been poured at dinner, so she was aware that she had consumed sufficient if not for intoxication, then for a discernible weakening of her normal composure.

She got to her feet, feeling the column of silk slide down her body as she moved. Felt it disconcertingly, as if her body had somehow become as ultra-conscious as her mind...

'Of course,' said Guy de Rochemont, getting to his feet as well.

Involuntarily, Alexa's eyes went to him.

The stark austerity of his evening dress etched him against the paleness of the decor, emphasised the flawless planes of his face, the extraordinary green eyes beneath the dark winged brows, the sable hair.

For one hapless fraction of a second she could not move her gaze. Could only remain standing there, with supreme consciousness of that arresting physical presence that drew all eyes quite helplessly. She could not drag her gaze from him. Her body seemed inert immobile, beyond her control. Then, wresting back her control with intense effort, she veiled her eyes and started to walk towards the door. Getting out of here was a priority. A necessity.

But as she gained the door Guy de Rochemont was before her, tall, and dark and dominating her senses. With a rigid stiffening of her spine she turned, holding out her hand, the gesture determinedly final.

'Thank you so much for this evening, Mr de Rochemont. I enjoyed it so much. It was extremely kind of you to invite me.'

Her voice was cool, her tone restrained, her manner formal—as befitted the situation. She was a guest—unexpectedly so, given the vastly different world she moved in from the gilded orbit that Guy de Rochemont inhabited— thanking her host for his hospitality.

For a moment she could see something flickering in those incredible eyes. It seemed to be amusement. But it was also something else. Something that suddenly, belatedly, sent a dart quivering along her nerve fibres. Then he was responding to her polite, formal leavetaking.

'It was my pleasure,' murmured her host. 'And this,' he continued, somehow closing the gap between them, 'is an even greater pleasure...'

His smooth, long-fingered hand slid around the nape of her neck, the other hand took hers, twining his fingers between hers to draw her to him. His mouth dipped to hers. For a fraction of a second shock, sheer and undiluted, sheeted through her. Then a completely different sensation took over....

It was like nothing she had ever experienced! She had been kissed before, of course she had, but nothing, ever like this...

The lightest, most velvet touch, the merest grazing of his lips on hers, the most subliminal pressure of the tip of his finger moving in the delicate fronds of her hair at that most sensitive point on her nape. She felt her body start to weaken, her pulse quicken, and her conscious mind simply dissolve.

Slowly, very, very slowly, his kiss deepened.

And the last dissolving vestiges of her conscious mind left her.

And then, some completely indeterminable amount of time later, by some quite unaccountable means which she could never afterwards explain, she dimly realised that she was no longer standing by the door, but was instead—quite mysteriously—in a room that was dominated by a vast brocaded bed. Onto the broad expanse of this bed she was being effortlessly lowered, and slowly, very slowly and expertly, being made love to by Guy de Rochemont.

And there was nothing, absolutely nothing, that she could do about it—because with every cell in her body she realised it was the most exquisite thing that had ever happened to her…

Now, as she gazed out into the dimness of the hotel room, the night gone and day come again, her conscious mind came into residence after its extraordinary absence all through the long, dissolving night. She felt incredulity open within her.

How had it happened? How had it *possibly* happened? Disbelief was still echoing through her. How *could* she be in bed with Guy de Rochement? It was impossible! Just impossible!

Except that it wasn't.

It didn't take the evidence of her eyes to tell her that.

No, her whole body could bear testimony…

Memory shimmered through her every cell. Memory of sensations so exquisite, so extraordinary that they, too, could surely not be real. Except they were…

Hands—cool, fleeting—grazing along her bared arms. The tips of long fingers slow-running along the striations of her skin. Lips as soft as velvet playing over the contours of her body so that her whole being became a symphony of sensations—sensations that she had not known a body could experience. Light, questing fingertips exploring every curve, every secret sensual place, and lips tasting and arousing—oh, arousing! The swell of her breasts to coral peaks, which he savoured and engorged. Then his lips brushing down over her satin flesh. He had parted her loosening thighs and with a touch like silk prepared her for his possession.

She felt her body flush with warmth evoked by the humid, arousing memories.

How had it been possible to feel such sensation? It

was beyond imagining! Beyond everything except experience. An experience that was completely beyond her comprehension.

I never knew! Never dreamed it could be like that— never!

Wonder soared through her, increasing her bemusement, her incomprehension of how this had come to be, her presence here. She knew with a frail, wavering fragment of her normal self that what she had done had been not only inexplicable, but total and complete folly—to have fallen into bed with Guy de Rochemont could be nothing else! Yet right now, as she lay cocooned at his side, there was nothing more she could do, than acknowledge these truths. She knew that if she had any vestige of sanity left she should leap from the bed, bundle herself into her clothes—*his* clothes—the clothes that he had first dressed her in then taken off her—and rush out of the hotel as fast as decorum could take her. Yet she could not do so. Not because it wasn't the sane thing to do, but because her body seemed so strangely, uncommonly inert…languorous…

That sense of wonder, mixed now with a strange new sense of extraordinary well-being, suffused her body and her mind, making her feel slumberous, supine. And now something else came over her—an overwhelming urge to turn her head, to see the man who had accomplished her presence at his side.

Slowly she tilted her head, and as her eyes lit upon his face she felt something very strange lift inside her—just the slightest ripple, as if a light breeze had moved across still, untouched water, setting in motion something she did not know. She could not tell what it might be—some ineffable current that might take her she knew not where? As her eyes came to rest on the face of the man lying beside her she felt again wonder and bemusement—and more.

She felt her breath catch. Dear God, the man was perfection! That face that she had drawn so often, sketching over and over again to try and capture its essence, that she had tried frustratingly, so frustratingly, to translate into paint on canvas, riveted her gaze.

She had never been so close to it—to him. The sense of intimacy overwhelmed her—that she should be centimetres away from him, their limbs still half entwined. His face was so close that all she had to do was lift her hand, as she found herself now doing without conscious volition, and brush with the lightest touch the lock of satin hair across his forehead. She gazed at the long lashes of his eyes, swept down over the sculpted plane of his cheek.

He was deeply asleep—she could see the steady, rhythmic rise and fall of his chest, see the pulse at his throat, feel the warmth of his breath on her hand. As she touched him he did not stir, and she was glad—for she wanted only this moment now, gazing at the extraordinary perfection of his face, a homage to male beauty that for this one night had out of nowhere been a gift of fortune to her.

And that was what it had been, she knew. Whatever the reason Guy de Rochemont had chosen not to send her home but to take her here instead, she knew it was no more than a passing appetite, no more than filling an empty night with someone who, for a night at least, was worthy of his possession however fleeting his desire for her. Yet it felt like a gift. She felt it with every sensuous memory still warming her body, flushed with the heat of their congress.

I was mad to let it happen! But it did, and I cannot regret it—not now, not here. I can regret it later, tomorrow—all those tomorrows—and think how weak and foolish I was. But for now, for this day, I cannot regret it.

A smile played at her mouth. Yes, she had been foolish beyond belief, foolish and weak, but what had happened she could not regret—not with her body whispering to her in every cell just how transformed she was. Her eyes softened as her gaze stayed upon that perfect face, displayed for her in deep repose.

Cliché it might be, but any woman chosen by Guy de Rochemont must surely take away from the encounter only her appreciation

'*Ma belle…*'

He had awakened, his eyes holding hers immediately, the intimacy of his gaze at once drawing her to him. As her eyes twined with his she started to drown in their green long-lashed depths, as if there were no more air to breathe in the world.

He kissed her, their mouths mingling, and a sweetness went through her that warmed her body. As he drew away his eyes were tinged with regret.

'*Hélas*—I cannot do what you must know I long to do. I cannot stay. *Je suis désolé.*'

With a single fluid movement he stood up out of the bed, supremely unconscious of his nakedness—and of his condition. Alexa could feel her cheeks flush as she realised.

'Yes,' he allowed ruefully, 'I do not need to lie to you—I would give much, *ma belle*, to stay. But it cannot be. So I must ask you only to excuse my neglect.'

He turned away, walking into the en suite bathroom, and a moment later Alexa heard the rushing of water as the shower started. For one timeless moment she lay there, feeling out of nowhere a desolation that was far beyond the polite utterance he had made on his own behalf. It was only for a fraction of a second, but it was like the tip of a whip across her heart.

No!

Where the admonition came from she didn't know. She only knew that it was essential that she administer it.

Essential, too, to take instant advantage of this window of opportune solitude. She threw back the bedclothes and stood up. Again, for a moment, she felt her body was different somehow—changed—but then she thrust the moment aside, casting around to see where her clothes might be. Gathering them up, she hastily got herself dressed. It seemed absurd—more than absurd—to be putting on evening clothes again, but there was nothing else to be done. As she finished zipping up the elegant, beautifully made dress—whose price was beyond her range even at her most self-indulgent!—a sudden depression of the spirits crumpled her. She shut her eyes. Hot chagrin burned her cheeks. Suddenly the sordidness of her situation hit her.

A one-night stand—that was what she had been. A passing convenience, a handy female—good enough to fill the night hours of a man who kept company with film stars, who'd dressed her up to his standard. And now, her purpose fulfilled, she had only to cover her nakedness and remove herself.

No! It hadn't been like that—it hadn't! Not for her, at least. She wouldn't let such thoughts intrude, wouldn't let the wonder of it all warp into something sordid and regrettable. Because it hadn't been! Yes, of *course* she was simply a passing fancy. How could she be anything but to a man like Guy de Rochemont? But that didn't mean it had been tacky or repellent. Every portion of her body told her otherwise.

She took a deep breath, straightening her shoulders. The beautiful line of the gown shimmered over her body, reminding her of how she had looked last night. With swift fingers she reached into the tumbled mass of her hair and plaited her tresses into a long pigtail over one shoulder, glancing in one of the many wardrobe mirrors as she did so. Yes, that was fine. Neat, tamed. Her eyes were still smudged with make-up, but a quick wipe with a tissue from the vanity unit removed a great deal—enough until she could gain her own flat. Slipping her feet into the soft leather shoes, she reached for the evening purse that went with the gown. There—she was ready to go.

Calm and composed again.

The door of the bathroom opened and Guy de Rochemont emerged, his showered body clad now in a dazzling white hotel bathrobe. His sable hair was damp, and diamond drops dewed his long eyelashes. Alexa felt her breath catch, felt a sense of wonderment that for a few brief hours he had been hers to embrace.

Well, now it was the morning, and real life took over again. *His* would, clearly, and so must hers.

'*Cherie*, there was no rush for you!' His voice was amused, as well as rueful, as he took in her dressed state at a glance as he strode to the wardrobes and threw open the doors. Inside, Alexa caught a glimpse of serried male garments hanging up. 'You should have stayed in bed—had breakfast. It is only I who had to make this infernal early departure—*tant pis!*'

'No, that's quite all right.' Alexa's voice was composed, beautifully composed, and she was proud of herself. As if there was nothing extraordinary about standing there in Guy de Rochemont's London hotel suite as he proceeded to get dressed. 'I must get going myself. I'll have the dress and accessories cleaned and returned. Should they go to your London offices, or…'

He gave her a questioning look as he shrugged himself into a pristine shirt. 'You don't like the dress? You should have said last night—the stylist would have found another for you. But I can assure you it suits you completely—you look *superbe* in it.' His voice changed a fraction. 'Just as I knew you would.'

'The dress doesn't belong to me,' she answered.

'Don't be absurd.' There was a flash of something that might be hauteur or irritation in his voice.

'Monsieur de Rochemont—' Alexa began. She hadn't actually intended to call him by his French name, but it had come out of her mouth automatically—out of habit.

His eyes flashed with green incredulity.

'Monsieur?' he echoed, his fingers stilling in the act of doing up his shirt. He stared at her. Then his mouth gave a wry smile. 'Alexa, I know you are English, and the English are very formal, but we have reached the point of first names—*je t'assure*!'

His clearly deliberate use of the intimate form of speech emphasised his assurance. She gave a slightly awkward lift of her hand. 'Well, it doesn't really matter anyway,' she said, 'since we shan't be seeing each other again. So—'

'Comment?' His expression froze.

Alexa's sense of awkwardness increased. 'I'm afraid I can't resume your commission…' she began, then trailed off, not actually wanting to put it into words. *Just because I've slept with you…*

He seemed to appreciate her unspoken point. Or at any rate ignore it. He gave a frown, as though something was not understood on her part.

'N'importe pas. The matter of the portrait, *cherie*, we can discuss later. However, the matter of moment now is that for some reason I have yet to comprehend you seem to think we "shan't be seeing each other again."' He echoed the intonation of her earlier words. *'Dis moi,'* he said, and his intonation changed again suddenly, as did the expression in his eyes, which all at once seemed to make Alexa's breathing stop. 'Did you find last night not to your liking?'

His voice—and his eyes—told her he knew the question

was as impossible to answer in the negative as if he had asked whether a rare vintage champagne might not be to her liking. Alexa made herself breathe.

'That isn't really the point,' she began, then stopped. She seemed to be beginning a lot of sentences and then stopping, not knowing how to proceed.

But her hesitation did not trouble Guy de Rochemont. He had resumed buttoning his shirt, and Alexa found her eyes going to the strong column of his throat, the lean twist of his wrists. Found her pulse somehow more noticeable. She really had to go—she really did. But Guy de Rochemont was saying something that brought her up short.

'*Bon.* Then we are agreed. Last night was exceptional, and we shall arrange matters accordingly. As I said, I am *désolé* that I am required to be on a pernicious flight to a tedious destination within the hour, but I shall return at the earliest moment—tonight, I hope. If not, then tomorrow at the latest. If you phone the London office my PA will give you my contact details for your convenience.'

He moved on to do up his cuffs, with swift, assured movements, then took out a tie and proceeded to knot it, continuing to talk to her as he did so. 'I shall endeavour to keep you apprised of my movements, but I must ask you to understand—as I am sure you do will—that I have commitments it is impossible for me to ignore, however much I may wish to do so. Accordingly, it is inevitable that there will be times—*hélas*—when I cannot honour my undertakings to you. I must therefore request your forbearance.'

He continued without a beat as he lifted his suit jacket from its padded hanger and shrugged himself into it, with an ease of movement she was burningly familiar with from all his sittings for her in her studio. 'Nevertheless, I trust we shall be able to spend sufficient time together, and that your work will permit you the flexibility required to ensure that. Have no anxieties for the moment. All can be arranged. For now, however…' He finished his knot, crossed to the bedside to retrieve the slim gold watch, wrapping it around his wrist as casually as if it had not been an item of masterly workmanship, with a price tag of several tens of thousands of pounds. 'I must fly to Geneva, and that is that. Already *le temps presse*, so I must ask your indulgence of my unseemly haste.'

He crossed towards her, buttoning his jacket as he did so, and Alexa found her hand being taken.

'Don't look so bemused, *ma belle*.' There was amusement in his voice, and a timbre that yet again seemed to make her breath catch. '*Tout sera bien. Tu vas voire.*'

He dropped the swiftest, most fleeting kiss on her mouth. As he started to move away, letting go of her hand to head for the door of the suite, she blurted out, her incomprehension evident in her voice, 'I don't understand!'

He paused by the door, in the act of opening it, and glanced back at her. Amusement was still in his eyes. That and something more—something that suddenly made Alexa's legs unable to support her.

'But it is very simple, *ma belle*—now we are lovers, *non*?'

And with that he was gone.

Behind him, staring blindly at the closed door, Alexa felt her mind go completely blank.

CHAPTER TWO

HER mind stayed blank all the way back to her apartment in the taxi she had climbed into at the hotel. She had walked with head held rigid across the marbled foyer, convinced that every eye in the hotel must be on her, seeing what she had done—for why else would a woman be leaving a hotel in the morning, still wearing the dress of the night before? She was sure, too, that the taxi driver had glanced knowingly at her in his mirror, and for that reason she'd stared blankly out of the window, before handing him a ten-pound note for her fare and walking into her apartment block as quickly as she could. She half ran up the stairs before any other occupant could spot her and jump to exactly the same conclusion. She had never done anything like this before—*never!*

'Well, of course you haven't!' she admonished herself as she gained the sanctuary of her bedroom and started to rid herself of the betraying dress. 'You've never been seduced by the likes of Guy de Rochemont before!'

But I have now...and I will remember it all my life.

Out of nowhere, she felt weak. She sank down on the bed, the reality of what had happened hitting her. Emotion came from all over—some that sense of wondrous bemusement, the almost physical memory of the hours entwined with him, and some sheer amazement about what had happened.

Playing over and over in her mind were the words he had left her with...

'Now we are lovers, non*?'*

Her expression changed. Confusion and incomprehension were in her eyes. What did he mean? What *could* he mean?

She found out within the hour. She had scarcely finished showering and changing her out-of-place evening gown for sensible daywear before her entryphone sounded. Heading downstairs to the entrance lobby, she discovered a delivery of flowers so huge that she could hardly carry them up to her flat. Inside, she fumbled for the note.

'À bientôt.'

It was all it said. All it needed to say. The phone call that came from Guy de Rochemont's PA five minutes later said the rest. The woman's dismissive style had not changed, but this time, instead of informing Alexa as she usually did that Mr de Rochemont either would or would not attend the next scheduled sitting, Alexa was given a mobile phone number 'as Mr de Rochemont instructed'. She was to use it instead of the London number, but only in reply to a call from its owner, and on no account must the number be made available to any other individual.

The woman finished with an admonitory flourish.

'Please ensure you do *not* call me, Ms Harcourt, in relation to Mr de Rochemont's itinerary. It will not be in my power to give you any information Mr de Rochemont has not instructed me to forward to you. Such information will be disclosed to you only on an "as necessary" basis, as Mr de Rochemont instructs.'

After the call, which Alexa had heard out in a silence that was partly due to her continuing inability to believe what she was hearing and partly because she had long since decided to ignore the woman's pointedly unpleasant manner, Alexa resumed her task of distributing the flowers into a variety of containers—for she possessed no single vase that was capable of holding the vast bouquet.

The scent of the flowers seemed overpowering. But her mind seemed strangely blank—as if too much had happened, too fast, and she could make no sense of it at all.

I don't know what to do, she thought. *I don't know what to do.*

Then don't do anything.

The words formed in her mind and brought a kind of relief. After all, nothing was required of her for the moment other than to place the vases around the flat. Then, knowing she was in no state of mind to go to her studio—where, anyway, no current commission awaited her other than Guy de Rochemont's, which, whatever the extraordinarily unbelievable events of the night before, she had resigned—she settled down at the desk in her living room and worked her way through a considerable amount of domestic paperwork, from utility bills to ongoing business expenses.

Then she vacuumed the flat, cleaned the kitchen, did some laundry and finally, after a light lunch, set off to the shops, having first despatched by courier the dress and accessories from last evening, with a note apologising because they had not been first cleaned, to Rochemont-Lorenz.

Her fridge restocked, she decided it would be a good opportunity to go to the gym, and spent several hours there. The exercise helped occupy her mind. Stop it falling back into vivid memory or that sense of blank incomprehension that seemed to be paralysing her brain. Back home again, she stayed in all evening, reading or watching back-to-back documentaries on television, before retiring to bed.

As she slipped between cool sheets she had a sudden searing memory of the previous night. For a moment she froze as heat flushed through her body. Then, with a decisive flick of the duvet, she reached for a book on early Italian art—her current bedtime reading. Pictures of martyred medieval saints would be an effective antidote to that betraying sensual flush—and to thoughts about the man who had caused it.

But about Guy de Rochemont she still didn't know what to do.

*I don't understand…*was her last conscious thought as sleep took her.

It was also her first conscious thought four days later, after days spent resuming her life as much as she was able, given her state of mental bemusement. She had come to the conclusion that the complete lack of any further communication by anyone remotely to do with Guy de Rochemont, let alone himself, could betoken only one thing: his parting words to her, the vast bouquet he had sent and the call from his PA with his private phone number, had not in fact meant anything. It was all beyond her comprehension, and continued to be so right up to the moment when, one Sunday, as she was passing a leisurely morning, the entryphone sounded.

It was Guy de Rochemont.

Numbly, she let him in. Numbly, she opened her front door to him. Numbly, she heard her own voice on her lips— 'I don't understand…'

He glanced down at her, wry amusement in his beautiful green long-lashed eyes that made her breath slow and her pulse instantly quicken. 'I told you, *ma si belle* Alexa, it

is very simple. As simple...' he lowered his mouth to hers
and took her into his arms '...as this.'

And so, over the next weeks, and then months, it seemed
to be.

Without any conscious decision on her part, Alexa
simply accepted the situation. Slowly, the sense of bemusement that it was happening at all seeped away, and having
Guy de Rochemont in her life became just—well, her *life*.
She did not look for words to describe it, she didn't want
to—she didn't want to think about it either. It was simpler
that way.

Simpler to accept this inexplicable affair. Simpler not to
question him, or herself, or wonder why it was happening.
For reasons known only to himself Guy de Rochemont
wanted this. Why, she could not fathom. Carla Crespi
seemed to be no longer on his radar. Alexa knew this
from seeing a photo in a celebrity magazine of the sultry
Italian star hooked onto the arm of a paunchy middle-aged
man—a film director, according to the caption, which described him as Carla's fiancé. Had she defected? Had Guy
tired of the actress? Alexa did not know. Did not want to
ask.

Asking Guy about his life was something she refrained
from doing. Again, why she was not entirely sure. One
element, she knew, was because his existence away from
her seemed so completely different from her life that she
preferred not to think about it. Another reason was because
she knew, with finely honed instinct, that Guy did not want
to talk about his life.

Sometimes it overlapped into their time together, with
a phone call to his mobile which he would take, talking
in one of several European languages, and sometimes
in English too. She caught snatches of conversation, but

always busied herself, even if it were only to pick up a book or a newspaper while he was occupied.

Sometimes the tone of his voice, whatever language he was speaking, sounded impatient and irritated, his manner abrupt and peremptory. Then, phone call terminated, so too would be that attitude, and he was his usual self with Alexa again—relaxed and attentive, and, in bed, passionate and demonstrative.

Yet there was a reserve about him that she recognised—recognised because it resonated with her own innate reserve. A reserve that made her glad, too, that Guy showed no inclination to socialise with her, take her out and about. She was relieved, appreciative of his discretion—she had no wish to be seen as Guy de Rochemont's latest paramour, with curious, speculative eyes upon her, and besides, her time with him was too thinly spaced for her to want to spend it anywhere but in his private, exclusive company—wherever that was. Sometimes it was in her apartment, or he'd whisk her to where he was, where his punishing timetable permitted him her company. For time with Guy was precious—and scarce.

And it would not last for ever.

Could not.

The knowledge sent chill fingers creeping over her, and with it another sort of knowledge that seeped into her like icy drops.

How it had happened, she did not know. Why it had happened, she could not tell. That it had happened at all filled her with a terrible sense of both inevitable heartache and yet present rapture too.

For somewhere along the way—unintended, unimagined—she had done what she had never dreamt she would do. She had fallen in love with Guy de Rochemont.

Doomed, hopeless love. For there could be no future

with him, no ending other than the one she knew must come—one day the affair that had started so inexplicably would end, and Guy de Rochemont would no longer be part of her life. He would tire of her, move on, and she would be left behind.

Left behind loving him. Helplessly loving him. Hopelessly loving him.

The knowledge dismayed her—but it did not lessen by one fraction of a fragment the power of the truth about what she felt for Guy. A truth that she knew, with every instinct in her body, she must mask from him, and even, as best she could, from herself. That mask was all the protection she would have—a mask of cool composure that had once been the reality of her emotion but was now no more than a frail, flimsy disguise.

She needed it right up to the final moment when, out of the blue, the blow that she had known must fall one day fell.

Guy was leaving her. Ending their affair.

It was over.

CHAPTER THREE

SHE could not go on cleaning the bathroom for ever. After some indefinite time she made herself stop. Made herself go into the kitchen and put on the kettle. Carefully not looking at the breakfast table. Not thinking about what had happened that morning. Not thinking at all.

Just feeling.

An ocean of emotion possessed her.

After a while—a few minutes, an hour? She didn't know, couldn't tell and didn't care—she started to make herself think. Started to try and seize the torn and tattered rags of her mind and sew them back together again—at least enough to make words come, make words take shape in her head. She had to force herself to say them, if only to herself.

You knew this day would come. You knew it. You knew it had to come—could only come. You understood nothing of why he started this affair with you—what made you his choice. He, who had all the world to choose from. You understood nothing of that. Nothing of why he kept the affair going. The reasons must have been there, but they were inexplicable to you. You always knew that he would at some point, a point of his own choosing, decide to terminate the affair. End it. Finish it.

You knew it would happen.

And now it has.

You have done all that you could do, all that it was essential for you to do. You accepted its ending with dignity, with composure, with your mask intact. So that never could he possibly know the truth—the truth that he can have no interest in. Because why should he? Whatever he was to me, he was not a man it was...sensible...to fall in love with.

No... The word tolled in her brain. It had not been *sensible* to fall in love with Guy de Rochemont.

It had been folly of the worst sort. A folly she now had to pay the price for.

And she *would* pay that price.

She had accepted his severing of whatever it was that had been between them with composure and dignity. That was essential. Quite essential. She stood stock still in the kitchen, instilling into herself just how essential it was.

The phone started ringing.

For a moment she could only stare at it. A name, unspoken, was vivid in her head. Then, knowing that it was not Guy—for why should he phone now that he had ended the affair as abruptly as he had started it?—she jerked her hand to pick it up.

'Alexa! I've just found something out that I *must* warn you about! You've got to listen to me on this!'

Imogen's voice sounded agitated. For a moment Alexa could not face taking the call. But she knew she would not be able to avoid Imogen.

'What is it?' she answered. Her voice was as composed as Imogen's was not.

'I don't want to tell you this—I really, really don't! But I can't *not*—it's about Guy.'

Of course it was about Guy. How could it not be?

It was so ironic, Alexa thought dispassionately. From

being someone who couldn't have waxed any more lyrical about the attractions of Guy de Rochemont, lavish in her appreciation of all his masculine allure, Imogen had become the very opposite.

When she had first discovered the fact that Alexa had succumbed to him, Imogen's initial disbelief had been overwhelmed by a vicarious but wholehearted gratification.

'*Oh-my-God!* Are you serious? You and Guy de Rochemont! Oh, that is just *brilliant*! Wow! It's amazing! Awesome! Totally brilliant!' Imogen had enveloped her in a bear hug. 'Oh, you are just *so*, so lucky! You jammy, jammy thing!'

But her views had changed completely as she came to know the circumstances of their affair.

'It's like he's *hiding* you!' she'd accused. 'Never being seen out with you!'

Alexa had been unperturbed by her friend's hostility. 'The last thing I want is anyone staring at us,' she'd said. 'Besides, we don't get much time together—why waste it going out? I'd rather be with him alone while I can.' She'd looked straight at her friend. 'Immie, this isn't going to last. I know that. I'd be a fool not to. But while it does—'

She'd broken off, and to her dismay, Imogen had stared silently at her. Then spoken.

'You've fallen for him, haven't you?' Her voice had been hollow.

Alexa had answered too fast. 'No—'

But Imogen had only shaken her head. 'Oh, hell,' she'd said.

Then she'd given a huge, heavy sigh, and gazed pityingly at her friend.

The pity was back in her voice now, audible down the line. So was a hesitation that was unusual for her. Alexa cut through it.

'Yes, he's getting married. I know.'

The silence on the phone was eloquent.

'The *bastard*!' hissed Imogen. 'The absolute *bastard*!' Then she launched. 'It's on one of those gossip websites! I've only just logged on. There's a huge pic of Carla Crespi, and then one of him, and then it says about how Carla can give up all hope of getting him back now, because he's just about to announce his engagement. And underneath that is the story about who she is—the fiancée of your precious Guy de bloody Rochemont! It's some cousin or other of his. One of the Lorenz lot. They've dug up some pic of her at some *schloss*. She looks like a painted dummy. Daddy's got one of the family banks, so they're keeping all the money in the family—nice and convenient!' Imogen's voice was scathing.

'Yes, well, that's how they've always stayed so rich,' replied Alexa.

There was so much calmness in her voice that it astonished her. Beneath the calm she could feel the information that Imogen was forcing on her pushing into the interstices in her brain. She tried to force it out—she didn't want to know anything about who it was that Guy de Rochemont had chosen to marry—but it was there, vivid in her consciousness. All she could do was ignore it. Turn away from it.

Imogen had cottoned on to another thing now. The fact that Alexa already knew about the engagement.

'So did he deign to tell you?' she demanded. 'Or did you find out the way I did?'

Of course she hadn't found out the way Imogen had! She never looked at such sites, or picked up the kind of magazine that followed the rich and famous in their glamorous lifestyles. Imogen, she knew, even when she'd realised just what was going on between Alexa and Guy de Rochemont, still made a point of being assiduous in her perusal of such sources.

'Believe me, Alexa, if that man is up to stuff you should know about, I'll be on to it!' she'd said, way back. 'I can tell you straight off that it's plain as my face that Carla Crespi is dead set on picking up with him again, for a start.'

But Imogen's vigilance had not been necessary. Nor had Alexa ever thought it would be. For why should Guy conceal anything from her? Let alone the fact that their affair had run its course, as she knew it must one fine day…

'He told me this morning,' she said. The calmness was holding.

There was an intake of breath from Imogen.

Alexa went on, pre-empting any outburst from her friend. 'So, obviously I wished him well, gave him my felicitations, and said goodbye to him. We parted perfectly amicably.'

There was another eloquent silence down the line. Alexa realised that she was gripping the phone hard, yet try as she might she could not make her fingers slacken. Instead, she concentrated on holding that calmness in her voice.

'Imogen, I knew this day would come, and that's that. Now it has. That's all there is to it. There's absolutely no point my making a fuss about it. Guy de Rochemont walked into my life, and now he's walked out of it. End of story. And I'm fine. Absolutely fine. Honestly. Completely fine. *Fine.*'

Again she tried to slacken her grip on the phone, and again for some annoying reason her fingers would not obey her. Something seemed to be gripping her throat as well. Choking her.

At the other end of the line she could hear her name being spoken. Then again. Then, 'I'm coming over,' said

Imogen. And underneath, as she was disconnecting, Alexa heard a sibilant, hissing expletive. '*Bastard*!'

'Guy! *Servus! Wie gehts, wie gehts?*'

The voice greeting him was jovial and welcoming. Guy's arm was taken, and he was all but steered in the direction his host wanted. Guy's jaw tightened. But then that was, after all, exactly what Heinrich von Lorenz *was* doing—steering him in the direction that suited him personally. And suited his damn investment bank. His tottering investment bank, brought to the brink of ruin.

Familiar anger bit within him. Deep and highly masked. Why the *hell* hadn't Heinrich come to him earlier? Why had he bluffed it out for months, getting more and more mired in toxic debt? Pride, that was why, Guy knew. Expensive, unaffordable pride.

Then his anger veered round to target himself. He should have picked up on the depth of the problems Lorenz Investment was having. Dammit, that was his job—taking the helicopter view of everything—*everything!*—that fell within the labyrinthine world of Rochemont-Lorenz. It was the job he'd inherited from his father, and the job he was stuck with.

A caustic glint showed temporarily in his eyes. How many people envied him? Not just those outside the Rochemont-Lorenz behemoth, but even those within. How many considered his position one they would love for themselves? The titular and *de facto* head of a vast, powerful, immensely rich dynasty.

Well, it was nearly ten years since the heavy mantle had fallen on his shoulders, in his early twenties—thanks to the premature death of his father. It was a death to which, Guy knew bitterly, the role he had passed on to his son had contributed in its ceaseless demands on him. Guy was no longer—if he ever had been—a willing occupier of that grandiose position. It might sound good—and, yes, it certainly came with wealth and power, with a social cachet and a historical heritage that lent glamour to the name and role—but it came with a weight of responsibility that exacted its own heavy price.

A price that had suddenly become crippling.

But I have no option but to pay it! No damn option!

His mouth tightened as he went into the ritual of greeting Heinrich and his wife Annelise, in the baronial hall of their Alpine *schloss*. It was Heinrich's residence of choice, for it had once belonged to an archduke and still bore Hapsburg arms above the mantel—arms which, defunct as they were, nevertheless intimated an association with royalty that Heinrich took pleasure in emphasising. The Lorenz quarterings might not have reached further back than a bare century and a half, but Heinrich took inordinate pride in them. Suppressed anger flared again momentarily in Guy. Just as Heinrich took inordinate and clearly unjustified pride in his financial acumen.

Pride goeth before a fall.

The sobering words of the Bible stung Guy's consciousness. Lorenz Investment was as near to falling as if it were a metre away from a precipice. But from the expansiveness of Heinrich's greeting it was impossible to tell how perilously positioned he was. Yet he knew, all right, just how bad things were, despite all his avuncular bonhomie. Again Guy's eyes darkened. He'd taken his eye off the Lorenz Investment balance sheet, targeted his attention at other parts of the operation that had seemed to be in more serious straits courtesy of the global recession, and by the time he'd knocked together the requisite heads, re-set the vulnerable financial thermostats to 'sound' across the multiple divisions and corporations that formed the complex corpus of Rochemont-Lorenz, the window of opportunity for a far less painless rescue package for Lorenz Investment had passed.

And now Heinrich had done what he should have done six months ago, and disclosed the full state of affairs.

And called for the ultimate rescue package.

One that would not just bail out his bank, but achieve his dearest wish…

Had Heinrich been planning this all along? Guy would not have put it past him. He had always known that Heinrich had ambitions to further his branch of the family by any means at his disposal—but Guy had always been uncooperative. Not just for business reasons—Heinrich's mismanagement at Lorenz Investment was proof that had been wise—but for far more cogent reasons. Heinrich's love of royal residences was not the predominant evidence of his fondness for the way royalty did things.

Dynastic marriages were.

For years Guy had simply ignored the subtle and less than subtle comments, insinuations and outright hints. So Heinrich had no sons, only a daughter to inherit his place within Rochemont-Lorenz? So what? This was the twenty-first century. Heinrich might think it impossible, but there was already a sprinkling of highly competent female Rochemonts and Lorenzs taking their place in the higher corporate echelons of the family, and there was no reason why Louisa, if she showed any talent, shouldn't join those ranks in time.

Not that—from what he recalled of Louisa—she seemed to have shown any signs of financial acumen. She was studying something like ecology, he vaguely remembered, and his impression of her was that she was quite shy.

But, shy or not, she should surely be in evidence this evening—as yet, she was not. Guy's brows drew together.

Despite the effusiveness of Heinrich's greeting, and the benign graciousness of Annelise's, Guy had seen the latter's eyes go repeatedly towards the staircase curling around to the upper floors of the *schloss*.

Of Louisa there was conspicuously no sign. Guy's initial reaction on realising she was not there was momentary relief, but as the minutes wore on, and he was subjected to the kind of irrelevant and time-filling social conversation on the part of his hosts that he found as hypocritical as it was irksome, he could feel irritation piercing through the predominant emotion of anger at Heinrich's machinations and the unacceptable fall-out from his incompetence. He could see Heinrich and Annelise getting tenser about their daughter's continuing absence even while they were determinedly not mentioning it.

Impatiently, Guy decided to cut through the flam. 'Where is Louisa?'

His blunt question brought an instant prevaricatory response, which only irritated him further.

'You must make allowances,' added Annelise in a saccharine voice. 'Of course she is anxious to make the very highest impression on you, Guy, knowing how demanding your taste in the fairer sex is. She is bound to want to look her very best for you. Your reputation is quite formidable, as you must well know. Ah, look—' the relief was plain in her voice as her eyes went to the staircase, '—here she is now!'

Guy turned. Descending the staircase was Louisa.

His intended bride.

And anyone looking less like the prospective Madame Guy de Rochemont it would have been hard to find.

For a moment, as vivid as a splash of scarlet in a monochrome photo, another image imposed itself—elegant, soignée, *superbe*...

He thrust it away. He had done with it now.

At his side, he heard Louisa's mother give a click of exasperation and dismay. And he could see why. Her daughter had clearly made no effort whatsoever for the occasion. She was wearing jeans, a jumper and trainers, her hair was in a ponytail and her face was bereft of make-up.

'Louisa, what are you *thinking* of?' demanded her mother.

Her father had gone red—a mix of chagrin and anger.

Wariness flared in the wide brown eyes as Louisa approached. 'I didn't have time to change,' she answered. 'And what's the point, anyway? I've known Guy for ever. He knows what he's getting.'

There was a flicker of defiance in her question, and Guy felt himself in sympathy. Louisa's preference for casual style might not fit with what he himself preferred, or what the world would expect of his wife—every eye would be pitilessly upon her—but that was not her fault any more than her father's ambitions for his daughter were—or the mess Heinrich had made of his bank.

Guy's frustration worsened. If there had been any way—any at all—of calling Heinrich's infernal bluff, he would have done so. But the damnable thing was that the man was right. Any visible sign of a bail-out—internal or otherwise—of Lorenz Investment would, at this delicate stage in consolidating Rochemont-Lorenz against the recession, send danger signals ricocheting around and beyond the confines of the dynasty. The potentially disastrous consequences could, at worst, have a domino effect, taking down a lot more than Heinrich's bank. With sufficient time Guy knew he could nail any potential danger, ring-fencing Lorenz Investment, but time was not what he or the bank had. Which was why Heinrich—damn him!—had argued the case for this archaic and Machiavellian dynastic solution.

'My dear boy…' It was a form of address that had set Guy's teeth on edge when Heinrich had disclosed his master plan for not just saving his bank and his own skin, but achieving personal advancement within the clan. 'It is the perfect solution! A union between our two branches provides the perfect occasion for closer financial ties— what could be more reasonable? There will be no occasion for press speculation or undue attention from the financial analysts. Any financial…adjustment—' his choice of anodyne term for *bail-out* had further angered Guy, already feeling the edges of a man trap closing around him '—can be made entirely painlessly,' Heinrich had concluded breezily, blithely skipping over the punishing financial cost of what it would take to protect Lorenz Investment against its toxic debts, incurred solely because of Heinrich's rash and greedy strategy for over-expansion.

He had provided in an unwise coda. 'Why, a hundred years ago such an…investment—' now he was presenting the bail-out as a commercial opportunity, Guy had thought viciously '—would have been regarded as a fitting bride-price! Cemented, of course—' he'd smiled with bland optimism at his prospective son-in-law '—with a position at your right hand on the senior global executive board.'

Guy's answer had been short and to the point.

'This is a salvage operation, Heinrich. Nothing more. And be aware, *very* aware, that I undertake it solely for the good of us all. This debacle is of your making—survival is your only reward.'

Heinrich had bridled, then changed umbrage to bonhomie.

'And yours, my boy, is my daughter. It's an ideal match!'

His words had rung hollow, and now, as Guy's gaze rested on Louisa, their echo rang even more hollow. Louisa was a pretty girl, and the casual outfit suited her brunette, gamine looks, but Guy knew with a sharpening of the knife that had been stuck between his ribs by Heinrich that they were not the looks *he* sought in a woman.

The image he had banned from his mind because it belonged to the past, not the future, tried to gain entry. Once more he thrust it aside. Alexa had been an affair, nothing more, he reminded himself brutally—that was all he must remember about her.

Now, like it or not, he had to come to terms with what his future was going to be. A future with Louisa von Lorenz in it. She was standing there, her unvarnished appearance making her look more suited to being a chalet girl than chatelaine of a hundred-room *schloss*.

Louisa's father barrelled forward, seizing her arm. 'Get back upstairs and get changed immediately!' he hissed at his wayward daughter.

Guy stepped forward.

'Quite unnecessary,' he said. 'Louisa—'

His eye contact with her was veiled, concealing his simmering frustration. He did not want to take it out on the hapless Louisa. Then he turned back to Annelise.

'Shall we go in to dinner?' his hostess said brightly, clearly wanting to move the evening on.

Wordlessly, Guy slipped his hand beneath Louisa's woolen-clad elbow to lead her forward towards the vast panelled dining room beyond.

With iron self-control, he tamped down the dark, bitter emotions scything through him.

CHAPTER FOUR

ALEXA was painting. Painting and painting and painting. She'd been painting all week. A new commission had arrived, and she had gone into overdrive. Imogen had lined up at least two more portraits, and Alexa was thankful, knowing that her friend had done it deliberately. So far she'd managed to hold herself together, though when Imogen had come round that first evening she'd come very close to cracking. Imogen had urged her on—but Alexa would not oblige her. Would not even let her call Guy a bastard. Let alone allow her to give all the details about his forthcoming marriage.

'You should *know*!' Imogen had wailed.

But Alexa had only said, 'What for?' and refused to let her friend say more.

Even so, it had been impossible to silence her completely.

'According to the internet and the press, quoting the girl's mother, this Lorenz cousin has been groomed to marry Guy de Rochemont for *ever*! There was a really yukky bit about how the daughter had been brought up to take her place at the head of the whole damn dynasty. Like they were royalty or something!'

'Well, there *are* some titles washing around,' Alexa had pointed out, keeping her answer reasonable—for being reasonable was essential. So was being composed. And calm. Very calm. 'And obviously there is the *"de"* and the *"von"* in the names. So they are clearly aristocracy in that sense.'

'Inbred, too!' Imogen had muttered darkly.

Alexa had not responded. Her consciousness had been filled with a memory of Guy, walking out of the shower, his honed, water-beaded torso as perfectly planed as his face. 'Inbred' was *not* a word to describe him…

Then, something Imogen had said snapped her mind back.

'…their only daughter—just turned nineteen…'

'What?' She stared at Imogen. 'What did you just say?'

Imogen nodded, glad she had finally pricked Alexa's calmness. She thought Alexa should be spitting with rage against Guy for having so unceremoniously dumped her. 'Yup, his precious family bride is only nineteen!'

Alexa had paled, shocked by the disclosure. 'She can't be! Guy's in his thirties. She'd be almost fourteen years younger than him. Nearly a whole generation!'

Imogen smiled nastily. 'So, cradle-snatcher as well, then—plus complete bastard!'

Alexa flinched. 'Immie, don't. Please.' Then she plunged on, 'But I can't, *can't* believe he'd marry someone that young.'

'He'll probably enjoy a young wife. Someone naive and easy to manipulate. Someone he can impress. Make a fool of.' She cast a dark look at Alexa. 'Though you don't have to be nineteen to be taken for a ride by Guy de Rochemont!'

But Alexa was still too shocked to react to the jibe. 'She can't be only nineteen,' she echoed.

'Well, she is. And don't tell me he won't find it conve-

nient. He'll be able to pocket her dowry—Daddy's bank!—
to add to his collection, and then after a night deflowering
her he can set up a sophisticated, grown-up mistress—like
you were, Alexa, whether or not you like that word—and
sow his oats with *her*, not some inexperienced little teenage
virgin!'

Alexa's lips pressed together. 'Immie, don't. That's a
completely unwarranted accusation! Guy would never do
that! Be unfaithful to his wife.'

Imogen laughed harshly. 'Oh yeah? Wanna bet?
Honestly, Alexa, you're as naive about him as if it was *you*
who was nineteen!' She glared at her friend. 'You just don't
get it, do you? Face the truth, Alexa—Guy de Rochemont
used you! He treated you appallingly. It's unbelievable. He
turned up whenever he wanted and there you were, waiting and willing. Or if he decided he could fit you into his
oh-so-busy schedule, he had you flown out to him—like
some whore!' Her voice sharpened, her expression fierce.
'He used you for on-demand sex, Alexa!'

'No!' Alexa's denial was automatic, instant.

'*Yes,*' insisted Imogen.

Alexa shut her eyes, twisting her head away. Imogen's
ugly words seared into her brain. *No!* she wanted to cry
out again. *It wasn't like that! It wasn't!*

Denial fought with doubt.

Imogen hammered home her condemnation.

'Guy treated you like dirt—why shouldn't he treat his
wife like dirt too?'

'Stop it—I won't let you say such things about him!'
protested Alexa, clinging to denial. 'You don't know him,
Immie. I do.'

Imogen looked at her. '*Do* you?' she said.

Alexa closed her eyes. Inside her lids, a thousand images
and memories replayed themselves.

Then, 'Yes, I do,' she said, as she opened them again and let her gaze rest unflinchingly on her condemning friend. 'Guy is not like that. I know. I know you didn't like the way he came and went, but I'll tell you, and I'll tell you again and go on telling you, I was OK with it. It suited us both.'

Imogen just nodded. 'Right. So will it suit you when he swans back into your life and suggests picking up again where you left off, because his honeymoon's over?'

For a moment as brief as the stab of a knife emotion leapt in Alexa's throat. Then, very carefully, she answered.

'That isn't Guy. Whatever the reasons he's marrying—and for all I know he's loved her for years and has been waiting for her to grow up—' She ignored the derisive snort from Imogen at this fairy-tale explanation. 'He'll treat her honourably. Why shouldn't he?'

Imogen just looked at her. 'Because,' she spelt out, 'he didn't treat *you* "honourably", that's why. And, Alexa, you're no Carla Crespi—she's as hard as nails and must have *ambition* written all the way through her like a stick of rock. So what excuse was there for the way he treated you? Apart from the excuse *you* keep coming up with? Saying you *liked* being treated like that! OK, OK, I won't go on about it any more—I'll just leave you to find out the truth for yourself. Because I'll bet you, hand on heart, that that painted little doll he's marrying won't keep him between her sheets. I will bet you the sum of one hundred pounds—cash down, Alexa—that he'll be running to another woman, wedding ring on his finger or not!'

'You're wrong,' said Alexa. Her teeth were gritted, her throat tight.

But Imogen had only levelled her remorseless gaze on her. 'One hundred pounds. On the table. And I,' she said, 'am going to win it.'

* * *

Hairpin bends snaked along the mountain side, heading towards the pass into Switzerland, away from the ducal *schloss* and his future bride. Guy drove fast and furiously, the powerful engine of his low, lean car eating up the curves along with the miles. The concentration it required to negotiate the precipitous Alpine road was a welcome— necessary!—diversion for his mind.

How the hell had he ended up in such a damnable situation?

But the question was pointless. Rhetorical. He knew very well how—had played it out a thousand times in his head. It didn't matter how he cut it, marrying Heinrich's daughter was the safest way to protect Rochemont-Lorenz. And protecting Rochemont-Lorenz was his job. His purpose. Just as it had been *his* father's and his father's before him, for over two hundred years. The weight of dynasty, destiny, pressed down upon him.

As he climbed the pass his eyes were bleak. It was nothing new, carrying such a weight. And for some it had been far worse than his burden. Only two generations ago his great-great-uncle Lorenz had liquidated his assets a week before the Anschluss of Germany with Austria, banking the remainder in a Swiss vault rather than let the Nazis sequester it. The gesture hadn't gone unpunished, and his great-great-aunt had become a widow, her husband 'disappeared' into Nazi prison camps.

Her sister-in-law had divorced the husband she'd loved to marry one of Hitler's top cronies, who'd fancied such a prestigious wife, in order to halt any further 'disappearances' in her branch of the family—and to preserve what she could of the Polish branch of the bank, first from Nazi and then Communist despoilation.

After the war another cousin had courted Stalin, funding Russian industry despite his father-in-law being despatched to the gulags for being a 'dissident intellectual' with his academic work suppressed. Even in less drastic times personal fulfilment had always been put aside for the sake of what was best for Rochemont-Lorenz.

His own father had wanted to be a professional sportsman—but what use would an Olympic rower have been to the family? So he'd become a banker instead—steering the family fortunes through the EC corridors of Brussels and Strasbourg and the opening up of the former Eastern bloc, and marrying a woman he did not love because it was a match that profited the family, whose perpetual requirements outweighed the petty emotions of individual members. Petty, transient emotions, that would not last if they were starved sufficiently, denied sufficiently.

Emotions as petty as desire. And more than desire…

That waterfall of pale hair, the slender, graceful body, the porcelain skin, and those grey, luminous eyes widening in wonder as the moment came upon her…

Guy's hand gripped the gear lever, shifting up to match the engine speed. What use to think of such things? To remember a time when he'd been free—free to have Alexa in his life? That was in the past. In the future was following in his parents' footsteps. Doing as they had done. He took another hairpin, faster than he should, as though by driving fast he could escape the inescapable, and thought about his parents' marriage. Neither had loved the other, but they had married all the same, and made a pretty good job of it along the way. Respect and consideration went a long way in a marriage.

Would it do the same for his?

The question hung in the high mountain air.

And found no answer.

Only as he glanced upwards, seeing an eagle soaring on

thermals, came the sure and certain knowledge that such freedom as the eagle had would never be his again.

Ahead of him, the dark mouth of the road tunnel started to open, swallowing all that entered. He depressed the accelerator and let himself be swallowed up.

'It's good that she is so young.' The voice speaking was beautifully modulated, and it was impossible to tell from it what its owner thought—other than the words expressed.

'Too young.' Guy's answer showed all too clearly his disquiet.

His mother paused momentarily in her needlework. Outside on the parterre an autumn leaf eddied intermittently. The sky was grey above the Loire château, but there was still light in the air, and the ornamental trees marching along the boundary of this section of the gardens still held their leaves, despite the season. Along the gravel, a peacock strolled disconsolately, his tail furled.

'It's an advantage,' Claudine de Rochemont said. 'It will make her impressionable to your charms. It would be good for her, Guy, if she fell in love with you. It would not be hard for you to make that happen, you know.' Green eyes, so similar to her son's, rested on him.

Her son frowned. 'God, no!' he exclaimed feelingly. 'How could you hope for such a thing? Unrequited love is the very last thing I would want for her! None of this mess is of her making, and I certainly acquit her of any ambition to marry me.' He gave a short, humourless laugh. 'Her appearance at dinner was enough to convince me of that. She had no design to attract me. She had neglected to change out of her jeans—Heinrich and Annelise were not pleased.'

'No, I imagine they would not be,' observed his mother. 'But Louisa is very pretty, Guy—Annelise took pains to send me the studio shots she had done in the summer. Too overdone, but that's just Annelise's taste. Underneath the bones are good.'

'Pretty?' echoed Guy condemningly, and said no more.

He did not want 'pretty'. His eyes veiled, masking memories.

His mother glanced at him assessingly. 'Not all women can aspire to the allure of Signorina Crespi,' she remarked dryly.

Guy gave a slight shrug but said nothing, aware that his mother was still looking at him. He glanced at his watch. He wanted out of this conversation, but knew he owed his mother the courtesy of letting her raise the subject. He could hardly exclude her.

'So, what are the plans in respect of the wedding?'

He glanced back up at her. 'I have no idea. It is not imminent.' His lips pressed tightly. 'Despite Heinrich's eagerness!'

His mother nodded. 'That is sensible. Such affairs should not be rushed. I must get in touch with Annelise. And of course Louisa must visit here too.'

'I suppose so,' said Guy heavily. He glanced at his watch again. 'Maman, you must excuse me. I have a dinner engagement in Paris. The helicopter is on standby.'

Again that speculative look was in his mother's eyes. 'A personal engagement?' she ventured.

Guy's expression closed. 'No. Business.' He paused, then said deliberately, 'I know enough, Maman, to follow the conventions! The only press coverage about me outside the financial press will be in respect of Louisa. And now, forgive me, I must go.'

He took his leave, dutifully kissing his mother on her scented cheek, and strode off. From her place on the Louis

Quinze sofa his mother watched him go. Her expression was troubled. A long engagement for a man like her son, fêted by women and used to their enjoyment, was not a good idea. Louisa von Lorenz *was* young—but a pretty, adoring young bride, swept off her feet by a handsome, sophisticated and experienced husband, could make a workable marriage. And who knew? A softening look in her eyes. Perhaps an adoring young bride would finally inspire her son to do what would be best for him—fall in love.

She picked up her needlework again, the troubled look gone, replaced by hope. Above all she wished her son the gift of a marriage based on love. Even if it took a *marriage de covenance* to achieve it, as it had in her case.

Would it be so for her son as well?

For now, she could only watch, and wait, in hope.

CHAPTER FIVE

'ALEXA, it's the best thing that could have happened to you. Richard Saxonby is seriously nice. Plus he's good-looking, well-heeled, and really keen on you. You couldn't do better!'

Imogen's encomium was a ringing endorsement of what Alexa already knew about the man who was asking her out. Richard was indeed seriously nice. Plus he was good company and intelligent, which was important to her—though Alexa did not regard as highly as Imogen his financial status and keenness on her. She liked him, and, yes, with her eyes she could see he was good looking, with his brown hair and brown eyes, and sturdy, muscular build.

But did that mean she should go out with him?

'Yes!' urged Imogen. 'You can't go on moping for ever!'

'I am not moping,' Alexa replied evenly.

'Just living like a nun.' Imogen said acidly. She rolled her eyes. 'It's been four months since Guy de Rochemont did the dirty on you. And since then—' she ignored the customary rejection Alexa always gave whenever she heard Guy criticised '—all you've done is work, work, work. If it hadn't been for me plaguing you, you wouldn't have seen a soul except your clients! C'mon, Alexa—it's time to rejoin the female race. Guy's history—and you're well out of it.

Find someone normal, with emotions, not just some jerk who thinks his zillions entitle him to treat women like disposable sex toys whenever he wants some personal R&R when he's not adding to his gold piles. That's why Richard Saxonby's so good—he's *nice*, for Pete's sake!'

'Too nice,' Alexa prevaricated. 'I don't want to—'

She stopped. Saying more would be revealing, and since Imogen was only too ready to find any reason to persist in her castigation of Guy de Rochemont Alexa did not want to add any fuel to the fire. But silently she completed the sentence in her own head.

I don't want to give him false hope...

Even as the words formed she felt the familiar scrape against her heart. If only familiarity lessened the pain—but it had never yet seemed to. For over four months her strategy had simply been to ignore the pain. Acknowledge it was there, but otherwise ignore it. After all, what else could she do? She had fallen in love—stupidly and unintentionally and rashly—with a man who was the very last she should have fallen in love with. He'd never expected her to, and if he'd known she had he would have been appalled with her. It wasn't his fault she'd gone and done it, which meant that the fall-out was hers and hers alone. She had to tough it out, that was all, because what else was there to do? At some point, surely, she would wake up one morning and realise that she was over him? Then, and only then, would she be ready to do what Imogen was vocally urging her to do—move on.

Move on to another man.

But that was the stumbling block. It was unimaginable still even to *think* of becoming emotionally involved with another man. The very thought was impossible. And for that reason she didn't want anyone becoming emotionally hung up on her. Especially not someone as nice as Richard Saxonby.

She'd met him at one of Imogen's frequent dinner parties, to one of which she'd finally been lured, and it was blatantly obvious he'd been carefully selected as a dinner guest by Imogen, purely to dangle in front of her. She'd been placed next to him, and Alexa had to allow that Richard ticked a lot of boxes. He was nice, funny, good-natured and good-looking.

But he wasn't Guy de Rochemont.

No one is! No one possibly could be!

Alexa laid into her own futile objection ruthlessly. No one was ever going to be Guy, and Guy was beyond her now—beyond her for ever. Her future lay without him, and nothing on earth could change that.

I have to get over him! I have to!

The pain still scraped away at her heart, familiar and futile. So damn, *damn* futile…

And Immie was right. Until she made a determined effort to remake the rest of her life she would inevitably go on 'moping', as her friend so cruelly described her decision to withdraw from the social world, turn in on herself, try and tough it out.

I have to get over him—I have no alternative.

A deep breath filled her lungs, and she lifted her chin. 'All right,' she said, 'I'll give Richard a go.'

Immie shut her eyes. 'At last. Thank God,' she said fervently. Then, less audibly but yet more fervently, she muttered, 'And maybe that bastard who treated you like dirt will finally get the hell out of your head! And stay out!'

Guy was meeting and greeting. As the customary social phrases flowed smoothly from his lips, so familiar to him that he could say them on automatic, his conscious mind was busy. Busy exerting what had become bleakly familiar to him over the last four months—iron self-control over his emotions.

Self-control had been an essential weapon in his personal armoury just about all his life, he recognised. It was what enabled him to function, and always had. It was as necessary as breathing. It enabled him to run the behemoth of Rochemont-Lorenz, bear the mantle that was his by inheritance, and cope with all the endless demands made on him—not only of ensuring that Rochemont-Lorenz would continue to survive and prosper in this uncertain new century but also far more tedious to endure, of being endlessly on call to just about every member of the entire damn clan.

So many relatives! So many gatherings of relatives! *Dieu*, he could have filled his days simply circulating around Europe, and further afield, on a non-stop diet of family social occasions from birthdays to weddings to christenings to funerals. His attendance was expected, his presence courted, and offence taken if he made too many repeated omissions. Ambitions were raised if he decided that relatives active in the myriad companies and enterprises within Rochmont-Lorenz were worth promoting, chagrin taken by those he did not consider sufficiently able.

Not to mention tracking and mitigating the endless politicking and jostling between the different branches—internecine rivalries and alliances alike. Not everyone had been of the opinion that a man in his early twenties—even though he was the son of the oldest branch of the family—should take over the helm from his father at so young an age. There had been plenty of older cousins who had challenged his succession. But Guy's dedication to his role, his cool head and formidable financial acumen, had proved him his father's son both in ability and determination, and now his place at the head of the dynasty was assured—taken for granted, even.

The bleakness in his face was visible momentarily. Just as it was taken for granted that he would continue to guard the fortunes of Rochemont-Lorenz, whatever that required.

Right to the very point of marrying for that purpose.

His eyes glanced sideways.

Louisa was standing beside him—conspicuously so—standing very still as the mill of people in the ballroom ebbed and flowed, and the cluster that Guy was meeting and greeting came and went. She looked ill at ease, saying little, and although Guy made allowances for her youth and inexperience at such formal gatherings, and had sought to reassure her that he would give her all the support he could, that did not mean she would not have to learn how to handle them with the assurance that would be necessary as his wife.

It did not help that she was clearly of marked interest to anyone who knew him, for this was her first appearance in London as his fiancée, and for once her parents were not here. Guy had finally succeeded in shaking them off for his visit here, and Louisa was staying with the family of an old college friend for a weekend in England. Guy would have preferred her not to be here at all—not to be putting her through what was clearly an ordeal for her—but on the other hand she had to get used to the life she would be leading once she was married to him: the endless round of socialising and hostessing. That would best be done without her parents endlessly hovering over her—and over him.

The bleakness flared in his eyes again, mingled with the other emotion that was his constant companion—an emotion that required every ounce of will to control. An emotion that being in London had brought dangerously to the fore. He hadn't been here in four months, and he was glad of it. It only reminded him of what he'd had to do without. Into his mind's eye flicked the image of the eagle soaring, free and unfettered, over the lofty Alpine peaks as he'd headed into the confines of the tunnel. Resentment bit into him at what he was no longer free to do. And what he had to do instead.

At his side, Louisa hesitantly echoed his greeting of whoever it was whose hand he'd just shaken. His glance went sideways again. His mouth tightened. Annelise might not be here in person, but she was here in spirit, given the choice of gown for her daughter tonight. The dress was far too overpowering, stiff and grandiose. Presumably Annelise had been intending to make Louisa look older, more sophisticated. Instead it just emphasised her youth—and her evident awkwardness.

She'd looked a whole lot better in the jeans she'd worn that first evening—casual teenage wear, Guy thought. Since then, whenever he'd set eyes on her, she'd always been wearing outfits obviously chosen by her mother, and never to her advantage. He'd made no comment, not wanting to make her even more unsure of herself, but had made a mental note to ensure that as soon as they were married he would put her in the hands of someone who knew how to dress her properly, to bring out the best in her.

Memory stung like an unwelcome wasp.

His murmured accolade—*superbe*…

The image was vivid in his mind.

A slender column of burnt sienna raw silk, sleeveless and high-necked, exposing graceful arms and accentuating the subtle curves of breast and hip…

His mouth tightened even more. Why was he remembering Alexa when she was gone from his life now? His future lay with Louisa and he must remember that, must banish distracting memories of his lost freedom.

At his side, Louisa's gaze suddenly flickered up to his, and he saw anxiety flare briefly. He curved a smile to his mouth to reassure her, and hoped he'd succeeded. As he'd said to his mother, none of this was her fault. A frown drew his eyebrows together. Despite the punishing demands of starting to sort out Lorenz Investment on top of all his other concerns, he'd made an effort to spend what time he could with Louisa, seeking to get to know her and, above all, establish that she was prepared to enter into such a marriage with him.

Like his parents, hers, too, had married for the sake of Rochemont-Lorenz, and he was as reassured as he could be in the circumstances that Louisa was willing to marry him, and that she understood that for now his first concern must be saving her father's bank. Once that was secure he would give Louisa the attention she deserved, get to know her better and draw her out of her shyness and reticence.

A young, adoring bride. His eyes frowned. Was that what he wanted? Even as the thought came, he knew the answer.

No.

But perhaps for Louisa—who, like him, had not sought this marriage—it would be the best way for her to find happiness.

The frown turned to bleakness. For him, happiness seemed unlikely.

Once more his eyes chilled. Once more his iron self-control hammered down—familiar and exacting. And absolutely essential.

* * *

'More champagne?'

Alexa gave a slight shake of her head. 'Not for the moment. I'm doing fine.'

She was, too—and not just in consuming the champagne that was circulating generously at this crowded charity gala. She was doing fine just being out for the evening with Richard. As fine as could be expected. She'd had cold feet half a dozen times since she'd given in to Imogen, but each time she'd gone through the same dogged loop of facing up to the unalterable truth that she simply could not go on living like a hermit for the rest of her existence. She had to get on with her life.

Even so, when Richard had disclosed that he was inviting her to be his partner at this charity gala, she had almost backed out. Something more low-key would have been preferable for a first evening. On the other hand as she'd gone on to consider, a charity gala was preferable to some kind of quiet, intimate *tête-á-tête* over dinner. Nevertheless, it had taken a stern degree of resolution to get herself ready for this evening and come here on Richard's arm.

Although he could not be faulted as an evening companion, she knew she was far from relaxed. The commercial property company where he was a consultant architect was supporting this event. At his table was a mix of fellow architects and their partners, and she was conscious of being reserved—even for her. Conscious, too, of the presence of so many glitteringly arrayed guests—the charity had clearly captured a good number of London's seriously wealthy people. The realisation made her uneasy. Evoked memories and associations she did not want. She felt the familiar scrape across her heart.

But the last thing she wanted was to spoil Richard's evening by being anything other than a good guest, and so, despite her reserve, she entered into the general conversation at the table. As the evening wore on, a sobering truth came to her. Had she not ever gone through that rash, misguided affair with Guy de Rochemont—or rather, she amended, had she not committed the folly of allowing herself to so stupidly fall in love with him—she would have enjoyed Richard Saxonby's attentions far more.

It makes such sense to fall for him…

Surely, with time, she could make herself do so? Surely, with time, she could start to feel for him, finally expunge the hopeless, dead-end love she'd felt for Guy that was keeping her in this pointless limbo? Surely, she thought, as she smiled pleasantly at Richard, accepting his invitation to dance as the dinner, speeches and charity auction finally gave way to a general mingling around the huge room, surely it would not be too hard to take pleasure in lifting her eyes to his, letting their warmth set a glow in hers, letting his well-made mouth kiss hers? It should not be too hard to come to desire him. To fall—one day, when the time was right and they had come to know each other and desire each other—in love with him?

Then the music ended, and the couples on the floor relinquished each other and started to disperse back to their tables. Across the wide expanse of the room, as Richard let go of her and she started to head to her seat again, the pattern of people shifted and her eyes went through a newly opened gap, far across the ballroom. She stopped absolutely, totally still.

And knew that never in a hundred years could she fall in love with Richard or any other man.

Because the man she still loved was looking straight at her.

It was Alexa.

For a moment Guy's line of sight encompassed only

her—a tall, slender column of wine-rich burgundy—then it widened to take in her arm, resting on the sleeve of one of the many tuxedos, and the wearer of the tuxedo looking proprietorially down at her.

Instinctively Guy moved forward. It took only moments, and Alexa hadn't moved. Only her expression had changed. The initial flare of shock in her eyes as they had lighted on him was now veiled, and she seemed to wait, immobile, for his approach across the floor of the ballroom.

'Good evening, Alexa.'

His voice was smooth, the accent, as ever, hardly noticeable.

Unlike the rest of him.

Her eyes, beneath their veil, were sucked to him. In her limbs she felt a sudden debilitating weakness, as if they might not hold her upright. But she must force them to. Must force herself not, *not* to let her eyes feed on that tall, effortlessly elegant figure that instantly, immediately, made every other man in the room look clumsy and lumpish. She must *not* feast on the fabulous planes of his face, the sable feathering of his hair, and *not*, above all, drown unstoppably in those deep green eyes that were resting on her and making her feel dizzy, weightless, breathless.

Oh, dear God, let this not be happening…

She could hear the call in her head, hear all the sense that she was possessed of decrying what was happening, what she was doing, and her fatal reaction. She was totally unprepared for this, her guard helplessly, hopelessly absent, so that there was nothing she could do except reel from the impact of his presence.

Another cry sounded in her head, coming from deeper yet.

It shouldn't be like this!

She shouldn't be so overcome like this. She shouldn't!

She'd had four months—four whole months to come to terms with the end of the affair. Four months to build up that vital, essential distance from what had been to what her life now had to be. Four months to do without Guy de Rochemont in her life. To get him out of her head.

And it took a single moment now to make her realise that all her efforts to get over him had been utterly in vain.

Dismay drenched through her, mingling with the emotion that had seized her throat, her lungs, as she'd recognised him—that was still seizing her now, making it impossible for her to speak, impossible to do what she must, which was simply to say his name, in a calm, level voice, suitable for the occasion, in acknowledgment of his greeting. Then they would exchange pleasantries, he would wish her well, and stroll away again. Back to his life. Back to his world. Back to the woman he was going to marry.

That was what she must do.

But there was nothing. She could not speak.

Then, like a knight to her rescue, Richard was speaking. Prompting her.

'Alexa?'

There was nothing in his voice but appropriate social enquiry, but thankfully it served to catalyse her into responding. A quick smile parted her lips.

'Richard—this is Guy de Rochemont. I had the privilege of painting his portrait a while ago.'

A glint showed in the green eyes. 'The privilege was mine, Alexa.' He paused minutely. 'I did not think you would be here this evening…' There was the slightest Gallic intonation in the comment, so that it sounded like no more than a passing remark.

She made herself give her quick smile again.

'Nor I,' she said. She glanced at Richard, encompassing him in her reply. 'Richard was kind enough to invite me.'

Her escort smiled acknowledgement. Without noticing it, Alexa leant slightly towards him. There was a flicker of enquiry on Guy's expression. Richard held out his hand.

'Richard Saxonby—Guy de Rochemont,' she said, her voice and manner relaxed.

Guy took the outstretched hand, which was firm and solid. Like the man. Good-looking, too, he acknowledged, with intelligent eyes and a face that found it easy to smile. Personable. Attractive. He could see why Alexa was with him. There was nothing to dislike in this Richard Saxonby.

Which made it illogical, therefore, that he should have a sudden impulse, ruthlessly controlled, to wrest Alexa's hand from the man's sleeve, clamp it in his own grip, and walk off with her.

Walk off with her, pile her into a car, take her back to her apartment, his hotel—any damn place, providing it had a bed in it and no Richard Saxonby or any other damn male!—and then strip Alexa of that utterly unnecessary evening dress, loosen the clips on her hair to let its pale waterfall cascade like silk over her shoulders, cover her opening mouth with his and get her beautiful naked body to himself. Completely, luxuriously, satiatingly to himself.

His jaw tightened, and he slammed down on his overpowering impulse. That wasn't going to happen. Despite the flash of desire momentarily possessing him, Alexa Harcourt was in the past. Everything to do with her was in the past. He'd made his decision, terminated their relationship. So if she wanted to have a relationship with another man, such as this Richard Saxonby, what was it to him? Nothing. *Rien de tout.*

The familiar sense of self-control settled over him, shutting out everything that had to be shut out, kept down. Smoothly he exchanged the socially required introductions

with the man who was now clearly enjoying Alexa's beauti
ful body—an enjoyment which was nothing to do with Guy
any more, nor would be ever again, and therefore some
thing about which he was unconcerned. Any other reaction
was inappropriate to the circumstances. He no longer had
Alexa for himself—a decision which had been his and his
alone—and therefore if she wished, as *evidemment* she did
wish, to bestow herself upon this man—any other man, in
fact—it was of no moment to him at all. None.

And, because it was so, all that was required now was to
do as he proceeded to do: loose the man's hand and give an
acknowledging nod of his head towards Alexa. He ignored
the fact that her shoulder was brushing that of this Richard
Saxonby, with his good-looking face and well-made body
and his air of masculine assurance—and why not? He had
Alexa in his bed—a presence which would make any man
satisfied. With a brief indentation of his mouth in farewell,
Guy took his leave and walked away from her and her
bed-partner of choice these days, and returned to his own
party.

It had been the work of a few moments only—a fleet
ing episode in an evening which was like a thousand other
evenings in his life spent at some social gathering in which
he had no particular interest, but where his attendance was
expected and therefore was provided. He had not even had
to take regard, for those few brief, inconsequential mo
ments, of his fiancée and her *gaucherie* at this first social
outing at his side. For, just before his glancing gaze had
lighted on the unexpected sight of Alexa Harcourt, Louis
had murmured her excuses and slipped away to what he
assumed was the ladies' room.

She had still not returned, but he did not begrudge her
her respite—indeed, he found himself glad she had no
witnessed his exchange with Alexa. Not that it was any

concern of his fiancée, or anyone else. Although he had never drawn attention to Alexa's role in his life, it would have been more marked had he *not* acknowledged the presence that evening of the woman whom he had commissioned to make his likeness in oils. He had no wish for Louisa to be in a social situation of any kind with any female who had occupied a place in his life that she, as his fiancée and then wife, would never occupy. They were orbits that would never meet, never intersect.

As he resumed the party, slipping back into the banal chit-chat of his company, for a few brief moments in his mind's eye he saw that eagle again, soaring away over the peaks, far, far beyond. Ahead of him opened the tunnel, leading into the mountain's stony depths.

'Richard, would you excuse me a moment?'

Alexa's voice was steady, her manner just as it had been five minutes earlier.

But only on the outside. On the inside her nerves were jangling as if a current had been set through them. She had to get away.

Hardly waiting for his acknowledgement of her intention, she turned away, threading through the throng towards the blessed respite of the ladies' room. There was a sickness in her insides, and her throat was tight. The moment she was in the Ladies she plunged into a stall, shutting fast the door and clinging to it. How long she was in there she didn't know—knew only that her heart was pounding, her mind ragged. Gradually, very gradually, the shock—more than shock—of seeing Guy again started to recede. With intense effort she forced herself to calm the hectic beating of her heart, banned herself from letting the scene replay in her head. It didn't matter—it didn't matter a jot that she had seen Guy again! She would not *let* it matter!

She dared not…

She took the deep breath, steadying herself. Then, unlocking the door, she stepped out of the stall. Running on automatic, she crossed to the washbasins and mechanically started to wash her hands. As she did so, she noticed a large, opulent ring, with a glittering stone inset, on the surrounding vanity unit. There was no other person present—not even an attendant. Alexa glanced around. It was not the kind of ring to be left lying there. The area was deserted, but just as she was wondering what she should best do, reluctant to pick the ring up in case she might open herself to accusations of theft, there was a bustle behind her and a little cry of relief.

'*Gott seie Danke!*'

Alexa turned to see a young woman dive on the ring and jam it back on her finger. As she did so, Alexa could not but help catch her eye.

'I'm not used to wearing it,' the girl said by way of explanation.

There was a slight Germanic cast to her accent. She smiled at Alexa, who found herself answering with a smile as well as she reached for one of the stash of folded linen towels by the basin.

'I'm glad you remembered it,' she remarked. 'I was wondering who I ought to alert that it was here. It's not the sort of ring one would want to lose.'

The girl made a face. 'I would have got into such trouble,' she said. 'It's some kind of heirloom. Every bride for a million years has had it!' She didn't sound very impressed by the fact, and as she examined it on her finger she didn't look very impressed by the ring either, despite the vast size of the diamonds in the opulent setting.

'It's a magnificent ring,' said Alexa politely.

The girl grimaced. She was pretty, a dusky brunette,

but the gown she was wearing was too overpowering for her, Alexa thought critically. It was in a very stiff lemon silk, with a sweeping panelled skirt and a tight bodice that seemed to crush the girl's breasts.

'It doesn't suit me,' the girl said flatly, still eyeing the ring.

'Well, perhaps you need only wear it for formal occasions,' Alexa answered tactfully. 'Maybe you could ask your fiancé for something simpler, more to your taste, for everyday wear.' Judging by the vastness of the gems, providing a second engagement ring for casual wear would not be a problem for what was evidently a very wealthy fiancé.

The girl's expression changed. 'No, he wouldn't do that. I have to be formal all the time.' She looked down at her dress. 'Like this dress. It doesn't suit me either.'

Alexa frowned slightly. It seemed a shame that the girl couldn't choose a gown she liked. Something in a more youthful style, in a softer material.

'*Your* gown's beautiful!' the girl said impulsively. Then she grimaced again. 'But that wouldn't suit me either—I'm not tall enough for it. Anyway,' she went on, her expression downcast once more, 'I don't like evening clothes. I'm too clumsy for them.'

'Oh, you don't seem clumsy at all!' Alexa said immediately. The girl seemed to do nothing but deprecate herself, which was completely unfair—just because she was wearing a dress that no one with any sense should have put her in.

'I am,' responded the girl. 'My mother always says so! And my fiancé thinks it—I can tell.'

Alexa frowned again. 'Surely not?'

'He does. I know,' the girl averred. 'And if he doesn't think me clumsy, he thinks me very gauche and boring, even though he tries to hide it. He's used to beautiful, elegant women. Women like you,' she said artlessly. 'But it doesn't matter.' She gave a heavy, resigned sigh. 'Because he's marrying me all the same—it's all arranged.'

Alexa felt her unease mount. Part of her knew she should not really be allowing this conversation, but part of her—the greater part—could not help but feel disquieted by this artless but clearly self-deprecating girl and what she was depicting about her engagement.

'You know, these days,' she ventured carefully, busying herself wiping her fingers on the handtowel, 'women don't *have* to marry men they've been "arranged" to marry…'

The girl only shrugged. 'Well, it's better than the alternative. Being nagged to death by my parents! They're actually pleased with me for the first time in my life—even though my mother keeps going on at me about how to behave, and so on and so on. My fiancé won't take any more notice of me when we're married than he does now—he'll keep a mistress, one of those beautiful, elegant women that he prefers. I won't mind, really.' She lifted her chin as if to confirm her assertion, but Alexa saw a bleakness in her eyes and felt her disquiet increase.

She opened her mouth to say something, but what she didn't know—because what *could* she say? Before she could speak, someone came into the area.

'Louisa! There you are! We were about to send out a search party!'

It was a middle-aged woman with the cut-glass voice of the English upper-class. The girl Alexa had been speaking to started, as if caught out doing something she shouldn't have been.

'I'm just coming,' she said hastily, immediately looking flustered. She threw a glance at Alexa, the bleakness in her face replaced by a fleeting awkward smile, then she was gone, ushered out by the older woman, who hadn't wasted a glance at Alexa.

Slowly, Alexa dropped the used handtowel into the basket provided. She felt a pang of pity for the girl, stranger though she was. It was none of her business, obviously, but no girl who was betrothed should be that downcast. She should be brimming with happiness, radiant with joy. The last thing that poor girl looked was *radiant...*

She sighed. Life was seldom as happy as people wanted it to be. Hers included. The exchange with the girl, disturbing as it had been, had served to distract her from her own situation, but now, as she forced herself to return to the ballroom, she felt the weight of it tear at her. Misery enveloped her. Why, oh, why had she had to see Guy again? How was she to do what she knew with every fibre of her being she must do? Free herself from the hopeless mire she'd fallen into and get her life together again, put Guy de Rochemont behind her, into the past, where he had to be.

I thought I was making a start! Thought that I was finally making myself move on, leave him behind me.

But it had been fool's gold, that hope. All it had taken to rip every frail tatter of that hope had been a bare few moments...

An ache scoured inside her, physical in its impact.

Hopeless in its longing for something that could never be.

One of his party had said something to him, but Guy hadn't the faintest idea what it was. He had hardly noticed when Louisa had returned to his side. There was only one thing that he was aware of—burningly, corruscatingly aware.

He was angry.

It was inside him, lashing like the tail of a tiger. His replies to conversation grew more abstract, his mood more impatient. He needed to get out of here. He needed to get rid of these people—Louisa included. In a remote corner of his mind he knew he was being brutishly unjust, because none of this was her doing. It was not *her* fault she was standing beside him, gauche and awkward, saying so little her lack of conversational ability was almost painful. It was not *her* fault that her father had got his damn bank into deep water, and it was not *her* fault that she just happened to be Heinrich's daughter. It was not her fault that she was going to marry Guy.

Above all—and he could feel the lash of his anger catching him on the raw, castigating him—it was not her fault she was not Alexa...

Into the mesh of anger another emotion speared—an emotion he did not want to feel, as he did not want to feel this lashing within him. An emotion that he wanted to push away, deny, ignore, disregard—any word would do, so long as he got rid of it. Disposed of it. Just the way he had disposed of his affair with Alexa Harcourt with a stark, effective severing. He had moved her out of his life because she could no longer be part of it—because his life had moved on.

Into the tunnel. The tunnel that was funnelling him forward to a marriage he could not avoid, to a future mapped out for him just as it had been for his parents, Louisa's parents, and so many more of his family over the generations, across the centuries.

Anger speared again, more intense. More intense, too, the other emotion—the one that was focussed like a dark, burning flame on what he had put aside to enter the tunnel. What he could not have again.

And what, with sudden consuming heat, he wanted once more...

One last time...

CHAPTER SIX

'THANK you so much, Richard, for a lovely evening.' Alexa infused warmth into her voice. It was a little forced, but she hoped Richard hadn't noticed. Just as she hoped he hadn't noticed her abstraction during the remainder of the evening.

She'd tried hard to be a good guest, the pleasant evening companion owed to someone as nice as Richard Saxonby, but her mind had had a will of its own. It had wanted her to wander off, wanted her to seek and find the object of its attentions, and she'd had continually to rein it back. So, too, her gaze. The knowledge that Guy was somewhere in this vast gathering, with scores of tables and hundreds of people, had been a constant torment to her. She had felt herself disastrously, damningly, wanting to seek him out with her eyes, searching through the mass to see if her eyes could light on him again…feast on him again. But they mustn't! She must not. That was all there was to it.

But it might be the very last time I see him in the flesh…

The plea came from somewhere deep inside her. She fought to crush it back, push it back where it had come from, but it kept trying to find its way out.

I've got to be strong! I've got to!

The admonition was fierce, the intent resolute.

Just don't look for him—don't try and see him. Leave him alone. He's nothing to do with you any more—nothing!

That was all she must hold on to. That time in her life, when Guy de Rochemont had been with her, was over. Gone. Finished. That was all there was to it.

But it was one thing to tell herself that, another to do what she was told—stop trying to see Guy somewhere in all this crowd.

In the end it had been a relief when Richard's party had started to break up and disperse. So focussed had she been on Guy's disastrous presence at the gala that she'd given no thought to what Richard might be thinking about how the evening should end. But now, as he helped her into a taxi in the hotel's forecourt, he said solicitously, after she'd thanked him for the evening, 'Would you like me to see you home?'

It was lightly said, no more than a polite offer, and Alexa was grateful. He was not going to chance anything this early, and it was yet another sign of how nice he was. Since she knew he lived in Highgate, quite a different direction from Notting Hill, she assured him she'd be absolutely fine, thanked him again for the evening, and waved him goodbye as her taxi pulled away. But once she was on her own, the taxi threading along Park Lane, she was instantly prey to her emotions. She sat back, her eyes shut, wishing she could shut out her thoughts as easily.

But it was impossible. Impossible to suppress, as she knew she must, the swirl of emotions in her head. Oh, *why* had she had to see Guy again? It had been the very last thing she'd needed!

I thought I was starting to get over him. Get him out of my system. Move on. Make new connections, put him behind me finally...

Her eyes shadowed.

I thought I was starting to make myself fall out of love with him...

Her hopes had been real, fervent—but all it had taken was a single, shocking sight of him to know just how useless those hopes had been. In anguish, the thought resolved in her head. Hollowing her out with hopelessness.

I'm still in love with him... And there's nothing I can do about it...

The truth, stark and painful, stared bleakly back at her, scraping at her heart with razoring pain. Guy was gone—gone from her life...

As the taxi deposited her on the pavement outside the house she lived in, she felt an empty longing in her, a hopeless tearing. She opened the front door into the entrance lobby. Dolefully, her feet leaden, she gathered her narrow skirt in one hand and headed heavy-hearted up the stairs. Never had life seemed so bleak.

A pall seemed to be hanging over her, slowing her steps. And what was there to speed up for? An empty flat awaited her. A lonely night.

A hopeless skein of yearning unwound in her. Heartache and hollowness.

In her head, as it had been over and over again, she saw Guy's image and felt her heart squeeze—but Guy wasn't there. Would never be there. Never again. Never—

The ache in her heart worsened.

At the door to her flat she paused, summoning the mental energy to open it and go in. When she did, she closed the door behind her, feeling the emptiness of the flat all around her. Dropping her evening bag on the hall table, she shrugged off her fake fur evening jacket and walked listlessly into the sitting room, intent on reaching the kitchen beyond to make herself a cup of herbal tea to retire with—and stopped dead.

Guy de Rochemont was there.

Her pulse froze. Then surged. She must have made some small noise in her throat, her hand flying upwards. Did she try and speak? She didn't know. Only that Guy had cut right across her.

'Where is he?' he asked, his voice casual. But there was the edge of a whip in it.

'Who?' Alexa's brow furrowed as she tried to breathe. Tried to reel in all her senses, emotions that were suddenly flying haywire, as if an electric field had arced through the room.

Guy—Guy is here—here!

The consciousness of his presence transfixed her. Stifled her lungs.

'Lover-boy,' said Guy.

Alexa stared. Stared at the figure seated as she had seen him so often, shadowed by the dim light. She didn't answer—couldn't answer. Had no idea what he was talking about. No idea about anything at all other than the overpowering consciousness of his presence.

With a sudden fluid movement he jack-knifed to his feet, crossed towards her. His pace was feral, and Alexa felt a flare deep within her.

'You didn't bring him back here?' The voice was harsh.

The question had tormented him all the way here—all the time since he had ushered Louisa to the steps of her friend's house, bade her goodnight, his mouth saying words that were appropriate, his mind somewhere completely different.

Making his decision.

Issuing the requisite instructions to his driver.

He still had the keys to Alexa's flat, and as he'd walked in he had known that the only thing on his mind was whether she was going to come back here alone, or go home with the man who had replaced him. Or bring the man back here.

Now, with a surge of raw, visceral emotion, he knew she had done all that he'd desired—come here, and alone.

Alexa still looked blank. Was still incapable of any coherent thought at all. Only of raw, surging emotion.

A rough sound came from him, as if dismissing his own question. He closed in on her, and Alexa felt raw emotion surge again. His hands clamped on her upper arms—hard, like a vice. Her eyes flew to his. She felt that surge seize her lungs. Felt her eyes arc into his, burning green, burning into her. He was saying something to her. Something she did not understand. Whatever language it was, the words were beyond her. Everything was beyond her. She knew only the emotion surging in her, only the hard clasp of his hands on her bare flesh, only the drowning of her eyes in his.

And the feral curve of his lips as he held her, pinioned. There was an unmistakable, irrefutable message in his burning eyes. To which she could give no answer other than the one her own eyes were giving.

For one long, timeless moment he held her, as her lungs seized, frozen, unbreathing, and then slowly, achingly, agonisingly slowly, his mouth started to lower.

'No man but me, *ma belle* Alexa,' he breathed. 'No man...'

Then his mouth was branding hers with his possession.

And in his tensed, steel-coiled body, the lash of his anger was finally extinguished. The hard, unbroken armour of his iron self-control finally pierced.

* * *

It was later. Much, much later. How much later Alexa didn't know. Couldn't know. Time had stopped.

Only her senses were alive. Senses once submerged, suppressed, for four long, empty, meaningless months.

Now released again. As if from a casket, buried deep. Broken open.

Limbs splaying, spreading; hands clasping, holding; mouths seeking, devouring; bodies winding, binding. Fusing.

Fusing into one. One living, moving body. Arcing. Moulding. Melding.

On, and on, and on.

Until all was gone. All. And now she lay there, in the slackening circle of his arms, her hair a shroud around his shoulder, her brow against the smooth, damask marble of his chest, with nothing left in her. Only the plunging of her heart.

Then, into the pulsing silence, Guy spoke. His voice was rough, distanced, speaking out into the darkness around them.

'This has changed everything.' The words fell into the pounding silence between them. 'Everything,' he repeated, and his voice was harsher than ever. 'I will not do without you.' A heavy breath escaped him, his chest rising and falling. 'It will be...difficult. I cannot be with you often. Even less than I was able before. You must understand that. Accept that. It will be when I can. As I can.'

His hand around her fastened on her hip, tightened.

'It cannot be as it was. You must understand that too. But what I can do, I will.' She heard a scissoring breath. Then the voice speaking out into the darkness continued. 'I will come to you—there can be no other way. Discretion is essential—I am sorry, but it must be so. No one must know that I have taken up with you again. There can be no breath of suspicion.' She felt his chest beneath her brow rise and fall again. Then he spoke again. Still into the darkness. Staccato, disjointed. 'Then later…later…afterwards… it will be easier. It will be understood. Accepted. By everyone.' He paused again. 'Including Louisa. My intended bride.'

His voice hardened.

At his side, in his arms, Alexa felt her blood thicken and congeal.

He was still speaking. 'Until then—' He fell silent. 'Until then only this is possible,' he finished. His voice was flat.

For a while, as the blood began to sluggishly force its way through her, bringing no heat but only a chill, draining cold, she just went on lying there, her head resting on him, her hand across the flat, taut plane of his abdomen as his arms encircled her.

Imprisoned her.

He said nothing more, only gazing upwards into the darkness above them. After a while he moved, lifted one arm to glance at the circle of gold around his wrist. Then with another scissoring breath he removed himself from her, reaching for his scattered clothes, pulling them on wordlessly. She watched him—watched him with nerveless limbs, numb. When he was dressed again he looked down at her.

'I am sorry—I have to go right now. Immediately. I should not be here—not with Louisa in London. There is too much danger of discovery—too great a risk that she might find out, be informed of where I went after the gala.' He took another heavy, distracted breath. 'I will need to talk to you, *evidemment*, to explain all the arrangements, the necessities… But right now I must go. It's unavoidable. And tomorrow I'm returning to Paris. Then everything will be impossible for at least one—two weeks. Then perhaps a possibility—that is all.' His voice was still flat. 'I will phone you when I can.' His expression changed minutely. 'You can no longer phone me. You must understand that.' He broke off, then with a rasp said, 'It is the very devil, but it is the only way. The *only* way! For now there can be no other, and I will take what I can. I am sorry—but it is all that is possible now.'

For one long moment he went on looking down at her. Then with a swift, fluid movement, one hand splaying on the wall behind the bed, he sealed her mouth.

Brief, dispassionate. Marking her as his.

'Until I can get here again,' he said.

Then, straightening, he walked out.

She heard the door shut behind him. Then nothing more.

Out on the street, damp from the rain, Guy walked—his pace rapid, his mind occupied. Racing ahead. Far, far ahead. He could see it. See what he had thought he would not see again. The tunnel, opening once more to space and air. Beyond, the freedom of the eagles beckoned.

'Alexa?' Imogen's voice was sleepy. Then a moment later anxious, despite the early hour of this morning visit. It was only eight o'clock, and as it was the weekend Imogen was still in her dressing gown. She had donned it when her bell had rung, the buzzer depressed unwaveringly until Imogen had groped her way to the door and opened it. She had seen, outside, Alexa—fully dressed, a small suitcase in her hand.

And a fistful of ten-pound notes.

Alexa walked in, holding out the notes to Imogen.

'One hundred pounds,' she said. Her voice was clipped. Unemotional.

But Imogen could hear an ocean of emotion in it.

She did not take the out-held notes, only pushed Alexa into the kitchen, sat her down at the breakfast bar, plonked herself opposite. She looked at the notes, looked at Alexa, at her drawn, immobile face.

'Oh, *hell*,' said Imogen. Then, as Alexa dropped the ten ten pound notes on the bar, she added another expletive. '*Bastard.*'

A strange noise sounded in Alexa's throat.

'I didn't believe you,' she said. 'I didn't believe anything you said about him. I *wouldn't* believe it. Well, now—' she took a breath that razored the cords in her throat '—now I do.' She let her eyes rest on her friend. They were expressionless. 'You said one hundred pounds. That was the bet. One hundred pounds that he'd be back, ready to carry on, despite the minor inconvenience of his forthcoming nuptials.' She swallowed as if a stone were lodged in her throat, large and immovable. Unbearable. 'He came back. Last night. He was at the charity gala. He let himself into my flat. We—' She halted. Swallowed again. 'Then he made his proposition to me. Informed me of his plans for me. For that wretched girl he's going to marry!'

Her face worked. 'I met her last night. I didn't know it was her—and thank God she didn't know who I was! But it was clear—clear as a bell—that she knew what she was in for in marrying him. Knew just how Guy was going to treat her. I didn't know it was him she was talking about— just heard about her cold-blooded brute of a fiancé, who thinks her clumsy and gauche, and who's going to set up a mistress and pay no attention to his bride and doesn't even damn well care! Doesn't care that he's going to humiliate her and neglect her. And I felt so damn sorry for her. But I didn't…didn't…' Her features twisted. 'I didn't realise that it was going to be me who was going to be set up to be the convenient mistress. To give her husband someone "beautiful and elegant—'" she mocked the description with bitter savagery '—to have sex with, because he'd be uninterested in his *ingénue* young teenage bride!'

She raked more air into her lungs. 'Immie, I thought you were cynical and mistrusting, but you were right—right all along! I thought that however...*odd*...you thought my relationship with Guy was, you were wrong about his treating me badly. I wasn't just convenient sex-on-demand as you said I was.' Her voice hardened, scraping along her skin. 'But you were right all along. That's exactly what I was. Exactly what he still wants me to be. The only difference is that this time—' she gave a harsh, humourless laugh '—I'm to be even more invisible! This time around I mustn't even phone him, mustn't contact him, must be totally unseen, unsuspected.' Her voice twisted. 'At least until he's got this convenient extra-marital sexual arrangement accepted by his bride. Which she will, poor kid, because it's what she's expecting anyway.'

Her face worked again, hands clenching.

'Oh, Immie—how could I have been such a damn *fool*?'

Across the breakfast bar, Imogen could only sigh heavily, squeeze Alexa's hands comfortingly, and say, with care and tact, 'It's always easy to blind ourselves to what we don't want to know.' Then, with even more care and tact, she said, 'Um, you mentioned that Guy let himself in? Which means he must still have your keys? I don't mean to panic you, but it might be a good idea to change the lock.'

Alexa gazed across at her friend. Her expression changed.

'Oh,' she said, 'I'm going to do a lot more than just that.'

* * *

Guy was in a good mood. An excellent mood. The best mood he'd been in for a long time.

Everyone noticed it. His staff, his friends, his family. He knew what they ascribed his good mood to, and he found it *fort amusant* that they did. Because it had nothing to do with his impending nuptials.

Just the opposite.

Marriage to Louisa no longer loured over his head like a heavy weight. Now, thankfully, he no longer had only its confines ahead of him. Instead, he had something very different. Satisfaction creamed through him. Why had he ever thought he'd have to relinquish his liaison with Alexa? Do without her? She'd suited him so well. Why had he ever terminated his affair with her just because he had been hog-tied by Heinrich into marrying his daughter to save his pernicious bank? Such a sacrifice was, in fact, quite unnecessary.

Oh, it would be tricky, he knew. Not easy to pull off, and requiring careful timing and finesse. Yes, it would involve deceiving Louisa—but, young as she was, she had been born to a family in which such arrangements were unexceptional, so why should she object to what he was planning? She understood the realities of the kinds of lives they all led, the privileges and the obligations alike. And, since she was no more in love with him than he with her, why should she care either way? Yes, she might perceive his arrangement as unflattering, but there was no question that she would be jealous, or feel rejected. Why should she not be accommodating about it all? Understand what he was doing, and why?

As for Alexa, she had already proved exemplarily discreet, so he had no reason to doubt *her* continuance on that score. He'd warned her that extra discretion would be required initially, but he was confident it would not be an issue for her. She would be as accommodating as Louisa, understanding the necessity for a low profile for the time being.

His mind raced ahead.

When can I be with her again?

Anticipation licked in him. The hunger of desire—desire that had burned within him that night of the charity gala when he'd seen her again after doing without her for four long months. He'd told himself that terminating their affair had been a necessity he could not avoid—unwelcome though it had been when she was so exactly what suited him—but seeing her again like that he had known, when the revealing anger lashed within him, that one thing was very clear about Alexa.

No man but me.

Well, now it was going to stay that way. No man but he in her life.

That was what he wanted—and that was now what he was going to get.

He just had to make it work, that was all. And he would. Of that he was confident.

He leant back in his chair, reaching out to the keyboard on his desk, tapping it briefly to pull up his diary, scrolling rapidly down the coming weeks. He looked for that all-essential window when he could get back to London—back to Alexa.

Back to her bed.

He paused the scroll. There—that was the opportunity he wanted. Ten days away. A mere ten days to wait before he got her to himself again. His good mood enhanced, he extracted his mobile and dialled hers. There was no answer. He gave a slight shrug, sliding the phone back in his jacket pocket. He would try again later. Because of this new, irritating need for discretion he would not leave a message, only speak to her—though he knew from previous experience that when she was painting, whether or not her subject was a commission or personal, she would not answer.

Tant pis—there was time in hand.

But as the days slipped by he was still not able to reach her. Three days before he was due in London his mounting irritation peaked, and he sent one of his security staff to convey the information about his imminent arrival.

The information was never delivered.

Alexa Harcourt, so he was informed by his security staff, no longer lived at that address. Alexa Harcourt, so his disbelieving enquiries further revealed, had disappeared off the face of the earth.

CHAPTER SEVEN

ALEXA flexed her fingers, trying to warm them and failing. The cold was biting, eating into her, making holding a paintbrush an increasing ordeal. The lone electric heater in the room she'd allocated as a studio, actually little more than a lean-to, made scant impact against the harsh weather outside.

But this desolate spot was exactly what she'd sought—somewhere to hide from the man who wanted to keep her as a handy side-dish for his tasteless marriage to a girl who was resigned to his infidelity even before her wedding day. Somewhere to hide from the man who'd treated her as a convenient source of sex-on-demand, accepting and acquiescent, whenever it had suited him.

A man who expected her to say yes to anything he wanted of her.

Her face hardened. Well, finally, *finally,* she'd learnt to say no.

The tight band around her heart, which had been there for so long now, tightened another notch. She'd learnt to welcome it, that crushing tightness. Knowing that it was like a stay around her heart, holding it together. Holding her together. Making her strong.

Strong enough to hate the man she'd once loved.

Because hate him she did. There was no doubt about that. No doubt in her mind whatsoever.

He treated you like dirt—and then he came back to treat you even worse than dirt!

All the arguments that she'd poured out at Imogen's that long, nightmare day when she'd fled to her friend's house, churning with emotion, sounded again in her head. Imogen had let her pour them out, let her purge herself, and then, making her a large, hot, strong mug of tea, she'd run through all the options that presented themselves.

This cottage in the middle of winter, in the middle of nowhere, had not been top of Imogen's list. Top of her list, Alexa knew, was simply changing the locks on Alexa's flat, changing her mobile and landline number, paying a solicitor to write to Guy de Rochemont informing him not to attempt any further contact with his client, and then, as a perfect remedy to all of Alexa's ills, going out with Richard Saxonby as often as it took for her to realise he was a perfect match, then moving in with him, settling down and, best of all, marrying him.

'He's absolutely ideal for you!' Imogen had waxed lyrical, running through, yet again, all the reasons why he was such a wonderful man and perfect for Alexa.

But Alexa knew that his main attraction, for her friend, was that he was not Guy. That was all that really mattered to Imogen. Keeping Guy away from Alexa, keeping him out of her life. Out of her head. Most importantly of all, out of her heart.

'Thank goodness he's shown his true colours—not that was ever in doubt anyway,' she seethed. 'But now even you, blind as you were to him, have seen him for what he is!'

To Imogen it was obvious, Alexa could see, that the way

to rid herself of Guy de Rochemont was by replacing him with Richard. But for Alexa it was not that simple.

'It wouldn't be fair on Richard,' she said. 'And anyway…' her chest heaved '…I don't want to be in London. It's too—'

Dangerous—that was what she meant to say. Too dangerous. Oh, she could change her locks and her telephone numbers, but that wouldn't make her feel safe.

Safe from Guy—safe from what he wanted of her.

Memory burned like a flame, licking over her flesh. It was agony—and worse, far worse, than agony.…

She shut her eyes, trying to stamp out the flame, stamp out the memory imprinted onto her body. *Her body fusing with his, melding, becoming one, becoming whole…*

Desperately she tore her mind away, forcing her eyes to open again. Imogen was talking, immediately sympathetic. 'I agree—a change of scene is exactly what you need. Somewhere completely different. A holiday—you haven't had one in ages. Somewhere tropical—the Caribbean, the Maldives, the Seychelles!' Seeing her friend's expression she hurried on. 'We'll go together. I can rearrange my diary today—there's nothing I can't get out of—then we'll hit the internet and book online. We can be at the airport tomorrow!'

'I don't think—' Alexa started hesitantly. What Imogen was suggesting was the very last thing she would possibly want.

'It's just what you need,' Imogen repeated. 'A complete change of scene, total relaxation. Getting away from everything—especially that adulterous bastard!'

Alexa shook her head. 'I want to move out of London,' she said.

Imogen was aghast. 'You can't run away! Why *should*

you? *He's* the one that's been a despicable rat. Why should you have to go? What about your commissions?'

'I've nearly finished the current one, and you'll just have to cancel anything else.'

Imogen bit her lip. 'I won't let you mess up your career for that creep.'

Alexa just looked at her. 'I've no heart for it any more. I don't want anything more to do with that world. All those rich, powerful men… It…it reminds me too much…'

'OK,' Imogen allowed, hearing the shaky note in Alexa's voice. 'Well, why not go on some kind of art-break, or something, for the rest of the winter? Move to Morocco, or Brazil, somewhere you can just paint your own stuff for a couple of months? I'll postpone any bookings and say you've gone somewhere warm for your health for the time being.'

Alexa nodded slowly, murmuring agreement, and Imogen was reassured. But she was aghast when she discovered just what Alexa had decided on.

'No, no, no, *no*!' she cried. 'That's just *not* what you need. Holing up in some godforsaken hovel in the wilds of Devon in the middle of winter!'

But her objections fell on deaf ears. Alexa packed her suitcase, and enough of her art materials to keep her going, put away the personal effects in her apartment, and handed it over to an estate agent to let it for six months. Then she hired a car, loaded it up, and set off.

'The estate agent has my contact details, but I've told him not to let you have them unless it's a genuine life or death emergency,' she told an appalled Imogen.

'I can't believe you're doing this,' Imogen said disbelievingly.

'I need to do it.' It was all Alexa could manage to say.

It had been true, and was true still, she knew, despite the

drear, cheerless countryside—or because of it. The leafless trees, the cold, raw weather, the grey, lowering skies and bare, muddy fields tuned in exactly with what she felt.

Desolate.

A desolation of the heart. Of the spirit.

Worse, much worse than before.

Then I thought it was simply that I'd fallen in love with a man who hadn't fallen in love with me. I accepted it— just as I accepted the limitations of the relationship—but I never thought ill of him.

The vice around her heart crushed tighter still.

Now she knew better.

She knew that she'd fallen in love with a man who wanted nothing more than adulterous, clandestine sexual congress. He regarded her as fit for nothing more. Humiliating his bride, holding both her and the woman he wanted to make sexual use of in callous contempt.

For a man like that it was possible to feel only one emotion.

Not love. Never love—not for a man like that. Love had to be not ignored, like last time, not starved or blanked out, but torn out by its roots, ripped out of her heart, bleed though it would. It did not matter. She had to be clean of such a tainted, toxic emotion. For such a man only one emotion should be felt.

Hatred. Hatred that would burn her clean—burn and rip that misbegotten love out of her. Hatred that could tear it loose.

Hatred that could free her from its thrall. Release her from this prison of desolation.

But hatred had to be channelled, or it would devour her.

With a set, granite face she reached again for the canvas. Blank, bare—

Then reached for her paints, her brush.

Reached for her hatred.

And let it loose upon the canvas.

'Well?' Guy's voice was harsh as he snatched up the phone.

'It's done.' The person at the other end of the line was brief, the way he knew his employer wanted him to be. He'd given the answer he knew his employer wanted. Just why Guy de Rochemont, who ran the vast financial and commercial empire of Rochemont-Lorenz, wanted to make this particular purchase his employee had no idea. It fitted in with nothing in the vast Rochemont-Lorenz portfolio, and was on such a small scale that even if there had been some logical reason for it, it was hardly of the order of magnitude that would draw the attention of the head of the empire. But it was not his job to ask questions—only to carry out instructions, and that was what he had done.

'Now, get me the following information,' came his next instruction down the line. 'I want it by tonight.' The line went dead.

In his London office, Guy dropped the phone on the gleaming mahoghany surface of his desk. His eyes stared out into the middle distance. They were very green. Very glittering.

Hard as emeralds.

They were harder still when he received the information he'd demanded. Still hard when the next morning, after a sleepless night—as so many nights now were—he climbed into the gleaming new vehicle and gunned the engine, keying in his destination to the satnav.

As he headed out into the London traffic the emerald glitter focussed only on the direction he was going.

Westwards.

* * *

It had been raining all night. Steady, relentless rain that had come down out of a leaden sky, turning the fields to a quagmire and the unmetalled lane up to the cottage to little better. Alexa was glad she didn't have to get in any shopping for a while. She'd got into a routine since she'd been here, of driving into the local market town some ten miles away and picking up enough groceries and household items to keep her going for a week.

Her lifestyle was simple, pared to the bone. She was uninterested in anything else. So long as the stash of logs neatly stacked in the outhouse extension behind the cottage's old-fashioned kitchen held out, so she could feed the log-burning stove in the sitting room that was the main source of heat besides the electric heater in the lean to, and so long as the electricity supply stayed operational, she was fine.

She wasn't lonely.

She was used, after all, to a quiet lifestyle. Even in London she'd been content with her own company, never craving the bright lights. Occasional dinner parties, lunch out, the theatre, concerts and art exhibitions were all that she'd wanted. Had it not been for her work and for the rich treasures of art that London housed she'd have been happier in the country anyway.

Though she would not want to live anywhere as remote, as desolate as this isolated cottage. It was doubtless an idyllically pastoral hideway in the summer for holiday-makers, but it now dripped water from the eaves on her head when she stepped outside. From under the doors a perpetual draught whistled, echoing the wind wuthering in the chimney in the evenings. The windows rattled in the bedroom, and she was pretty certain that mice were scuttling in the cob walls.

Not that they bothered her either, provided they kept out

of sight. Nor did the spiders that emerged from the wood basket, scuttling across the sitting room to take refuge under the sofa.

Unless the rain was a deluge, she made the effort to get outdoors every day, pulling on the pair of sturdy gumboots she'd bought in the market town, with a thick waxed jacket and a scarf to hold her hair down in the wind that blew in from the west, whatever the weather. She tramped down the muddy lanes and across fields, where incurious cattle continued to graze, and weather-beaten sheep lifted heads to stare unblinkingly at her as she crossed their domain.

The bleakness all around her echoed her own.

How long had she been here now? The days had merged one into another, and then into weeks. It must be four, five weeks already.

But time had no meaning for her. She was living in a world of her own, bare and bleak, but it was what she wanted. What she needed.

She crossed to the log-burner and crouched down to feed it. She'd mastered the art of keeping it alight, damping down all night, then building it up again in the morning. Now, by midday, the little sitting room was warm, despite the raw cold outside and the sodden, chill air.

Closing the door of the log-burner, she straightened. And turned her head sharply. She could hear a car approaching.

It was a car, definitely, not the tractor in which the local farmer sometimes lumbered past the cottage on his way to his fields. Warily, she crossed to the little deep inset window and peered out across the lane. A huge four-by-four was drawing up, its sides covered in newly spattered mud from the unmetalled lane, its wheels half a foot deep in a waterlogged rut.

Was this the letting agent? The local farmer? Someone

who was completely lost down this dead-end lane? Someone
was getting out. She heard a car door slam, but she couldn'
see from this side. She quit her post and headed for the
front door, pulling it open.

And froze.

Disbelief drowned her. She could *not* be seeing wha
she was. She couldn't…

*It can't be him—it can't, it can't! It's impossible
Impossible! He can't be here. He can't, he can't, he
can't!*

But he was. Striding up to her.

Her vision swam, and she clutched at the doorframe
to steady herself. He stopped in front of her. Tall. Overpowering.

Intimidating.

A shot of emotion bolted through her. It wasn't fear—i
couldn't be fear, surely it couldn't be fear? But it was strong
and sharp and it seized her lungs.

'Alexa.'

It was all he said, standing there, confronting her.

'How—how did you…?' Her frail voice failed.

But he didn't answer, merely steered past her, going into
the cottage. Numbly she followed him. He seemed far too
tall for its low-pitched confines. He strode into the living
room, where the log-burner beckoned, and positioned himself in front of it, looking around the room. Then his gaze
swept back to Alexa, standing frozen by the doorway. His
eyes glittered.

'Why?'

A single word, but to Alexa it held a universe of demand
Shock was still seizing her, but she'd gone into that ultra
calm that accompanied the condition. Everything seemed
to have stopped around her.

'Why?' she echoed. Her voice seemed calm too. Preternaturally calm. 'Why what, precisely, Guy?'

'Why did you run?' His voice was less controlled than hers. Deeper. Harsher. And his eyes still burned green.

Alexa tilted her head. Very slightly, but discernibly. 'What did I have to stay for? Your…offer…didn't appeal.'

His eyes narrowed, pinpointing her with laser focus. 'No? That wasn't the message I got when I had your body beneath mine. You gave me a quite different message then, Alexa.' His voice caressed her like the tip of a whip.

She felt colour flare in her cheeks. 'That shouldn't have happened.'

'But it did. It did, Alexa, and now I want an explanation of what the *hell* you think you're doing!'

He was angry. He was actually angry. Alexa stared at him. Inside, she felt a leashed, powerful emotion at seeing him standing here, in the very place she had sought refuge from him. But she would not let it loose. She would keep it smothered. Controlled.

'How did you find me?' Her voice was clipped. 'No one knows I'm here.'

'Your letting agency knows. I found them through the tenants in your flat.' His tone was offhand.

'I instructed the agency to disclose this address to no one!' she snapped. 'How dared they tell you?'

His eyes glinted sardonically. 'I have access to all their files. As of yesterday, the agency belongs to me.'

'*What?*'

'I bought the agency, Alexa. It was clearly the only way to find out where you were.'

She stared. 'You *bought* the agency to get my address?' There was incredulity in her voice. Then, with a lift of her

chin, she bit out, 'You wasted your money. I don't know
what you think you're doing, but—'

'I'm doing what I clearly ought to have done that night—
making things clear to you!'

Her eyes flashed. 'Oh, you made things very clear—
don't worry. I got the picture, I promise you. But like I
said, I didn't like the offer, so I turned it down. And now—'
her face hardened '—you can just get out—get out of my
life!'

His expression changed. 'You don't mean that.'

It was the calm assurance with which he spoke that lit
the touchpaper. Exploding her fury.

'My God,' she breathed, 'you arrogant, conceited pig! Do
you really think that just because you're Guy de Rochemont
you can behave any way you want? Do you think that just
because like a complete *idiot* I fell back into bed with you
I'll do whatever you want? Do you? You think you can
have an affair with me, and then calmly tell me one fine
day that you're getting married, and that's it—and then
months later turn up again and just pick up again where
you left off, not worrying about anything as trivial as your
fiancée? *Do* you? Because—'

'Stop—Alexa, listen to me.' His hand had flown up, as
if to silence her passionate outpouring with an autocratic
command.

'What for?' she bit back. 'So you can tell me how *discreet* you're going to have to be when you pick up with me
again?'

His eyes flashed. 'I can't help that, Alexa! Do you think
I *want* to be clandestine in that way? I have no choice. And
if you will simply *listen* to me, I will explain why—'

'Oh, I'm sure you will!' she thrust witheringly. 'To you
it's all totally straightforward, isn't it? Well, it is to me too. I

don't want anything more to do with you. There is nothing, *nothing* you can say that will change that. So go—*go*!'

She could feel her heart pounding in her chest, adrenaline pumping. It was unbearable—unbearable that Guy had walked in here.

'Just *go*!' she repeated, because he hadn't budged at all, was still standing there, looking like the lord of the manor in the humble cottage of one of his countless peasants. Rich, arrogant, conceited—thinking he only had to find her to dictate his terms to her again.

'Just *go*! You pushed your way in here. It's unbelievable! You actually went and bought the letting agency just to find me. Your ego is monstrous—monstrous! Just because you're Guy de Rochemont, born with a whole canteen of silver spoons in your mouth, and just because women swoon at your feet, you think you can do anything you want, get anyone you want. Any woman you want. Well, not me—not any more! There is nothing, *nothing* you can say to me that would *ever* change my mind.'

His face was stark as she threw her bitter words at him. Two white lines flared along his cheekbones.

'Then I won't waste my time talking.'

He was in front of her in an instant. He seized her arms, lowering over her. Panic, rage, fury, convulsed her. She threw herself backwards.

'*No!* Not this time. Don't touch me.' She took a shuddering, shaking breath. 'Whatever we had, it's over. I'm not going there again. Ever. I don't *care*,' she spelt out, her words cutting like stone knives, hard and heavy, 'whether you have a tame, cowed little fiancée in tow or not. I don't want anything to do with you.' Her face worked. 'You were bad news right from the start, though I was too stupid to see it—and you're bad news now. You always will be. I don't want you. I don't want anything to do with you. On any terms.' She took one last shuddering breath. 'Any terms at all.'

Her voice was flat. Final. She stared at him. She was back under control now. Back from that dangerous maelstrom of emotion. She'd mastered it, quelled it.

His face was stark, his jaw set like steel, the white lines along his tensed cheekbones etched like acid. His eyes were unreadable. Completely unreadable.

They always were. I never knew him. I loved him, but I never knew him. How stupid can a woman be, to love a man she doesn't know? Who keeps her out of his real life...

Pain twisted inside her. All she'd ever had of him had been brief, bare snatches. Making do with scraps. No wonder he'd thought she would accept that vile adulterous offer of his. He'd had every expectation she would comply. After all, all he had to do was seduce her, just as he'd done that first time, and she would acquiesce in anything he wanted.

But no more. No *more*.

The desolation she was long familiar with swept through her. This had to end—now. His eyes were on her. Masked. Unreadable. The pain twisted again—the pain of seeing him, wanting so much to reach out and let him take her in his arms, let his mouth lower to hers, let him do what every cell in her body suddenly, flaringly, vividly, oh, so vividly, wanted him to do—let him make her forget everything that her head knew about him, everything that she must not forget. To melt her flesh and melt her mind, so that they were only bodies, bared and beautiful, twining together, made one together...

But they weren't one. They were as separate from each other as it was possible to be.

'Alexa—'

There was something in his voice. Something that she blocked out. Had to block out. Something dangerous.

'No.' She shook her head. 'No—I'm not going there. This ends, Guy. Now.'

She moved away, making the move deliberate, controlled. Heading for the kitchen and the lean-to beyond.

'At least your journey won't be wasted. I've no idea whether you still want this, but I know I don't.' Her voice was cold—as cold as she could make it.

Her painting equipment was in the lean-to, and resting on a chair was the object she was going to fetch. He might as well take it now—it would save her having to courier it at some point, whenever the time came when she could no longer hole up here in the middle of nowhere. She'd wrapped it up already. She didn't want to look at it. She'd finished it—the ability to do so had come to her, and she knew why it had, and hated herself—and it—for that very reason. But then, and only then, had it released her from its loathesome power....

She gathered the parcel up and turned, ready to take it out to him. But he had followed her. He wasn't looking at her, however. Not even at the object she was holding. He was looking to the canvas on her easel.

She stilled.

His face was immobile. Silently she held out the wrapped painting in her hands to him. It was his portrait. The one she'd not been able to do. Now she had.

But not on its own. The portrait—quite deliberately and intentionally—was one of a pair.

Its companion was still on the easel. As finished as it would ever be.

His eyes were fixed on it, and in them Alexa saw a shadow flicker deep, deep within. Something moved in her, something even deeper inside her than the shadow in his eyes. Something even darker.

'That one I'm keeping,' she said. Her voice had no emotion in it. The emotion was all in the paint on the canvas.

In the twisted, demonic image of his face. The face of a man she had once loved.

But now only hated.

'It's to remind me of you,' she said.

For a second, an instant, his eyes went to her. But there was nothing in them. Nothing she could discern. The mask over them was complete.

He took the wrapped portrait—the other one, the one that bore the face that Guy de Rochemont showed to the world. To the women in his bed.

Then, slowly, he inclined his head to her. 'I won't trouble you again, Alexa.'

There was nothing in his voice just as there was nothing in his eyes.

He turned and left. Walking out. Out of her life.

Leaving only the dark portrait to keep her company.

Slowly, haltingly, she went back into the sitting room. The fire was still blazing fiercely in the log-burner, and she could feel the warmth after the chill of the lean to.

But she was shivering all the same.

Guy drove. The long motorway back to London stretched before him, and the powerful car ate up the miles. On either side of the motorway the drear wintry landscape stretched, monotonous and rainswept. Grey and bleak.

Just like his life.

It stretched out ahead of him—swallowing him up.

He had seen hope—hope almost within reach, within his grasp and he'd stretched out his hands to take it.

Seize it.

Instead—

Instead it had been like a shot through the skull. Instant, total destruction. The work of a second. All it had taken for his eyes to light on, to focus on that square of canvas resting on the easel.

A mirror—a mirror held up to him.

In the few brief moments when his eyes had rested on it he had known—searingly, punishingly—that Alexa was gone. Out of his life.

She would never come back into it.

He pressed the accelerator, increasing the speed taking him away from her. Back to all that was left to him now.

His hands tightened on the steering wheel. Alexa was lost to him—he could not have her on any terms. She had shown him that in a square of canvas.

So now a heaviness settled over him, a weariness. All he could do was continue on the course he had resolved on. Ahead of him waited the girl he had said he would marry. He would do what he could for her.

What else was there for him to do? With Alexa gone—nothing.

Only Louisa.

CHAPTER EIGHT

SPRING came. The days lengthened, the tender shoots of new growth peered between the blasted stalks of last year's vegetation. In the garden and in the hedgerows primroses pushed their way out of the dark, confining earth, new leaves unfurled on bared branches. Life returned.

And Alexa returned to London.

But not to live. Only to pause, then pack again, and head to Heathrow. She'd booked a desert safari—a tough one. Bumping across endless dunes in a Jeep, sleeping in a bedroll underneath the stars which burned through the floor of heaven, revealing blisters of brightness, cracks showing the existence of a realm impossible to reach.

By day the sun burned down, hazing the horizon so that it was impossible to know if the Jeep were making progress or not. Yet each day they were a little further on. Each day a little further from their starting point.

They reached their goal—old ruins of an ancient city that had once been filled with living, breathing people, each one of them with their own life, their own aspirations, hopes and dreams, their own dreads and losses. Now only the desert dust blew through their emptied houses, along their deserted streets.

Alexa stopped and stared out over the desolation. Lines, bleak and spare, tolled in her head.

"'For the world...hath really neither joy, nor love...nor peace, nor help for pain...'"

No, there was no help for pain, she knew. But the cruellest lines of the poem she could not say: *'Ah, love, let us be true to one another...'*

Could not even think them. Could only envy the poet who'd had someone to be true to, someone true to him.

Beyond the city's ruins, the bare and boundless desert sands stretched far away, and she stood looking out over their loneliness, encircled in isolation, filled with a quiet despair.

And a new resolution. This could not go on—this endless desolation. It could not. Or it would destroy her. Somehow she had to find the strength to get past it. She had done it once before, when her parents had been killed, and she had found the strength to renew her life. Whatever it took, she had to do it again now.

So, at the end of the safari, when the Jeep returned to base, she did not head for the airport with the others. She found a small *pension*, simple but respectable, and stayed there awhile, going out every day with paints and inks and sketchbook, her body shrouded to keep attention from her, her head covered against both the sun and male eyes. The locals thought her mad but let her be, unmolested and unchallenged, and she was grateful.

Each day she worked, depicting in starkest lines the empty vastness of the lifeless desert, and each day, in the dry, relentless heat, little by little the endless pain in her desiccated a little more, a little more.

Until she could feel it no longer.

Had it gone completely? She couldn't tell. Only knew, with a deep, sure certainty, that the work she had done was good. Spare, stark, bare. But good.

Then and only then did she pack up her work and head

for home. The six-month lease of her tenants had expired, and they had moved out. She was wary, deeply so, of returning to London, lest it plunge her back into the vortex of memory again. Above all she knew that she would not—could not—simply return to the life she had had. She would put the flat on the market, move away, right out of London, for good. Find a future in her work.

It was hard to walk into her flat. Hard to see its familiar contours. Hard to block out the memories that went with it. But block them she did. Not bothering to unpack, she left her suitcase in the bedroom, with her newly created portfolio of desert art, and took a quick shower to refresh herself after her long flight. Then she changed into a pair of well-cut grey trousers and an ice-blue jersey top, knotted her hair into its usual neat chignon, took up her handbag and went back downstairs.

She needed to go to the shops to refill the fridge. On the way back she would look in at the estate agents—*not* the agency that Guy had so arrogantly bought!—and talk about marketing her flat for immediate sale. In the evening she would go through all her finances to see what her options for the future would be. At some point, too, she knew she would have tell Imogen she was back—but not until she had a good idea of what her plans were going to be. Her mind busy, determinedly so, she stepped out of the front door and headed down the short flight of steps to the pavement.

'Miss Harcourt—'

A car had pulled up in front of her at the kerb, and a man was getting out. The car was nondescript, and so was the man accosting her. In broad daylight, on a busy pavement, her only emotion was puzzlement.

'Yes?' she said.

'I work for a security firm,' the man said. He handed her a business card, with an upmarket-looking name on it that even she had vaguely heard of. 'My client has requested a meeting with you.'

'What client?' said Alexa. Warning bells were ringing now.

'Madame de Rochemont,' said the man.

Alexa froze. Madame de Rochemont. Guy's wife.

Despite the heat of the afternoon, a chill went through her. A chill she forced to subside. She had not spent all that time away, purging herself of the past, only to be felled at the first reminder of what was no longer a part of her life, a part of her. But her insides churned for all her resolution.

He had a wife.

It was done—Guy was married.

Married to that poor girl—the one who'd looked the antithesis of 'radiant' at the prospect. With good reason. Alexa's mouth thinned. Louisa von Lorenz had known what kind of man she was marrying. What kind of marriage she was in for. What kind of husband she was getting.

The adulterous kind.

Alexa's thoughts were like knives. But why on earth should Guy's wretched new wife have asked for a meeting with *her*? What for?

How does she even know of my existence?

And how could she possibly know I'd be walking along this pavement today?

'How,' demanded Alexa frigidly, 'does Madame de Rochemont come to know of my whereabouts?'

The man was unfazed by the question. Maybe it was a familiar one to someone in his line of work. 'When your tenants moved out, Miss Harcourt, your flat was put under surveillance on the chance you might be returning shortly. As indeed you have.'

Alexa's mouth twisted. Of course. Guy had bought the lettings agency, hadn't he? When you moved in the stratospheric circles that the de Rochemont family moved in such things were unexceptional. Just like hiring people like this man to wait until she showed up.

But how Guy's wife had found her was inconsequential—the question was why on earth did Louisa de Rochemont want to meet her?

Cold went through her suddenly as realisation struck.

Does she think I'm going to take up with Guy again now that I'm back in London? Is that what she fears?

Had that poor girl somehow found out—or been told—just who the last woman was that her husband had had a liaison with before he'd become engaged? Had she then, knowing what her husband was going to be like, speculated that he might well carry on after their engagement and their marriage with the same woman he'd been seeing before?

The chill in Alexa's veins deepened. Had all this security surveillance and private investigation shown up a photo of her? It was more than likely. And then—she swallowed horribly—then Louisa would recognise her from that evening at the charity gala.

She'll know that she spoke to me—will she think that I knew all along who she was?

But, whether Louisa had seen Alexa's photo or not, Alexa knew that one thing was clear—she was not going to have Guy's bride think the worst of her. Whoever was providing Guy's adulterous sex, it was not her! And any attempts, by any of them, to subject her to surveillance and investigation could stop right now! She was clear of Guy de Rochemont and she would stay that way. She would not be sucked back anywhere near that maelstrom. Wasn't she doing everything she could to be free of it all?

She looked straight at the man. 'Where is your client?' she demanded.

'Madame de Rochemont is currently in London, Miss

Harcourt,' he answered, in his professionally neutral tone. 'She has indicated that it would suit her to see you this afternoon.'

London? Well, that was convenient. And so was getting this over and done with right now. Another thing she could put behind her.

'Very well.' She pulled open the rear door of the car and climbed in. The man got into the driving seat and restarted the engine. The car set off, heading out onto Ladbroke Grove, and thence towards Holland Park. Cutting across Kensington, it made its way into the pristine, elegant squares of Belgravia, pulling up outside a vast white-stuccoed terraced house set on an elegant square with a private garden in the centre. It was a location where, Alexa knew, only the richest of the rich could afford to live. But then, Guy de Rochemont *was* in that ultra-exclusive echelon.

I knew he was rich, but I hardly saw it, Alexa thought as she got out of the car. So was it really so surprising that a man like that, so blessed by the gods—not just with vast wealth and the highest social position, but by incredible good-looks and searing masculine attraction—should have thought that she, or any woman, his wife included, would do whatever he wanted of them, without question or demur or objection? Would such a man not naturally have a natural arrogance that expected others to comply with his every wish, every desire?

Like the way she'd just rolled over into his bed the moment he'd indicated he wanted her there...

But even as she thought that memory intervened. Not the memory of Guy casually informing her that he'd bought a lettings agency as he might buy a bar of chocolate, simply in order to locate her, or informing her that she had been selected to provide his sexual amusement and compensate for his being required to marry a teenager for dynastic purposes, or demanding to know what the hell she thought she was playing at by objecting to his plans for her.

Not that Guy.

The Guy who took me to bed—breathtakingly, wonderfully, amazingly! The Guy who held me afterwards, slept with me, woke with me. Ate with me, smiled at me, talked with me about art and history and culture. Who would sit and check his e-mails on his laptop, or look through business papers, while I watched a TV documentary or read a book. Nothing much, nothing extraordinary.

Yet precious—so precious…

The old, familiar rending ache scraped at her. She had to wrest it away, make herself think of Guy as she had to think of him now.

Above all, a married man.

A married man whose wife—young, naïve, innocent—did not deserve to have her marriage, as difficult as it must be, blighted even more by worrying about whether her husband was going to take up with his former lover again. A wife who, though she might call a house in Belgravia only one of what were doubtless half a dozen palatial homes around the world, deserved the reassurance that only Alexa could give her.

Yet as Alexa walked up the wide steps of the multi-million pound house, stepping into the grand hallway beyond, she felt anew the gaping distance between the world she moved in and the world that Guy and his bride inhabited. She had been kept far apart from it.

He's a world away from me—he always was.

Like a spear in her side, she felt the force of how pointless it had been to fall in love with such a man.

Reluctance at being here filled her. But this had to be done. Head held high, she followed the member of staff who had admitted her as he proceeded up a graceful sweep of stairs to the first floor. She was ushered into a vast drawing room.

She stopped short, her eyes going instantly to the walls. It was the paintings that drew her first, not the opulence of the Louis Quinze decor. She heard her breath catch as she took in enough priceless artworks to fill a small museum. Fragonard, Watteau, Boucher, Claude, Poussin—

Instinctively, without realising she was doing so, she walked up to the one closest to her and gazed at it. A riot of Rococo art, a *fête galante*, with girls in clouds of silks and satins, and young men as lavishly adorned. A fantasy of the Ancien Régime that took her breath away with the exquisite delicacy of its brushstrokes to catch the richness of the fabrics, the hues of the fruits and flowers.

A voice spoke behind her.

'Rococo is no longer fashionable, but I confess I have a particular fondness for it. It embodies all that is most *charmant* in art.'

The voice that spoke had the crystal quality of the upper classes, but with a distinct French accent. It was not the voice of the young girl that Alexa had encountered in the powder room at the charity gala. She swivelled round.

A woman who must have been in late middle age, but who had the figure of a woman no more than thirty, chicly dressed, was standing before a huge marble fireplace, on an Aubusson rug, between two silk-upholstered facing sofas. Her dress was a couture design, Alexa could see instantly, and several ropes of pearls were wound around her neck. Her hair was tinted, immaculately styled, and her *maquillage* was perfect.

And her eyes were green. As green as emeralds.

Alexa started.

'Yes,' said the woman, acknowledging why Alexa had reacted. 'My son has inherited his eye colour from me.'

Her son—?

Alexa swallowed. *Madame de Rochemont...*

She had assumed—of course she had assumed—that it could only be Guy's wife.

The woman who was not Guy's wife—who was his mother, could *only* be his mother—walked forward several steps, holding out her hand. Alexa found herself walking forward as well, to take it briefly.

'Won't you sit down, Mademoiselle Harcourt?'

With a posture that was regally elegant, Madame de Rochemont indicated one of the pair of silk covered sofas. As Alexa lowered herself down, her head in a whirl, Guy's mother took her place opposite her. Her green eyes flicked briefly over Alexa's habitually groomed appearance, as if she were assessing her.

Alexa's thoughts were reeling. What on earth was going on? Why was she here? Why on earth had Guy's *mother* wanted to see her?

'Thank you so much for coming, Mademoiselle Harcourt. I have wanted to meet you for some time.'

Alexa could only stare, nonplussed. All her expectations had been overset, and she could make no sense of what was happening. Then, a moment later, enlightenment dawned.

'I wanted to thank you in person,' Madame de Rochemont said, 'for the portrait you made of Guy. He presented it to me for my birthday last month. I am very pleased with it.'

'I...I'm so glad,' Alexa managed to get out.

'And I am also,' said Guy's mother, and now there was a different note in her voice which Alexa could not place, 'very grateful for it.'

Alexa gazed at her. For a long moment, Madame de Rochemont simply looked back at her. Alexa had the strangest feeling she was being placed in a balance and weighed. Then, abruptly, the moment ended.

'I understand you have been traveling?' said Madame de Rochemont. 'The Middle East. An unusual choice for a young woman.'

'I—I wanted somewhere different,' Alexa managed to say, wondering why Guy's mother should have gone to the trouble of finding out where she had been these last weeks.

'Indeed. But it is not a part of the world where young women tend to go on their own,' observed Madame de Rochemont.

Still reeling, Alexa tried to gather enough composure to make an appropriate answer. 'I was treated with great respect, *madame*—I did not court attention in any way, and my hosts were kindness itself.'

'You were there some time?'

'I worked, *madame*. Painted. The desert has a beauty of its own.'

'Of course. Tell me, do you plan to exhibit your work?'

Alexa shook her head. 'My talent, such as it is, is moderate only. Portraiture allowed me a comfortable standard of living, and I am grateful.' How she got the words out, made this simulacrum of normal conversation when her head was reeling, was quite beyond her, but she did it somehow.

'You are very modest, *mademoiselle*.'

There was a tone in her voice that Alexa could not interpret. Her eyes went automatically to an exquisite seventeenth-century Claude beside the mantel, depicting a classical mythical episode in a vast landscape. 'It takes only a single great work, *madame*, to make anything else impossible,' she replied candidly.

Guy's mother inclined her head slowly. 'Yet modesty,'

she said, 'may go hand in hand with not inconsiderable natural gifts. The portrait you made of Guy confirms that to me. You have captured him well.' She paused, her eyes never leaving Alexa's.

Alexa swallowed, fighting for composure, remembering all that had come about because of that portrait. Remembering, with burning pain, how she had finally come to complete it, her heart torn to shreds by the man she was depicting. Then… 'Thank you,' she managed to get out, her eyes dropping to the floor. She could not look at Guy's mother.

'I wonder, *mademoiselle*, if you would consider painting me, as well as my son?'

Alexa's eyes few upwards. She swallowed again. Madame de Rochemont was regarding her, her gaze slightly questioning.

'I—I am sorry. No.' Alexa's reply seemed staccato, blunt, even to her own ears.

'No?' The arched eyebrows rose delicately. The questioning look was still in the eyes. More than questioning. That sense of being evaluated came over Alexa again. She felt her cheeks colour slightly. More than ever she wanted to get to her feet and walk out—as fast and as far as she could.

'I—I am sorry,' she said again.

There was a pause—the very slightest. 'Perhaps you would tell me why, *mademoiselle*.' It was politely said, but there was a hauteur in it that Alexa could hear clearly. She knew why—a *grande dame* such as Madame de Rochemont would not be used to hearing blunt refusals, especially to a commission that was intensely flattering, not to say valuable and prestigious.

Alexa pressed her lips together, trying to find an answer. 'I no longer practise portraiture, *madame*. I am so sorry.'

'I see. Would I be correct in thinking, therefore, that my son's portrait is the last you have made?'

Into Alexa's mind came the vivid, violent portrait that was the demonic twin of the one that had been a birthday gift for Guy's mother.

'My last professional portrait, yes,' she replied. 'It was a commercial commission. Done only for money.' Her voice was flat.

'Of course,' said Guy's mother. 'Why else would you wish to paint my son's likeness, *mademoiselle*?'

Alexa looked away. Back to the Claude beside the fireplace. She studied the figures, tiny against the broad pastoral expanse. One of the figures, at least, was blending into the landscape. It was Daphne, at the moment of her transforming into a laurel bush to escape the attentions of Apollo.

I escaped as well—becoming a recluse, hiding from life. Hiding from Guy. From what he wanted of me.

She looked away again, her gaze colliding with that of Guy's mother. The air froze in her lungs and dismay drowned her. Realisation dawned.

She knows. She knows what I was to her son…

Her face paled. Panic rose. Without conscious volition she got to her feet. She had to go now. Right now.

'I am sorry, Madame de Rochemont, but I must go.'

Guy's mother did not stand up. 'Before you do, I have a favour to ask of you.'

There was something different in her voice. Alexa didn't know what it was. Didn't know anything except that she had to go. Escape.

'I'm so sorry, but I really can't undertake the commission you mentioned—' she began, her voice hurried.

Madame de Rochemont held up a hand. A graceful, imperious gesture, cutting her off. 'That is not the favour,' she said. Her voice was dry. Her expression was as unreadable as ever, but there was a tension in it suddenly. She paused a moment, then spoke. 'I would like you to go to France. To talk to Guy.'

Alexa froze, disbelief in her eyes. Had she really heard what she had? Had Guy's mother really said that? Why? Why on earth…?

Words formed in her throat. Words that were impossible to say—impossible to get out—certainly not in front of this formidable *grande dame* who was Guy's mother and who *knew* about Alexa and Guy. But she must say something…

'That isn't possible.' Alexa's voice was flat. As flat as a butterfly crushed by a rock.

'Why?'

Alexa's face closed. 'I think you will agree, *madame*,' she said, with stony formality, 'that it would not be *comme il faut*.'

The green eyes, so like the eyes she had once drowned in, widened slightly.

'I do not understand you,' said Guy's mother.

Alexa pressed her lips, clenching her hands in her lap. She looked directly at Madame de Rochemont. 'But your daughter-in-law would, *madame*,' she said.

The older woman's face stilled.

'Ah,' she breathed slowly. Her eyes were fixed on Alexa. She got to her feet. 'You must forgive me for insisting,' she said, 'but it is imperative that you talk to Guy.'

'I have already said everything necessary.' Alexa's voice was clipped. This was unreal—surreal. Standing here in front of Guy's mother, who was telling her to talk to her son.

About what, precisely? About how his marriage is

going? Is that it? What on earth is going on here? It doesn't make sense—any of it.

'But my son has not,' said Madame de Rochemont. 'And that is why you must go to France, to talk to him.'

Alexa stared, giving in. 'Look, what *is* going on?' she demanded, the edgy formality gone completely. 'I'm sorry if I sound impolite, but nothing here makes sense. Why am I here? What do you want of me, and why? I will be open with you—as I take it that you know that, much to my regret, my relationship with your son progressed beyond the professional one of client and artist. I had a brief affair with Guy last year—that's all. It meant...' She swallowed, but ploughed on. 'It meant as little to him as you might imagine. He informed me of his engagement, and terminated the relationship the same day. And, *madame*,' she emphasised, restraining herself from saying anything about Guy's subsequent attempt to restart it, 'the relationship remains terminated. If that is your concern, then you have my assurance that—'

Again, an imperious gesture with the hand silenced her. 'The only assurance I ask for is that you accede to my request to talk to my son.'

Alexa's chin went up. 'To what purpose?' she said bluntly. Her eyes met those of his mother—defiance in hers, his mother's unreadable.

'For the future happiness of my son,' said Madame de Rochemont.

Alexa's eyes closed. 'He may be as happy as he wishes, *madame*—it is nothing to do with me. I hope...' She took a breath, opening her eyes again to look straight at the woman who was asking something of her that was inexplicable and impossible to agree to. 'I hope he has a long and happy marriage.'

Something moved in the emerald eyes.

'So do I, Mademoiselle Harcourt. Any mother must wish that for their child. Which is why it is essential for you to talk to Guy.' She started to walk towards the door, and Alexa followed. 'It will take very little of your time,' said Guy's mother, talking over her shoulder. 'A car will take you to the airport, and you will be at the château in under two hours.'

'*Madame*, I cannot—'

Guy's mother stopped. Turned. 'Please,' she said.

What was it in her face, her eyes, that made Alexa stop as well? She bit her lip a moment, then simply nodded and said, 'All right. If you insist.' She gave a bewildered sigh, half throwing up her hand in concession. 'I don't understand why you are set on it—I cannot begin to imagine what you think it will achieve.'

'I think that Guy's wife,' said his mother, and her eyes met Alexa's full on, 'will find it the making of her marriage.'

So that was it. Now Alexa understood. She might have assumed the wrong Madame de Rochemont earlier, but it was indeed Madame Guy de Rochemont who needed assuring that Alexa did not pose a threat to her marriage. So, in order to allay her fears, the woman her husband had set up to provide an adulterous liaison had to be flown in so that Guy could tell her to tell his wife—who had somehow found out about Alexa—that she was not, in fact, her husband's mistress.

She took a breath. 'I will do this, *madame*, but only on the condition that I will be free of further contact with any of your family. I want nothing more to do with any of you. I'm sorry if that sounds rude, but my life has moved on and that is that.'

The unreadable look was back in Madame de Rochemont'

eyes. 'As you wish, *mademoiselle*,' was all she said.
'Come—'

She led the way out of the room. Outside, one of her
members of staff was waiting, and Guy's mother spoke
to him in rapid French. Then she held out her hand to
Alexa.

'Thank you.'

Reluctantly, Alexa shook the outstretched hand.
'*Madame*,' she said formally. Then, clutching her bag more
tightly than was necessary, she followed the member of
staff back down the curving marble staircase. Her mind
felt quite, quite numb.

CHAPTER NINE

ALEXA was still feeling numb as she took her seat on the private de Rochemont jet. It was familiar to her. She must have travelled on it half a dozen times, perhaps, during the months with Guy. The extravagance of it had shocked her but he had been blunt about it.

'It saves time,' he had said to her.

And time was what he'd had least of. At any rate for her. So she had gone along with it, this outrageous extravagance, burning who knew how many carbon units, paying half a dozen salaries for the personnel required for a flight, simply to get herself, the woman Guy de Rochemont currently wanted to have sex with, to him at the time he wanted her.

I put up with it. I went along with it. I colluded with it.

Condemnation of her own behaviour bit at her.

I was as complicit as he was. Because I wanted to be. I wanted him on the terms he offered—because they were the only terms on offer. I told myself it was all right. It worked for both of us. That that justified it.

But it didn't.

I should have had the strength, then, to say no to those terms. To say no to him.

But she hadn't. She had gone along with it, made no demur, no question. Accepted it all.

Well, she had paid for it in the end, though. Paid for it even sooner than the end. Paid for it the moment she'd realised, with dawning dismay, that she had started to fall in love with Guy de Rochemont. And from that moment onwards he had held her to ransom. Held her heart to ransom. And her self-respect.

Well, she had her self-respect back again now. She had said no to being the mistress of an adulterous bridegroom, and she would make that clear to Guy's bride—as it seemed he now wanted her to do. Alexa should be glad that he cared, glad that he was finally showing consideration to the poor girl he'd married. Perhaps their marriage stood a chance now.

She must be glad of that.

What else could she be?

As the plane winged its brief way across the Channel, she made herself say that over and over. Ignoring the fingernails that were trying to scratch at her heart.

Let me get through this. Let me get through this and come away again. Back to the life I am going to lead now. The only life left to me.

A voice spoke at her side, making her turn her head.

'Miss Harcourt? The captain's compliments. We are starting our descent, and should be landing on schedule.'

The stewardess smiled politely at Alexa, and Alexa murmured something appropriate. Inside, her stomach started to knot. She took a breath, and then another. She could get through this. She *would* get through this. She must.

It was a mantra she repeated as the plane landed at a small private airfield west of Paris, and repeated again as she was escorted to a waiting limousine. It whisked her quickly and efficiently away, down a brief stretch of major roadway, to turn off after some miles onto a smaller country road. The weather was glorious, a perfect late afternoon in early summer, with the sun dipping low, turning the world to ripeness all around her. As the car slowed and turned down another narrow road, then drew up briefly to pass through ornate iron gates set in a two-metre high perimeter wall, she felt the knot tighten. She looked about her as the car moved along the smooth, long drive, curving through ornamental woodlands until it was clear of them to make visible a sight that made Alexa's breath catch.

Château Rochemont, a Loire château, was like something out of a fairy tale—palest grey stone and pointed towers, surrounded by vast, ornate parkland. As the car drew up at the front entrance and Alexa was ushered out, she glanced around as if she must surely see sauntering lords and ladies of the court, dressed for the very *fête* she had seen in the painting in Madame de Rochemont's London drawing room a bare two hours ago.

It's a different world—unutterably, incomparably different!

And it was the world Guy lived in. The one he'd visited her from, dipping into her modest bourgeois life to collect what he wanted from her, then leaving again to come back here. His home. Where he lived.

With his bride. His wife.

Her face closed. That was all she must remember—all that she must hold in her head. Nothing more than that.

She was ushered indoors—expected, that much was obvious. The huge entrance hall, with mirrors and gilt and chandeliers and a vast double staircase, took her breath away, but she showed no visible reaction. Her expression stayed closed. Composed.

Sang-froid—that was what she needed now. What she called upon.

Outwardly calm, she followed a member of staff along a wide *enfilade* stretching along to the right-hand side of the hall, then through into what seemed to be a separate wing. Her low heels tapped the parquet flooring and seemed to echo in the panelled corridor. Deliberately she did not look along the walls, though she was aware there were paintings everywhere, and niches holding statuary, which instinctively wanted to draw her eyes to them. But she steeled herself not to, steeled herself only to keep walking, ignoring the knotting in her stomach, until at length a pair of double doors was reached at the end of the corridor and the servant knocked discreetly at them.

A muffled, terse, *'Entrez—'* and the doors were opened for her. She walked in.

The room was double aspect, at the far end of the wing, and at first she saw only the huge sash windows in front of her and to her left-hand side. Then she saw a desk—huge, ornate.

Behind it sat Guy.

For a moment, just a moment, she saw his expression as it had been before her entry. Something like a blow struck her. There was such a bleakness in his face, such wintriness in his eyes! It was sudden pain, hurting her. Then, as he took in her presence in the doorway, his expression changed.

His face was transfixed. Completely immobile. As if a mask had dropped down over his features, shielding them from her. Then slowly, very slowly, he got to his feet. Distantly, Alexa heard the double doors behind her click shut.

'Alexa.'

Her name, nothing more. She had heard him say it in that bare, stark way before. But that time, at the cottage in Devon, it had been said differently. Emotion, dark and turbid, had been heavy in it. Now it was blank—completely blank.

She turned to face him fully. Face him, but not see him. She refused to see him. Refused to see his tall, lean figure sheathed in a hand-made suit that fitted him as if it were moulded to his broad shoulders, his svelte hips. Refused to see the perfect planes of his face, the fall of his sable hair, the shape of his mouth, his jaw. The emerald, long-lashed eyes…

She refused to drown in them.

Her face was stony, as blank as his. Beneath the surface she could feel her stomach knot itself again, her lungs tighten. But she ignored it. It was imperative to ignore it.

'I was told you wanted to talk to me.'

Her voice was brusque.

His eyebrows drew across sharply. 'By whom?' he demanded. His voice seemed rough. She didn't care. Didn't care about its roughness. Didn't care about him. He was lost to her. For ever. And she did not care about that either. Must not care…

'By your mother,' she answered.

The mask vanished. Astonishment whipped across his face. 'My *mother*?'

'Yes, this afternoon. She invited me to visit her and told me you wanted to talk to me. She said it was important.' A heavy breath escaped her. 'So I have come.'

He seemed to be gathering his control.

'I find it…hard…to believe that,' he said slowly. His voice was harsh, grating at her. His eyes bored into hers and she felt their force making her stance unsteady. 'When last I saw you, you made it very…clear…that you wanted nothing more to do with me.' He stood looking at her, his gaze like a knife to her flesh. 'I know what you think of me, Alexa. You made that unmistakable. Convincing.' His face tightened. 'Every line in that portrait on your easel told me that. Told me of your hatred for me.' His eyes darkened like a sunless forest. 'I should have told my mother about it. Then she would not have wasted her efforts getting you here.'

Alexa took a breath. Hard and heavy. Ignoring what she saw in him. Ignoring what it did to her.

'She said—' she took another breath '—it was important to your marriage. That's why I came—only for that reason.'

Guy stilled. 'My marriage...' He echoed the words. His brows snapped together disbelievingly. 'My mother talked to you about my marriage?'

She gave a rasp in her throat. 'It wasn't my idea—don't worry,' she said scathingly. 'She raised the subject. She said it was important I come here. Talk to you.' A heavy breath escaped her. 'So I have. I can only assume—' Her lips pressed tightly as she made herself say what she had to say. 'I can only assume that she means it's essential that your bride—' she said the word without the slightest trace of emotion, despite the knot in her stomach tightening like a ligature around a bleeding vein, oozing her lifeblood out of her body '—hears from me that I am no threat to her— that I never succumbed to your adulterous offer.'

'My bride.' His voice was flat. Stark. His eyes were veiled again, all emotion gone.

'Yes.' Alexa took another effortful breath. 'I don't know what chance of happiness she has, but what little I can give her I do. I wish her happiness—all that she can find.'

His eyes were on her. She could not read them. They were masked, opaque.

'That is...generous...of you,' he said slowly.

There was something different about him, but she could not tell what. She dared not look at him, dared not meet his gaze. But there was something different in his stance somehow, though he had not moved. He was immobile behind his desk, one manicured hand resting on its mahoghany surface. He was speaking again, and she made herself listen. Made her eyes meet his.

'Well, I can tell you,' he was saying, his eyes on hers, unreadable and veiled, but seeming all the same to be boring deep, deep into her, 'what I hope will reassure you, Alexa.' He paused, his eyes resting on hers like lead. 'Louisa is very happy in her marriage. Blissfully happy.'

Alexa swayed. Pain bit like a wolf, tearing at her throat. She made her mouth work. Forced it to work.

'I'm…glad. I'm very glad for her.'

'So am I,' said Guy. His eyes were still holding hers. 'She is deeply in love with her new husband.'

The wolf was tearing now, biting out her throat. 'I'm… I'm very glad for her,' she said again.

I must be glad. I must! She deserves that—every bride deserves that!

And every bride deserved a husband who loved her. Her expression changed, emotion rising in her throat, making her take a half-step towards him.

'Guy—' she spoke impulsively '—be…be kind to her! Don't do to her what you were planning on doing. Not with anyone. Please don't. If she's in love with you, don't hurt her—don't hurt her the way you hurt—'

She broke off. He was looking at her strangely, through that veiled mask.

'Did I, Alexa?' His words were slowly spoken. 'Did I hurt you?' There was something strained in his words. Did he feel bad that he had hurt her? she wondered.

She pressed her lips. Tried to look away, but could not. Yet she could not meet his eyes either. Then she spoke—admitting all, her voice drear, her words heavy.

'You didn't mean to, Guy. I know that. I know that the affair we had was…what it was. You were not responsible for my reaction to it. I chose to go along with it, with the affair, and the responsibility for my reaction is mine and mine alone. I should never, that night after the charity gala, have let you…let you…'

She swallowed, unable to finish. Then, with a shuddering breath, forced herself onwards. 'You have never been responsible for my feelings. And even if I deplored what you proposed—some adulterous, clandestine liaison—then that still does not make you responsible for what it did to me.' Her hands clenched at her sides. 'When you hunted me down, turned up at the cottage assuming I would come back to you simply because you wanted me to, I was glad you saw that second portrait. It spoke for me. Said everything!'

His eyes were pressing in on her, but they had changed. She could not tell how, or why, but they had all the same. She shut her eyes to shield herself from what was in his that she could not bear to see, then opened them again.

'What you wanted of me I no longer wished to give,' she said. Her words fell like stones. 'Even without the adulterous offer I would not have wanted it.' Her face worked. 'Flying here in your private jet reminded me all over again. How I'd been flown to you when you wanted me, and then flown home again. How you'd arrive when it suited you, and then leave again. I didn't want that.'

His expression tightened. 'You knew the limitations I was under from the start,' he said.

'I knew what they meant about what I'd thought I'd had with you.' She lifted her chin. 'It took me a long time, Guy, to face up to that. It wasn't until you made your…proposition…to me that I made myself see it. It showed me what I'd been to you all along—'

'What I'd been to you?' he echoed, cutting across her like a blade falling. He moved suddenly, abruptly, coming around the corner of the desk to face her.

He was too close, much too close, but she was too frozen to move.

'Do you know what you were to me, Alexa? Do you?' His voice was animated, urgent suddenly. 'You don't seem to know at all! I thought you did—but then—' his face twisted again '—I thought a lot I no longer think…' He spoke again, his eyes flashing now, green fire burning in his face. 'Look about you,' he ordered. His hand gestured, encompassing the high-tech equipment along one side of the room, the wide mahogany desk behind him, the lavish decor of the room, the vast domain of the château beyond the sweeping windows. 'What do you see?'

His eyes burnt greener. 'You see wealth, don't you? A château on the Loire. Stuffed with treasures. With art that could populate a museum. And this is only *one* of the de Rochemont properties! There are dozens of others— more!—all over the world. And you know what keeps them all? Keeps all the scores of de Rochemonts and Lorenzes living in the lap of luxury? Money—money that my family have been making for over two hundred years. Two centuries of accumulation, of wheeling and dealing and loaning and banking, to anyone and *everyone*. We're a byword for survival—we've survived *everything*! Because we guard everything we've got. No matter what history has thrown at us. Wars and revolutions and confiscations and proscriptions and competition and governments and commercial rivals. Every damn thing!'

He took a scissoring breath. 'But there's a price to be paid. Oh, it's a trivial one compared to the price that the mass of humanity has to pay for their survival, but it's a price all the same.' He looked at her, his expression bare.

'I pay in time, Alexa. *Time*. It's time that's my luxury—nothing else.' He glanced around at his palatial surroundings. 'Yes, mock if you will, but that is the truth to me. It is time that is my greatest treasure. And something more, as well.'

He took another breath. 'Do you know how many people there are in my life, Alexa? In my family?' He gave a short, abbreviated laugh. 'Too many. Too many. And they all want something of me. Namely: time. Business time and private time. I am deluged with relatives—deluged. And they all want my time. All of them.'

His expression changed again. 'Which is why my time with you—my brief, fleeting time with you—was so very precious.'

He shut his eyes a moment, then opened them again, and in them was something that made Alexa's breath catch.

'You were my haven, my respite. My repose. When I came to you, or you came to me, I could escape everything about my family, and just be with you. Only with you, Alexa. No demands on me. Only the two of us, together—the world shut away from us. All that I wanted. You with me. I thought…' His voice stumbled a fraction, then he went on. 'I thought it was what you wanted too. Just to be with me. It worked so well—so easily. It just seemed to happen. Without effort or difficulty. As natural as if it was ordained.

'Then I realised what you were—something I'd never found before in all my life. A woman who was not setting her cap at me, a woman who was actually indifferent to me, who didn't care whether I commissioned her or not, who paid me no attention other than to study me for her work, for whom I held no fascination other than deciding how to capture my likeness, who didn't even notice…' his voice became drier than ever '…that I desired her. And then—ah, then, Alexa—I knew what I wanted.' He paused.

'*You*. I wanted you. Just you. And you were everything that I wanted—in bed and out of it. In bed… Well, how could any man want more? Out of it… Ah, out of it you were peace and comfort, ease and quiet companionship. And I thought—'

There was a break in his voice now, an uncertainty that made Alexa's throat tighten. But not with the tearing of the wolf, with something quite different that she didn't dare think about. She dared not do anything other than stand and hear him speak to her.

'I thought that it was the same for you. That you understood what it was you gave to me that was so precious, and I hoped so much that I gave to you in return. That you understood why I wanted you—and that you understood…' his voice now had an edge in it, an edge that was a blade turned not against her but against himself '…why I had to end our relationship.'

He looked at her. 'I did not do that well, Alexa. I know that, and I am sorry for it. That morning when I severed you from my life, brutally and ruthlessly, because there was no other way I could bring myself to do it, it went against everything I wanted. I had to force myself to do it! Fighting every instinct that told me not to say those words to you! I had to force them out of me. The only way I could—'

She wrapped her arms around herself. It might help to stanch the wound. A wound he had reopened—a wound that had gouged so very deep in her, though she had tried so hard not to let him. Her eyes fell to the floor, picking out the lustrous blue and gold in the priceless carpet's pattern. Her breathing was shallow, difficult. Her expression anguished.

What was the point? What was the point in hearing this?

It was only torment—torment beyond any that she had thought possible—to hear him speak like this. And yet it was a treasure to her beyond imagining to know what she had once been to him.

But could never be again.

She lifted her head. Gazed right at him.

For a moment so brief, so precious, she felt emotion sweep through her—the emotion she had drained out of herself, forced out of herself, because there was no place for it, no point to it.

'You should have left it like that,' she said heavily. 'Let it go when you let me go.'

'I tried to. But I failed. I saw you again, saw you with another man, and I knew then that I could let no other man have you. I knew then that I could not let you go.' His eyes were holding hers again, as if it was essential to him, vital. 'I could not,' he said again.

'And I,' she answered, and her words were crystal clear, cost her what they would, 'could not comply with what you wanted. An adulterous affair. I never hated you till then. But then I did. It was all I felt for you.' She let the lie fall into the space between them, a space that could never now be bridged, that forever parted her from him.

For a long moment he just looked at her. Then, as if something had snapped inside him, he crossed to the window in front of his desk, looking out over the gardens of his château. There was tension across his shoulders. Abruptly, he turned, looking back at Alexa.

'Do you know,' he asked, and his tone was almost conversational, 'how many people work for Lorenz Investment? How many depositors it has? How many business loans? To how many firms? Employing how many people? Have you even *heard*,' he asked, 'of Lorenz Investment?'

'I take it,' Alexa replied, 'that is the bank owned by Louisa's father?'

'It is the bank,' Guy said, 'taken to the brink of *ruin* by Louisa's father. And because of that every single person employed at that bank, every firm that borrowed money, every organisation that lent it money, was at risk—of unemployment, of collapse, of ruin!' His face worked. 'Heinrich Lorenz, Louisa's father, had me at gunpoint. He knew that I would not, *could* not risk Lorenz Investment failing—or even merely to be at risk of failing—lest it start a fatal ricochet through all the other parts of Rochemont-Lorenz. He knew that the only way to allay suspicion was for me to have a convincing reason to invest in his bank.' He paused heavily. 'Like becoming his son-in-law.'

He looked across at Alexa, so far away now—so very far from this world in which vast amounts of money flowed, from this family that was a dynasty, a complex network of wealth and power.

'I didn't want to marry Louisa. But then...' his eyes shadowed '...I saw nothing strange about doing so. For two hundred years, Alexa, we have been making such marriages—both within the family and outside it. Louisa's parents made such a marriage, and she had been brought up to expect the same. My own parents had no particular desire to marry—but they did, and very successfully. When you are used to something like that it seems...normal. Unexceptional. Expected.'

He fell silent. All Alexa could hear was the subdued hum of the PC on Guy's desk. And the pulse of her heart. Telling her something she did not want to hear. Did not want to listen to.

Then, in a low voice, he spoke again. 'I went on thinking that—thinking that such a marriage was unexceptional, acceptable,' he said, 'right up until I had you in my arms again that night when I saw you at the charity gala. And I knew then, like lightning ripping through my being, that everything had changed! I wanted you, and I had to have you. I had to have you in my life. I could not do without you.' His jaw tightened. 'But I also could not let Lorenz Investment fail. Too much was at stake.'

She spoke.

'So you didn't. You didn't let it fail. I understand, Guy. Truly I do.' Her voice had hardened. 'I also understand why you thought you could have your bank-saving, emotionally empty dynastic marriage *and* have an adulterous liaison with me as well. I understand—but didn't condone. Never condone. And that is why—' she took another breath '—why I came here now. Simply to make it clear—as I know your mother must want me to, or else why should she have arranged all this?—to assure your bride of that.'

'Ah, yes, my bride.' There was no emotion in Guy's face.

'Yes. You said…' It was impossible to speak, but speak she must, with a strength she had to find. 'You said she was in love with you. That she was happy after all in her marriage. So if she needs to know about me—about what I am no longer to you—then I will tell her.' Resolution steeled her. Too much emotion was in her, but this had to be done. 'Where—where is she?'

There was a curious light in Guy's eyes. 'Louisa's on her honeymoon,' he said. For a moment time hung still, then Guy started to walk towards her. 'I told you—she's blissfully happy, in love with her husband. A husband,' he said, 'who doesn't happen to be me.'

CHAPTER TEN

ALEXA heard him say the words. Heard them clearly. But they made no sense.

Guy reached her. Lightly, very lightly, he cupped her elbows. Slowly her tightly crossed arms lowered, as if they had become too heavy—which was odd, because the room seemed to be swirling around her.

'I told you,' said Guy, 'that Louisa had agreed to marry me. Saw nothing to object to. But it seems—' his voice was dry '—someone else objected. Someone she'd known for a while. Someone who told her that a loveless dynastic marriage was anathema to the soul. Someone,' he finished, 'who persuaded her to marry him instead—because he was in love with her, and because she, after he'd pulled the scales from her eyes, was in love with him. So—' the green eyes glinted '—she jilted me and eloped.'

Too much was going through Alexa. It was as if electric currents were passing through her, overloading all her circuits.

'What about the bank? Lorenz Investment—?'

It was all she could think to say. All that was safe to say.

'Back from the brink,' said Guy. 'Just as I'd planned.'

She frowned, trying to make sense. 'But you had to marry Lousia—'

'No.' His eyes were holding hers. 'I had to let the world *think* I was marrying Louisa.' His expression changed. 'That was what I realised that night after the charity ball. When I knew that everything had changed. When I knew I had to have you back in my life. I could not marry Louisa.'

His hands cupping her elbows tightened. 'That was when I realised what I was going to have to do. Somehow I had to have it all—I had to protect the bank and have you, too. And I realised that I could do it if I could just keep the engagement going—because that would give me vital time, under cover of the betrothal, to pull together a rescue package. It was going to be a race, and it was going to be risky, but it could be done. I knew it could be done!'

Abruptly he loosed his grip, turning away from her, knuckling his fists on the mahogany surface of his desk. He twisted his head to look back at her.

'I thought myself so clever—thought I had found a way to make everything work out. Because I had to, Alexa.' His voice changed. 'The stakes had just become higher than I could bear to lose. That night—' his face worked '—that night when I made love to you again, I knew that I could *never* let you go! And I thought…' He paused, then went on, forcing himself to speak, 'I thought it was the same for you. That you would agree to what I was proposing. I was scared, Alexa—scared that it would be all too easy for you to take up with another man, like the damn man you'd been with that evening. So I had to keep you—any way I could!—while I sorted out the bank, got myself free of my engagement to Louisa.'

He went on raggedly. 'I was intending to tell you everything—talk to you—bare myself to you—make you understand the trap I was in. But you disappeared.'

He paused again, then made himself go on, his eyes

burning into hers. 'When I found you I discovered what a fool I'd been—an arrogant, conceited fool—to think you felt for me what I felt for you. And when I saw that portrait—' He broke off.

'Then I knew.' His voice was heavy, as heavy as a weight crushing him. 'I knew I was too late. I had made you hate me. And I had lost you.'

There was bleakness in his face—as bleak as the desert sands blown by witless winds.

The room, despite its cooling air-conditoining, was suddenly airless. Alexa's throat was blocked. She couldn't breathe.

'I—I need to get some fresh air,' she said faintly.

At once he was there, crossing to the pair of large French windows that opened on the other side of his desk out to the gardens. He threw them open and she hurried out, dragging in lungfuls of summer air. There was a little ornate garden bench, and gratefully she sank down on it. Her legs did not seem to be working.

Nor her mind.

Thoughts, emotions, swirled like a maelstrom, and she could make no sense of them—no form, no order. All the certainties she had lived with for so long now—certainties that had been like blades in her heart—had suddenly in a few moments, dissolved to nothing...nothing at all. Desperately she tried to still the swirling maelstrom, make order of it, sense. She seized the one thought that swirled most vividly, most tormentingly. Seized it and stilled it and looked upon it.

Guy wasn't married. He hadn't married Louisa. He was never going to marry Louisa. And since the moment he had taken her to bed again he had never been going to marry Louisa.

The enormity of the realisation was like a tsunami going

ver her. She seemed to sway as she sat, too weakened
o move.

As arms came around her. Guy had lowered himself
own beside her, his arm over her shoulder, steadying
er.

'Alexa—'

There was anxiety in his voice. At least it sounded like
nxiety—but what did she know? What did she know of
iuy de Rochemont at all?

She twisted her head, looked at him.

'I don't know you,' she said.

His arm dropped from her, his expression transfixed.

'I don't know you,' she repeated. 'I've never known
ou.' She pulled a little away from him. 'But then…' Her
hroat tightened, and the words were so difficult to say, but
he had to say them—she must look right into his face, his
yes, and say those words to him. 'I never tried to know
ou. Not in those months we were together—though the
ctual time we spent together was probably little more than
few weeks. But you had barriers all round you, keeping
ie out—keeping everyone out. I respected them, under-
tood them, knew why you did it—because you were—
re—a very private person. I am too. I…I keep myself to
iyself. Keep my emotions to myself. I'm…used to it. Just
ke you. That's why…at the time…I didn't mind the kind
f relationship we had. It was only afterwards, when you
ame to me again, that I saw it differently. Made myself
ee it differently. As demeaning. Exploitative. With you
ist using me for convenient on-demand sex.'

She looked at him, looked into the troubled green eyes
iat held hers.

'But it wasn't. I had been right before. I'd understood
/hat there was between us, and I should have trusted that.
should have trusted *you*. Instead—' her voice was heavy

'—I simply ran away, giving you no chance. No chance at all. No chance to talk to me, tell me what you intended.'

He disengaged his gaze from her, looking out over the gardens. The last of the sun caught the water in the stone girded pond, which rippled lazily in a lift of air.

'But I never did talk to you, did I?' he said. 'Not about us. I just accepted what there was and was glad of it. Grateful for it. Grateful to have found a woman who could be, for me, an oasis in my life. So when I had to end it, had to agree to marry Louisa, all I could bear to do was—walk. Walk away. Leave that precious oasis you had become and instead walk out into a desert. Seeing you again...' He glanced at her now, a gaunt look on his face. 'It was like seeing a mirage, beckoning to me—promising me all that I could want. All that my life did not have any more. So I reached out, and I discovered—' his voice was strained '—discovered it was, in truth, nothing more than a mirage. My own imagining. Not real at all.'

He leant forward, back hunched, forearms on his thighs, hands loose, staring at the water rippling in the stone basin, slowly draining of its light as the sun slipped away, off the gardens, behind the shadowing trees that marched along the borders.

She sat beside him a while, saying nothing. The maelstrom had gone now, sunk down through her, absorbed into her veins. Quieted. Somewhere she could hear birdsong.

She looked about her. It was so very beautiful, this spot, with the vista of the level gardens spreading all about her, the ancient mass of the château behind, and the lingering sunlight just catching the tops of the protecting trees. An oasis of beauty. Of quietness. And peace.

Peace of the heart.

Slowly, very slowly, in the warm, peaceful quietness, she reached for his hand, closing hers over his, winding her fingers into his. He pressed his into hers, holding her hand. Such a simple gesture. Saying nothing.

Saying everything.

He turned to her.

Tears were running down her face. Quietly, silently.

He gave a soft rasp in his throat. Then he put his arms about her, drawing her to him, holding her against him as they sat together, side by side. And still her tears came—so quietly, so silently.

Making words unnecessary.

Then he kissed away her tears and kissed her trembling mouth, kissed the hands he took again in his, raising them to his lips in homage, and she clung to his hand, and to him, and to his heart.

'*Ma belle* Alexa,' he murmured. Then he drew back a little. 'I thought you hated me,' he said wonderingly.

'So did I,' she said. 'But I was wrong.' She kissed his mouth. 'So wrong. It was still love…all along.'

'Still?' There was a questioning in his voice. Uncertainty.

'For so long. I don't know since when. Only that I fell in love with you knowing I should not—that it was…unwise beyond all things. A *folie d'amour*. There was no point in loving you—not even before I knew you were going to marry Louisa. Because what hope could there be in loving you—you who were who you were, from so different a world, wanting only what you did from me and for so brief a time? And when I knew about your betrothal, when you came back and I ran from you, refusing to listen to you, then there was no point in love at all. Only in hatred. And I poured it all—all my hatred—into that portrait of you. The one you saw.'

A voice from the French windows spoke. 'Just as you poured all your love into the one Guy gave me.'

Both started—Guy getting to his feet, drawing Alexa with him, her hands were still entwined in his.

'Maman—?'

Madame de Rochemont stepped out on to the gravelled terrace. How she had suddenly arrived, Alexa had no idea. But then, as a de Rochemont, what was there to stop her having a second private jet at her disposal?

'*Mon fils,*' she acknowledged. Then, coming up to Alexa, she kissed her on each cheek. 'Why do you think,' she asked her, 'I made sure I would know exactly the moment you returned to London?'

She took a step back, her regard encompassing them both.

'When it became clear to me that on no account should my son do what his father had done—what I had done— marry someone he did not love, I knew I must ensure it did not happen. Quite how to do it gracefully, I did not know. Sometimes, yes, such a marriage can be successful. But mine, Guy, was so because in the end I came to love your father, and he me. When I saw your portrait—the one you gave me—I knew.' Her voice changed. 'I knew you were already in love—and were loved in return.'

She met Alexa's eyes. 'That was why I told you I was grateful to have been given that portrait. Because it told me all that I needed to know.' She paused, her expression softening as she spoke to Alexa. 'I can tell who loves my son as much as I do. And I can tell—' she looked at Guy with the same look '—when my son is looking at someone with as much love as—from time to time!—he looks at me. And so,' she went on, 'there was only one last mystery to solve. Why the two of you were not together. A mystery,' she finished, with the air of one delivering a *coup de théâtre*, 'solved not three hours ago, when you, *ma chère*, recommended I consult my daughter- in-law on the action

I was—in desperation to resolve this *impasse*—urging you to take.'

She glared at Guy. 'How could you not have told her Louisa had eloped, and solved your problem *tout court*?'

'Maman,' he answered, tight-lipped, 'it was not that simple—'

Madame de Rochemont gave another imperious wave of her hand. 'Love is always simple. It is men who are fools to think it is not! Do you not agree, *ma chère* Alexa?'

'I think, *madame*, it is also women who can be fools—as I was.'

'Well, I am sure Guy gave you cause. But now I can see that finally all is resolved, and that is a great relief to me. Ah…' her voice lifted '…perfect timing.'

Guy and Alexa turned to see what the cause was. Guy's face blanched, and Alexa could only stare, eyes widening.

Along the façade of the château a grand procession was approaching, its lead a resplendent personage in a velvet jacket, bearing a vast silver salver held in front of him with both hands. On it nestled a champagne bottle in an ice bucket, next to three flutes, and behind him three equally resplendent but lesser personages bore aloft silver salvers groaning with dishes of canapés and *hors d'oeuvres*. They were followed by a dozen uniformed staff carrying between them a gilded antique table and three matching chairs, which they proceeded to set down, with great precision, on the terrace. Upon the table with a practised flourish, the salvers were placed, one after another, and then the champagne bottle was opened and the flutes filled to perfection.

All the attendant staff stood back, apparently staring fixedly ahead, as well-trained staff would always do, but Guy knew they were actually riveted with full and absolute attention on Alexa. They clearly realized—given the dramatic circumstances not only of her sudden unscheduled arrival, but also the arrival of his mother, not to mention the fact that he was still clasping her hand—that she was, *evidemment*, to be their new *châtelaine*.

With admirable composure Guy thanked them, his expression a picture, and they withdrew in good order.

'I'm sorry,' he apologised to Alexa. Embarrassment was clear in his face at all this over-the-top grandeur.

'Quite unnecessary,' said his mother airily. 'Alexa is perfectly familiar with the concept of a *fête champêtre*. We have already discussed my predilection for the art of the Rococo—and I confess I am much looking forward to showing her all the paintings hanging here, too. It is always enjoyable to discuss these matters with professional artists. Their eye is quite different from that of a mere amateur such as myself. But that is for later—we have many years ahead, my dear, for you to give me your opinions, and of course to choose your own additions to the collection. Guy is far too much of a barbarian for it to be necessary to regard *his* tastes, so I never do,' she finished dismissively, and she led the way forward to the table.

'Come!' She lifted her hand to them, seating herself regally at the foot. Guy pulled out the chair beside him for Alexa, and sat himself down at the head of the table. He handed a glass of champagne to his mother, and another to Alexa.

She was in a daze—a daze of incredulous happiness—happiness so full, so complete, that it was carrying her on an iridescent rainbow to heaven. She tried to think, to understand—but it was impossible. Impossible to do anything other than what she was doing: letting Guy take her hand once more and hold it loosely, possessively, across the table, as they raised their glasses at his mother's instigation.

'To you both,' said Madame de Rochemont, her eyes suddenly soft, and full with emotion. 'To your love. And to your long and happy marriage.'

Together, Guy and Alexa tilted their flutes to drink, and the setting sun turned the champagne to molten gold. As golden as their happiness, and their future yet to come.

EPILOGUE

'DON'T move. Stay just like that—'

Guy stilled, lounging back against the sun-warmed roc[k]
behind him. The instruction to stay still was not a problem[.]
Nothing in the world was a problem any more. He relaxe[d]
gazing out over the incredible Alpine panorama of soar[-]
ing mountains. Some rocky peaks were still topped wit[h]
pristine snow, even now in the high summer, and the lowe[r]
slopes were garbed in verdant green, plunging down t[o]
deep valleys far below. Here on the upper slopes, wher[e]
they had walked on this wonderful sunlit day, the air wa[s]
like breathing crystal—clear and sharp. Making him fee[l]
so alive…

His gaze went out over the soaring vista, focussing o[n]
the eagle rising lazily on the thermals. As free as the win[d]
that bore it upwards. As free as he now was. Free to liv[e]
the life he wanted—and, oh, more than that! The life tha[t]
he hadn't even dreamt could ever be his. The life that wa[s]
like a precious, precious jewel—and that jewel was her[e]
so close he could reach out his hand and stroke the tende[r]
curve of her calf. Her legs were half drawn under her as sh[e]
rested the sketchpad on her knees, her wide brow furrowe[d]
in concentration as her pencil worked across the paper. H[e]
gazed lovingly at her as she worked.

Alexa—his Alexa! His beautiful, beloved Alexa! He fe[lt]

his heart fill with emotion, with love. Oh, she was a jewel indeed. He had thought her lost—thought he had driven her away—but she had come back to him, given him the gift of her heart, her love. And he would treasure it all his life. His eyes softened. For a moment he saw her as he had first seen her—lifting her gaze to his and doing exactly what she was doing now: reeling! He had seen it then, at their very first meeting, and it had sent a shot of lightning through him, a satisfaction so intense he had known even in that moment that getting this beautiful, wonderful woman to gaze at him with the same rapt expression was worth everything in the world to him.

For a moment that raptness held, and then he saw her expression change—liquefy and transmute—into something so much more than what it had first been. Now, as his gaze mingled with hers, and hers softened to his, between them flowed the message of their love—strong and pure and eternal.

Then her expression changed yet again, and her mouth pursed.

'Stop it—I can't concentrate,' she admonished sternly.

A smile played at his mouth. 'Of course you can,' he replied. He stretched back, lengthening his legs and crooking his arms behind his head, lean and relaxed. 'You just concentrate on me, *ma belle*.'

His evident satisfaction at this state of affairs drew an answering smile. Alexa put aside her sketchpad.

'It's hopeless,' she said. 'I want to draw you, but I can't. You are far, far too distracting. I don't want to draw you—I want to kiss you.'

She leant forward, her hand cupping the outline of his jaw, and brushed his mouth with hers.

He folded her to him, nestling her against his heart as they both gazed out over the breathtaking vista all about them.

'It was so good of Louisa and her gorgeous young bridegroom to lend us their chalet for our honeymoon,' she said.

A frown creased Guy's brow. 'Gorgeous?' he growled, in mock anger.

She glinted up at him. 'Well, he *is* gorgeous—if you like those sort of looks. Which Louisa obviously does. Even though I—' she gave a mock sigh '—am utterly addicted to green eyes, and so sadly young Stefan leaves me quite unmoved.'

'That's better,' said Guy, and hugged her more closely against him. 'I'm glad you like Louisa, though—she's a nice kid.'

'Pretty, too—much prettier now she isn't being forced to wear those formal clothes her mother chose for her,' said Alexa.

She'd met Louisa properly now, when Alexa and Guy had arrived from their lavish wedding reception at the château the day before and the young couple had shown the honeymooners around their chalet before heading off down the mountain themselves, to visit Stefan's family on the far side of the range. Louisa had been first astonished, then delighted, and then smug when she'd recognised Alexa from their initial anonymous meeting in the hotel powder room.

'Didn't I tell you that you were exactly the sort of woman Guy would go for? Elegant and *soignée*—unlike me!' She'd grinned. 'And that ring looks far, far better on you than it ever could on me.'

Alexa had glanced down at the huge betrothal ring glittering on her finger. 'I'm afraid I've done what I advised *you* to do—asked for another one for everyday wear. I'm keeping this for best!'

Now, as she sat within the circle of Guy's arms, high on

the alpine slope, only the simple gold band of her wedding ring adorned her hand. She glanced at it wonderingly.

'Are we really married?' she asked dazedly.

Guy smiled, humour tugging at his mouth. 'How could you doubt it? Did our wedding not have sufficient impact on you? A packed cathedral, a wedding breakfast that could have graced a Renaissance feast, and enough champagne to float a battleship! I lost count of how many hundred guests there were. And even I do not know just how many relatives I have. Even more than those who decided they could not bear to miss seeing you make me the happiest of men!'

He moved her more comfortably into the circle of his arms and she nestled close against him. More happiness than she could bear filled her.

'Will your family forgive you for marrying an outsider?' she asked.

Guy shrugged a shoulder. 'It's of no importance to me,' he said, 'and besides…' wry humour tugged at his mouth again '…one good thing about marrying you is that it means I am not favouring one branch of the family over another. But if we are talking of forgiveness,' he went on, and his voice was serious now, 'although she was very civil to me as your bridesmaid, will your friend Imogen forgive me for my treatment of you? When I was desperately trying to find you after you'd run from London, and I contacted her to see if she knew where you were, she was not…well-disposed…towards me.'

'I think,' said Alexa mischievously, 'that you have now convinced her of your honourable intentions! Besides, she is deliriously in love herself now, and that makes her charitable.'

Guy laughed. 'Ah, yes—that man I thought might threaten my claim on you. It was actually Imogen who interested

him! How blind can the man be?' he said, his prejudice
blatant.

'Richard agreed to ask me out as a kindness, because
Imogen was so keen to take my mind off you—but, so
she's told me now, it was *her* he was hoping to impress.
And eventually she got the message.'

'These obdurate women, *hein*!' he exclaimed humour-
ously. 'So, *dis-moi*...' He smoothed the pale fall of her
hair from her shoulder. 'Are you truly happy to spend your
honeymoon on a mountain miles from everywhere? In a
humble mountain chalet?'

'Completely,' Alexa assured him. 'I like living in the
back of beyond—I've done it in Devon, and I've done it
in a desert. An alpine mountain is a welcome addition to
my list. But are *you* sure,' she asked, and the mischievous
note was back in her voice, 'that you can acclimatise to
this after all the splendours of your natural environment.'
She waved an arm around the airy vista.

'I revel in it,' Guy assured her. His eyes softened. 'Don't
you yet believe how much I crave the quiet life—not the
three-ring five-star circus I usually have around me?' His
expression changed again—a more serious note entered his
voice. 'Now that Heinrich's bank is safe—and so, thank
goodness, are all the other parts of Rochemont-Lorenz—
I'm going to ease off. Running everything hands-on brought
my father to an early grave, I'm sure of it, and I won't go
that way, Alexa.' His voice was resolute. 'Our wealth is
quite enough,' he went on dryly, 'and I'm going to set up
a more federated management structure—spread the load
more. The bank nearly cost me the most precious treasure
of all—you.' He tilted his head, cupping her cheek in his
hand. 'I could not live without you, Alexa *ma belle, mon
coeur*—not for a day—not for a lifetime.'

He kissed her tenderly, and she kissed him back. Then

they both relaxed back against the rock. All around was silence, with only the occasional tinkling of a cowbell from far away, or the wind soughing in the bare rocks of the peak towering above them.

'It's a good mountain,' said Guy approvingly.

'Better than a global historic banking house?' Alexa queried wryly.

'If I had to choose, then, in the end, yes. I am proud of my heritage, I will not deny that, but mountains last a lot longer than banks. I think Stefan is richer than I in that respect.'

'They'll be happy, won't they, the two of them—Louisa and Stefan—turning this place into a nature reserve?' said Alexa.

'Blissfully,' Guy assured her.

'Will Louisa's parents forgive her, do you think? Jilting you to run off with Stefan?'

'Oh, yes,' Guy said dryly. 'Annelise and Heinrich are two of the biggest snobs I know, and they've got far, far more than they deserve. Louisa told me they went ballistic at first, hearing she'd run off with some drop-out green crusader she'd met through those friends in London she'd been staying with. They saw all their hopes of having a grandchild of theirs running the whole of Rochemont-Lorenz evaporating before their ambitious eyes. But then—' his eyes glinted mordantly '—they realised that I'd bailed out Heinrich's wretched bank for them anyway. And then they realised that they'd snaffled a much, much bigger prize for their wayward daughter. One to set their snobbish hearts aglow. I would have just *loved* to have seen Louisa introduce him when she finally dragged him to that ducal *schloss* of theirs!'

'Prince Stefan of Andovaria,' supplied Alexa, her eyes laughing.

'Yes, indeed. Only a younger son, but it's the title that counts,' said Guy sardonically. 'And now Stefan can be as green as he likes, with their blessing, and live in any eco-chalet he wants—for he owns his own mountain and his cousin is a sovereign prince, so their daughter takes social precedence over every person in *this* family! Heinrich and Annelise are very pleased with Louisa.'

'I'm glad,' said Alexa. 'And I'm glad, and so relieved that your mother, Guy, doesn't mind my marrying you.'

'She approves of you enormously.' His voice was wry again. 'And not just because you have made me the happiest of men. You are unimpressed by all our wealth—but *very* impressed with our art collection. And best of all—' he kissed her affectionately on her nose '—you are polite about her saccharine Rococo paintings!'

'Well, they have their charms,' allowed Louisa.

His mouth curved. 'And so do you, Madame Guy de Rochemont.' A new note entered his voice, doing what it always did to her, what she knew it would always do, all her days—weakening her limbs like honey. 'Charms so plentiful, so alluring, so…enticing…that there is only one thing to be done…'

The jewelled green eyes poured into hers, reaching her soul. Her heart.

'This…' said Guy.

His mouth was soft as velvet. His touch as fine as silk.

His love as long as life.

And so was hers for him.

A sneaky peek at next month...

By Request

RELIVE THE ROMANCE WITH THE BEST OF THE BEST

My wish list for next month's titles...

In stores from 16th May 2014:

❑ Misbehaving with the Millionaire –
Kimberly Lang, Margaret Mayo & Lee Wilkinson

❑ Hot Summer Nights! –
Kelly Hunter, Cara Summers & Emily McKay

In stores from 6th June 2014:

❑ Royal Seductions: Diamonds –
Michelle Celmer

3 stories in each book - only £5.99!

❑ Wedding Wishes – Liz Fielding,
Christie Ridgway & Myrna Mackenzie

Available at WHSmith, Tesco, Asda, Eason, Amazon and Apple

Just can't wait?

Special Offers

ery month we put together collections and
ger reads written by your favourite authors.

re are some of next month's highlights—
d don't miss our fabulous discount online!

On sale 6th June   On sale 6th June   On sale 6th June

Join our *EXCLUSIVE* eBook club

FROM JUST £1.99 A MONTH!

Never miss a book again with our hassle-free eBook subscription.

★ Pick how many titles you want from each series with our flexible subscription

★ Your titles are delivered to your device on the first of every month

★ Zero risk, zero obligation!

There really is nothing standing in the way of you and your favourite books!

Start your eBook subscription today at www.millsandboon.co.uk/subscribe